BLACK ICE

Julia Blake

Sele Books
www.selebooks.com

This is a work of fiction. All characters and events in this publication, other than those in the public domain, are either a product of the author's imagination or are used in a fictitious manner. Any resemblance to actual persons, living or dead, or actual events is purely coincidental.

ISBN: 9798563714786

Black Ice is written in British English and has an estimated UK cinema rating of 12+ containing mild fantasy violence, mild sexual references, and mild language

Black Ice is an Authors Alike accredited book

A Note from the Author

Like many little girls, I grew up on a steady diet of princesses and princes, magic, and true love. Then I grew up and realised that real life isn't like that. Yet I still hanker for those days of wonder when "Happy Ever After" meant precisely that.

This grounding in fairy tales, my long and abiding love for epic fantasy, and a newfound fascination for all things steampunk, eventually coalesced into the germ of an idea for Black Ice. Six weeks later the book was written – all 147,000 words of it – and the world of the Five Kingdoms had been created.

Will I ever go back there? Well, as we all know, in fairy tales anything and everything is possible. But for now, why not settle back and let this tale be told... Once Upon a Time.

By necessity, Black Ice is told from multiple points of view, and I am aware that some readers may struggle with this. To indicate when the POV has changed, you will see the following icon.

As ever, I always appreciate comments, thoughts or maybe even simple shout outs on my Facebook page, Julia Blake - Author.

You can also follow me on Instagram @juliablakeauthor and Goodreads. And why not sign up to read my humorous blogs about life, parenthood and writing on "A Little Bit of Blake"

https://juliablakeauthor.home.blog/

Finally, there is my website for information about me, as well as background on all my books.

www.juliablakeauthor.co.uk

All the best

Julia Blake

A Table of Contents

Dramatis Personae

House White

Princess Snow	Heir to the throne of House White
King Elgin	Snow's dead father
Queen Raven	Snow's dead mother
Prince Hawk	Stepfather to the Princess Snow
Princess Jay	Younger sister of Queen Raven, wife of Prince Hawk, and aunt to Snow
Mirage	Advisor to Princess Jay
Pontifex Slie	Head of The Contratulum
A Young Man	Slie's Secretary
Duncan	The Contratulum's Head Technician
Tibby	Greta's Serving Maid
Matron	Runs the city orphanage
Heyes	Contratulum Commander
Barnabus	Contratulum Commander
Cradoc	Dungeon Gaoler

House Avis

Princess Robin	Third in line to the throne and Snow's cousin
King Falcon	Snow's Grandfather
Queen Wren	Snow's Grandmother
Prince Peregrine	Heir to throne and Snow's Uncle
Princess Magpie	Snow's Aunt
Clara	Robin's Lady's Maid
Lady Franki	Robin's Lady-in-Waiting
Lady Tegan	Robin's Lady-in-Waiting
Miss Cooper	Avian Schoolmistress
Jacobson	Chief Engineer
Mabel	Communications Officer on ***The Kittiwake***

The Dwarvians

Ronin	The Captain
Lissa	Ronin's dead sister
Arden	The Storyteller
Eli	The Apprentice
Kylah	The Mechanic
Fae	The Witch
Grein	The Alchemist
Nylex	The Trickster
Greta	Snow's old nurse and Arden's sister

Glossary of Terms

Pontifex	High Priest/Chief Minister of the Council of Elders – Head of the Contratulum
Chatelaine	Set of short chains attached to a woman's belt used for carrying keys and small items
Fortnight	Two weeks
Lollygagging	Aimlessly idling, dawdling
Frick/Fricking	A swear word
Breosts	Slang word for a woman's breasts
Chemise	Simple garment worn next to the skin, akin to a long slip or petticoat
Sweetling	Term of endearment for a female friend
Nameday	Day a baby officially receives its name which is celebrated each year
Quisling	A person collaborating with the enemy, serving as their puppet
Petrichor	The smell of the earth after rain
Cuz	Slang term of endearment for a cousin

A Brief History of The Contratulum

The Contratulum was one of a few religions within the Kingdom of House White. Approximately 200 years ago it began to assume dominance over all other faiths until eventually it became the only faith openly practiced. Sanctified by the throne as the official religion of the kingdom, the Contratulum amassed great wealth and power.

Vocal in their condemnation of all believed to use the Dark Power, the Contratulum was especially hostile towards the race of people called the Dwarvians. Primarily living in the Great Forest and the Dwarvian Mountains, they were a peaceful, progressive, and tolerant people. However, their possession of elemental magic and the advances they had made in airship technology and the like, made the Contratulum view them as a threat.

One hundred years ago, the Contratulum claimed to have knowledge of a secret plan by the Dwarvians to invade and impose their rule over the kingdom. With the full weight of the throne behind them, the Contratulum set out to eradicate the Dwarvian race. It is believed they were successful, and the Contratulum's power continued to grow. However, with the ascension of King Elgin to the throne and his questioning of their function, they were forced to become more covert about their intentions.

The Contratulum is ruled by a Council of Elders lead by a Pontifex, currently Pontifex Slie. He has held power for over thirty years and under his control, the Contratulum has expanded its reach and its ambitions. He is the acknowledged face of the Council of Elders. Indeed, no one can claim to have ever seen these shadowy figures although their influence is felt by all.

Any believed to have magical abilities who come to the attention of the Contratulum tend to vanish, and any with ancient knowledge of the technology of the Dwarvians know best to keep quiet about it.

THE FIVE KINGDOMS
HOUSE URSA
HOUSE WHITE
FEATHERWELL
ARROWFORD
WINGHAM
HOUSE NARWHALE
HOUSE AVIS
THE CITY
THORNFIELD
RONIN'S COTTAGE
THE CAPITAL
DWARVIAN VILLAGE
HOUSE CORAL
LARKHAVEN
THE SOUTHERN TERRITORIES

Chapter One

A Fateful Encounter

It was a scream that demanded attention. He froze, his ears straining to listen. His eyes scanned the forest depths and followed the path of a flock of birds that had taken off in fright. Cautiously, he moved one soft footstep in front of the other, edging in the scream's direction. Swinging the crossbow from his back, he fumbled a bolt into position, long years of practice making it so second nature, he did not need to look at his hands.

A flash of colour and movement through the elongated tree trunks made him pause. There, in a small clearing up ahead – someone was there. Reaching the edge, he peered through the foliage at the unlikely sight.

A woman, barely more than a girl, her long hair ripped from its elaborate styling to tumble freely in coal-black waves over her shoulders. Her cloak was wrenched to one side, the lacings at the front of her corset half yanked free, her breasts heaving with terrified exertion. She was incredibly beautiful – a small portion of his brain noted and filed the fact away. She was also splattered with blood.

Shockingly red, it stained her face and clothes, standing out starkly against the purity of her pale skin. As he watched in stunned amazement, she stumbled back from something lying on the floor. It looked like a body.

He moved closer.

It was a body.

It was a man, dressed in palace guard uniform, his hands clasped over a gaping abdomen wound from which his entrails were pulsing. Staring at her hands, saturated in scarlet, the girl moaned aloud and wiped them down her silk skirts, tripping on their length as she staggered away from the mess on the ground before her.

Reluctantly deciding this was something he couldn't walk away from, Ronin stepped into the clearing, crossbow loose at his side so it didn't threaten, but was there if necessary. Although he doubted this girl would be much of a threat. At the sound of his approach, she spun to face him, eyes widening in terror, her stained palms held out as if to ward him off.

"Who are you?" she gasped.

"No one you need fear, Milady," he reassured, figuring a nod to her obvious high status to be a diplomatic move. It seemed to work. Relaxing a fraction, she gestured to the downed man.

"He attacked me, I ... I fought back, but I didn't mean ... can you help him?"

Silently, Ronin moved to kneel beside the panting man, swiftly assessing his injuries. The wound was brutally big. Blood had already puddled under the body, and the slippery mess of his insides was more out than in. He had seen wounds like this before. The man was already dead, he just hadn't stopped breathing yet.

He glanced at the girl. Only a little thing, yet she had gutted her assailant like a fish. Admiration briefly flared. Looking down, he saw the knife lying at her feet and picked it up, just in case. A quick examination showed the insignia of the royal legion. She had used the man's knife on him. He slipped it into his boot.

The man groaned, his eyes blinking open. Focusing on the girl, a look of hatred settled on his strained features.

"Whore!" he snarled. "No wonder she wanted rid of you, bitch. You've done for me, you piece of sailor's seconds, you used up trollop." Ronin blinked at the dockside expletives being levelled at a lady, and a deep crimson flush stained the girl's porcelain cheeks.

"I'm sorry," she sobbed. "But I had to do it; you were going to kill me."

"No, I wasn't." Red gushed from his mouth, and Ronin knew by the shadows darkening his eyes that the end would not be long. "I felt sorry for you, was only going to have a bit of fun, then I was going to let you go."

Under the man's hands still desperately trying to hold in his guts, Ronin saw the laces of his britches were undone, his manhood resting on his thighs. He could guess what kind of 'fun' the man had planned to have with the girl.

"Stupid bitch, I know what you are, we all know ... disgusting whore, you're nothing but a stupid slut," the man muttered, seeming determined his last words were to be anything but noble. He coughed, red gushed, his hands dropped to his sides, and he spoke no more.

A long moment passed. Behind him, Ronin heard the girl gasp.

"Is he ...? Is he dead?"

Ronin swept his fingers over the man's staring eyes, then stood, looking at her curiously.

"Aye, he's gone, a wound like that ... well, there's no coming back from it."

The girl looked at the consequences of her actions, any vestige of colour draining from her cheeks. Then her eyes rolled back into her head and Ronin jumped forward to catch her as she fainted dead away.

Carrying her through the darkening patches of light between the trees, Ronin wondered what the blazes he had gotten himself into. Why hadn't he left her where she lay? It was none of his business. Let her sort her own mess out.

A single howl sounded in the twilight behind him, and he quickened his pace, the girl's slight weight barely slowing him down. That was why he hadn't left her. After dark, in the middle of the forest, a lady used to gentle living. There was no way she would survive the night, and he would not have her death on his conscience. Besides, he had to admit he was curious. The words the guard had spoken, the accusations he levelled – Ronin was interested to know what this business was about.

She didn't stir as he loaded her into the back of the scoop, which was just as well. Trying to explain quite why he had such a contraption when even the merest notion of them was a crime punishable by death would have been awkward, to say the least.

Thinking further on that, Ronin fumbled in his pack and drew out a pinch of the herb Midnight Sleep, which he crumbled in his fingers and then gently blew up the girl's nose. It would be best if she slept the whole journey, only awaking long after they were safely home. He needed a chance to hide away certain ... items ... that would be difficult to explain.

He pulled the chain to start the motor and the scoop coughed into life, drops of precious oil spattering the nearby ferns. With a lifelong caution that was engrained bone-deep, he took the time to pluck the soiled leaves and frowned at them, before dropping them into the cart on top of the girl.

Damn it. Kylah had promised she had taken care of that. Best he took it back to her for more tinkering. It was risky enough using it this close to the forest's edge, but to leave evidence behind of its existence was foolhardy to the point of suicide.

Although Ronin knew most would have no idea what the slick, sticky black deposits meant, there would be some who would still remember the old stories and they might very well report their findings, keen to collect the reward for such information.

Now eager to be gone from this place, he straddled the crossbar and settled gingerly onto the small, narrow seat. The weight of the girl in the back was pulling the scoop to one side, so he had to lean his weight the other way to compensate, which put a strain on his spine.

Ronin sighed. It was going to be a long journey home.

Reaching his cottage some three hours later, he carried the girl carefully through the door. She stirred as he settled her on the bed. Closing and locking the door firmly against night-time predators, he swiftly built up the fire, swinging the pot of stew that had been slowly cooking all day back over to bring it to temperature.

Putting away his pack and crossbow, he tossed the now wilted fern leaves into the fire, where they hissed upon contact with the flames. The scoop had already been hidden in the old, tumbledown stable at the back of the cottage, its door locked against any exploration.

Moving swiftly about the small room, he removed anything that might be odd or incriminating to an outsider's eyes, then took a moment to examine the royal knife. He determined to get rid of it as soon as possible and cursed his stupidity for not leaving it with the body.

Pouring warm water from the kettle into a bowl, he washed his face and hands, blood darkening the water. Glancing at the girl as she stirred, he tipped the water into the spill bucket and poured some fresh. Placing it on the table, he jerked his head at it.

"You might want to wash the blood off yourself."

The girl shuddered as she silently examined her torn and blood-stained clothes and skin, then looked around his dwelling in growing confusion.

"Where am I?"

"This is my home. I figured I'd better bring you here for the night, rather than leave you to the wolves." He paused, nodding towards a pile of clothing he had placed at the foot of the bed. "I found a few of my sister's bits left that might fit you. She was a little 'un, like you."

Silently, the girl picked up the long dark skirt and a white blouse, together with a leather corset. Not such fine quality as her own, but beggars couldn't be choosers.

"I'll be outside. Call me when you've finished, and we'll have supper."

"Thank you." He heard her soft reply as he let himself out. Settling in his chair on the porch, he ran his mind over the day's strange events. After supper, he wanted answers. She would get no more aid from him until she had supplied them to his satisfaction.

When they'd eaten, and Ronin had cleared away the dishes, noting that although she'd eaten little, she appeared to have enjoyed the tasty rabbit stew, he leant back in his chair and levelled an enquiring gaze at her.

"I think you owe me a story, Milady, and it had better be a true one."

"Yes," she agreed slowly, hands nervously playing with her hair. His eyes followed them. Never had he seen such luscious hair – so black it seemed to shine blue, like a glossy raven's wing.

"You've been so good to me I suppose it's only fair." She shook her head slowly. "I don't know where to begin."

"Well, why not start with your name? Who are you?"

"I'm Snow White."

Whatever he was expecting, it hadn't been that, although he didn't consider for a heartbeat that it wasn't the truth. He had heard the tales of the princess's beauty – her raven hair and snow-white skin, her red lips, and large black eyes.

The sole heir to the throne, the last remaining member of House White. The cherished princess who held out hope for the future was sitting at his table. Wearing his sister's clothes, and watching him nervously, pearly white teeth gnawing at those famed ruby lips.

"Snow White?"
"Yes."
"Princess Snow of House White?"
"Yes."
He sighed, then slowly nodded. "All right, so you're the princess. What were you doing in the forest with that man? And why do you think he was trying to kill you?"
"I don't think he was trying to kill me; I know he was. Probably ordered to do so by my stepmother."
Shaking his head in confusion, Ronin's mind quickly flew over the complex history of House White. When King Elgin White had taken as his bride Princess Raven from the neighbouring kingdom of House Avis, the whole nation rejoiced. Yet their joy had been short-lived. Always reckless and wild, the young King had been killed whilst out hunting, leaving his bride of six months shattered and pregnant.
Being delivered of a baby daughter had given Queen Raven new purpose, and the kingdom had slowly come to terms with events. Believing the succession to be secure, the people thought that the wise and kindly Queen would rule as regent until Princess Snow came of age.
It was even agreed Queen Raven would be allowed to marry again – a distant cousin and minor princeling from her own kingdom. Her husband was named prince consort, on the understanding that he was to be no more than a companion to Queen Raven. Bearing no real power, he acted as a father figure to the young princess.
However, Queen Raven was lost to fever when the Princess was only five years of age, and the kingdom was once again thrown into turmoil. Her husband hurried to reassure the people that the succession was still secure. Princess Snow was their heir and always would be. To ensure that the Princess was raised in a manner fitting for her future responsibilities, he would take another bride – none other than Queen Raven's younger sister, the Princess Jay.
And so, the unusual situation came to pass. The heir to the throne was being raised by her stepfather and her aunt, and that had seemed to be an end to the matter.
But now that very heir was sitting at his table, a mere two weeks before her coming of age when she'd be named as Queen Snow of House White, crowned in the ancient cathedral, and proclaimed before all to be the ruler of the land.
"Why?" he asked, slowly. "Why would Princess Jay want to kill you? You're her niece and the heir to the throne."
"I'm not sure she did, but she wants me out of the way, and death is a pretty final way of achieving a person's permanent absence." She paused and took a deep breath. "It is not common knowledge yet, but my aunt has recently discovered she is with child."

"But her child can't inherit in your place – they'll have no drop of White blood in them."

"Then who would inherit? With me gone, out of the picture, who would be left?" Under her level gaze, he paused, considered her words, saw the truth of them and reluctantly nodded.

"But I've always believed Prince Hawk and Princess Jay to be kind mild-mannered people," he said. "Not the type to plan murder and insurrection to put their offspring on the throne."

"They are, or rather, they were. But both are weak, both governed by other forces. Hawk has ... appetites, that he cannot control. His wife, my aunt, is not enough for him so he seeks satisfaction elsewhere, and over the years this has driven my aunt to the brink of insanity. Seeing the bellies of her young maids' swell, knowing that they carry his bastards when for so many years she appeared barren. The humiliation of my stepfather carrying on his tawdry affairs under her very nose – one can almost pity her."

He knew there was more she was not saying, yet held his tongue, letting her tell the tale in her own time and her own way.

"And then there is Mirage."

"Mirage?"

"My aunt's advisor. He acts as her liaison, her counsellor, and her spymaster. He gathers information for her and seems to know everything that happens, almost before it has come to pass. It appears almost ... magical."

Ronin's head jerked up. "You do not believe he possesses the Power?"

"Yes," her eyes glinted fiercely. "I have seen him do things when he believed himself unobserved. I have witnessed the way his control over my aunt has grown until now she is his puppet, his plaything. She does his bidding – it is as if she has no control over her thoughts and actions anymore. She has become so completely his creature."

"Magic is strictly forbidden in this kingdom. If Prince Hawk or the Contratulum knew ..."

"They do know, or at least suspect, yet do nothing. Any who speak out against him mysteriously die or disappear soon after, so all are too terrified of the consequences to take any action. And now that my aunt is pregnant, he sees the throne within his grasp."

"The people would never agree to a commoner, much less one using the dark Power, taking the throne ..."

"No, but my aunt being crowned queen, they would accept that, and then he'd rule through her. There was one tiny fly in this ointment of power he was concocting, though."

"You?"

"Yes, me. I should have known when my aunt agreed to let me visit my old, sick nurse, and when the guards she assigned me were all from her private legion ... I was so stupid. I should have realised."

"Where are the other guards?"
"I do not know. I was dragged away from them by that man, I suppose he drew the short straw to do the deed, to kill me. He carried me to that clearing, where he ... but you know the rest."
Ronin thought he probably did not know all the details of what had happened. Of how she had got hold of his knife, and how she had been in a position she had been able to slice upwards through the man's stomach.
"So, you see," she concluded, resting her elbows on the table, and staring intently at him. "I cannot go back. I dare not. My life wouldn't be worth one gold piece if I went back."
"But if you told the Contratulum what had happened, what your aunt tried to do ..."
"They'd do nothing. In truth, they would welcome my demise. As for the court officials, I told you – they are all afraid of Mirage, and my aunt controls her legions – they are loyal only to her."
"What do you intend then? Is there somewhere you can go? Anyone who'd protect you?"
"No," she whispered, and something shifted inside him at the glint of tears in those dark eyes. "There's nowhere, there's no one. I am all alone."
"Well, I suppose you could stay here for a bit," he heard himself say, and could have bitten off his tongue for its damned foolishness.
"Could I? Please? Until I think of something else," she looked around the small, firelit room. "I like your home. It's cosy and I feel safe here – thank you."
He nodded brusquely, inwardly cursing himself, but acknowledging it was said now and could not be unsaid. Truth be told, he would probably do the same again. Something about her innocence and purity had touched that part of his heart he had believed to be locked away after the death of his family so many years before.

Chapter Two

The Path to the Throne

Despite her protests, Ronin insisted she have his bed for the night. It didn't sit well with him – the notion of a princess sleeping on the hearthrug, or in his old chair. Besides, it wasn't as if he hadn't spent many a night sitting there, fully clothed and staring into the fire, his mind roaming over the past and what his life had come to.

"It doesn't seem fair, though," she continued to protest. "You've done so much for me already. Depriving you of your bed as well seems wrong."

"It'll only be for the night," he promised and jerked his head towards the ladder in the corner of the room. "Tomorrow you can clean out the old attic bedroom and use that. Reckon that'll be more fitting for a lady such as yourself."

"Why don't you use it?" she asked innocently, and his jaw tightened. Turning away from her, he busied himself making up the fire to last the night.

"It was Lissa's room," he finally said. "I don't like to touch it, not since ..."

"Was Lissa your sister?" she asked.

He nodded, unable to speak. Unwilling to look her in the eye lest she saw the emotions her harmless comments had stirred up.

"What happened to her?"

Ye gods, she would not leave things be. Could she not understand that it was a subject he was reluctant to prod at? He feared the barely healed scabs cracking open and the festering pus of memory oozing out.

"Will I meet her? I hope she doesn't mind me borrowing her clothes."

"She won't be coming back, so she won't be needing them anymore."

"Why not? Where is she?"

"She's dead," he snapped, and hearing the tone in his voice she finally subsided. Guilty at having snarled at her, he opened the chest and pulled out a blanket. "It gets cold at night, so deep in the forest," he told her. "Best you have this as well. I don't expect you've ever been cold before, living in the palace."

"It snowed the day my father died," she told him, taking the blanket, and placing it on the bed. "My nurse told me the tale of how my mother and her ladies were sewing in the garden when a freak fall of snow occurred. My mother hurried to gather up her embroidery and pricked her finger on the needle. Seven drops of blood fell onto the snow at her feet and in that instant, she knew her husband was dead – but that her child was a girl and would be born strong and healthy. An heiress to the throne. Isn't that a wonderful story?"

“Tis a pretty tale,” he agreed. “If it be a true one?”

“My nurse was deeply superstitious and prone to exaggeration,” Snow agreed with a shrug. “So, it may be a fairy tale she told to make me go to bed at night. But I like to think it’s true.”

Ronin merely grunted, unwilling to spoil her memory by informing her that if her mother had been foolish enough to admit to using the magic of prophecy, then queen or no queen, she would have been hanging from a gibbet by nightfall, courtesy of the Contratulum.

“Try and get some sleep,” he ordered. “We’ll see what the morrow brings and make our plans then.”

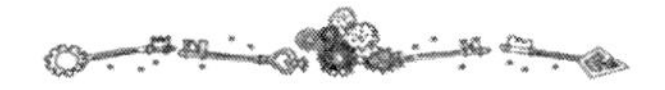

Much to her surprise, she did manage to sleep, and for the first time in months, it was a sound and dreamless slumber. She had left behind the almost nightly terror of watching the handle to her chamber turn. Hearing the rattling at the lock, and the pleading, whimpering tones of her stepfather begging her to admit him. Now she felt safe and protected because instinctively she knew that this man, Ronin, meant her no harm.

She had seen the raw flash of remembered devastation in his eyes at her heedless questioning about his sister. Cursing herself for her clumsiness, she had meekly obeyed his command to go to bed. Convinced she would be unable to sleep, she had dropped like a stone into deep slumber the moment her head hit the pillow.

Awaking once in the night and shivering as a chill crept into her bones, she opened her eyes to find him carefully laying another blanket over her. As he tucked it under her chin, his piercing blue eyes were gentle in the firelight.

Murmuring her thanks, she watched him toss another log on the fire and settle back into his chair. His head turned in the direction of the door and his body tensed at a noise out there in the darkness. It came again, and he relaxed at the realisation it was only an owl hooting its intentions to the moonlit night.

The last thing she saw as sleep dragged its lacy wings over her eyes, was his face silhouetted against the firelight as he listened and watched, protecting them from all that might do them harm.

Morning came. She lay for a moment in the still quietness of relief that this day would not be one spent in hiding and avoidance. She was spared her daily activity of seeking out private places. Of finding company that would spare her the acerbic comments and insinuations of her aunt, and the cloying and unwanted attentions of her stepfather. Of avoiding the attempts by Mirage to corner her alone and whisper his insidious and treasonous proposals into her unwilling and disbelieving ears.

She shuddered, remembering also the thrice-weekly visits from Pontifex Slie, the head official of the Contratulum. Ostensibly to instruct her in the ways of leadership and prepare her for her coronation. In truth, scrutinising her every word and thought. Always looking for a weapon to use against her.

Snow knew she might be innocent of the ways of the world outside the high palace gates, but she had learnt political intrigue and machinations the way any other child would learn their letters.

She knew that the Contratulum wanted the royal houses gone. That they viewed the line of succession, and the power held by the legally crowned monarch, to be an outdated anachronism belonging in the dark ages – along with alchemy, prophecy, elemental magic, and all the other traits associated with the Power.

Her father had controlled the Contratulum, using the power of the throne to keep them in check, and the Contratulum had quietly and insidiously filled the power vacuum left by his death.

Slowly, bit by precious bit, they had stolen for themselves crumbs of power, until now almost the whole loaf sat upon their table.

The death of her mother, queen regent and widow of the last legally anointed monarch, had cemented their position as an undeniable fist of power in the land. As the rightful heir, only she stood between them and absolute control.

When she reached the age of sixteen and was formally declared heir-in-waiting, the 'lessons' of Pontifex Slie lost even the thinnest veneer of education. They became little more than propaganda and occasionally outright attempts at mind-control.

Yet Snow was the child of her parents. Tempering her father's strength and canny stubbornness with her mother's cautious wisdom, she had walked a fine line every day for the past two years.

Murmuring platitudes of appeasement to the Pontifex, maintaining levels of civil decorum with her aunt, and ignoring the blatant intentions of her uncle. She made sure she was never alone with him. She kept her chamber door locked, and the key safely secured in the chatelaine which was always chained around her waist.

Snow had settled down to wait them out. The ancient and engrained laws of the land dictated that upon attaining her eighteenth birthday the throne would be hers – as would the absolute power afforded to the ruling monarch.

It wanted but a fortnight until her birthday. She should have known that the players in this game of power would be desperate enough to try anything, including arranging her murder. Snow did not doubt it for a moment, although was unsure whether it had been her aunt acting alone, her jealousy aroused by her husband's obvious preference for her young niece, or her aunt acting under the control of Mirage to fulfil his own twisted, mysterious agenda.

Or even by order of the Contratulum, rightly suspecting that for all her apparent biddability to the Pontifex, once she ascended to the throne Queen Snow would make life very uncomfortable for them. That under her rule they would find their hard-won powers eroded, or even snatched away altogether.

No, she had been careless.

Relief at how close she was to being safe had affected her judgement. When the messenger brought news of her old nurse's sickness, she had seen it as a respite from the unbearable tensions within the palace.

She should have been suspicious that she was permitted to go at all. When she saw that her escort was hand-picked from her aunt's private legions, she should have hurried back to her chamber and locked the door.

But she hadn't, and consequently had almost been defiled and murdered by a man who plainly believed the evil rumours that had been spread about the palace. Tales that whispered how Princess Snow was not so pure after all. That she willingly joined her stepfather in bed-sports. An accusation which, if proved true, could have barred her from being crowned.

Yet another reason why the Contratulum had been so eager to bend her to their will and make her their puppet. The monarch ruled through the power of the people, and those same people would never allow the Contratulum to seize control.

Snow saw now that a longer game had been played. One which stank of corruption and sly manipulation. With her safely out of the way, either dead or discredited, nothing now stood between them and absolute power.

Her stepfather was a foolish letch who posed no threat to them. As for her aunt, Snow shivered at the thought of what Pontifex Slie and his evil consorts would do to Princess Jay if she were ever stupid enough to oppose them.

No, she had been the only obstacle that stood in their way, and through her carelessness, she had effectively removed herself. The path to the throne now stood open to them.

Snow wondered what she could do to stop them. She was but one young woman with no friends or powerful allies to aid her.

Even if she did return to the palace, she would not last five minutes. Her death and the discreet disposal of her body was a certainty – the only question being who would get to her first.

No, returning was not wise, yet she was unsure what other option she had.

Ronin knew she no longer slept and wondered what thoughts were keeping her so still, her eyes squeezed tightly shut. Curiously, he studied her face. There was no doubt she was the most beautiful woman he had ever seen, her features so perfect they were almost unreal. But he was aware of the ways of the world enough to realise that such outstanding beauty could sometimes be a curse, rather than a blessing.

Wishing to give her privacy to arise and attend to her morning ablutions, he boiled some water and poured it into a bowl on the table. Placing a fresh towel beside it, he loudly announced his intention to go and attend to something, declaring he would be gone some time but would knock upon returning.

Then he left her alone in the cottage and went to check his nearby traps, pleased to discover a fine buck rabbit in one. Meat had been running a little scarce, and now he had two mouths to feed instead of one, he would need to hunt more frequently.

Coming back via a tangle of wild brambles, he filled his hat with plump berries hoping their sweetness would please her. Then he scolded himself for caring whether her new living arrangements were to her liking or not. The fact of the matter was she had little choice, relying totally on him for her very survival. Still, the berries were a welcome addition to their diet that he, too, would appreciate.

Arriving back at the cottage, he was pleased to discover her standing on the front porch with the empty water bucket, peering around curiously. Her face relaxed with relief when she saw him, her smile deepened when he showed her the rabbit, and her eyes lit up when she peered into his hat and spied the berries.

"Oh my," she cried. "I remember having them, a very long time ago, when one of my maids had family who lived within the forest. She brought me back berries once. I remember they were delicious." He smiled. Her pleasure at his simple gift making him happy.

"I used all the water," she continued. "If you point me in the direction of the well, I will fetch us some more."

"No well, Your Highness," he replied. "But the stream is a few yards in that direction." He nodded his head to the east. "Follow the path and you can't miss it. I will start breakfast while you are gone."

She smiled at him again and set off down the path, the early morning sunshine caressing her unbrushed raven black hair. He watched her go, then went inside to see what could be arranged to break their fast.

By the time she came back, the front of her skirts suspiciously damp, showing her unfamiliarity with filling buckets from streams, he had made a pot of tea and sliced some bread. Placing butter, cold ham, and a small bowl of blackberries on the table, he looked up as she stood the bucket in the corner and slid onto the bench on the other side of the table.

"Hungry?" he asked.

"Very," she replied.

"Well dig in, it's simple but there's plenty."

"Thank you." Her hand hovered over the fare, then, as he had expected her to, she couldn't resist taking a blackberry and placing it in her mouth, her nose wrinkling at its tart sweetness. She had pretty manners, he noticed. But then, she was a princess used to courtly ways, so he would have expected nothing less.

"I saw a very strange thing when I was at the stream," she said, daintily finishing her crust of bread.

"Oh?" Instantly alert, he placed his cup down and looked at her. "What sort of strange thing?"

"It was a butterfly, I think, only like no butterfly I have ever seen before. It landed on a branch quite close to me and did not fly away even when I drew near to it. It had the strangest markings, almost like tiny interlocking wheels. As I bent closer to examine it, I could have sworn that one of the eye markings on its wing opened and stared back at me. Truly, it was a most extraordinary creature."

Ronin groaned and dropped his head in his hands.

"Is something wrong? Is there some meaning to my sighting?"

"Meaning? Well, it means that I'd better get that rabbit onto stew and see what other provisions I have in the larder."

"I do not understand."

"Brush your hair, Your Highness, we'll have company by nightfall."

After their breakfast had been cleared away, he took her up the ladder and showed her the small room tucked away under the eaves that had been Lissa's domain when she lived. Opening the large chest standing under the dormer window, he gestured to the pile of bedding and clothing inside.

"Use whatever you need," he invited her. "There are more clothes in there, and I know Lissa would not mind you having them."

He paused and swallowed. The faintest scent of lavender had wafted from the folds of clothing as Snow knelt and gently touched them. Lavender had been Lissa's favourite flower, and she had used to distil them to an oil, as well as making sachets of the fragrant flower to protect her clothes from moths.

Snow pulled out Lissa's Flying Corset and held it up, her face registering her confusion as her fingers explored the softness of the well-cured leather, the straps and chains to which Lissa had attached the various tools of her trade, and the high leather throat guard and wrist braces.

"I have never seen such a corset as this before," she exclaimed.

"Nor will you ever again," he replied, then hesitated. How much of the truth could this princess be trusted with? He did not believe she would ever betray them, indeed, could not, as it would place her own life in peril. But telling a stranger their most closely held secrets was a direct violation of their most sacred oath.

"Lissa was the best aviatrix you could ever hope to meet," he finally said.

"Aviatrix?"

"Airship pilot."

"Airship ..." Her words faltered, and she stared at him, her eyes pools of disbelief. "But airships are a myth, a fable – they never existed."

"Oh, they were far from a myth, princess. They existed." *Still do,* he thought, *even if they no longer take to the skies.*

Speechless, Snow looked down at the leather, form-fitting trousers that lay underneath the corset. They were intended for a woman, but Snow had never seen any garbed in such apparel. She looked back up at him.

"Airships ... And your sister piloted one?"

"Yes, she was the best pilot of her generation."

"What happened to her?"

"She went down with her ship, defending her people." Ronin turned abruptly away. He had said too much already, enough to get them all swinging from gibbets if the princess ever opened her mouth to the wrong people.

"I'll leave you to settle in," he said. His tone leaving Snow in no doubt that the subject was now closed.

Chapter Three

Marvellous Devices and Surprising Secrets

The day passed. Each busy with their tasks, their conversation was limited to enquiries from Snow as to the whereabouts of various cleaning necessities, and Ronin answering her queries with as few words as possible.

Having never cleaned a room in her life before, Snow was at a loss as to where to begin. Pushing open the small window in the roof, she noticed how dirty her hands were from touching it and decided to start there. Mayhap if the room were lighter, it would illuminate what she should do next.

With Ronin glancing over frequently in concern, she filled the large kettle with water and set it to heat over the fire. Gathering cleaning rags and soap from the cupboard he pointed to when she asked, she waited impatiently for the water to heat.

Forgetting that the handle would now also be hot, she yelped in shock and snatched her hand away when her fingers touched it. Ronin came instantly to her side. Frowning, he plunged her hand into the bucket of water standing by the door and made her keep it submerged until the pain had subsided. Then he passed her a thick gauntlet to wear to pick up the kettle, which she now realised lay always by the fire expressly for that very purpose.

Slopping water down herself as she tried to climb the ladder with the full bucket, she realised she had overfilled it. So, she came carefully down, tipped some back into the kettle, and tried again.

Feeling Ronin's eyes upon her endeavours, she wondered if he was holding back mirth at her ineptitude. But each time she glanced in his direction his mouth was set in its usual grim line. She thought of asking for his help. But then her father's stubbornness came to the fore, and she decided she'd be damned, rather than admit to him she was so spoilt she did not know how to perform a simple task such as cleaning a room.

The sun had passed over the roof of the cottage and was slanting directly through the attic window before she was satisfied with her efforts. She stepped back in exhaustion. She had gained a deeper appreciation of the maids at the palace, vowing that in future she would show her gratitude to anyone who had to clean up after her. Snow also realised that half the grime she had cleaned from the room had transferred itself to her face, hands, and hair.

Ruefully scrambling down the ladder, she wearily poured water into the kettle and swung it over the fire to heat for the umpteenth time that day. Feeling her clothes sticking to her sweaty body, she pulled a face with distaste. Did she smell? She was convinced that she did and glanced surreptitiously around the cottage.

There was no sign of a bathtub of any description. She wondered if it would be indelicate to enquire of Ronin how he managed his ablutions when more than a quick washing of the face and hands were required. Probably bathed in the stream, she concluded glumly and considered it as an option.

As she thought of him, he appeared in the doorway with a basket of salad crops in one hand. Raising a brow at her bedraggled and begrimed state, he entered the cottage and placed the basket on the table, before putting his hands on his hips and quirking a rare smile at her appearance.

"You finished?"

"Yes."

"Most of the dirt now appears to be on you."

"I am aware of that fact." Looking down at herself, Snow's lip quivered with dismay and she flinched as he reached up to gently untangle a cobweb from her hair. "I am boiling some water to wash. May I ask you to leave so I can do so."

"I think it will take more than a splash of water," he commented dryly, and her lip quivered down even more. He hesitated, then his expression softened, and he seemed to come to some sort of decision.

"Go and fetch fresh clothing," he ordered. "I can offer better than a bucket of warm water and a flannel."

Curiously, she ran to do his bidding, pulling out an embroidered red skirt, a white blouse with matching embroidery around the collar, and a corset of the softest black suede she had ever felt. Descending the ladder, she found him waiting for her at the open door with a towel folded neatly over one arm and a small wooden pot in the other containing some sort of sweet-smelling lotion.

"Soap," he said as she peered into the pot and looked at him in enquiry. "For your hair and body. Now, follow me."

"Are we going to the stream?" she asked, lifting her skirts to hurry after his long-legged stride. "I did consider going there to bathe but thought it might be a little cold."

"The stream?" They had reached a tumbledown stable located at the back of the cottage, and he turned to face her. "It would be far too cold, Your Highness. I think the chattering of your teeth would be heard all the way back to the palace."

"Then what were you suggesting?" she enquired, as he snapped open the padlock on the door and ushered her inside its dim and dusty interior. It was conspicuously empty, containing only two stalls where horses, mules, or other such beasts had once been housed. Along one wall, a line of gardening implements was neatly arrayed, and a stack of wooden buckets and boxes stood along the other wall.

Confused, she watched in silence as he carefully padlocked the door behind them. He took a broom from the wall and proceeded to sweep the straw away, revealing a large pair of doors set into the floor. These were also padlocked shut. Ronin selected the largest of a bunch of ornate keys hanging from his belt and unlocked the doors.

He threw them open onto the wooden floor with a muffled bang. Snow stepped forward and peered curiously into the opening. To her surprise, it was a lot deeper than the mere root cellar she had been expecting. Instead, a slope made of firmly compacted soil led away into the darkness with two deep wheel ruts bearing witness to its regular use.

"Follow me," he ordered and took a lantern from where it hung from a hook on the ceiling. Lighting it with a spark from his tinder pouch, he beckoned to her and set off down the slope into the depths, with Snow following him uncertainly.

The slope descended for ten feet before flattening out into a wide room with a variety of strange devices and contraptions lined up along the walls. Using the lantern to light candles dotted around the room, Ronin watched as Snow went from device to device, letting her hand wander over each one and trying to guess its purpose.

"Ronin, what is this place?" she finally asked. "And what are these things?"

"They are mechanical transportation devices," he told her, then smiled as the confused frown on her brow deepened. "See here."

He gestured to a device that at first glance looked like some sort of cart. "We call this a scoop. See the carrying compartment? Look how the back can be dropped to form a ramp to make it easier to load it with heavy cargo. See the engine at the front?"

"Engine?"

"This, here." Kneeling, he gestured to cogs and wheels that were interlinked and connected incomprehensibly, behind a large waterskin fixed under an uncomfortable-looking seat.

"Water goes into the pouch. When the chain is pulled the engine turns and draws water through into this chamber. It is heated until it produces steam, which propels the scoop along. It is slow and a little cumbersome, but useful for carrying heavy loads quietly through the forest. It's how I transported you back here yesterday."

"I was in that thing?" she asked incredulously, waving a disbelieving hand towards the carrying compartment.

"Yes."

"Like a load of potatoes, you had harvested?"

"Well," he smiled, "I wouldn't put it quite that way, but yes."

"Oh." Stunned by his words, Snow silently examined the other three devices in the room. There was another contraption very like the scoop, but without the carrying compartment and with no waterskin visible.

"And this? What is this thing?"

"That's a mechanised bicycle."

"Like the little ones that children play with?"

"Exactly like. Only this is no child's toy. This can go faster than any horse and is a great deal more fun. It's also very noisy, which is why I don't get to ride it nearly as much as I would like to."

"Does it run on heated water?"

"No, it runs on oil."

"Oil?"

"It's a black substance, like the stuff we burn in lamps. But it burns much hotter and propels the engine forward at speed."

"Where does this ... oil ... come from?"

"From deep underground, or it can be extracted from coal."

"Coal?"

"It's a form of black dirty rock that produces a lot of energy when heated. It burns hotter than wood and is more consistent. Coal is what is used to power an airship."

"And where do you find coal?"

"Also, from very deep underground."

"I see." Snow slowly rose to her feet and looked at the last two devices. "And these ones?"

"This right here is a skimmer."

"It has wings!"

"That's right, it does."

"Can it fly?"

"Yes, it's a light aeronautical device. It can carry two – three at an absolute push. It doesn't have much of a range but it's much more manoeuvrable than an airship, and of course, being so much smaller, it doesn't attract attention the way an airship would."

"Flying." Snow breathed out the word on a sigh of longing. "Ever since I was a little girl, I've dreamt of being able to fly. My old nurse used to tell me tales of wings that could be worn like an article of clothing and could give one the ability to soar above the treetops."

Frowning, Ronin gestured towards something hanging on the wall. "Something like that?" he asked, lifting the lantern higher so Snow could see them.

"Oh, my." Snow clasped her hand to her breast and eagerly stepped closer. "Yes, they are exactly as she described them. But how could she possibly have known?"

Delighted and intrigued, she examined the outstretched wings. Gently, she touched the fine membrane that was stretched taut over thin metal struts, the whole attached to some sort of device – no, engine – she corrected herself, that bore straps to attach to one's body and arms.

"I don't know," Ronin admitted. "But I think we need to discuss this nurse of yours, she seems to have known more than she should have done. But for now, let me show you why I brought you here."

Reluctant to leave these marvellous devices behind, Snow followed him from the cavern down a corridor that snaked away into the darkness, ending in a junction with three stout doors arranged one on each wall. Ronin put the lantern down carefully on a wooden stool positioned by one of the doors and fumbled at his belt for another key.

"Ronin, what is this place?" Snow asked, and he paused to look at her steadily.

"It's a hiding place and an escape route. If you are going to be staying here for any length of time, I will give you your own set of keys, and if ever I tell you to hide, you come here and lock all the doors behind you. If ever I tell you to run, well ..."

He opened the door facing them, and Snow followed him through as they emerged into another passageway. This one was a great deal narrower. Following Ronin's broad back, Snow felt the pressure on her knees as it rose sharply. The passage ended at a small hatchway, big enough for a grown man to crawl through. Opening it with yet another key, Ronin invited her to peep through the canopy of thick ivy which completely concealed the hatch. Carefully pushing to one side the fronds, Snow peered through and saw a portion of the forest on the other side.

"Where are we?" she murmured.

"Listen." Ronin said in reply, placing a hand on her arm. "What do you hear?"

Closing her eyes, Snow took a deep breath and tried to still the frenzied pulsing of her heartbeat in her ears. She listened, hearing all around them the low rustling of the undergrowth as a breeze whispered through the forest and flirted with the branches of the trees above their heads. Under that, there was another sound – a constant roaring and burbling.

"The stream," she said, opening her eyes and looking at him. "We're near the stream."

"Aye," he agreed. "We've gone under the stream, and we're on the other side. If they have tracker dogs, they will find it harder to pick up your scent."

"Tracker dogs?" Her voice faltered as she heard his words and added them to all the other strange and wonderful words, he had uttered that day. Slowly, pieces of the puzzle clicked into place. She remembered the old tales her nurse had told her as a child. The whispered stories she had overheard the servants exchanging.

"Ronin," she began slowly. "How far into the forest did we travel yesterday?"

"A goodly way," he admitted.

"And we were on that device thing – the scoop – so we would have travelled much further than any man could have done on foot."

"We did," he agreed, his eyes never leaving her face.

"So, we are deep into the Great Forest?"

"Aye, almost to its heart."

Snow swallowed hard, her heart pounding so loudly she felt sure he could hear it. Her palms were clammy with nervous realisation.

"Ronin are you ..." She stopped. The notion was so impossible. She could not believe it was one she was even considering voicing.

"Are you a Dwarvian?"

"I am," he said.

"But that's impossible," she whispered. "You don't exist, you can't exist. The Dwarvians were completely wiped out a century ago."

"And yet here I am, Your Highness." His words were mocking, but his smile was kind and Snow could not pull her eyes away from his – from the pain she saw lingering at her words, the acknowledgement of the fact that his people were all gone. Destroyed for the power they were rumoured to bear by an entity that was in its infancy at the time. An entity that was hungrily clawing its way up the hierarchy of control and believed the Dwarvians to be an obstacle to that ascent.

The Contratulum.

Their weapons ones of insinuation, slander, and lies, the Contratulum set out to destroy an entire race of people – and within one generation had done so. Until now, a hundred years later, the Dwarvians had been banished to the realms of fable and myth. Stories to be whispered around the fireplace by foolish servants, none believing they had ever existed for real.

Snow herself had been told such tales, her nurse swearing her to absolute secrecy and claiming the stories to be true. When Snow was a child, she had believed her. But then she grew up and learnt otherwise, and assigned such tales to the stuff of childhood, along with giants, unicorns, mermaids, and other fantastical creatures.

But now here was Ronin, claiming that not only were the stories true – that the Dwarvians had indeed existed – but that he was one himself. Gazing in disbelief into his face, Snow saw the truth there and realised that nothing was as she had thought it to be. That the very bedrock of belief upon which her entire life was based, was a lie.

"How ..." she began, then stopped.

"How did we survive? Now, that, Your Highness, is a tale best left for later. The others will be arriving soon, and it is a story that concerns them as much as it does me, The telling of it should be shared by all. And besides, I am not the storyteller of our group. That is a task best left for Arden."

"Others? There are others?" At his nod, she shook her head in dazed wonderment. "There are other Dwarvians? And I will meet them this very day."

"Aye," he confirmed.

"But I cannot," she exclaimed, looking down at the ruinous condition of her clothes, the grime encrusted into her hands, and thinking of the bedraggled and begrimed state of her hair. “Not like this.”

“Oh vanity, thou name art Snow.” he laughed, closing, and locking the hatchway and ushering her back down the passage to the junction of doors again. “Now this,” he continued, unlocking the door to the left, “is one device I believe Your Highness will approve of much more.”

“What is it?” she breathed, gazing in bemused wonder at the tall cylinder made of iron. Walking around it, she discovered it was open on one side. Peering up inside, she marvelled at the large, dish-like structure that protruded from a complicated arrangement of smaller cylinders, gears, and cogs, which in turn hung from the ceiling.

“We are right beneath the stream here,” Ronin informed her, placing the towel and pot of soap on a nearby stool. Rolling up his shirt sleeve, he reached inside the cylinder and twisted a metal wheel all the way around. There was a hiss and then water was crashing down into the cylinder from the dish, which Snow saw was punctured with many holes.

“Oh, my,” she exclaimed weakly, wondering how many more surprises this day would hold.

“It’s called a shower,” Ronin explained. “And do you want to know the best thing about it?”

Bemused, Snow glanced up at the twinkle in his eye, not objecting as he took her hand and held it under the stream of water crashing down onto the floor.

“It’s hot!” she squeaked.

“It’s hot,” he agreed, his smile broadening as she nodded her head in anticipation, her hands flying to her corset laces in obvious eagerness. “I’ll leave you the lantern. Take your time, I have a few chores to do. When you are finished, follow the passageway back up. I’ll leave the doors unlocked for you this time, but in future, they are to be kept locked at all times.”

“Yes, of course, I understand. I suppose if this was to be discovered, then ...”

“Then my life would be worth even less than yours, Highness.”

Chapter Four

The Gathering of the Seven

Twenty minutes later she returned. Her hair was a damp curtain of black silk down her back, her cheeks were glowing with colour from the hot water, and her soiled clothing and wet towel were bundled under one arm. He looked up from where he was tinkering with the scoop, trying to see why it had sprayed lubricating oil when he had pulled the starter chain. Being forced to admit that he could see nothing wrong, he decided he should wait until Kylah arrived and ask her to look at it.

"What a miraculous device," she announced, almost dancing in happiness at being clean. "I do not believe I have ever felt so fresh in my life. I took long baths regularly in the palace, of course, but they cannot compare to this marvellous shower contraption of yours."

"Well, the problem with a bath is that you're sitting in your own dirt." He scrambled to his feet and rolled down his shirt sleeves.

"I suppose that is true," Snow agreed, her nose wrinkling at the thought. She then peered curiously at the box of tools by his feet.

"What is it that you are attempting to do?" she enquired.

"The scoop spilt lubricant oil yesterday. I was trying to see why."

"Oil? I thought the scoop ran on water?"

"It does, or rather it runs on steam. But the engine also needs a drop of oil to keep all its parts running smoothly."

"Oh, I see," Snow replied, although he suspected that she didn't. "When do you think the others will arrive?"

"At sundown. We should go and ensure there is enough food for all. Although I wager, they will not come empty-handed."

She chatted to him as they returned to the cottage, her spirits high with all the wonders he had shared with her. The secrets she had learned, her excitement at the coming evening, and the sudden release from the almost unbearable strain she had lived under since she was a child.

Listening to her talk, and dropping in the odd comment, Ronin realised he was also looking forward to seeing the others again. He had decided to live so far away from them, and he still believed that the only way to ensure their survival was to rarely all be together in one place.

Do not repeat the mistakes of the past was a lesson acquired tragically hard. Ronin intended that none of them should ever have to go through such heart-breaking and crushing loss again. Still, for one evening it would be pleasant to be in the company of his friends.

He glanced at Snow as she helped him lay the table with almost all the food from his pantry. She arranged bowls and platters in a manner pleasing to the eye, then darted out to the edge of the forest to collect wildflowers. These she styled attractively in a jug and placed in the very centre of the large wooden table. He wondered what she would make of the others. He wondered what they would make of her.

At last, all was prepared, and Ronin wandered out into the cool stillness of the evening to sit on the porch in anticipation of the merriment that was to come. Following him outside, Snow folded herself down onto the porch steps and clasped her knees to her chest. She fell silent in the face of the glorious sunset that splashed gold across the treetops and spilt beams of fading warmth on the ground by her feet.

"It's so peaceful here," she finally murmured. "I don't think I have ever known what it is to feel safe and content. To not have to guard my every word, and look, and thought. To not always be cautious and doubt the motives of all around me."

"Was it always that bad?" he asked.

"I barely remember my mother," she confided. "But I think things were very different then. My mother was a queen in her own right. As the heir to her own father's kingdom, she would have inherited if she had not died before him, and as the legally anointed queen, married to the King of House White, she wielded considerable power."

"If she had not died, do you think things would have turned out the way they did?"

"No." Snow shook her head. "She would have controlled the Contratulum. She was so strong, even though she was a woman, and she was absolutely convinced of the monarch's right to rule. She never would have brooked any attempt by them to take power away from the throne."

"Why did she marry Prince Hawk, then? She did not need a male figure to give her power – she already had it. I never did understand why a queen such as Raven ever agreed to marry a weakling like him. After your father, he must have seemed a poor substitute."

"Perhaps she was lonely," Snow mused softly. "Perhaps because he was family, he reminded her of home. You did know that Hawk and my mother were second cousins?" At his nod, she continued. "Or maybe it was simply a diplomatic alliance that served to strengthen both kingdoms."

"And then she died," Ronin remarked, a random thought occurring. "It was natural causes, wasn't it? The queen's early demise?"

"Why yes – I mean, I have always been told it was a fever. It took her so quickly there was nothing the healers could do. What else could it have been?"

Ronin stayed quiet, unwilling to share the unpleasant notion that had flittered across his mind.

Snow fell silent, and into the dusky hush, there crept a sound he had been expecting – a roar far away amongst the trees. Barely audible at first, it grew louder, until Snow lifted her head and stared in its direction. Their attention caught by the sound, neither noticed the quiet arrival in the clearing of a man and a pig, until they were almost at the porch steps. Snow started at the sight of them.

"How now, Ronin," the man said, swinging a large pack off his shoulders and staring at Snow with unabashed curiosity. "What do we have here?"

"Arden!" Leaping down from the porch, Ronin reached the other man in one quick stride, clasping him in a fierce hug of greeting.

"How goes it, my friend?"

"Well, it goes well," Arden smiled, his gaze swinging back to Snow who remained frozen to the steps, her eyes wide as she took in his bizarre appearance from top to toe.

She saw a man, no longer young in years, but with a youthful sheen to his eyes that instantly reassured her, he was a friend. His clothing was an odd assortment of stout woollen trousers with a leather waistcoat from which a variety of chains draped from pocket to pocket. He wore knee-high sturdy boots with buckles and straps, and a long leather coat that almost touched the ground. On his head, he wore a close-fitting hat with straps that could buckle under his chin. A pair of goggles perched on top.

Returning her gaze, he tugged on one of the waistcoat chains and pulled out a small pair of spectacles, which he put on and peered at her through.

"Well, well," he said again. "What do we think of this, Cesil?"

This was addressed to the pig, which Snow now saw was likewise attired in clothing to match its companion's. She bit her lip at the unlikely sight of a pig clothed in a waistcoat of much-worn leather, with a pair of goggles perched on top of its head.

"Cesil?" she asked, wondering if the pig were a magical creature from myth as well, and fully expecting it to open its snout and talk to her.

But whatever Arden, or Cesil, had been about to say was swallowed up in a roaring explosion of sound and movement at the edge of the clearing. A contraption that she recognised as being like the mechanised bicycle Ronin had shown her earlier, burst through the treeline, skidded in a wide circle before them, and then fell silent. The quiet was shocking after so much noise.

The device bore two riders. The one in front kicked down an iron stand to hold it upright, as the one clasping their waist from behind swung a leg over and clambered off. He ripped off goggles and a helmet much like Arden's, and Snow saw the features of a comely young man, little more than a boy, as he grinned and waved at them.

"Ronin," he cried happily. Ronin embraced him with obvious joy.

"Eli, how fare thee?"

"G-g-good," stuttered the young man. As he turned to look curiously at Snow, she noticed a childlike innocence to his face. She smiled, wishing to put him at ease. A painful blush laid claim to his cheeks, and he ducked his head in acknowledgement, then glanced at Ronin, obviously seeking an explanation for her presence.

"Later," Ronin said. "For it is a complicated tale and one I only wish to tell once. Let us wait for the others."

"Fae left before us, but said she had something to do on the way." This was from the rider of the machine as they dismounted and pulled off their helmet and goggles to reveal the dark blonde braided hair of a hard-faced woman. She eyed Snow with suspicious dislike.

"Kylah." Ronin nodded his head. "I'm guessing the automaton butterfly this morning was one of your latest creations?"

"It was," she agreed. "Nifty little thing. It has a range of fifty leagues and a surprising turn of speed if the wind is in the right direction. The only problem is larger birds keep trying to eat it."

"I wasn't aware you were using your toys to spy on me now." Ronin's voice was casual, but even Snow heard the underlying steel.

"Normally wouldn't dream of it," Kylah replied cheerfully, seemingly unabashed at his implication. "But when Fae said you had unexpected company, we thought it prudent to judge the lie of the land before calling out the troops."

"Well, as you can see," Ronin nodded to where Snow still sat on the porch steps, "I'm not in any danger."

"No, indeed." Kylah looked Snow up and down with an appraising look that made Snow's hackles rise and had her straightening and returning the other woman's stare with an equally assessing one of her own. "I can see that. You old dog."

"Kylah," Ronin growled. "Enough."

Kylah shrugged innocently, then proceeded to pull packs from her machine, tossing them to Eli as he lurked awkwardly. He stared, open-mouthed, at Snow, in such obvious awestruck admiration, that she was amused rather than insulted.

"Eli," Kylah snapped, "stop lollygagging with the pretty lady. I could do with a hand."

"S-s-sorry, Kylah," he mumbled and jumped to help her.

At a persistent humming sound, Snow looked up to see a young woman descending from the sky. Her mechanical wings were spread to steady her descent, and her buttercup-yellow skirt billowed in the breeze as she neatly landed in the middle of the clearing. Folding the wings behind her back, the girl removed her helmet and goggles to reveal a small, enchantingly pretty face, with soft auburn hair gathered into a nimbus around her head.

She smiled when she saw Snow. A dimpled smile of such open welcome that Snow instinctively smiled back, rising to her feet as the girl strode towards her. She dumped the pack that she was wearing across her chest at Arden's feet, gently stooped to pet Cesil, then shrugged her arms out of the winged device and handed it to Eli.

"There you are," the girl exclaimed. Her voice was light and lyrical, with a lilting accent that lifted her words at the end of the sentence. "You are exactly as I imagined you. Come, I have a gift for you."

"I'm sorry, a gift?" Confused by the girl's apparent familiarity with her, Snow stared in puzzlement at the item held in the girl's outstretched hand, then glanced up into the girl's vivid green eyes. Fringed with thick long lashes, they slanted at the corners, giving the girl's face an otherworldly cast.

Fascinated, Snow gazed into them, noticing the light tattoo of entwined leaves and flowers which decorated the girl's temple and sprawled onto her cheekbone.

"Yes, a gift for you," the girl repeated. She placed the item into Snow's reluctant hand and closed her own briefly over it in a gesture of friendship. "You must wear it always," she continued. Snow opened her hand and examined the fine pendant of sparkling quartz strung on a thin leather cord.

"It's beautiful," Snow murmured, holding it up to the setting sun and watching as light glittered deep within its rose-pink depths.

"Thank you."

"I am Fae," the girl told her. "There is someone who has been watching you all of your life, and I do not believe he means you well. You are important to him. Very important if his plans are to succeed. He does not realise yet that you have escaped him, but when he does, he will look for you and he will find you unless you wear this next to your skin at all times."

Snow stared at her, cold terror trickling down her spine at Fae's words. "Someone watching me?" she began, her throat tight with fear. "Who? What does he look like? And how do you know?"

"I do not know his name. As for what he looks like I only saw inside his soul and found it to be a dark and miserable place. He is cold – so cold – and as treacherous as a snake."

"Mirage," Snow whispered and looked up at Ronin. "It must be Mirage. I must go. I've put you all in great danger by being here."

"Has she?" Ronin looked at Fae in concern. "Will her presence put us in danger?"

"No." Fae shook her head. "He knows nothing of us. It is only her he is interested in. Tell me," she turned those amazing eyes back to Snow. "This Mirage, have you ever seen him stare into a mirror for long periods, or maybe even into a bowl of water?"

"Yes," said Snow. "He always carries with him a small mirror attached to his belt, and once when he believed himself unobserved, I saw him screw it into his monocle eyepiece and stare intently into it for many minutes."

"It's as I thought." Fae looked at Ronin. "He has the Power to scry."

"Scry?" Snow interrupted. "What does that mean?"

"It's the ability to spy on someone at a distance," Ronin explained.

"Then I have brought danger to you all. I need to leave immediately."

"It's all right," Fae reassured her. "It is only possible to scry on that which you already know. As he knows nothing of us, nor this place, he cannot observe us. So long as you always wear the crystal it will block him from finding you. It has shielding properties which I have enhanced with a little protection spell of my own."

"Protection spell ..." Snow's voice trailed away as she stared at the pendant as though it might bite her. "Then that means that you're a ..."

"A witch? Yes, that's right." Fae's eyes twinkled with amusement. "But fear not, I don't have the power to do harm even if I wanted to. I felt your presence in the forest last night and knew that forces had been set in motion that are now impossible to stop. I told the others we needed to come right away, but Kylah insisted on sending an automaton first."

"An automaton?"

"Yes, the butterfly you saw whilst you were fetching water from the stream."

Snow bit her lip, remembering the strange markings of the creature, now recognising them as cogs and gears in a device like the ones Ronin had shown her – only much smaller.

"So, when I thought it had opened an eye on its wing and was looking at me?"

"It was, yes," Fae confirmed with a smile.

"Oh," Snow responded weakly, unsure how much more strangeness she could take. Gently, Ronin took the pendant from her hand and fastened it around her neck. Looking down at it resting on her skin, Snow sensed its warmth and felt reassured by its presence.

Fae pressed her palm over the crystal and murmured words in a language that Snow did not recognise, yet instinctively felt was old – very old. Heat blazed through the crystal into her skin and Snow cried out in shock as the other girl's eyes flared with an intense bloom of vivid green, before subsiding to normal.

"It's all right," Fae reassured and removed her hand. "I had to bond the crystal to you. It recognises you now as the one it must protect, and if it ever senses someone trying to scry you, or that this person is close by, it will turn black to warn you."

"Thank you," murmured Snow.

Ronin snapped a pocket watch out of his waistcoat pocket and glanced briefly at it. "Do you think the others will be much longer?" he asked Fae, who closed her eyes, then opened them with a smile.

"Here is Grein now," she replied. Once again, the clearing was filled with the sound of an engine and Snow watched in fascination as a large device, that looked for all the world like a horseless carriage, trundled into the clearing from the forest.

There was a muffled explosion, and a cloud of black smoke belched from its nether regions, causing Kylah to groan and shake her head in despair.

"How many times have I told him not to let it get so low in oil. He'll seize the engine and then no doubt expect me to work a bloody miracle and fix it for him."

The contraption shuddered to a halt. The door swung open and a helmeted and goggled head appeared. Raising a hand to them in salutation, he turned and scrabbled about inside, gathering up packs and bundles, accompanied by a frenzied barking.

Eli scuttled over and pulled open the other door, releasing a wiry bundle of canine energy which bounded about the clearing excitedly greeting everyone. It sniffed at Cesil in a way that had the little pig squealing in offended dignity and hiding behind Arden.

Finally, the creature stopped in front of Snow and sniffed at the hand that she had stretched out in thrilled hope. A princess was certainly allowed no pets of her own, and the closest she had ever come to one was secretly feeding the kitchen cats scraps saved from her plate.

But this was a dog. An actual large and boisterous dog that appeared to be no respecter of boundaries – be they human or porcine – and Snow was delighted by him. Especially when he sniffed at her hand and allowed her to stroke his brindled head, before prancing back to where his master had managed to struggle free of his device.

"Ronin, my dear fellow," bellowed this newest addition to their gathering, striding over to give Ronin a hug of greeting and leaving a trail of bundles and packages behind him.

"No, Dog, drop it!" he cried, as the dog eagerly grabbed up a parcel secured with string and tried to abscond with it. "Catch him somebody!" he roared. "That's our sausages in there ... sorry Cesil," he added, as the pig gave an almost human grunt of disapproval.

Eli and Kylah both made grabs for the hound. But he dodged between their legs, sending Eli sprawling to the ground. Kylah let loose a string of barrack-room expletives that had Snow's brows shooting up in surprise at a woman using such words.

Arden got in on the act, making a desperate grab for the dog's collar as he bounded past. He missed, causing the creature to race in even faster circles, avoiding all hands that reached and voices that commanded.

Judging his moment, Eli threw himself upon the hound, only to miss and end up flat on his face in a puddle. Even Ronin made an unsuccessful attempt at grabbing the creature, who dodged him easily. Lolloping away with his tail wagging furiously and his tongue hanging out around the package, looking for all the world as if he were laughing at them.

A bubble of laughter erupted out of Snow's throat, and then another. It was quite possibly the funniest, most carefree moment of her life, and she couldn't help the laugh that burst forth. Picking himself up from the puddle, Eli looked down ruefully at his muddy clothes, and then a grin erupted onto his face and he began to laugh.

Arden was already chuckling, a hand going down to steady Cesil, who had taken refuge behind his master's sturdy legs and was peering out at the shenanigans in obvious disapproval. Ronin looked down at Snow, pushing his long hair out of his eyes and wiping his dusty hands on his trousers. A glint came into his eyes at her obvious joy, and she saw a smile play about his usually controlled expression.

Fae had sat down beside Snow on the steps and was laughing wholeheartedly. Exchanging a happy grin with Snow, she held out a hand and started to hum. A high-pitched, soothing, tuneless melody settled over the clearing, and Snow felt herself being drawn irresistibly towards Fae.

Pulling back in confusion she glanced around at the others and saw wistful looks on their faces. Eli even stumbled a few steps towards the pretty young witch, as Dog calmed his crazed circuits of the clearing and ambled over to the steps. He dropped the package at Fae's feet, then thrust his muzzle into her lap, looking up at her with eyes of absolute devotion as she flicked a look up at Ronin.

"Thank you, Fae." Grinning he stooped and retrieved the package. "That's breakfast saved anyway." And Snow realised as the group gathered around and all heads turned to gaze with naked curiosity upon her, that the moment of shared merriment was over. The time of reckoning had come.

"Well, Ronin." Grein pulled off his helmet and goggles and stared at her. His short hair spiked all over his head and his face crinkled into lines of enquiry through his begrimed features. "Who is this? And what is she doing here?"

"Her name is Snow White," came a voice from the edge of the clearing. "And she's come to damn us all."

The seventh member of the group had arrived, and Snow's heart sank at the hatred gleaming in his dark eyes.

Chapter Five

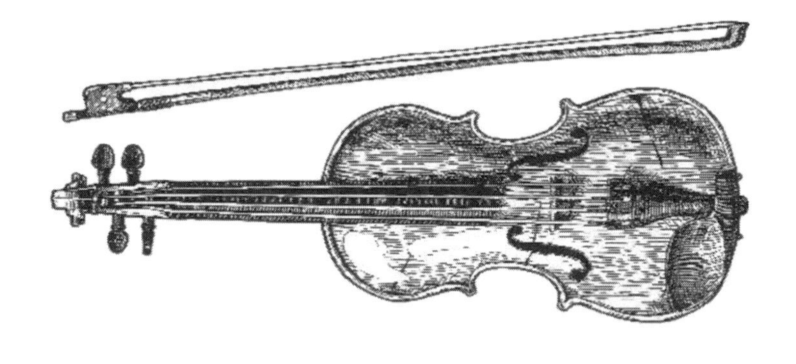

A Destroyed People

A man, younger than Ronin but older than Eli, dressed in unrelieved black. His long leather coat swirled about his ankles as he strode towards them, and his simmering resentment of Snow was an almost tangible aura about his wiry body.

Beside her, Snow heard Fae give the tiniest of gasps. Ronin moved as if to shield her from this newcomer, whose face was set firm into an expression of utter contempt and loathing.

"Nylex ..." Ronin began, as the young man reached them and stood, hands upon hips, surveying them coldly.

"Ronin," he retorted sarcastically. "Don't tell me you are unaware of who she is? Nor of the danger her very presence places every one of us in?"

Flustered and feeling accused, Snow rose to her feet, but Fae stood and slipped an arm reassuringly through hers.

"There is no danger, Nylex," she said, her voice calm and reassuring. "None but us know she is here, and I have placed protection about her so none can discover her presence."

"They will come looking for her though," he insisted angrily. "And kidnapping the princess is a crime for which we will all hang."

"Wait! Wait just a fricking moment." By now the others had gathered their wits and were congregating around them, their incredulous faces all turned upon Snow and Ronin.

"Snow White? She's Snow White? The fricking princess?" Kylah's voice was shrill with angry accusation and she thumped Ronin on the arm. "What the frick were you thinking of, bringing her here? Much as I hate to admit it, I'm with Nylex on this one."

"A princess?" Eli's eyes were round with wonder. "You're a p-p-princess?"

"Yes, I am," Snow sorrowfully admitted, for the first time in her life ashamed of her status.

"No wonder you're so b-b-beautiful," Eli breathed in genuine awe and handed her a single yellow wildflower that seemed to suddenly appear in his hand.

"Thank you, Eli," she whispered, taking the flower, close to tears at the boy's kindness.

"Protection?" Grein glanced at Fae. "A crystal?"

"Rose quartz," she confirmed and lightly touched the gem that lay snugly against Snow's chest.

"Nice," he agreed, pulling a magnifying glass from one of his many waistcoat pockets and examining it closely, much to Snow's embarrassed discomfort.

"I added a little something extra to it," Fae admitted and Grein nodded distractedly, his attention still caught by the quartz.

"Never mind about the fricking rock!" Kylah erupted. "I want to know what the frick you were thinking of, bringing her here?"

"Kylah." Eli squinted at her in disapproval. "Mind your language, she's a p-p-princess." Kylah growled with annoyance and thumped him on the arm, then for good measure thumped Ronin again.

"Men!" she exclaimed in disgust. "A big pair of eyes and a pretty pair of breosts and you forget all sense or reason."

Snow had no idea what breosts were but judging by the way every man's eyes swivelled to the front of her corset, she could have a pretty good guess. Her temper – rarely experienced but always there – began to surface. Drawing herself up to her fullest height, she looked the angry blonde woman up and down, in the way she would a cheeky serving wench who required a good dressing down.

"Now see here," she began, her voice on the freezing side of chilly. "I do not know who you think you are, but I am Princess Snow of the House White, soon to be your queen. I am the anointed ruler of this land and all who dwell within it. As such, I demand your respect and your allegiance."

There was a stunned moment of silence, then Eli sank clumsily to one knee, his expression one of childlike admiration.

"Your Highness," he murmured.

"Your Highness," repeated Fae and dipped into an elegant curtsey.

Grein bobbed a bow, his face lined with amusement. "Your Highness," he echoed.

Snow looked at Ronin helplessly. Unsure of what she had started but not wanting him to kneel before her, because that would be designating him as inferior to her and she did not want that. She could not explain why, but the idea of being his superior was distasteful to her.

But Ronin did not kneel or even bow. Instead, raising an eyebrow at her in a gesture of shared amusement, he took her hand and brushed his lips gently across it. "Highness," he said. But it was his usual teasing tone. A mere repetition of the pet name he had been using all day, and she smiled in tearful relief.

"Little Snow," Arden said with unexpected familiarity, his eyes crinkling with warmth. "You have your mother's looks, but I see your father in your face as well. His strength and his humour."

"You knew my parents?" Snow whispered.

"A long time ago, in another life, I knew them very well. I was sorry, so sorry, to hear of their passing. They were two beautiful people whose love burnt brighter than the stars. As their child, I offer you my support, Your Highness, and more importantly, my enduring friendship."

"Thank you," Snow murmured, a lone tear sliding down her cheek at his words.

"Oh, I don't fricking believe this." Kylah exploded. "Have you all gone fricking mad?"

"Kylah," Ronin snapped. "They tried to kill her."

"What?" Kylah looked at him, then at Snow. "But you're the princess, who the frick would want to kill you?"

"There are quite a few candidates," Snow confided sadly. "But the guard who dragged me to the clearing and tried to ... well, he ..." She stopped and flushed, looking down and biting her lip in remembered fear, not seeing the searching look that Kylah gave Ronin, the subtle nod of his head, nor the way Fae gently touched Kylah on the arm.

"This guard," Kylah began gruffly, "I hope you killed the despicable pig, Ronin?"

"I didn't need to," Ronin told her wryly. "Snow had already finished him off with his knife by the time I got there. But I couldn't leave her alone in the forest. Even if she had managed to evade the rest of the guards, the wolves would certainly have got her."

"You killed him?" Kylah looked Snow up and down in thinly disguised disbelief. "How did you manage to do that?"

"He had me on my knees." Snow said, her cheeks aflame in agonised shame. "And I took his knife from his belt and I ... I ..."

"Gutted him like a fish." Ronin finished for her, and Kylah's eyes gleamed with admiration.

"Good," was all she said though, then turned to Fae. "And you're sure they can't trace her here?"

"Absolutely sure," Fae reassured her. "Not with the rose quartz and my protection spell. Nothing could see through that."

"Well then," Kylah reluctantly conceded and stepped back, "I guess it's all right."

"How can it be all right?" Nylex interjected fiercely. "When it was her family that sanctioned the extermination of our people?"

"House White cannot be blamed for the genocide of the Dwarvians," Arden insisted. "They were lied to and mislead by the Contratulum. When presented with undisputable proof of the treachery of our race, they had no way of knowing that the evidence was false. So, they agreed that measures of control over the Dwarvians had to be imposed."

"Measures of control?" Nylex sneered. "They massacred us – men, women and children – none were spared. If that were not enough, the Contratulum set about erasing all memory of us from history. You, Your Highness," he demanded of Snow. "Before meeting Ronin, had you ever even heard of the Dwarvians?"

"In myth, fables," she admitted. "Stories told to me late at night by my old nurse. She swore they were true, yet when I grew older, I was informed that they were merely fairy tales." She paused and looked sorrowfully at them all. "If my family was responsible for this atrocity, then I beg your forgiveness, for I did not know."

"How could you have?" Arden said. "The Contratulum took great care to cover its tracks. They thought they had wiped us out entirely, yet a small number of us survived. Enough to begin to rebuild our society, deep within the great forest where none but us ever ventured."

"There are more of you?" Snow whispered. "Where? Can I meet them?"

"Alas, Princess, five years ago the Contratulum somehow gained knowledge of our continued existence, and in the dead of night laid waste to our village. Although we tried to defend ourselves and many heroes were created that night trying to fight back, we were no match for the might of the Contratulum. This tiny band you see before you are all that remains of a once proud and powerful people."

"Just you?" Snow whispered in horror. "You're all that's left?"

"Aye." Arden nodded. "Just us." He waved a hand around the group. "A mechanic." Kylah shrugged. "An alchemist." Grein's eyes twinkled once more at Snow. "A witch." Snow returned Fae's smile. "A trickster." Nylex pulled away in angry denial. "An apprentice." Eli flushed with pleasure at being mentioned. "And myself, a teller of stories."

"And you?" Snow looked at Ronin. "What are you?"

"Our Captain," Arden continued, "and the best of us all."

"I would dispute that," Ronin smilingly protested, "but as your Captain, I say why waste this precious time together in raking up old hurts and arguing the whys and wherefores of them? When there is food to be had, and ale to be drunk, and tunes to be played."

"Yes." Fae clapped her hands. "Let the evening commence. And let us show Princess Snow that although we may not live in a fancy palace, we still know how to throw a party the likes of which she will never forget."

"Indeed, that would not be difficult," Snow confessed. "For I have never attended a party of any sort. My aunt believed me too young to be exposed to the company that attended the gatherings my uncle held. A fact for which I am eternally grateful."

"Come then." Fae slipped her arm through Snow's. "Let us see what type of feast we can assemble while the others build a fire, for it looks to be a chilly evening."

"Chilly?" Kylah looked around the sun-warmed clearing. "Why, Fae, I plan to sleep out under the stars tonight it's so warm ...."

A brisk breeze blew through the trees, scurrying old leaves and a nip of autumn before it.

Kylah pulled a face and Grein laughed, slapping her companionably on the back. "Kylah, Kylah," he said. "Why do you insist on contradicting Fae? You know she's always right."

"Not all the time, she isn't," Kylah muttered quietly by Snow's side and shot a sour look at Nylex that Snow did not understand, and which went unnoticed and uncommented upon by the others.

Ronin had been right; the others had not come empty-handed. Besides Grein's sausages, Snow watched in wonder as various packages and bundles and jars were produced from knapsacks and from Grein's commodious horseless carriage. Several jugs of ale also appeared, which Grein informed her with a wink was of his own making and the best ale in the kingdom.

Delicately sipping some, Snow pulled a face at its sour hoppy taste. Ronin laughed and swapped her tankard for a small glass of something smooth and yellow.

"Try this," he offered. "I believe this will be more to your liking."

"What is it?" she asked, sniffing at its pleasing honey aroma, and daring a sip. Finding it pleasantly sweet, with a warming after burn, she took another larger taste, her nose wrinkling at the flavour.

"Mead made by Fae. She keeps bees and makes it from their honey."

"It's delicious," she agreed, watching as the pile of food on the table kept increasing. "So much food," she exclaimed. "We will surely never eat it all."

"Oh, we will," Ronin assured her and ruffled Eli's hair as he wandered towards the table with an empty plate and a gleam in his eye. "Whilst there's an Eli about there can never be too much food, right Eli?"

"I'm hungry," protested the boy.

Ronin laughed and let him go. "Aye, Lad, feed the termites in your belly. Perish the thought they should starve."

"T-t-termites?" Eli stared down at his stomach in concern, then hurried over to Kylah's side and whispered something in her ear. She rolled her eyes in exasperation and flicked him about the ear, before scooting him back towards the table.

"Ronin?" Snow murmured.

"Aye?"

"What is wrong with Eli? Was he born this way?"

"No. Up until five years ago, he was a bright and intelligent lad. He was learning to be a mechanic, like his big sister, Kylah, and had his sights set on learning to fly airships. And he would have done. Lissa frequently told me he had the right aptitude and the brains to make a fine pilot."

"So, what happened?"

"The Contratulum happened. That night, Kylah was working late on something in her workshop some way out of the village. She sent Eli home to get some sleep. Then the airships of the Contratulum arrived and opened fire on the village. By the time Kylah reached her home, it was well ablaze. She plunged into the building to try and rescue her family – her parents, her older sister, and Eli – but the fire was too intense, and she could only save one of them."

"Eli," Snow said.

"Eli," he agreed. "But something had happened to him. Grein says he inhaled too much smoke and that it damaged his brain. I know not if that is true, but Grein's the alchemist. If he says that is what it was, then I have no doubt he is correct. But ever since then, Eli has had the mind of a child and it is doubtful he will ever progress any further."

"It's such a shame," she said, watching the young lad as he carefully and precisely loaded up his plate to maximum capacity. Finding no room on top for one of the honey cakes also brought by Fae, he stuffed it whole into his mouth.

"It is," Ronin agreed. "And it explains much about Kylah and why you must forgive her prickly ways. We all lost so much that night – Kylah as much as anyone – and I know the guilt of not being able to save them all weighs heavy on her."

"I can imagine," Snow agreed, her gaze moving to the blonde woman who was downing a pint of Grein's ale and laughing about something with Arden and Fae. "Actually," she corrected herself, "no, I cannot imagine what she experienced – what any of you did. Excepting my old nurse who was sent away many years ago, I have never loved anyone. There has never been any whose loss I would mourn, or indeed who would mourn the loss of me. Is that not sad?" She turned her dark eyes onto Ronin, emotion swimming in their inky depths.

"Is it not pathetic that for all my riches and jewels and silken gowns, I envy you – all of you – for having each other? And even though they are now lost to you, for once knowing the love of family and friends?"

"No, Your Highness." He shook his head, his eyes as serious as hers. "It is not pathetic, although it is sad. But maybe now there are those who do care whether you live or die, for I know the others like you and are willing to accept you as one of us."

"Kylah doesn't like me."

"Kylah doesn't not like you. She is merely cautious and deeply protective of the only family she has left. Give her time. She will come to include you in their ranks and then you will have no fiercer or more loyal friend."

"And Nylex hates me."

"Ah, Nylex. Yes, well, he is a deeply troubled young man with a burden of guilt so large it threatens to smother him every day."

"Guilt?"

"On the night it happened, Nylex should have been on sentry duty. Despite it being almost a century since the Contratulum massacre, the memories still ran deep. Every night a sentry was posted, ready to sound the alarm should any approach the village. But on that night Nylex had been drinking with a group of friends to celebrate his upcoming nuptials, and he fell asleep when he should have been standing guard."

"Oh." Snow's eyes flew to where the young man stood alone, clasping a glass of mead. He was watching the others almost hungrily. As if he wished to join in with their revelry but would not allow himself to do so.

"He was awoken by the sound of the village burning, and the screams of his family and friends as they died in their homes. He lost everything and everyone."

"His fiancée?" Snow breathed.

"Was lost to him too."

"That is truly awful, no wonder he ..."

"Hates himself and punishes himself more than any other could?"

"Yes," Snow agreed, a pang of empathy for the lonely and bitter young man piercing her breast.

"Ronin." Fae appeared before them and clasped Ronin's hand. "Music. Please let us have music, for I have a desire to dance."

"Very well." He crossed to a chest pushed against the wall, reached in, and took out a fiddle, it's wood smooth and rich from the passage of time. "Allow me a moment to tune it, for it has been some time."

"Wonderful." Fae clapped her hands. "Come, Eli," she cried, taking the young man by the hand. "You will dance with me first."

Quickly stuffing one last piece of honey cake into his mouth, Eli nodded in eager anticipation and followed Fae from the cottage. Outside the bonfire was blazing brightly, its warmth and moving energy instantly attracting Snow as she followed Fae and Eli outside.

"Do you dance, Your Highness?" called Fae over her shoulder.

"I'm not sure," replied Snow, uncertain whether the formal dances she had been instructed in would be the kind that could be danced around a bonfire, under the stars, to the strains of an old violin.

Chapter Six

When Evil Meets in a Darkened Room

He was not followed. Of that, he could be certain. Slipping quietly through the shadows of the slumbering palace, he muttered a few words of concealment and walked past the men guarding the gate. They did not see him. Would not remember that a few heartbeats after midnight, a dark and menacing figure had oozed by like oil on water.

Mirage paid no heed to the men whose minds he had so easily manipulated. Peasants. Their simple brains were incapable of grasping anything beyond their next meal or having enough coppers for a turn in the bawdy house. It had been child's play to convince them they saw nothing, heard nothing, felt nothing.

But then, he found most lacked the strength to refuse him. They would go slack-jawed and glassy-eyed in dumb agreement every time he whispered a direction into their ear, his wishes rapidly becoming their own. Only one was his intellectual equal, and at the thought of her black hair and perfect skin, her dark eyes that pretended acquiescence but harboured defiance, Mirage's breath quickened, and his fists clenched.

The clock struck the quarter-hour, and he accelerated his pace. It would not do to keep the Pontifex waiting. Mirage feared no man, but it would not be prudent to annoy Pontifex Slie, and it would be detrimental to his health to give the Contratulum reason to view him as anything other than an ally.

Mirage reached his destination – a little-remarked upon stout wooden door at the end of a nondescript side alley. He paused to ensure he was alone, then removed his gauntlet and placed his palm on the wood. He murmured the words of entry under his breath, and there was a click deep within the door. It silently swung open to reveal a long, dark passageway stretching away into infinity, lit by a single flickering globe of light strung on a wire from the ceiling.

The door closed behind him. Mirage waited impatiently until with a hiss the next globe on the circuit spluttered into life. He walked forward, hearing the click as the first light was extinguished behind him. Understanding it was a necessary line of defence, but still wanting to scream with impatience at the time it took to traverse the passageway.

He amused himself by imagining the superstitious fears of those peasants outside if they ever saw such marvels as the light globes – let alone the other wonders that the Contratulum hoarded with all the greed of a miser clutching his chest of gold.

Reaching the end of the eternal passageway, Mirage paused in front of ornate double doors guarded by a pair of elite soldiers who studied him dispassionately. It would be no good to try and bypass them with mind-control trickery. Handpicked by Slie himself as children, they had been raised to be able to close their minds to such manipulation.

"Counsellor Mirage for Pontifex Slie," he murmured, although there was no need for such an announcement. Slie knew he was there – had known he was approaching the moment he placed his hand on the outer door, maybe even before then.

One of the guards nodded.

"Counsellor, you are expected." His tone was barely the correct side of respectful and Mirage clenched a fist, longing to be able to stop the man's heart at his impudence. Swallowing down such rash impulses, he merely inclined his head and waited for the guard to open the door and step aside.

Once through the doors, any pretence that this was a residence like any other was dropped, and Mirage was awestruck as he always was, at the sheer scale and audacity of the Contratulum. To have such a vast base of operations, right under the nose of House White sitting in their pretty palace above, was mind-blowing.

Passing through the doors, he emerged onto a balcony that ringed the entire huge atrium. The biggest enclosed space Mirage had ever been in, it was easily twenty times larger than the palace throne room. Just to walk around the balcony overlooking it would take twenty minutes. Leaning over the railing to look down into the vast area below, Mirage felt his head swim at the deadly drop to the floor.

Completely lit by artificial light globes, the temperature was permanently maintained at a pleasant level by means of vents set into the wall at regular intervals, which blasted warm or cold air depending on the season.

His footfalls muffled on the rich thick carpet beneath his boots. Mirage wished for such luxuries within his suite of rooms in the palace, but such a notion was an impossibility, at least for the meantime. His thin lips pressed into a smirk of anticipation at the thought of the changes he would make once their plans had come to fruition, and the kingdom was under their command.

Glancing over the railings, he saw a team of mechanics far below, fussing around a mighty airship, like worker bees about their queen. Again, another marvel from the realms of myth, which the Contratulum had believed was true, they had then painstakingly set about acquiring the technology for themselves.

He had heard the tales of how many Dwarvians died under extreme torture and mind-stripping before a complete set of plans had been created. Then the many years of training their mechanics to build and fly such incredible contraptions. But it had been worth it – oh, yes – it had certainly been worth it.

When intelligence had been gained – at great cost to himself – of a last miserable settlement of Dwarvians deep within the forest, there had been no question that it would be these mighty sky leviathans that would be deployed to clear out this final infestation.

And what a success they were. The Contratulum's mighty fleet caught the Dwarvian rats completely by surprise. They had laid waste to the entire village and sent the rebels own hastily launched airships crashing to the ground in vast fireballs of death. None survived. The entire Dwarvian race was utterly destroyed this time and with it the only people who might have had the technology and the mental acumen to pose a threat to the all-encompassing stranglehold the Contratulum must acquire over the kingdom.

He walked for ten minutes around the circuit of the atrium before reaching an ornate golden door recessed into the thick wall. A small desk was posted outside, at which sat a young man, his black robes with a single band of gold on the collar indicating he was still only in his first five years of prelateship.

"May I be of assistance?" He raised his brows in officious enquiry as Mirage stopped before him.

"Counsellor Mirage to see the Pontifex Slie," Mirage repeated, barely containing his impatience as the young man searched down a scroll in front of him, seeming to linger deliberately over each name.

"Of course, Counsellor Mirage. Please leave any weapons you might have." He gestured towards the large basket positioned to the left of the door.

Mirage drew his lips back in a mirthless smile, and withdrew his sword, placing it blade down into the basket, along with his belt knife. He went to enter the door, but the young man discreetly coughed and glanced down at Mirage's feet. Perhaps not so green after all, Mirage thought, and removed the daggers from both of his boots and tossed them resentfully into the basket.

"Thank you for your cooperation, Counsellor," chimed the young man and operated a lever under his desk that creaked the door open wide enough to admit entrance.

He was good, Mirage thought, passing through into the room beyond. He smiled to himself as he gently ran his thumb over the ring on his index finger – a ring that had a sharp needle in its large central stone with enough poison on its tip to stop a man's heart in seconds. But he wasn't *that* good.

The room was dark, as it always was. Its sole source of illumination a bright lamp on the large desk in the middle of the room. Mirage walked softly towards the light. The door closed and locked behind him, and he knew he was trapped in this room until its occupant decided he may leave.

The Pontifex sat at the desk, ostensibly busy with some paperwork, but Mirage knew him to be fully aware of his entrance. The room echoed beyond the darkness, and Mirage reflected how he had no real idea of how cavernous the chamber was. Certainly, there was a sense of a vast echoing space all around him and he wondered what secrets this chamber held beyond his vision.

He reached the desk and waited, knowing it would be foolhardy to address the Pontifex before he was ready to bestow his attention upon Mirage. A movement flickered in the shadows, and to his surprise, a fire lizard crawled onto the desk and squatted upon a pile of paperwork.

Curiously, Mirage studied it. A small, brightly coloured creature, they were native to the warmer lands of the south and he wondered at its unlikely presence here in Slie's inner sanctum. The creature looked at him and flicked out a long pink tongue as though tasting the air. It was theorised that such creatures could be the basis for the dragon tales of old, and Mirage supposed that made them mildly interesting but could not imagine that being the reason why Slie should possess one. Surely, the Pontifex had not grown sentimental in his advancing years and acquired one as a pet.

The creature blinked. Mirage startled at the slight delay to the blink, the faint, almost imperceptible click as its eyelids snapped shut. Fascinated, he leaned closer to examine it. Yes, that almost too-perfect sheen to its skin, the stilted awkwardness to its gait. Surely, this was no natural creature, but one of mechanical construction.

"Beautiful, is it not?" Slie murmured without raising his head. "Of course, it is one of the early prototypes, but still not without merit."

"It's incredible," replied Mirage in genuine admiration, and touched the creature with his finger. Its hide was rubbery and chilled, its textured surface giving it the appearance of a reptile's leathery skin. "I had no idea our experiments with such devices had advanced so far."

"Oh, my dear fellow." Finally, Slie lay down his pen and looked at him. "We have advanced so much further than this amusing child's toy, and that is one of the reasons why I have summoned you here. I feel it is time that you knew the final stages of the plan. Time that you were entrusted with secrets beyond your reckoning."

"Your Grace?" Mirage felt his heart give a surge of anticipation. Was he finally to be recognised for the key player that he was in this endeavour? He was growing frustrated with the scraps of knowledge he was doled out in miserly portions and had chafed at not being trusted with the whole grand plan. *When the time is right,* Slie had promised him. Was the time right now? Were the schemes of over a century finally coming to fruition?

Logic dictated that it must be. With Snow's ascension to the throne a scant fortnight away, Mirage had believed that time was running out, that under no circumstances would she be allowed to claim the crown. But with the Contratulum, nothing was ever a certainty, and it did not do to assume anything.

"Sit," Slie ordered. Mirage eased the other chair away from the desk and settled upon it as comfortably as he could. Compared to the vast winged and padded construction of the chair the Pontifex rested his not inconsiderable frame in, Mirage's seat was hard and unyielding, designed to not allow its occupant to relax even for a moment.

"Now then. First thing first," Slie began. "Your mission to the Northern outpost? I trust you were successful?"

"Of course, your Grace. Our units there are ready and waiting to advance south on your command."

"Good, good. And was everything there to your liking?"

"Quite – only ..." Mirage paused and Slie quirked a brow at him.

"Only?"

"The Commander there, Barnabus. I am unsure as to how committed he is to the cause. I sensed a certain reticence about the man."

"Hmm. We cannot have any hesitation on the day. What do you suggest?"

"His second-in-command, Heyes, seemed an ardent and devoted believer, Your Grace. I believe him to be more fit for the task at hand."

"Heyes?"

"Yes, Your Grace."

"Very well. Your instincts have never let us down before. Replace Barnabus and have Heyes fully instructed in what he should do."

"A wise decision, Your Grace." Mirage hid a smirk behind his hand. That would teach a much-needed lesson to those arrogant backward northerners. Sensing that their loyalties lay more with their commander, Barnabus than to the Contratulum, Mirage had concerns that the chain of command would stop with him. No – the fanatically loyal, ambitious, and sycophantic Heyes was a much better man to be in charge.

"Now then. While you were off gallivanting around in the north, there has been a rather unfortunate development."

"Development?" Mirage sat upright, something in Slie's tone sparking unease in his soul.

"Yes, we appear to have misplaced the princess."

"Snow? You've lost Snow?" Mirage couldn't help the accusatory note that underlay his words, and Slie's eyes narrowed in annoyance. "I apologise for my outburst, Your Grace." He quickly tried to pour soothing oil onto the situation. "I was shocked by your words and spoke too hastily. Of course, I did not imply any criticism of you, but merely wished to know what you meant?"

"It appears that Snow requested, and was granted, permission to go and visit her old nurse in Thornfield."

"Granted by whom?"

"Your protégé, the Princess Jay. Did you have any prior knowledge of this, Mirage?"

"Of course not, Your Grace. As far as I was aware, Snow was to be kept busy with her duties until the coronation, I gave strict instructions – she was never to be left with idle time on her hands."

"Yes, well. Obviously, there was a lapse in your control somewhere. Two days ago, a message arrived from the old woman informing Snow that she was ill – dying even – and would like to see her one last time to bestow her blessing upon her for her ascension."

"I see. And Jay let her go?"

"Not only did she let her go, but she sent along a full legion of her guard to escort her. Our informant within the palace did not get wind of the plan until they had left. By the time they got a message to us, it was too late to intervene."

"This is merely a setback, Your Grace. Snow is no fool. She will not risk missing her coronation. She will be back within a day or so. She was very fond of the old woman, so, naturally, she would wish to see her before her demise. Has your spy in Thornfield confirmed her arrival?"

"That is the problem. She never did arrive. And the old woman is reported to be hale and hearty, and certainly not at death's door as the message claimed. Not only that, but all of Jay's battalion arrived back in the palace last night – all bar one that is."

The two men exchanged level looks across the desk, and Mirage's mind raced with the implications of these tidings.

"So, where is the princess?" he asked, and Slie again levelled a shrewdly assessing stare at him.

"*That* is what I was hoping *you* could inform me."

"The message was plainly a ruse to get Snow out of the palace," Mirage murmured, trying to arrange all the parts of the puzzle to make a logical whole. "The Princess Jay has become increasingly irrational about Snow. Her jealous suspicions that her husband prefers the company of her niece have been growing, and her moods have not been improved by her current, delicate condition."

"Yes – good work on that matter, by the way. I do not wish to know the details of how you achieved the impossible, but Jay being with child could be crucial to the plan."

"Thank you, Your Grace," Mirage smirked, remembering a dark night, a transformation spell, a woman desperate to reclaim her negligent husband, and a sleeping potion to ensure the hapless Prince Hawk had no memory of what he had – or rather had not – done that night.

"It was a challenging task, but one that was not without its pleasures."

The Pontifex grunted in amused distaste, but Mirage fancied he saw a flash of well-concealed lustful interest behind the man's eyes. The Contratulum was supposed to be a chaste order, yet there were rumours and whispered accounts of this dictate not always being strictly adhered to.

"Do you believe Jay to be behind Snow's disappearance?"

"If it was not by your doing, Your Grace, and it certainly wasn't by mine, then Jay is the only other candidate."

"What about Hawk? It is no secret that he is desperate to get into his stepdaughter's undergarments. Is there any chance she returns his affections? Could he possibly have smuggled her out of the palace and secreted her in a secret love nest somewhere?"

"No." Mirage dismissed the possibility without even giving it a second thought. "Snow despises him. She would never have agreed to go anywhere with him. And it is inconceivable that Jay would have given him her soldiers to transport her rival for his affections to a love nest. No, it is Jay who is behind this. I fear she may have taken Snow with intent to do her harm – may already have killed her."

"Pray for all our sakes that is not so, Mirage. We need the princess alive a little longer for the plan to succeed."

"What attempts have been made to find her?"

"The usual, but if Jay's soldiers know what happened to her, they're keeping it to themselves. All my spies could find out was that one of them disappeared whilst out on patrol, and they later found him dead – apparently attacked by a wolf. Although my thinking is it was more likely a she-wolf."

"You believe Snow killed him?"

"It's the only thing that makes any sense. What do you think? You probably know the girl better than any. Is she capable of such a thing?"

Mirage considered the question carefully, remembering those dark eyes, that quietly contained manner that hid her father's strength and determination. The treacherous path he had watched her skilfully traverse these past few years. Her refusal to bow to his suggestions.

"Yes," he agreed slowly, nodding his head. "Under the right circumstances, and given the right provocation, I do believe Snow White could be capable of anything."

Chapter Seven

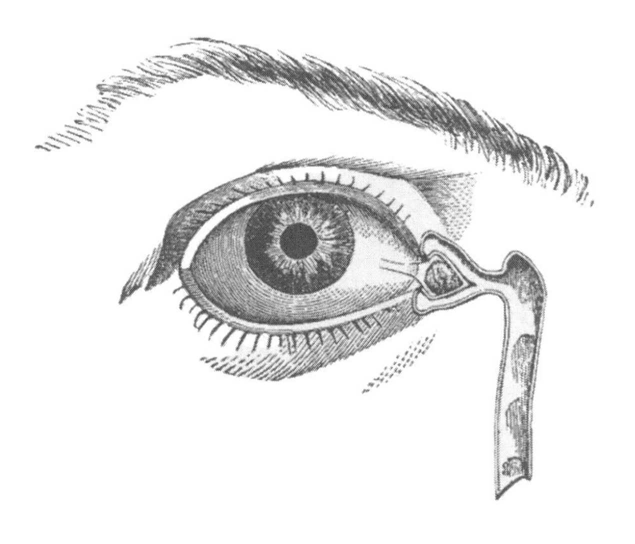

A Clockwork Princess

There was silence in the room at his words. Slie leant back in his chair and nodded, absentmindedly toying with the tail of the mechanical lizard as he considered the implications. He sighed and met Mirage's concerned gaze.

"So," he began. "Working on the assumption that the princess did indeed manage to kill the guard, we need to find her and find her fast. She will be lost somewhere within the Great Forest, alone and vulnerable. We need to get to her before the wolves do – always assuming they haven't already."

"Do you wish me to ...?"

"If you wouldn't mind."

"Of course." Mirage reached for the small mirror hanging from his belt. Unscrewing the protective lens from his eyepiece he fixed the mirror in its stead, took a deep breath, and cautiously opened his eye.

Damaged beyond repair in the incident, his eye had been replaced with a mechanical one, but of course, none but the Pontifex and the head mechanics of the Contratulum knew this. To the rest of the world, it seemed to be an ornate eyepatch that he wore out of vanity to hide his disfigurement – when in truth with his mechanical eyepiece he could see better than any human.

Now he gazed into the mirror and thought of Snow. Feeling a twinge of amusement, he imagined her horror if she ever discovered just how many times, he had spied on her in the past. In her chambers when she believed herself alone, in her bath ...

Pulling himself back to the moment, Mirage frowned as he spied nothing but a swirling storm of white shapes and images. Removing the mirror, he carefully wiped it clean on his kerchief, screwed it back into the fixing, and tried again.

Still nothing.

Seriously perplexed, he removed the mirror and looked in concern at the Pontifex. "I cannot see her," he admitted, and Slie's eyes narrowed even further.

"What does that mean?" he demanded. "Is the girl dead?"

"I am uncertain," Mirage replied slowly. "I have scried on corpses before and have seen nothing but blackness, as though looking into the abyss where their soul now resides. But this is different. This is something I have never seen before. It is as if another image is being superimposed over that of the princess."

"A barrier of some kind?" Slie demanded in surprise.

"Perhaps," Mirage agreed.

"But how can that be? Can the girl somehow be blocking you?"

"I do not believe so. She possesses no knowledge of my ... gift ... so I do not see how she could have learnt to block me from seeing her. It may be that where she is within the forest, there is some natural element that is working as a barrier. But if that is so, I do not know what it is, and I have never come across its like before."

"But you do not believe her to be dead?"

"I cannot be certain, but I do not think so."

The Pontifex was silent for a moment as if reorganising strategies in his head.

"This is ... unfortunate," he finally said. "All attempts to find the girl must be made. But, if she truly is lost to us, there is an alternative plan. Come with me – and remember that not a word of this is to be breathed beyond these chambers."

"Of course, Your Grace," replied Mirage, following Slie's example and rising to his feet. Outwardly calm, inside he was a seething mass of anticipation that secrets were finally to be revealed, and previously locked doors thrown open to allow him entry.

Trailing the Pontifex, Mirage now saw there was another door into the room. Hidden in the shadows in the furthest corner, it was plain and unadorned with the usual trappings of the Pontifex's power. Mirage could barely contain himself as Slie pulled a chain from around his waist, selected a large key, and inserted it into the lock.

Beyond the door was yet another passageway – this one brightly lit by glowing globes to its conclusion some twenty feet away. Mirage noticed with a twist of wry amusement that they stayed lit even after he had passed beneath them.

At the end was another door – this one thick and imposing. Yet again, Slie fumbled with his keychain to find the right key for the lock. It swung open, and Mirage followed the Pontifex through, his eyes darting about the large room he now found himself in.

It was a workshop, but not like the usual Contratulum workshops where he attended for regular checks on his mechanical eye and other ... parts. Always, he had been slightly in awe of these places, feeling somewhat intimidated at being in the presence of such devices and such men of knowledge. But this workshop made those he was used to appear clumsy and backward, an airship compared to a horse and cart.

The walls were gleaming white. There was a low, persistent hum from the hundreds of light globes that hung from the ceiling, bathing every workbench in bright light, and banishing all shadows to the very outer perimeters of the room.

All around were men in white, working on various projects on those well-illuminated workbenches. Following the Pontifex, he noticed none of the workers spared a glance for the most illustrious figure in the whole organisation. Then his eye was drawn to *what* they were working on, and he understood their total absorption. Why Slie had impressed on him the need for absolute secrecy.

Body parts. They appeared to be working on body parts. There was a human hand attached to a device, with a mechanic working at the open wrist end. As Mirage watched in fascination, the fingers of the hand uncurled, then curled back up again. Over there another mechanic was working on what looked like a disembodied leg, smoothing down its skin and ensuring it was not so taut over the kneecap that the joint could not move smoothly.

Unthinkingly, Mirage's hand crept up to touch his eyepiece. Although a marvel of ingenuity, it did not look human, thus necessitating the wearing of his eyepatch. But if the Contratulum had advanced to this level of sophistication, perhaps it could be replaced with something more lifelike.

"Come on, keep up." snapped the Pontifex. Mirage realised in his distraction that he had stopped walking and was staring, open-mouthed, at all the wonders around him.

"Sorry, Your Grace," he mumbled and hurried to catch up as Slie led him out and down another corridor and into an ornately decorated parlour. Looking around in barely concealed surprise, Mirage realised it was a replica of Princess Snow's receiving chamber in the palace far above their heads.

Beckoning him to come all the way in, Slie closed the door behind them and motioned him to sit in one of the gilded chairs pushed against the wall.

"Sit down and be quiet," he instructed. "And watch."

Confused, Mirage did as he was ordered. Pushing his long, heavy locks over his shoulder, he felt a prickle of sweat spring up between his shoulder blades, as an instinctive unease crept over him that he was about to witness something of monumental importance.

For long moments, nothing happened. Then a curtain moved on one side of the room and a woman stepped out from behind it. Lavishly clothed in a richly embroidered silk gown, she moved into the room, her face turned away from the watching men. Her step was quick and light. Her long, dark curtain of silken hair was instantly familiar as she went to a table placed in the centre of the room, pulled out a chair and sat in it, her spine ramrod straight.

"Good evening, Your Highness," said Slie.

There was a pause, then, "Good evening, Pontifex Slie," replied the figure.

Mirage sharply sucked in his breath. The hair, the body, the voice, the manner, were all hers – were all Snow White's. He darted a quick, confused glance at the Pontifex, who smirked, but held up a hand for silence.

"How are you this evening, Your Highness?"

"I am well, thank you, Your Grace."

"Good. That's good. Tell me, Your Highness, how was the weather today?"

"The weather was most agreeable, and I very much enjoyed my turn about the gardens."

It was undeniably her voice – and yet, and yet … something was amiss. There was no spark to her tone, no variance in the cadence of her sentences. Delivered in a flat, monotone manner, it was almost as if she were a … Mirage leapt to his feet and in one stride crossed the room to where the figure sat so still and stiff in her chair.

"Your Highness?" he asked. "Snow?"

There was an almost imperceptible click as she turned her head to look at him, and he saw. And knew. And understood in a flash of wondering dread, what they had accomplished.

He backed away. Turned to look at Slie who had remained seated, watching him intently. Looking back at the creature seated in the chair calmly gazing at him, Mirage noticed little tell-tale signs that this was not the real princess, was not *his* Snow.

Her hair was black – certainly as black as Snow's. But it lacked that blueish sheen that had always fascinated him. Those large, dark eyes did not have the fire swirling in their depths which so tantalised him to explore her mind and bend her will to his. And she was calm – too calm. When he was with Snow, he could sense the emotions churning within her soul. Although he appreciated it was his gift that allowed him that exclusive glimpse under the surface of the perfect princess, the lack of it made this thing appear flat and two-dimensional.

Then there was her scent or rather lack of it. Entering a room Snow had left, with his heightened olfactory system, Mirage could always taste her scent upon the air – roses and cinnamon – it was unmistakable. Yet this creature was scentless and instantly rendered sexless and inert.

Still … even with these flaws, it was enough like the real thing to fool any but those who knew the princess intimately and could certainly pass at a distance.

"It's incredible," he finally murmured. Slie arose from his seat and joined him at the table to stare at Snow's doppelganger. It stared back, coolly, and dispassionately.

"Yes," the Pontifex agreed. "This latest model is almost perfect."

"Latest model? How many models have there been?"

"Since work began five years ago, over one hundred." Mirage swallowed, imagining a hundred mechanical Snows. "Yet, it's still not quite … there. The eyes are lacking humanity, would you agree? After all, the eyes are the windows to the soul, but this creature looks as though nobody is in residence."

"Perhaps," Mirage cautiously agreed, reluctant to appear too critical.

The door opened behind them, and a mechanic shoved his head through the gap, raising his bushy eyebrows at Slie as the men turned to confront him.

"How did she do, Your Grace?" he asked.

Mirage frowned at the man's familiarity. Either the man was a complete fool or knew his worth to the Pontifex to be so great he could take a few liberties.

"The eyes, Duncan. It's as we discussed. The eyes let her down."

"Ah, I have been working on something that might overcome that, Your Grace. May I ...?"

"Yes, by all means." Slie moved to allow the man access and said in an aside to Mirage, "I must confess to an absolute fascination with all things mechanoid and have spent many an hour watching Duncan, and his team, work. Have I not, Duncan?"

"You have indeed, Your Grace," Duncan confirmed with a friendly smile at Slie that had Mirage swallowing down his resentment at this evidence of a relationship beyond that of master and subordinate. Then all such petty matters were forgotten, as Duncan unrolled a bundle of tools and took out a small pair of forceps.

Feeling about the figure's temple, he pushed on some hidden catch within the device and there was a faint click. To Mirage's queasy fascination, a channel opened under the eye socket, which Duncan then inserted a small syringe into.

"Fascinating," rumbled Slie. "Absolutely fascinating. And what are you doing now, Duncan?"

"Well, Your Grace, I've been giving the lack of spark in the eyes some thought and realised it's because they always stay the same. Now, in humans, our eyes are constantly changing colour as our mood and emotions change, and as external forces such as sunlight and brightness affect the pigmentation of the eye. So, I thought if I could insert a vial of a gaseous substance under the surface of the eye, it would make it appear as if the eyes were changing colour."

All this time, Duncan had been busy injecting into first one eye and then the other, carefully closing the concealed channel under each eye socket as he did so, to leave the skin as perfect and blemish-free as the real Snow.

"Close your eyes, Your Highness," he ordered the puppet princess, who obeyed instantly. Gently, Duncan massaged first one eyelid then the other. "Now open them," he ordered.

Slowly, the thing opened its eyes and looked at them.

"Good evening, Your Highness," said Slie again.

"Good evening, Pontifex Slie," it replied. But this time warmth stirred in her eyes and apparent emotion shone through them.

"Better," breathed the Pontifex. "Much, much, better. Do you not agree, Mirage?"

"Yes," began Mirage, then hesitated, unsure how honest he could be. "It is, only ..."

"Only?"

"Well, the hair is not quite right. Snow's hair has a bluish sheen to it, like a raven's wing. It is particularly noticeable in sunlight, and

I know others have remarked on it." He rolled his eyes. "At last count, there were at least four sonnets praising the Princess Snow's hair."

"Right." Duncan had produced paper and pencil from somewhere and was busy writing down notes. "This is very helpful, sir, anything else?" Normally, Mirage would not have hesitated to correct the man, and insist on his correct title being used, but was far too interested in the subject at hand to worry about such petty things.

"The voice needs more variation. It is too monotonal. And then there is her lack of scent."

"Lack of scent?" Both men stared at him and Mirage hurried to explain himself.

"Yes, Snow has an aroma all her own. Surely you are aware of this, Pontifex?"

Slie raised his brows in distaste. "I cannot say I have ever noticed it, but then I do not get as close to the princess as perhaps you do?"

"It is a pleasing mix of roses and cinnamon. Maybe you can replicate it?" This last was to Duncan, who nodded his head thoughtfully.

"We can certainly try, sir. Anything else?"

"She lacks Snow's spark, her energy. This creature may look like her, but a person is made up of much more than mere outward appearances. Snow has a presence, an energy about her that this mechanoid lacks."

"That is precisely why we need to find the girl and find her fast," replied the Pontifex. "To achieve that spark, as you call it, within our princess, there is something we need to take from the original and insert into the copy."

"And what is that?" Mirage asked curiously.

"Her heart, sir," said Duncan. "We need her heart, preferably still beating at the time of extraction."

Chapter Eight

Images in the Firelight

She had never known that such times could be had. That such friendly companionship could lift one's spirits so, it seemed possible to touch the stars glittering fiercely above. Stars that Snow had never noticed before, having spent her whole life within the high palace walls. Especially in the last few years, when she had ensured that by nightfall, she was firmly ensconced within her chambers with the stout door locked against all who might wish to gain entry.

Ronin struck up a lively jig on his fiddle and Fae and Eli danced joyfully around the fire – Fae as light as thistledown, and Eli capering about like a loon, a broad grin all over his open face. Snow clapped along to the tune, laughing at their antics. Giggling with pleasure when Eli twirled Fae to one side and bowed to Snow, holding out his hand in obvious invitation.

Protesting that she did not know the steps, she still bounced around the clearing with Eli, laughing so hard she felt sure her corset laces would burst. Fae dragged Grein up to perform a slightly more dignified, but no less energetic, turn about the bonfire, and Kylah and Arden laughed and clapped along to keep time.

Only Nylex stood apart, his face registering such poignant and bitter loneliness that it was all Snow could do to stop herself from running over to him and pulling him into their merriment. But she did not, knowing full well he would not appreciate it. Besides, she was unwilling to spoil the joyful mood of the evening.

The dance ended, and Snow collapsed onto the porch steps, breathless and clasping at the stitch in her side. Arden murmured something in Ronin's ear, who nodded, tucked the fiddle under his chin and began to play a tune Snow instantly recognised. Slow and dignified, it was an old waltz tune that had long been popular at court. It was the first dance to which, as a young princess, she had been taught the steps.

Arden bowed courteously to her and held out his hand. Surprised, Snow allowed herself to be guided to a level part of the clearing where Arden assumed position in front of her, one hand in the small of his back, the other held up at shoulder height with his palm facing her.

Snow stepped closer, placing her opposing hand in the small of her own back and lightly touching her palm to his. Slowly and precisely, they began to dance. Surprisingly graceful on his feet, Arden proved to be an expert at the steps, and Snow relaxed into the dance. The familiarity of the tune took her back to happier times as she remembered learning this very dance with her old nurse.

Gracefully they moved, twirling apart and re-joining, their palms remaining lightly touching throughout all the complicated manoeuvres.

Out of the corner of her eye, Snow was aware of the others gathering closer to watch, their smiling faces sharply illuminated in the leaping flames of the bonfire. In perfect alignment, Arden twirled Snow around into a deep curtsey as the fiddle wept to a halt, and bowed over her, their palms still touching.

"Oh, well done," cried Fae, clapping her small hands in delight. "That was wonderful."

Smiling up at Arden, Snow rose to her feet and impulsively threw her arms around him in a friendly hug. "Thank you," she whispered.

"I am amazed I remembered the steps as well as I did," Arden admitted with a twinkle. "It has been many a year since I danced it."

"You were perfect," she assured him, then shrieked as Eli bounded over and grabbed her hand. The fiddle sang into life again, and the dancing continued until all were left breathless and thirsty. Then the remaining jugs of ale and mead were brought from the cottage, and they collapsed around the bonfire, mugs in hand, gazing silently into the flames.

Ronin once more lifted the fiddle, nodding at Fae, who moved to sit beside him on the porch steps. She arranged her skirts neatly and, taking a deep breath, began to sing.

Snow had never heard anything like it. Haunting and twisting, the tune was unfamiliar. Fae sang in a language she could not understand, yet the mournfulness of the melody set tears pricking at Snow's eyes. Instinctively, she knew this to be a song of loss and longing.

She glanced at the others, at the heartbreak and grief evident on their faces. Softly, one by one, they joined in, their voices merging in the still, dusky evening to become a harmonious entity that rose to the stars.

Snow looked for and found Nylex. Alone and apart, standing beyond the circle of firelight, he appeared statue-like in the darkness, apparently unmoved by the nostalgic moment being shared by his friends. Then he sharply turned his head.

In the glow of the full moon that had pulled itself over the rim of the treetops and chose that instant to beam down upon them, Snow saw his lips silently moving, and watched as he wiped a hand over his face.

Her heart ached for him. For all of them, and for all that they had lost, and she continued to watch as he visibly pulled his scattered senses together. Seeming to feel her scrutiny, he looked up, straight into her eyes. At the utter hatred and seething resentment Snow witnessed there, she turned away in sorrow, not wishing to intrude on his private suffering any longer.

The fiddle quivered into a final note that hung in the air, before softly fading. There was a sense of people coming back into themselves, as throats were cleared, and eyes surreptitiously wiped.

Snow realised that during the song, Dog had crept closer and was now resting his large head on her lap, his eyes closing in delight as she gently petted his soft ears.

Eli crouched down before her. "P-p-princess Snow," he said, and Snow smiled at him.

"It's Snow, Eli, I'm just Snow out here."

"S-s-snow," he said, struggling to get her name out through his stutter. He held out his cupped hands before her and gently opened them to reveal a moth perched on his palms. Large, and beautifully decorated, it sat there seemingly unafraid, opening, and closing, its wings as if showing off its exquisite apparel to Snow.

"Oh, Eli," she breathed. "It's beautiful, but where did it come from?"

"I c-c-called it to me," he tried to explain. Snow frowned in confusion as the moth seemed to tire of Eli's palm and fluttered into the air to land on Dog's muzzle. Confused, the animal crossed his eyes trying to see the tiny creature that was perched upon his nose, and Snow smiled as dog and insect stared directly at one another.

Then Eli cupped his hands about it and when he opened them again, the moth was gone. Snow gasped, and Eli's face flamed beetroot red in embarrassment.

"Eli, how ...?" she began, but he had gone, bounding away with Dog in hot pursuit. Ronin saw her dumbfounded expression and moved to sit beside her, placing his fiddle down on the steps between them.

"Does Eli have the Power?" she asked in concern, remembering the old dark tales about the Dwarvians. Ronin's eyes were troubled as he studied her in the flickering light of the bonfire.

"Not the Power in the way you mean. None of us does. That was the vicious rumour spread by the Contratulum to excuse their genocide of our people."

"But Eli ... Fae ...?"

"All Dwarvians possess elemental magic to one degree or another."

"Elemental magic?"

"It's a gentle, natural skill. We are so in tune with nature and the elements that we can draw upon its strength and bend them slightly to our will."

"So, the moth ...?"

"Was a real moth. Eli merely summoned it to him and then sent it back to wherever it had come from. He can do it with plants as well, which is a very useful talent should someone have a craving for blackberries but is too lazy to hunt for them." Snow smiled at the gentle tease, but her thoughts were in a whirr.

"And Fae? Her talents seem much more than merely summoning flora and fauna."

"Yes, Fae is strong with magic. She comes from a long line of witches. Her mother was the most powerful witch of her generation, and Fae's father was a talented empath. She inherited both their skills."

"I see. And you all have this magic?"

"Yes, although it is stronger in some than in others."

"So, Grein?"

"Understands the inner workings of the world. He can see things right down to a cellular level. He can even manipulate them to a certain degree."

"What about Kylah?"

"Her talent is not so obvious, although she does have an affinity with iron and can feel where is a good place to mine to find it. She is also adept at working with it and can persuade it to her will."

"I see. And Arden?"

"Ah, he has an unusual talent. He is a storyteller, and his words can bring forth images from the very ether itself."

Snow looked at where the others were sitting by the fire, chatting to one another, their bonds of family and comradeship obvious in the easy connection each one had to the others. That made her think of Nylex.

She sought him out in the darkness beyond the ring of firelight, finding him sitting on a fallen log by the forest's edge. A grimly still figure in the gloom – Snow shuddered at the loneliness he wore like a shroud.

"And Nylex?"

"Our Trickster? He is cunning and bold. Set him any riddle or puzzle and he can solve it. He can also draw upon the element of fire whenever he wishes."

"And you?" Snow looked at Ronin.

"Me, Highness?"

"Yes, what is your skill?"

He didn't reply and instead stared intently at the soil by her feet. Following his gaze, Snow was startled when there was a faint rumble beneath the ground and the soil moved to form a small peak, before flattening back down.

"You can move the earth?"

"To a degree. A mountain would be beyond me, but I can manipulate earth and stone to my will."

"Could you use your magic to harm another?"

"Not without real intention to do so, and the Dwarvians were a peace-loving people. We merely wished to be left alone. But that was something the Contratulum could not allow."

"But why? Why did they consider you so much of a threat to them?"

"To best answer that question, Princess, I must tell you a tale."

Snow looked up at Arden's words. Whilst she and Ronin had been talking, he had emerged from the cottage with Cesil by his side and now moved down the steps to stand in front of them, the firelight casting his features into shadow.

"A tale?"

"Aye, a tale. One that will help you understand the motives behind the Contratulum's actions."

"Arden's g-g-going to t-t-tell a s-s-story, everyone."

Eli's words tripped over his tongue in his excitement, and the others moved closer to the fire, their eyes shining in anticipation.

"Once upon a time ..." Arden began, then stopped and looked at Snow. "That is how all tales should begin, Princess. For all times were once – be they the past, the present, or the future. Once upon a time," he said again.

The fire roared upwards into life, its flames twisting into images. Mesmerised, Snow leant forward and stared intently as Arden's words, and the pictures he conjured in the fire, took her to another place and another time ...

Once upon a time, there were two villages that had existed on either side of a vast meadow for many centuries. One village was lucky enough to have a stream running through it, that had its source high in the mountains above.

Now, the waters of this stream always ran crystal clear and pure. It was believed that it was a stream touched by magic, for it never ran dry, not even in the hardest drought, and the villagers who relied upon its water for their survival were a healthy, hardy, and happy people.

The other village was not so lucky, for its water came from an underground spring accessible only through an ancient well. This water was dank and bilious. Constant bellyache was the villagers' lot, so they were a sour, cantankerous, and unhappy people.

Now, the people of the first village, seeing how ill and miserable their neighbours were, generously offered them access to their stream, wishing only to help. For a time, it seemed the two villages could co-exist in harmony and both take advantage of the delicious fresh water of the mountain stream.

But all too soon a discontent spread through the second village. It was not fair, they grumbled to themselves. Why should they be beholden to the first village for the very water they drank? And they began to perceive imagined patronage where none was – a feeling of unwanted charity growing each day that the villagers had to draw water from the beautiful shining stream belonging to the first village.

After a time, this jealousy and resentment grew so intense that the second village resolved to do something about it. To this end, a group of their strongest men set off into the mountains to discover the source of the spring.

They climbed for many days, always following the stream as it cascaded and frothed over rocks and waterfalls. Finally, they came to a craggy outcrop and saw, at the base of it, the shining white waters of the stream gushing forth, and realised they had discovered the birthing place of the stream.

Working together, they dug away at the rocks above the source until there was a great cracking, tearing sound and the mighty rocks fell, blocking the hole so that the water was denied exit and the stream was no more.

Going back to their village in spiteful triumph, the villagers waited for the first village to realise that its stream flowed no more. When they would be forced to come begging to their neighbours for access to their well.

Sure enough, the next day a group of elders from the first village came in a delegation. Their stream had stopped flowing, they explained, and they were without water. They respectfully requested access to their well, until such time as the stream began flowing again, or they could discover the reason for its disappearance.

Confident that their neighbours would be only too willing to help – after all, they had been freely partaking of their stream for many months – the delegation was shocked and dismayed to be told that if they wished to draw water from the well, they must first pay a tithe of crops and livestock.

Saddened and angry, the delegation from the first village realised they had little choice in the matter – their need for water was desperate and the nearest other source was many days away – so they reluctantly agreed to the second village's terms, and a deal was struck.

However, the black well water was so tainted by foulness that the residents of the first village very quickly sickened and died, having not built up the immunity that the second village had acquired over many centuries of drinking it.

Once the first village was no more, the second village realised that without the rich crops and livestock the first village had produced from their healthy, well-watered fields, and which they had bartered with the second village for the iron and copper goods the second village was famed for, they too fell prey to various ailments that soon left their own village a desolated and abandoned shell.

Thus, the story of the two villages passed into legend as a lesson to us all ...

Arden's voice fell silent. The images in the flames died away. Snow slowly came back into herself, imagining that she had been transported far, far away to a vast meadow surrounded by high mountains, where two villages had fought to the death over water.

Taking a deep breath, she looked down, considering Arden's words, and thinking about their meaning. Dog had returned during the tale to lie once more by her feet. To Snow's amusement, she saw that Cesil had sprawled himself out on the ground by the canine. As she watched, Dog licked at Cesil's ear and Cesil twitched in annoyance.

"So, Princess," Arden continued. "Why do you think the second village destroyed the other village's source of water?"

"Because they were jealous," she began slowly. "But, also, because they wanted power. After all, he who controls the water controls everything."

"True," he agreed.

"In the same way that the Contratulum were jealous of the Dwarvians," she continued. "They wanted control over something that you also had ... your magic. They were jealous of your magic, and believed with you out of the way that they would be the only ones with access to it?" Snow stopped and stared at Arden in disbelief.

"But that would mean that the Contratulum also has access to magic somehow? And that unlike your magic that is natural and pure theirs is ... dark and tainted."

She stopped, as her words and their meaning were laid out clearly before her.

"The Power," she whispered shakily. "The Contratulum has access to the Power. It wasn't you who were practising the foul dark arts – it was them. It *is* them! The Contratulum are warlocks."

Then she cried out in shocked pain as the crystal lying on her chest pulsed heat onto her skin and black swirled deep within its depths.

Chapter Nine

Whispers in the Night

Clasping her hand to the crystal as it pulsed its warning into her skin, Snow was aware of Fae kneeling before her and gently pulling her hands away. "What is it?" Snow gasped. "Why is it doing that?"

"He's trying to scry you," Fae replied, her smooth brow furrowing in concern. "But it's all right, my spell is strong. He cannot see you."

"Mirage?" Snow whispered.

"Aye," Fae nodded. "He must know you're missing, so he's looking for you."

"But he definitely can't see her?" Ronin insisted uneasily.

"No," Fae reassured him – reassured them all. "We are safe."

"For now," Nylex snarled from the darkness. "But what if he finds a way around your protection? We all know how strong the Contratulum are. I say we should get rid of her."

"And how exactly do you suggest we do that, Nylex?" Kylah's voice was ripe with sarcasm. "Turn her loose in the forest for the wolves to find? Or are you suggesting we simply kill her here and now and hide her body where no one will ever find it?" Snow shrank back at the suggestion, but Ronin dropped a reassuring hand onto her shoulder and Fae patted her arm.

"Don't worry," she whispered. "No one will harm you."

"No," Nylex ground out. "Whatever you may think of me, I'm no murderer. But maybe Fae could remove us from her memories and then we could take her to the edge of the forest. She could make her way back to the palace from there."

"And go back to what?" Kylah scoffed. "Have you forgotten they all want her dead? That's not an option, Nylex, and you know it."

"Besides," Fae interjected. "Even if I could alter someone's memories, once the Contratulum got hold of her, I doubt that alteration would be able to withstand their Power. Remember, they dare to call upon dark forces that no one who values their soul would meddle with." She lightly tapped the crystal, which was once again shining with a pinkish-white light.

"He has given up," she informed them, "although I do not know what conclusion he has drawn from being unable to see you."

"Perhaps he will believe she is dead?" Ronin suggested.

"Perhaps," Fae agreed, "or perhaps not. Either way, he will not be able to locate you using that method."

"I think it is time to turn in for the evening," Arden suggested. "We will speak more of this in the morning."

Wondering where everyone was going to sleep, Snow watched as Kylah and Fae made up beds on the floor of her attic room. Grein and Dog disappeared into the back of his strange contraption, and Nylex, Eli, and Arden were thrown blankets and pillows by Ronin to make up beds for themselves downstairs.

Having never had anyone sleep in the same room as her before, Snow was hesitant about undressing. Discreetly, she watched the other two women out of the corner of her eye as they unlaced corsets and removed their outer clothing, before tumbling wearily into their makeshift beds.

Hastily stripping down to her chemise, Snow crawled between the covers into her little trundle bed and lay for a moment gazing out of the window at the stars twinkling far away above. She sighed. It had been a good day, she decided. She was exiled from her home knowing that should she ever return she would likely be killed. She had no money, allies, or plans for her future, and yet she felt secure and at peace.

"Snow," Fae murmured into the soft gloom of the attic. "What was it like? Living in the palace and being a princess? It must have been wonderful – all those beautiful gowns, and balls, and meeting new and exciting people all the time."

"No," Snow replied, rolling over in her bed to face the pretty young witch. "It wasn't like that at all. I was so alone. There was no one I could talk to. No one I could trust not to report my every word and action back to *them*."

"Them?" Kylah asked, looking at Snow with interest.

"My aunt, my stepfather, Mirage, Pontifex Slie. They all wanted to control me, they all wanted something from me. Slie wanted me to be the puppet of the Contratulum. To be so under his control that when I ascended to the throne, they would rule the kingdom absolutely through me. Mirage confused me. I was unsure where his true allegiances lay. He purported to be Jay's advisor, but I have seen him in secret conference with Slie, and there was something about him that stank of the Contratulum. I would not be surprised if he were Slie's lapdog – sniffing around, hoping to gather secrets for his master. And if the Contratulum has the Power, then it would be no shock to learn Mirage is one of them." She fell silent, thinking about Mirage.

"But there was more to it than that. The way he spoke to me, the way he was with me – it was almost as if ..."

"As if?" Kylah prompted.

"As if he wished to possess me," Snow admitted and looked into Kylah's understanding and concerned eyes. "As though I were his plaything, and he did not want to share me with any." She shuddered at the memory. "Even when I was not in his presence, I would sometimes have the strongest sensation that he was watching me still."

"Perhaps he was," Fae said, and Snow stared at her.

"What do you mean?"

"Perhaps he was scrying you. Those times when you sensed his presence, perhaps somehow you were aware that he was watching you."

"But some of those times I was in bed, or in my bath ..." Snow's voice ground to an abrupt halt and a shudder of intense loathing shook her body.

"Try not to think about it." Fae soothed her. "So long as you keep the crystal on you at all times, he will never be able to watch you again."

"What about your aunt?" Kylah asked. "What did she want from you?"

"My throne." Snow gave a wry smile. "My absence."

"She was your aunt – your only blood relative in the palace," Kylah protested. "Why did she wish you gone?"

"Because her husband, my stepfather, made no secret of his feelings about me."

"Which were?" Kylah persisted. "Did he hate you? Did he want you out of the way, so Jay did too?"

"Oh, no," Snow corrected her sadly. "Quite the opposite. Ever since I became a woman, Hawk has made it quite plain that what he wanted was me."

"But he's your father." Kylah protested in disgust.

"Stepfather," Snow clarified. "And you don't understand what it's like at court. It is not how it is here, where you are all simple and good, and you all care about one another. At court, it is twisted and complex, and everyone is looking to promote their own standing within the ranks. Honesty, decency, and honour – they are all things that are looked down upon as being weak and undesirable."

"And yet you're not like that," Fae said.

"If I am not, it is only because my old nurse taught me the ways of my parents. Each time someone would harm another for their own gain, my nurse would tell me my parents would not have tolerated anyone in their court behaving in such a manner. That they were good and honest people, and if they had lived, then the palace would have been a very different place. It made me grow up determined to be like them. To behave in a manner that would make them proud, even if nobody else around me was acting in the same way."

“What happened to your nurse?” Fae asked, and Snow smiled sadly at the memory.

“They sent her away from me when I was only ten years old. I never knew why, and I was not even given a chance to say a proper farewell. She was there one evening and gone when I awoke the next day.”

“Are you surprised they sent her away?” Kylah sat up and clasped her knees to her chest. “If she was the only person in your life that was showing you an alternative path to the twisted one, they were trying to force you down, is it any wonder they got rid of her? I’m only surprised they didn’t kill her.”

“I had never considered it that way,” Snow exclaimed. “But thinking about it now, I believe you are correct, Kylah.”

Kylah grunted in affirmation and settled herself back down. There was silence in the room for a moment, as each woman thought about what had been said. Moonlight crept softly through the window, and Snow stared in fascination at the dust motes it illuminated in its radiant beam. Swirling and dancing – she had never seen anything so beautiful, and her eyelids drooped with tiredness watching their strange, ethereal dance.

“Maybe,” Fae began softly. “If your parents had still lived, the Contratulum would not have dared to attack our village. I am sure King Elgin and Queen Raven would never have allowed such slaughter of the innocents.”

“No, they would not have done,” Snow agreed fiercely. “And if I had been on the throne, I wouldn’t have allowed it either. And if I somehow still manage to claim the crown, I can put a stop to your persecution, issue a royal apology, and tell the truth.”

“I wish I could see your coronation,” Fae sighed wistfully. “I imagine it would be a magnificent occasion, watching as they place a beautiful crown upon your head. Is the crown beautiful?”

“The Crown of Purity?” asked Snow. “Oh, yes, it’s very beautiful. It shimmers with a silvery light and it is imbued with the magic of the ancients. When it is placed upon the heir’s head, it judges whether or not they are pure enough to rule.”

“So, what are you saying?” Kylah enquired in interest. “Are all of the monarchs of House White virgins when they are crowned?”

“No – of course not. It’s not virginity that it means by purity – indeed, some of the monarchs were married by the time they ascended to the throne.” Snow tried to explain.

“It’s more that it is examining the contents of their heart and judging whether they are free of all malicious intent. Pure of the soul – if you like. It is the final test of the heir before they can be crowned.”

"The Contratulum are not going to allow you to claim the throne now," Kylah told her. "If you ever show your face outside the forest again, you'll be as good as dead."

"I know," Snow agreed sadly. "I do not know what my future holds, but you are correct that it would be unwise to go back."

"You could stay here, with us," Fae offered. "You could be one of us – our sister. Maybe marry Ronin and bear him lots of children, for he is lonely living here by himself and I know he likes you."

"Fae!" Kylah spluttered. "You cannot matchmake like that. People do not love to order, and the heart must be free to choose its own mate."

"I know that," Fae protested. "It would be rather wonderful. That's all I was saying."

Snow was silent, unsure how to reply. Some tiny part of her agreeing with Fae – that yes, it would be rather wonderful to remain here with Ronin and never leave this cosy cottage and this enchanted clearing, but to live out the rest of her days in his soothing, undemanding company. Then she thought of his teasing, brotherly conduct towards her and sighed quietly.

Whatever her fledging feelings were about him; she knew they were not reciprocated.

"What about you two?" she demanded, desperate to shift the subject away from herself and any romantic notions she might have towards Ronin. "Will there be any settling down in your future?"

"Hardly," Kylah snorted. "You have seen the pool we are fishing in. It is not exactly teeming. When our village was attacked ... we all lost so much to the Contratulum that night."

"I am so sorry," whispered Snow. "I cannot begin to imagine what you went through. Did you both lose your heart mates that night?"

"There was a man – still a boy really," Fae admitted. "We were to be married, when our village was destroyed, he was lost to me."

"And you?" Snow looked at Kylah in the darkness, seeing the blonde head of the other woman as it faced away from her on her pillow. There was a long silence, and Snow berated herself for her tactlessness. Plainly Kylah did not wish to rake over such painful memories – but then she turned and looked at Snow, the sadness etched into her features visible in the gloom.

"My love went down with her ship, defending her people," she said, then closed her eyes and turned her head once more into her pillow, making it plain that there was no more to be said.

Downstairs, stretched out in his armchair by the fire, facing Arden as he snoozed lightly in the chair opposite and listening to the soft breathy snores of Eli fast asleep in his bed, Ronin thought about Snow upstairs with the other women. He wondered how great a culture shock it would be for her Highness to share such humble quarters with others. Then he smiled to himself, remembering the way she had laughed at that evening's shenanigans.

"She is Elgin's child, there's no doubt about that," Arden remarked softly, not opening his eyes. At his feet, Cesil grunted quietly in his sleep, his belly facing the warming embers of the dwindling fire. "He was always one for a party," he continued, "and yet I see much of her mother in her. Her beauty of course – but also her compassion and her wisdom."

Ronin nodded thoughtfully. Arden pulled himself upright in his chair, disturbing Cesil. The pig lifted his head from where it lay on Arden's foot and fixed a balefully reproachful gaze upon him, before laying back down with a grunt. Pulling an ornate pocket watch from his waistcoat, Arden snapped it open and surveyed the time.

"An hour past midnight. It makes sense that Mirage would be trying to find her at this time. When else would he be having secret meetings with his puppet master, but when all are abed?"

"Was I wrong?" Ronin asked, leaning forward in his chair to peer into Arden's face. "In bringing her here, have I endangered us all?"

"Perhaps." Arden shrugged. "But there is danger all around, and you cannot let fear dictate your actions. You did the right thing – the only thing you could do. Tell me – if you had left her well alone, do you believe she would still be alive now?"

"No." Ronin shook his head. "If the other guards had found her, they would have killed her, especially after she was responsible for the death of one of their own. And they probably would have made her pay for his death before dispatching her." At the thought of Snow at the mercy of a group of angry, brutish men, Ronin's jaw tightened.

"Even if she avoided capture by the guards, then wolves would have found her, or a bear, or she would have wandered alone until she died of thirst or starvation. Simple exposure to the elements, as inexperienced as she is, would have been the end of her."

"Then what else could you have done?" Arden snapped his watch shut and tapped it on Ronin's knee to emphasise his point. "No matter what Nylex says, you chose the only humane course of action there was." Ronin looked around the cabin at the mention of the young man's name, not wishing to stir up yet more resentment within his troubled soul.

"It's all right." Arden gestured towards the door. "He slipped out a while ago. Probably gone to do a bit more brooding by himself under the stars."

Ronin smiled in sad acknowledgement of Arden's words, then his eye was caught by the intricately decorated back of Arden's watch as it glinted in the firelight. He put out a hand to stop the older man from slipping it back into his waistcoat pocket.

"That watch," he murmured.

"What of it, my boy?" Arden enquired. "Tis one you have seen many times before."

"Yes, but I never noticed those carvings before. I didn't realise they were ..."

"The crest of the Royal House of White?"

"Yes."

"It was a gift bequeathed to me a very long time ago, by a young man who would be king."

"It sounds as though there's a tale there that needs to be told?"

"Maybe, but not tonight – and not to you. However, you are right that Snow should hear the truth, and on the morrow perhaps I shall tell her."

There was silence as Ronin considered the older man's words, then he released his hand and watched as Arden returned the watch to its correct pocket. A log shifted in the fireplace and seizing the poker Ronin carefully stirred up the embers, tossing on more wood to keep the chill at bay.

Both men turned their faces to the flames as renewed warmth leapt and light danced over their features. Looking into Arden's kindly, knowledgeable eyes, Ronin spoke out loud the question that had been running through his mind ever since Snow had sat at his table and openly confessed her name and lineage.

"What is to become of her, Arden?"

"Snow?"

"Yes, what is to become of her? She is Princess Snow of the Royal House of White. Her parents were the king and queen. In a fortnight she should be ascending to the throne to become Queen Snow. But here she is, sleeping in a rough cabin, in clothes borrowed from another, and with not a shilling to her name. She is friendless and powerless. If she returns to claim her birthright, the likelihood is she will not live to ever sit upon the throne. And yet, if she stays here, she is giving up her crown forever."

"Maybe," Arden said again, then smiled enigmatically. "But you are wrong about two things, my boy. Snow White is not friendless, and she is far from being powerless."

Chapter Ten

The Family of the Phoenix

When she awoke the next morning, Snow was alone in the attic room. She stretched and basked for a moment in the early morning sun that was streaming through the window onto her face. Looking around, she saw the neat piles of bedding left by Kylah and Fae and wondered where they were. As she lay there, thinking about all that had happened the day before, and all that she had learnt, an enticing aroma of sausages frying crept through the open hatchway.

Sniffing the air in eager anticipation, Snow marvelled that she could be hungry again after the amount of food she had consumed the evening before. She giggled, as she wondered if Eli's termites were contagious.

Unable to resist the temptation, she scrambled out of bed and hastily pulled on her borrowed clothes from the day before. Lissa's clothes. That made her remember what Ronin had said about his sister, and how Kylah had said she had lost her soulmate, and she drew conclusions that made her eyebrows rise.

Carefully climbing down the ladder, Snow discovered the cottage was empty, except for Grein. He stood by the fire expertly frying sausages in a large pan, watched in drooling anticipation by Dog.

"Good morning, your Highness," he said, without turning around. "Help yourself to breakfast," he added, as Snow's hand sneaked out to steal a blackberry from the bowl set upon the table. Guiltily, she paused, wondering if another of Grein's magical skills was the ability to see behind him.

"Where is everyone?" she asked, and he threw a warm smile over his shoulder.

"I believe Kylah and Fae went to take a shower. Ronin, Arden, and Eli are outside, and Nylex ... well, Nylex will be somewhere, I have no doubt. Here," he thrust an earthenware mug of tea into her hand, "why don't you go out and join them?"

Emerging into the bright, crisp sunlit morning, Snow discovered Ronin, Arden, and Eli were outside. Sprawled on the porch steps with mugs of tea, they chatted easily as Cesil ran around the clearing in high agitation, letting out the occasional mournful squeal.

"What's the matter with him?" Snow asked, settling herself onto the highest porch step.

"He's up-p-pset because Grein's frying s-s-sausages," Eli explained.

"Oh, of course," Snow agreed. "I can see why that would be distressing for him."

“Did you sleep well, Your Highness?” Arden enquired, his kind eyes twinkling at her as she took a cautious sip of her tea and found it to be a pleasing blend of camomile, mint, and honey.

“I did, thank you.” She returned his smile, the tea becoming more agreeable with each sip. “Will you all be staying much longer, or do you have other tasks to attend to?”

“We have much to discuss,” Arden informed her. “But such conversation is best done on a full stomach, so it has been agreed to save all such discourse until after breakfast.”

Snow nodded and forced a smile. Suddenly, the morning seemed to lose its newness, for she knew full well that any such discussion could only have but one topic – her.

Kylah and Fae returned from the direction of the old stables, their wet hair, and glowing red cheeks, a testament to the showers they had taken. Helping themselves to tea, they joined the others on the porch until Grein bellowed that the breakfast was burning. They all trooped in to load plates with fat, glistening brown sausages, thick slabs of bread spread with butter, blackberries, and leftover honey cakes from the night before.

There not being enough room for them all to sit around the table, they sprawled easily over the porch steps again, eating their breakfast from their laps, licking at greasy fingers with contentment when every morsel had been consumed.

Nylex had returned from wherever he had been roaming and consumed his breakfast with them, yet still, Snow was achingly aware of the distance he kept. The mantle of outsider he insisted upon wearing was so glaringly apparent that her soft heart hurt for the punishment he imposed upon himself.

Occasionally, she would feel his gaze upon her. But no matter how warm and genuine the smile she returned, his face would pull into lines of stiff resentment, and he would turn away in obvious disgust.

With breakfast finished and cleared away, Snow’s heart quickened with anticipation. Despite Ronin’s reassurance and Fae’s promise, she was still terrifyingly aware that her very survival depended upon the kindness and acceptance of this small group of strangers. That no matter how tolerant they appeared it was her family who had sanctioned the extinction of their people. Even if it had been due to false intelligence, and had occurred five generations before Snow’s birth, it was still House White – her house – that had allowed such an atrocity to occur.

Even as recently as five years previously, it had been due to the weakness of her family – her stepfather and aunt – that the

Contratulum had amassed enough power to mount yet another attack upon the Dwarvians. This time succeeding in annihilating them, apart from this tiny group of seven.

Snow wouldn't blame them if they withdrew their offer of sanctuary and ordered her to leave, although she swallowed in fear at the thought. Finishing the last mouthful of her tea, she swirled the dregs around in the bottom of the cup and surveyed the leaves intently.

"It will rain by nightfall," she murmured.

"I didn't know they taught princesses how to read the tea leaves." Fae glanced at her with interest, and Snow flushed in embarrassment.

"They don't, and I can't read them, not really. But my old nurse used to read her tea leaves every morning. She was very often right – especially about the weather. I remember avoiding many a soaking because she knew precisely when to take an umbrella."

"Again, I feel we are long overdue a conversation about this nurse of yours." Ronin looked at her in renewed curiosity. "She seems a very unusual choice to raise a princess. She also seems to have an alarming knowledge of things I believed to be known only to those within this clearing."

"You're right. She was unusual," Snow replied. "But she came with my mother when she married my father, and no one liked to question my mother's wishes that she be responsible for raising me. She told me many myths and stories which I later dismissed as mere folktales, but now I am not so sure. You are correct that she seems to have known much she could not have simply guessed at."

"Another time," Ronin promised her, "you will tell me all you can remember about her. It could be that her parents or grandparents remembered stories from the old days and passed them down to her, but still, it is concerning."

"Your Highness," Arden interrupted Ronin. "There are things you need to know, things concerning your parents and even further back. Your grandparents, and your great-grandparents. Connections and ties of loyalty and friendship that went beyond crowns and Houses. I must tell you a tale of love, family, and the secrets that we keep, to protect the ones we love."

"A story?" Snow asked, and beside her, Eli beamed with joy.

"Yes-s-s, yes, Arden, a s-s-story. Is it the one about the b-b-blacksmith and his wife? Or the one about the donkey stuck in a gate?"

"No, Eli. Tis a new story that will be unknown to any of you, and it goes like this ..."

Once upon a time, three siblings lived in a cottage on the edge of a deep, dark wood. Now, these three by rights should have lived in the village with the rest of their kin. But bad things had happened to their people some forty years earlier, and the children's grandparents and then their parents had chosen to live separately, only returning occasionally to the village to barter for goods and visit with family and friends.

The little family felt safe enough though, living at the very edge of the forest's northern border. This was in the kingdom of the newly crowned young King Egret of House Avis, who was known for his tolerance, and hatred of persecution.

Sadly, when our tale begins, the parents of these three siblings had died of a fever the previous winter, leaving the three children to fend for themselves. But they were of an age to be resourceful and resilient, and the three fared well enough.

One day, the eldest of the three – a beautiful maid named Rosalyn – was foraging in the woods for mushrooms and berries, when she was approached by a giant dog of the kind nobility used for hunting and hawking.

Alarmed, for the dog was indeed large, Rosalyn was surprised when the dog took her hand gently in its mouth and pulled. Clearly, it wished for her to follow. So, Rosalyn let the dog lead her deeper into the wood to a small clearing where a horse lay upon the ground, its sides heaving with pain and its front leg broken.

Saddened by the horse's distress, Rosalyn noticed a young man lying on the ground. He had been thrown by the horse when it had stumbled and fallen. Quickly, she knelt by his side, concerned by the gash on his forehead and the fever upon his brow.

Hurrying home, she fetched her younger brother and sister and a makeshift stretcher, and together they returned to the clearing and carefully loaded the young man onto it. Rosalyn and her brother then carried him back to their cottage, whilst the youngest sister gently led the horse as it limped after them. The dog followed, occasionally licking at his master's hand where it lay on the stretcher, and Rosalyn was touched by the animal's devotion.

Once home, Rosalyn tended to the man's ailments for she was much versed in the healing arts, possessing the natural magic of growth and renewal. For many days though, the young man's soul hovered between this world and that. On the

fifth day, he opened the most vivid pair of green eyes she had ever seen and looked upon the face of his saviour.

For a further fortnight, the young man stayed with them, growing stronger every day. The three siblings grew to care very much for him, especially Rosalyn. Falling deeply in love with the young man's merry ways and kind heart, she fought to hide her feelings from him, knowing by his clothing and the quality of his steed, that he was a member of the nobility, and ranked far above her in terms of station.

When it was time for the young man to return to the life he had left beyond the forest's boundary, he went for one final walk with Rosalyn where he declared that she had his heart completely and asked her to become his wife. Sobbing with devastation, Rosalyn denied her feelings and refused him – citing the disparity in their backgrounds as her reason – vowing to never love another and sending him on his way.

For a week Rosalyn pined for her lost love, neither eating nor sleeping. Her younger brother and sister worried that she would grieve herself into an early grave and begged her to forget the young man. But their pleas fell onto deaf ears. Rosalyn had given her heart away irrevocably and could not bear the thought of life without her heartmate.

Then early the next morning a party of richly dressed nobility arrived at the cottage, the young man at their head. To the astonishment of the younger siblings, he helped a gracious older woman down from her milk-white mare and demanded to see Rosalyn.

Rosalyn's brother led the unlikely pair to where she was seated by the fire. The young man gathered her in his arms and declared that he could never love another and that he would die without Rosalyn by his side. To prove his intentions were noble, he had returned with his mother to convince Rosalyn to reconsider.

Softly, his mother spoke with the young woman. Rosalyn's beauty and pretty manners soon reassured the lady that she was indeed a fitting heart mate for her son, and she gave her blessing to the pair.

Weeping with quiet joy, Rosalyn allowed the young man to embrace her. This time, when he asked for her hand, she did not refuse but accepted with a tender wholeheartedness that brought tears to the eyes of all who heard it.

The young man led her outside, where the nobles accompanying him unfurled their banners to show a proud phoenix arising from the ashes. Only then did the young man reveal to her his identity. He was King Egret, noble ruler of the kingdom, and he wished Rosalyn to be his queen.

And so, Rosalyn became Queen Starling, and her brother and sister moved into the castle with her. But her brother never forgot his origins and was in the habit of roaming the land, gathering stories, and visiting his kin in their far-off village. Her younger sister became the lady-in-waiting of the royal nursery, in charge of the three children that Starling bore King Egret.

When the throne passed to their eldest son, King Falcon, he relied much upon the wise counsel of the brother, his uncle. And the sister, his aunt, became chief nurse to Falcon's children, especially his daughter and heir, Princess Raven.

In time, the Princess Raven came of age and news of her beauty, kindness, and wisdom travelled far and wide, catching the attention of King Elgin, the new, young ruler of the neighbouring kingdom, who was looking for a wife. Arrangements were made for him to visit, with the intention of wooing the princess into agreeing to marry him.

Princess Raven had other ideas. Not wishing to relinquish her freedom, she begged her parents not to force her to wed where her heart did not lead, and they agreed that she should be entrusted with choosing her own husband.

However, when King Elgin arrived it was immediately apparent to all that the stars had been kind to the young couple, for love, instant and eternal, sparked between them. A grand wedding was arranged, to be followed by an elaborate reception in King Elgin's kingdom.

Now, during the month before the wedding, a friendship sprang up between King Elgin and his bride-to-be's great-uncle, who had returned from one of his many travels to attend the wedding of his beloved great-niece, Raven. Upon parting from each other, the two men exchanged gifts – King Elgin's gift being a fine pocket watch with the royal crest of House White upon its lid.

And when Princess Raven travelled to King Elgin's palace, with her came her much-loved and valued old nursemaid, for companionship and her wise counsel. In turn, Queen Raven was delivered of a beautiful little girl whom she named Snow, and the old nursemaid whom none realised to be her great-aunt, took over the care of the child.

Arden's voice ended. Snow came back into herself, blinking her eyes to clear the images that had swirled and formed from the dust on the ground before her. Thinking of all she had heard, she looked into Arden's eyes as he smilingly took something from his waistcoat pocket and held it up for her inspection.

Snow looked at the pocket watch, instantly recognising her family's crest upon its lid, and blinked back tears of disbelief and wonder.

"Uncle?" she whispered.

Chapter Eleven

One of Us

Grasping the porch railing for support, Snow gazed at Arden. There was indeed something of her old nurse around his eyes and the shape of his mouth, and she knew instantly in her heart that his story was true.

"You're my uncle?" she asked again, and Arden's smile deepened.

"Well, technically, I'm your great-great-uncle, but 'uncle' will do."

"So that means my old nurse ...?"

"... is my younger sister, Greta – and your great-great-aunt."

"Family? You're my family?" Snow choked back a sob of shocked happiness, and Arden's hand came gently to rest over hers.

"Yes, we are your family."

"But ... but that means ..." Snow's mind was racing, as the implications of this revelation spread like ripples on a pond. "That means I'm part Dwarvian?"

"Yes, Dwarvian blood runs through your veins from your great-grandmother, Queen Starling. That was my elder sister, Rosalyn. You are one of us, Snow." Arden looked at the others.

"She is one of us."

Fae placed her hand over Arden's where it rested on Snow's hand.

"One of us," she repeated.

"One of us." Ronin was next with his hand and his vow.

"One of us." Grein twinkled a smile at Snow as he, too, placed his hand on top of Ronin's.

"One of us." Eli was next, quickly followed by Kylah.

"One of us," she said, her tone fierce. Snow knew it meant more than mere words to the other woman – that this was an eternal pledge of clan loyalty. There was a pause, then as one, they all looked to where Nylex stood apart. His face twisted into a disbelieving sneer as he stared from one to the other, at the stack of hands, and all it represented.

"She is *not* one of us," he stated and walked away.

"Nylex Greenblade!" Arden roared. "As my mother and your great-grandmother were sisters, we are kin – and that makes her your kin too. The same blood runs through your veins. She is your family, and as such is entitled to your vow of family loyalty."

Nylex turned and walked over to where they stood.

"All right," he spat furiously. "I will make the vow, but it means nothing. She is nothing to me."

He slapped his hand on top of the pile. "Snow White, I recognise you as kin of my kin, blood of my blood. I vow to protect and honour you until death takes one of us from this world. I give you my pledge. You are one of us."

Then he ripped his hand violently away, stalking off into the forest before Snow could say another word. Shaken to the core by all that had happened, Snow's knees buckled, and Ronin eased her down onto the steps.

"Are you all right, Your Highness?"

"Yes, it's just ..." She looked up at them all standing there. "I can't believe this. A few moments ago, I had no family other than an aunt who wants to kill me, and a stepfather who wants to ..." she paused in embarrassment and ducked her head down. "And now – now, I have family and a clan ... It is all a little overwhelming."

"We must prepare," Arden stated.

"Prepare?" Ronin looked confused. "Prepare for what?"

"Why, prepare to go and visit my sister, of course." Arden reached down a hand and pulled Snow shakily to her feet. "It has been almost two decades since I last saw Greta. I did not dare come to the palace and risk exposing her for Dwarvian, and I was unaware she had been sent away or else I would have tried to find her. Although I confess, would not have known where to look."

"Thornfield." Snow wiped away her tears in sudden determination, her heart thumping at the thought of seeing her beloved nurse again. "She resides in the village of Thornfield."

Ronin and Arden exchanged glances, Ronin's mouth a grim line of disapproval.

"Aye, I know it," he said. "It lies to the north, a small hamlet almost to the borders of the forest."

"It would make sense that Greta would choose to live out the rest of her days as close to the forest as she could," Arden murmured.

"But it is still too dangerous." Ronin insisted.

"The danger is minimal," Arden reassured him. "That far from the palace and that close to the forest, it is unlikely there will be a Contratulum presence, and none will recognise us for what we are."

"W-w-where are we going?" Unable to contain his excitement any longer, Eli pulled at Ronin's arm in enquiry.

"You, my boy, are going nowhere," Kylah informed him, and Eli's face dropped. "If you are set upon doing this," she looked from Arden to Ronin, "then I suggest the skimmer. It's quick and can be easily hidden in the forest while you go into the village on foot."

"I haven't said if we *are* going." Ronin insisted.

"We must," Arden insisted. "She could be in danger. The Contratulum might go there looking for Snow. We have to warn her."

"All the more reason to stay away."

"Please." Snow spoke quietly into the rising disagreement. "Please." She looked at Ronin. "I want to see her. I must see her again. She is family. I never knew that before, but now that I do it changes everything, and I must see her one more time."

Ronin looked into the large, dark eyes that shivered with barely held back tears, and sighed, knowing he was beaten.

"Frick," he muttered. "All right, but a quick visit, and at the first sign of danger, we're out of there. Oh, and Highness ..."

"Yes?"

"You may be a princess, and the future ruler of this kingdom, but out here, and on this mission, I am the captain. What I say, goes. You will obey my orders instantly and without question."

"Of course," Snow hastily agreed. "You are the captain, Ronin."

It seemed to take forever to prepare for the journey, and Snow watched with mounting impatience as Ronin and Arden unrolled a large map of the forest on the table and conferred about the best route to take.

Kylah had vanished off to the stables to check over the skimmer and make sure it was flight-worthy, barking an order at Eli to come and help her when the young lad bounced from foot to foot, grinning inanely at Snow.

Grein had requested a pinprick of blood from Snow's finger, and then vanished into the back of his contraption to 'run some tests on it'. Although about the precise nature of these tests, and what exactly he was looking for, he was not forthcoming.

Nylex had not returned from the forest, and Snow found herself musing on the fact that they were related. Even though she knew Nylex was none too pleased about it, a quiet glow of warmth arose at the thought.

Nylex would come around to the idea – she was sure of it – and then she would have an almost-brother, or at the very least a sort of cousin.

Dog and Cesil seemed to pick up on the growing tension. They charged around the clearing like creatures possessed, squealing, and barking in frenzied delight, until Ronin bellowed at them to "shut the frick up" and they abruptly sat down in the grass.

The only calm member of the group was Fae. She had drifted off with Ronin's fiddle to perch on a fallen tree at the clearing's edge.

Realising that hovering over Arden and Ronin's shoulders would not speed up the proceedings, Snow wandered over to where the pretty witch was sitting and scrambled up to sit beside her.

For a while they sat in silence, then Fae raised the fiddle and drew the bow expertly across the strings. A sweetly lilting tune drizzled from the instrument, instantly making Snow inexplicably happy and light-hearted. Half-closing her eyes in delighted bliss, a tiny movement had her opening them again to find a mother doe and her fawn standing among the trees, watching them.

Snow drew in her breath and glanced at Fae, who half-inclined her head to indicate she had seen them too and then continued to wring the beckoning melody from the fiddle. Slowly, softly, the pretty creatures stepped over to the two women, until they were so close Snow could have reached out a hand and touched them.

Frozen to the spot with delighted joy, Snow could hardly believe her eyes when a shaggy pony stepped from the forest and joined the doe, its rough head nodding as if in time with the music. There was a flitter and a chirp, and a little blue bird swooped down to land beside her on the tree, then another, and another, until a whole flock were perched all around them, chirruping in time with the melody.

Softly, the tune ended, and Fae lay down her bow. For a wonderful moment, every creature remained still, then quietly and without fuss they disappeared once more into the forest, the birds sweeping up into the sky in one glorious mass of brightly coloured feathers.

"That was incredible," Snow breathed, and Fae smiled.

"It's a friendship tune that lets any animals nearby know we are no threat to them, and they should come and listen to the music."

"I wish you were coming with us," Snow said, and Fae shook her head.

"The skimmer will only carry three, and that will be Ronin, Arden, and you."

"I cannot believe I will soon see my nurse again. I had forgotten how much I missed her when she left. She was like a mother to me, and without her, I felt vulnerable and so alone."

"You will never be alone again, Snow. I promise." Gently Fae took her hand, then Snow felt the witch's body spasm into an arch of agony, her eyes turning milky-white.

"Fae?" Snow cried out in fear as the other girl's grip on her hand tightened. "Fae, what's the matter? You're hurting me. Help! Somebody, please help."

Alerted by her cries, Ronin and Arden bolted from the cottage and ran towards them. Even Grein stuck his head out of his contraption, his eyes covered with strange, thick goggles.

"Snow?" Ronin reached her first, concern roughening his voice. "What's the matter?"

"It's Fae. Look at her."

"It's all right." He took her other hand to reassure her. "It's something that happens to Fae sometimes – don't be scared. Fae," he said gently to the witch, "tell me what you see?"

"Danger. You must beware." She ground out the words as if in intense pain. "There is one who watches. Be careful of them for their mind is not their own and they follow the orders of those who seek to harm Snow White. Look for the wine stain, for by this you will know it is them. Look for the red wine stain..."

Fae's head lolled onto her chest and her hand released Snow's. Seeming to faint, she crumpled from the fallen tree trunk, and Ronin caught her as she fell against him.

"Ronin?" she whispered.

"It's all right, sweetling," he replied. "I have you."

"My head," she gasped. "Ronin, my head." She began to weep as Ronin swung her up easily into his arms and carried her swiftly to the cottage, where Arden waited in concern.

"A vision?"

"Yes, a hard one this time. It's taken its toll."

"I have the potion ready." Grein reached them, holding out a vial of thick, greenish liquid, and Ronin sat down on the porch steps with Fae upon his knee.

"Here we go, sweetling," he reassured, one hand removing the cork from the vial and holding it to her lips. "Here's the potion. Get it down you and it will help." Desperately, Fae groped for the vial and gulped it down in one, frantic mouthful, retching as she tried to force the foul-looking liquid down her reluctant throat.

"Uggh," she gasped and wiped a hand unsteadily across her mouth. "You forgot the mint," she accused Grein.

He shrugged sheepishly. "Sorry. I did prepare it somewhat hastily."

Fae drew a deep breath and opened her eyes. Snow was relieved to see that they were her normal fresh green again.

"What happened?" Snow murmured. "What was that?"

"Fae gets visions," Ronin explained, helping the witch to her feet. "But they are usually vague and inconsequential, like when she felt that you were here. But then sometimes a pivotal vision will grip her, and then they tear her apart with their intensity."

"A pivotal vision?"

"It's when I see a moment in the future which is pivotal to how events will play out," Fae tried to explain. "When there are two possible outcomes, but one defining action that will decide which outcome will occur."

"I see." Snow was not sure that she did – not really. "You said there was danger? Is it dangerous for us to make this journey?"

"Yes, but it is a journey that must be undertaken, for much depends on it. I sensed that someone is not what they seem, that their eyes look not only for themselves but for others who do not have your best interests at heart."

"A spy, in other words," Ronin stated grimly. "How far into the future will this occur, Fae? Is this spy in Thornfield, or some other place?"

"I cannot say for certain." Fae shook her head sadly. "I only know it is soon, and that you must beware of the red wine stain."

"The red wine stain – what sort of red wine stain?"

"I am sorry, that's all I can tell you."

"I am not happy about this trip at all," Ronin began. "I wasn't before, and I'm even more certain now that we are walking into a trap."

"That may be so," Arden replied cheerfully. "But is a trap still a trap, if we know it's there?"

Deciding it would be best to travel at dusk, the group passed the rest of the day slowly, and Snow helped a now fully recovered Fae to prepare an early evening meal for everyone.

Watching as the young woman moved lightly around the kitchen, the ease with which she located all she needed suggesting a familiarity with Ronin's home, Snow wondered if she dared to ask the question in her heart.

"Fae?"

"Yes, Snow?"

"How much of the future can you see?"

"I don't see the future. That's not how it works. I see possible outcomes, but the future isn't set in stone. Too much depends on the actions taken now, in the present, for me to see what will happen."

"I see."

"No, you don't." Fae smiled at her, pushing back a strand of hair from her cheek, and leaving a smear of flour in its place. "I will try to explain. What would have happened if you had not gone to visit your nurse?"

"The guard wouldn't have tried to kill me, I wouldn't have killed him, and Ronin wouldn't have brought me here. I would never have met you all."

"Exactly. You would have stayed in the palace and that future would have played out instead."

“So, the present we are living now all hinged on my spontaneous decision to get away from the palace for a few days?”

“Yes.”

“Was it a pivotal moment?”

“Yes, it was.”

“I see.” Snow said again, and this time she did.

The women worked on in silence, Fae putting the finishing touches to an enormous pie, which as far as Snow could see consisted of every leftover from the night before in a rich, meaty gravy, topped with a slab of thick pastry.

“Fae?”

“Yes?”

“Can you see when people are going to die? Can you see when I’m going to die?”

“No.” Fae looked at her steadily. “And please do not ask me to try.”

Chapter Twelve

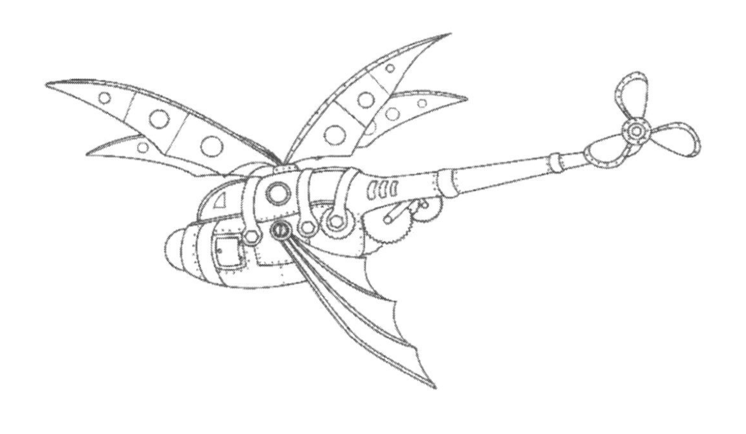

Truths Discovered at Dusk

That evening's meal was less jolly and carefree than the previous one. Snow knew they were all thinking of the journey she, Ronin, and Arden would soon be making – its possible outcome, and the dangers that Fae had foretold. All too quickly, it was time to go, and Ronin was handing her a cloak from a peg on the wall.

"It will be cold up there," was all he said, but Snow's stomach clenched at the thought that soon she would be flying in a flimsy contraption that did not look strong enough to bear the weight of a mouse, let alone three grown adults.

"Here." Fae passed her a pair of goggles. "The wind blows particles into your eyes. It is best to keep them covered."

Nodding her thanks, Snow silently took them, put them on, and then pushed them to the top of her head, as she saw Ronin and Arden had done. Trailing after them out of the cottage, her unease intensified. At the sight of the skimmer sitting in the clearing, her stomach roiled unhappily, and she was miserably aware it was highly possible she might vomit.

"Well." Kylah wiped at the skimmer with a grimy rag. "She's all ready for you. Tank is full and I realigned the flanges on the right wing." She cast Ronin a beady eye. "When were you going to tell me, she was listing to the right?"

"She wasn't," Ronin protested. "Much," he added as Kylah raised her brows.

"Goodbye, Snow." Fae enveloped her in a warm, reassuring hug. "Take care, and I'll see you upon your return."

Snow nodded, her teeth chattering as she followed Ronin to the skimmer and allowed him to help her scramble into the narrow seating area between the pilots. Pretending not to notice the flimsiness of the membrane that was all that stood between her and the air, Snow tried to steady her shaking hands enough to do up the buckle on the restraining strap on her seat. Warm hands steadied hers and she looked up into the quietly concerned gaze of Ronin.

"You don't have to do this," he murmured, under cover of ensuring her belt was fastened tightly enough.

"Yes, I do," she replied, meeting his gaze with a confidence she was far from feeling.

He sighed, then nodded, swinging himself easily into the seat in front of her and buckling himself in. Immediately, he began twisting and pulling on the various switches and levers arrayed in front of him, and Snow hoped he knew what he was doing. There was a grunt, and the skimmer dipped alarmingly as Arden crawled into the seat behind her. His long legs cramped in the confined space, he muttered curses under his breath as he struggled to fasten his belt.

Looking over the high side, Snow managed a brave smile for Fae, Grein, Kylah, and Eli as they stood watching. Returning Eli and Fae's waves with a nervous flutter of her hand, she gasped and gripped onto the side as the blades above her head began to whirl at a faster and faster rate. The skimmer gave an almighty lurch, and the next moment, they were airborne.

"Oh, no," she cried, as the skimmer shimmied upwards in a series of alarming and stomach-gripping hops. Arden placed a comforting hand on her shoulder.

"Don't worry, it gets smoother."

Clenching her teeth together and praying frantically to all the gods that her dinner wouldn't make an unwanted reappearance onto Ronin's shoulders, she squeezed her eyes shut until abruptly the skimmer levelled out and hung motionless, before turning mid-air and gliding forward.

"Open your eyes," Arden instructed her. "Open your eyes and look, Snow."

Reluctantly, she cracked open first one eyelid and then the other, and instantly something flew into her eye. Wiping away the tears, she pulled the goggles down into place and tried again.

It was magnificent.

Below her stretched the forest. Snow held her breath at how vast it was. Stretching in all directions as far as the eye could see, it appeared endless. For the first time, she appreciated how lucky she had been that Ronin had found her at all in this immense ocean of green.

Over her left shoulder, far away in the distance, loomed the Dwarvian Mountains. With their feet clad by the forest and their snow-draped shoulders disappearing into the clouds, they were unbelievably colossal. Snow remembered all the legends told to her about them by her old nurse – Greta, her great-great-aunt – she corrected herself.

The sun was on the verge of vanishing below the horizon, spilling glorious streaks of pinks and reds over the treetops, and painting the clouds with sugar-plum hues. Its fading warmth dappled her cheek and Snow took a deep breath of exhilaration.

She felt alive. For almost the first time in her nearly eighteen years, Snow knew what it was to feel utterly and completely alive. Aware of every tingling sense, her body hummed with elation and a broad grin spread across her face.

Glancing over her shoulder at Arden, wanting to share the moment, she found him beaming back at her. Leaning closer, he put his mouth by her ear to be heard over the soft whirring of the blades above and the rushing of the wind over them.

"Pretty something, hey?" She nodded enthusiastically, her eyes shining behind her goggles. "We're like birds in the sky," he bellowed and again she nodded.

Settling back in her seat, she allowed herself to relax slightly, her hands unclenching. She realised she had drawn blood with her nails and rubbed at the row of perfect crescent marks in her palms. Ronin banked the skimmer to the right, and Snow instinctively clutched at the sides again, before realising it was intentional and that they were not about to crash into the forest canopy mere feet below them.

Straightening once more onto an even course, the little craft flew steadily on through the gathering dusk. Snow wondered if Ronin could fly in the dark. The thought of flying merely by the light of the moon and the stars was enough to make her shiver in terrified anticipation.

They flew for what felt like forever before eventually, Ronin angled downwards. Snow saw below them a small clearing amongst the trees, big enough for the skimmer to set down in. Skilfully, Ronin held the craft above the clearing as he adjusted its angle. Snow wondered how long it had taken him to learn to fly the skimmer. She wondered how long it would take her to learn, the idea of being able to soar into the sky herself thrilling her into goosebumps.

Gently, the skimmer landed in the middle of the clearing with a small bump, and the blades above their heads slowed their frantic spinning until at last they stopped and were silent. In the sudden hush, her eardrums thrummed from the constant vibration of the blades, and she gently pressed at her ears, attempting to relieve the pressure.

"We'll stay the night here," Ronin informed her, turning around, and removing his goggles. Oil had splattered from the engine mounted at the front of the skimmer onto his face and Snow giggled at the comical sight.

Grinning back, he climbed down from the skimmer and held out his hand to assist her as she gathered up her skirts and scrambled out. Arden followed her down with a loud groan as he struggled to unfold his long frame from the cramped space.

"This skimmer was definitely only designed for two people," he moaned, arching his back, and pressing his hand to his side as he attempted to ease out the kinks in his spine.

"Would you care to walk the rest of the way?" Ronin asked casually, pulling their knapsacks from the tiny storage compartment set into the back of the skimmer. Arden grunted in reply and pulled off his goggles. Looking at the dirt encrusted into his face, Snow wiped at her own, wondering if she, too, were now that grubby.

She was once again made painfully aware of her inadequacies, as Arden and Ronin set about making camp for the night with practised ease that spoke of long years of familiarity with such a task. Laying a small fire on a bed of flat stones he had placed in the centre of the clearing; Ronin took the flint from his pouch. He was about to set light to the kindling, when he noticed Snow watching him with a wistful expression and hesitated, then beckoned her over.

"Come, Highness," he said, handing her the flint as she knelt beside him. "It is time you learnt how to make and light a fire. You see here, how I have made a very small pile of twigs and dried pinecones from the ground? These will make good kindling and will catch quickly. Larger pieces of wood take a while to catch, so you need to get a good, small fire going first and then gradually feed on the bigger pieces."

He watched as she fumbled unsuccessfully with the flint. Patiently, he placed his hand over hers and helped her to strike at the right angle to create a spark. He smiled at her cry of triumph when she eventually produced a spark big enough to set the small pile of kindling alight.

"Where's Nylex when you need him?" Arden had been watching the proceedings with interest.

"Nylex?" Snow asked, observing with proud fascination as Ronin carefully fed the baby fire she had created until it was crackling and burning at a steady pace.

"Yes – remember I told you Nylex can control fire?" Ronin said, sitting back on his heels and looking at her. "Well, Nylex never requires a flint. He can start a fire with the snap of his fingers."

"Goodness," Snow exclaimed, then fell silent as a new notion grew in her mind. "Ronin ..." she began.

"Yes, Highness?" Ronin was laying out bedding rolls close to the fire.

"As I have Dwarvian blood in my veins, do you think I have any magical skills?"

"It's possible," he said, and Arden nodded.

"Very possible," he agreed. "The skill runs strong in our family. Even diluted as it is with non-Dwarvian blood. I would not be surprised if you discovered you had an affinity for some form of elemental magic."

"Oh." Snow fell silent, hugging the thought to herself, examining it from all angles and deciding that she quite liked the idea of having a secret magical power. "But wouldn't I know by now?" she asked, looking from one man to the other.

"Not necessarily." Ronin frowned. "Very often a person's skill does not become apparent until early adulthood, and you would not have known how to look for the signs of a latent power."

"So, I could still develop one?" she persisted.

"You could," he agreed, and she fell silent again, thinking it over.

"We'll set off at first light," Ronin told her. "We should reach Thornfield early in the morning. There is a small clearing I know at the edge of the forest where we can land and leave the skimmer. We will approach the village on foot so as not to raise the alarm. Do you happen to know which cottage Greta resides in?"

"No, I don't." Snow shook her head. "I have never been permitted to visit her before. Other than a brief letter sent with dried flowers every year on my nameday, there has been no contact between us since she left eight years ago."

"Dried flowers?" Arden looked up with interest. "What type of flowers?"

"They were small and yellow." Snow wrinkled her nose in remembrance. "I was unfamiliar with them, so I asked the head gardener. He told me they were a form of witch hazel."

"Witch hazel, hey?" Arden looked thoughtful.

"You think it has some significance?"

"I am unsure." Arden shook his head at Ronin's question. "Witch hazel is a powerful protection plant, and it is also a symbol of magic and mysticism. It could be she was trying to give you some sort of clue."

"In her letter, she begged me to always keep it close to me. In fact, here ..." Snow fumbled at her chatelaine that she had automatically placed about her waist. Opening it, she pulled out the two keys that hung on short chains and plucked from it a small, dried morsel of yellow flower which she handed to Arden.

He took it, and his brows flew up in surprise. Stroking a finger softly over the almost desiccated bloom, a wistful look of nostalgic longing crossed his face. He handed it to Ronin, before pulling a kerchief from his pocket and rubbing it across his moist eyes.

"By the gods, I can feel the power of the spell this flower contains," Ronin exclaimed, and handed the bloom back to Snow who looked at it in wonder.

"Yes, it bears the stamp of Greta's magic," Arden agreed. "I would recognise her touch anywhere."

"A spell?" Snow asked. "What kind of spell?"

"It's a protection spell, yet it is more than that. Oh, so complex and twisted an incantation has been placed over this bloom to enhance its natural properties that I do not know where to begin to figure it out. At its base is an invocation to keep you safe from harm and lend you the strength to defeat those who would hurt you."

"When that guard thrust me to my knees," Snow exclaimed, "I knew he intended to kill me and from somewhere I gained the wit and strength to grab his dagger and kill him first. Do you think that was all Greta's doing?"

"No," Arden reassured. "It is more that the spell gave you the courage of your convictions – the push to do what needed to be done. But there is more. Interwoven through the base note of the spell is another. This one is more subtle, helping you to strengthen the walls of your mind, to put you above being coerced and manipulated."

"And it does." Snow exclaimed in excited realisation. "I have oft wondered how it was that Mirage could control the minds of all those around him yet could not do so with me. And I know it irked him. He would subtly suggest I take some action I disagreed with, and I would see the flash of surprise and annoyance in his eyes when I refused to do so."

"And finally, there is a summoning spell – a 'blood calling to blood' incantation. It does not have a very wide range, but it would call those of your kind to you." He looked at Ronin. "Tell me, why did you choose that day to visit the mines in that particular part of the forest? So close to the forest perimeter and near to the palace? Why did you choose that day to visit mines I thought you believed had been mined out?"

"I don't know," Ronin rubbed a hand thoughtfully over his chin. "I recall a sudden urge mid-morning to examine them one more time. But of course, there was nothing left to extract from them, and I was angry with myself for wasting my time. I was on my way home when I heard Snow's scream."

"It was about mid-morning when we first entered the forest," Snow confirmed, and the three exchanged telling glances.

"Even though Greta could no longer be with you, still she protected you from afar," Arden murmured. "Tell me, Snow, did you receive the same flower with every nameday letter?"

"Yes, with a renewed plea to always wear it about my person."

"And the letter you received from her telling you of her illness and begging you to visit?"

"No," Snow began slowly. "That letter was barely more than a note. It contained no flower and indeed was not even in her hand. I assumed it had been written by another at her direction because she was too ill to write herself, but now..."

"Now you wonder if it even came from Greta at all?" They fell silent at the thought, then Arden gestured towards Snow's chatelaine as she carefully placed the flower back inside it. "I see you inherited your mother's chatelaine?"

"Yes, she gave it to me the very last time I saw her." Snow looked at him in surprise. "But how did you know it was my mother's?"

"Because I gave it to her the night before her wedding. It was my gift to her, to hold the keys of her new home." Snow nodded, then bit her lip in painful memory.

"I remember Greta coming to me in the middle of the night. She shook me awake and told me I had to come quickly. That there was no time to dress, and that I had to be as quiet as possible. Then she led me to my mother's room, but I was unfamiliar with the route we took to reach it, and we slipped in through the concealed servant's entrance."

Aware that the attention of both the men was focused intently upon her, Snow blinked back tears as that long-ago night swam to the top of her memories and begged for attention.

"My mother was lying on the bed. Even though it was a warm night, the bedclothes were piled over her and I remember thinking how strange that was. She turned her head and looked at me, and for a moment I did not recognise her – so strange was her expression. But then she smiled and held out her hand to me, so I ran to her and clambered upon her bed and lay down beside her."

"Go on," Arden urged when Snow hesitated. She was reluctant to share such an intimate moment – her final memory of her beloved mother. Yet Arden's eyes were warm, and she realised that her mother had also been his great-niece. He was family. It was his right to know.

"She held me close and told me how much she loved me, and how proud she was of me. It was almost as if she was saying farewell, which, of course, she was. Then she bade Greta fetch her chatelaine from the drawer and gave it to me. She told me it was my birthright. But I didn't understand, because all the keys were missing, and I was upset. I believed it meant she did not trust me with the palace keys. But she said it was because they would simply be taken away from me. That it was the chatelaine itself that was important, and the single key it still contained. That they wouldn't be interested in that one because it fitted no lock in the palace."

Snow fumbled the key out on its chain and held it up for the others to see. Curiously, Ronin reached out a hand and took the chatelaine from her, running his fingers gently over its embossed surface and examining the intricate fretwork design on the key.

"What lock does it fit then?" he asked, and Snow shrugged.

"That I have never been able to discover. Although for many months afterwards, I tried every lock I could think of."

"What does the second key fit?" he asked, tapping the second key in the chatelaine.

"That is the key to my chamber door," Snow told them. "I was in the habit of keeping it locked at all times, and ensuring the key was upon my person. My stepfather, he ..." She broke off, looking down at her hands with a painful flush staining her pale cheeks, and Ronin felt a clutch of anger at the thought of all she had endured in her short life.

"What happened next?" Arden persisted. "The last time you saw your mother. What happened after she gave you the chatelaine?"

"She told me to trust no one, but my nurse, or my own heart, and that I was always to tread the path of goodness and humility, no matter how hard it might become. That I was to trust in love, and that when I found it, I would know. Then she began to cough, and she seemed unable to catch her breath. Greta eased her up and tried to give her water, but she couldn't swallow, and the coughing grew more painfully pronounced, and there was a strange odour ..."

"An odour?" Arden's head, which had been between his hands, jerked up at her words. He fixed her with a stare of such intensity, that Snow clasped a hand to her chest as her breath caught painfully in her lungs.

"What is it?" she cried. "Why do you look so?"

"What sort of odour?"

"Just an odour. It was unpleasant, sickly. I could smell it on my mother's breath when she coughed. I later understood it must have been the sickness that would kill her that very night, but at the time... I was only a child," she whispered. "I did not know what I was doing. I wriggled away from her and would not return even though she held out a hand and begged me for one more embrace. It was the smell of her. It disgusted and frightened me."

"Yes, but what exactly did it smell like?" Arden persisted, and Snow shook her head in confusion.

"It was the sickness inside her, it smelt like things rotting after the rain has fallen ..."

"Petrichor? It smelt like petrichor?"

"Petrichor?" Snow looked wildly from man to man in confusion. "I do not know what that is."

“Tis the way the earth smells after it has been raining,” Ronin explained.

“Oh, I see. Yes, it smelt like that, only not in the wholesome, pleasing way that ... petrichor, normally smells. Instead, it was a rank, vile smell ... with a bitter orange undertone.”

“Death’s Trumpet,” Arden sighed.

“No.” Ronin protested. “That would mean that Queen Raven ...”

“Was poisoned, yes.”

“What?” Snow’s head whipped wildly from each of their faces and back again. “What are you saying? My mother died of a fever.”

“Child,” Arden murmured, and gently took her hand. “If your mother had a fever so virulent it took her life that very same night, you would have seen signs of it in her. Yet, she was coherent and conscious. She spoke with you. Twas no fever that killed your mother. It was poison.”

“Poison? But how can you be so sure?”

“The odour you spoke of, like bitter orange after rain. Tis unmistakably Death’s Trumpet.”

“Death’s Trumpet? What is that?”

“It’s a plant,” Ronin spoke up, his eyes warm with sympathy. “It grows in graveyards and anywhere that the dead be buried. Ground to a powder it can be mixed with food or drink and its victim will be oblivious to it until it is too late.”

“But who?” Snow cried. “Who would have done such a thing?”

“It bears the mark of the Contratulum,” Ronin continued, and Arden nodded his head in agreement.

“Aye, with their network of spies and assassins it would have been child’s play for them to poison Raven’s food or drink.”

“Did she know?” Snow demanded. “Did she know she was dying?”

“Raven had been well tutored in the ways and uses of plants. She would have realised. Even if she had not, Greta would have known.”

“So, when I went to her, she knew it was the last time she would ever see me,” Snow murmured. She dashed a hand angrily across her eyes and bowed her head to her knees. “They killed my mother,” she whispered, then raised her head and stared at them, the light of anger dancing in her eyes. “They killed my mother.” She spat the words out again, her hands clenching into fists.

“Yes, Snow, I’m afraid they did.” Arden’s voice was sorrowful, and his own eyes sheened with unshed tears.

“But why?”

“With Raven out of the way, there was no anointed monarch on the throne. Hawk doesn’t have a drop of White blood in him. Only

Raven had the authority and the will to stop the Contratulum from achieving their goal."

"Which is?"

"Total power."

"Yes," Snow agreed. "I see that now. So why didn't they kill me as well?"

"They saw no need to." Ronin joined in the discussion. "You were a child – easily mouldable, or so they thought. Much easier to put the genuine heir onto the throne as a puppet, a quisling to do whatever they commanded. Only ... you proved less easy to control than they expected."

"Frick knows they tried though," Snow ground out, and Ronin raised his brows at her language. "All those lessons with Pontifex Slie. All those attempts by Mirage to control my thoughts. That's what they've been doing all these years. Trying to control me. Make me their doll. But thanks to Greta's magic, they couldn't."

"Not only Greta's magic," Arden broke in. "Give yourself some credit, Snow. Her spell could only strengthen what was already there. I have no doubt even without her spell you would have been able to stand against them."

"They killed my mother, and then they tried to kill me. They should pay for that." Snow looked steadily at them. "I swear to you both, on the memory of my parents, the Contratulum will pay for their crimes. I, Princess Snow of House White, do promise that if there is any way I can bring about their downfall I shall not hesitate. No, not until every stinking last member of that foul nest of vipers is exterminated."

Chapter Thirteen

The Poisoned Apple

Shaken awake by Ronin before dawn the next morning, Snow struggled to contain her yawns. Crawling from the bedroll he had laid by the fire for her, what felt like only an hour previously, her teeth chattered from the chill of the early morning.

"Time to go, Highness," he replied to her grunt of enquiry, offering her his hand to pull her to her feet. "Here." He passed her a square of rough towel. "Go through the trees a few feet in that direction and you will find a small pool and privacy for your morning ablutions."

Ducking her head in embarrassment at his implied meaning, Snow took the towel and headed in the direction he pointed, passing Arden as he stepped into the clearing.

"Good morning, Snow." He greeted her with a friendly smile which Snow returned. "I trust your first night sleeping under the stars was comfortable."

"The ground was a little hard," she confided, and his grin broadened.

"I would say you get used to it, but alas," he stretched and creaked his back straight, "I am afraid you never do."

Feeling better after a quick wash in the crystal-clear waters of the small pool, Snow stood for a moment by the water's edge, gazing at the beauty of the dawn mists which wisped the tips of the trees. There was a flicker of movement. To her delight, a stag stepped from the forest on the opposite edge of the pool. Seeing her, he froze in place, his magnificent head with its antler crown proclaiming his royal status. Then he bent his head and drank, before slipping silently back the way he came.

Her spirits lifted by the encounter, Snow hurried back to the others, wondering what the day would bring, and excited at the prospect of seeing her beloved nurse again.

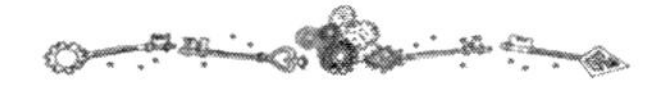

They flew for an hour through the gathering dawn, and Snow drank deeply of its flaming wonder. The golden glow of the brilliant sun as it heaved itself ponderously over the rim of the world reflected into her enchanted eyes, and she almost wished she could live in this moment forever.

She had never seen the sunrise before. Ensconced within the high palace walls, with heavy drapes at every window, she had never realised such beauty could exist. Snow reflected on how many simple joys she had discovered over the past two days. She realised, if it were not for the effect on her people of the Contratulum gaining power, she would be happy to walk away from her birthright and stay in the forest forever with her newly found family, and with Ronin.

She let her eyes rest for a moment on his broad, leather-clad back. Confused by her growing feelings for the Dwarvian leader, Snow only knew she had never dreamt she could feel this way about a man. Could feel so safe and protected by any member of the sex for which she had hitherto only felt distrust and fear.

Such thoughts are best put aside, she told herself fiercely. Now is not the time or the place for silly girlish notions, not when our lives are in danger and the future is so uncertain. Still, she allowed her eyes to linger sadly on him a moment longer, until Arden tapped her on the shoulder, guiding her attention to a stork taking off from its untidy nest high in a tree and flapping away from the skimmer in alarm.

Snow realised they had reached the forest's perimeter as the trees petered away and the thatched rooftops of a small hamlet came into view. Expertly holding the skimmer motionless in the sky, Ronin then eased it down into a tiny clearing. Snow braced herself for the now familiar, stomach-churning bump as the skimmer landed on the rough ground.

Taking a deep breath in the sudden silence, Snow shakily clambered from the skimmer and stood on legs that wobbled with nerves. They were here – there was no going back now. Removing her goggles and brushing down her cloak, Snow gratefully accepted the towel that Ronin had dampened with water from his flask. Wiping it around her face, she waited for his smile of approval that she had removed all the grime, before passing it onto Arden so he could do the same.

Shouldering their packs, the two men led her to the edge of the clearing and Snow realised once again how dependent she was upon them. Even though she had seen the hamlet from above, now on the ground she had no idea which direction it lay in. Without Ronin and Arden leading the way, she could have wandered deeper into the forest and been lost forever.

They walked silently through the trees for several minutes, until Ronin held his hand up for them to stop. Softly, he paced to a wall of tangled undergrowth and peered through. He motioned them forward, and Snow copied Arden as he stepped lightly, mindful of dried twigs and brush underfoot that might crack if trodden on.

Looking down onto the hamlet which lay in a slight depression a short way from the treeline, Ronin tapped Arden on the shoulder.

"Any idea which cottage will be Greta's?" he asked.

Arden let his eyes roam over the huddle of cottages clustered around a village square, then his face lit up and a grin spread across his face. "That one," he murmured.

Following the direction of his gaze, Snow saw a small, neat cottage standing apart from the others and close to the forest's edge. A garden bloomed with vibrant plant life, and by the front gate was a bushy, living example of the dried bloom in her chatelaine.

"Witch hazel," she whispered, and Arden nodded in agreement.

"I'd say that's the one," he declared.

"Right. Let's work our way around staying within the trees," said Ronin. "If we approach the cottage from behind it should shield us from view."

Quietly and carefully, they walked along the forest's edge, always staying a few trees in, and constantly looking for any sign of life within the sleepy hamlet. It was still early. Snow imagined the village inhabitants waking up. From chimneys curled ribbons of smoke which hinted at fires being roused to cook breakfast and heat water for washing.

It was a pretty village, each cottage well maintained with a small garden attached containing vegetables, fruit trees, and herbs. Beautiful flowers nodded over wicker fences, and there was an air of quiet gentility to the place.

"This is where many of the palace staff come to retire," Ronin whispered in her ear, and Snow nodded, already aware of the fact.

Finally, they were behind the lone cottage Arden had chosen as being his sister's. Ronin cautiously led them from the trees, across a short patch of coarse grassland and through the small gate that opened into the spacious back garden.

It was a pretty and well-kept space. Sunflowers turned their heads towards the sunrise from their places against the cottage walls. Herbs tumbled over one another in a pleasing display, and an old wooden bench had its place by the open back door. A large ginger tomcat snoozed in a patch of sunlight on the stone doorstep and raised his head to look at them as they approached.

A young voice was tunelessly singing a ditty about a farmer and his flighty love from inside the depths of the cottage. An arm appeared around the corner of the door to empty a pan of water onto a patch of mint that was vigorously growing there in an old wooden bucket.

The cat yowled in protest when droplets of water splashed his sun-baked belly.

“Oh, hush your mouth, Arden,” the voice said, and the three exchanged glances. Arden’s brows shot up in amused surprise as he and the cat surveyed each other, before the cat got lazily to its feet, stretched, and wandered off into the garden searching for a safer spot to snooze.

“Arden?” The voice said, and a young female face followed the voice around the corner of the door. Her wide mouth gaped in shock when she saw the strangers, her honest ruddy cheeks paling under her freckles.

“Who are you?” she gasped, clutching the empty pan to her chest as if for protection.

“Is your mistress at home?” Arden asked, ignoring her question.

“My mistress? Yes, but she left strict instructions she wasn’t to be disturbed.”

“Oh, I think she’ll make an exception for us,” Arden assured her and took a step over the threshold.

“No, wait!” The girl thrust herself in front of him as if her small form could make the slightest difference to his intentions. “You can’t march in here as if you own the place,” she cried angrily. “The mistress said she wasn’t to be disturbed.”

“Tibby, who is it?”

The voice that sounded from deeper within the cottage was old but firm, and Arden gently pushed the girl aside and followed it. Exchanging glances, Ronin and Snow shadowed him, moving by Tibby who stood with the pan dropped to her side, clearly out of her depth.

“Who is it, Tibby?” the voice said again, and Arden paused at the kitchen door, his hand clutching the frame so tightly Snow saw his knuckles whiten.

“It’s me, Greta,” he said.

There was a brief second of silence. Then hands were pulling Arden further into the room and encasing him in a fierce and long hug. Bending his height down to that of his smaller sibling, Arden hugged her back as hard, and Snow swallowed at the intensity of the reunion.

“Thank the gods,” Greta mumbled into Arden’s chest. “I heard of the massacre and feared the worst, and when the years passed with no word, I was convinced you were all dead and that I was alone.”

“No, a few – a very few of us survived – I had not dared try and contact you whilst you still resided in the palace for fear of placing you in danger.”

“But how did you know where to find me?”

“I do not come alone, Greta.”

Gently he pulled his sister around him to see the others and her hands flew to her face in shocked joy.

"Snow?" she whispered.

"Aunt," Snow whispered back, then was encased in Greta's familiar arms, breathing in that forgotten scent of peppermint and bergamot that had so comforted her as a child.

"Aunt?" Greta questioned, shooting Arden a look over Snow's shoulder. "Then you know ...?"

"That you are my family? Yes, I know."

"Come and sit." Greta released Snow and gestured into the small, pleasantly furnished, sitting room behind her. "I feel there are many stories to be shared. I have yet to break my fast so you shall join me, and we can become acquainted with all that has occurred since I last had news of you."

Greta gently cupped Snow's face, her eyes soft with love. "My little Snow," she murmured. "You have grown so. You are even more beautiful than your mother. I never thought I would see you again, not after they sent me away." Snow smiled and rested her forehead briefly on her aunt's.

"Tibby." This was to the young maid who still stood gawking, her simple face twisted with confusion at the morning's events. "These are my long-lost family, come to visit. Please prepare breakfast and make sure there is enough for all."

"Yes, mistress." Recovering herself enough to bob a sketchy curtsey, Tibby scuttled to fill the large kettle from the pump and place it onto the range.

"Come." Greta ushered them into the other room. "Sit. We will have tea and break our fast and you can tell me everything."

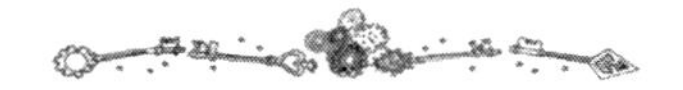

Not realising how famished she was, Snow let the others do most of the talking as she filled her plate with chewy bread slathered with fresh butter, hard-boiled eggs, crispy fried bacon, and a cheese so mature it stung her eyes to tears. All washed down with several cups of strong black tea sweetened with honey.

Snow finally pushed her plate away and sighed in contentment as Ronin raised his brows at her in amusement.

"Feeling better, Your Highness?"

"Much," she grinned in reply.

"Only seven of us are left?" Greta asked again, clearly in shock.

"Eight, now," Arden replied, and placed a hand over her own where it lay trembling on the table. "You cannot know how relieved

I was when Snow told me you still lived. I was afraid you may have been discovered as Dwarvian."

"No," Greta assured him. "That secret, at least, Raven managed to keep from them. But they suspected her of enough to ..." she paused and glanced at Snow in concern.

"It's all right, Greta," Snow told her. "I know the Contratulum murdered my mother."

"But how?"

"Death's Trumpet," Arden said grimly. "As soon as Snow told me of the odour she detected on Raven's breath, I knew what had occurred."

"We had been so careful," Greta said, a lone tear rolling down her wrinkled face. "We neither ate nor drank of anything that had not been prepared by me. But one day in the orchard she plucked a ripe red apple from a tree and took a bite. The moment she swallowed it she knew what had happened. We hurried back to her room and I prepared a purge for her, but it was too late. The poison was in her system. All that night I tried everything I could think of. In the end, we realised it was futile, and she sent me to fetch you so that she might see you one last time."

"They poisoned all the apples in the orchard?" Ronin exclaimed in shock.

"Next day, all the trees were felled by order of Pontifex Slie, and cherry trees were planted in their stead." Greta sighed and shook her head. "I knew then it was only a matter of time before they removed me as well. So, I tried to make myself invisible. I blended into the background, did my best to appear almost a simpleton, and for a while, it worked. But then when you reached your tenth nameday, I was given a choice. Retire here in comfort or be sold into slavery at the southern borders."

At Snow's gasp of horror, Greta clasped both her hands in her own. "I am sorry I had to leave you, Snow, but knew I could do no good far away as a slave, so I took their bargain and left. I hoped that the lessons I had taught you were enough to keep you on the right path, and every year I sent you a fresh charm to help protect you. I still had one or two friends within the palace whom I trusted to ensure you received my letter each year."

"Your charm saved me in so many ways," Snow reassured her. "When Jay sent me into the forest to be murdered by her guards, it gave me the courage and the strength to fight back. And it called Ronin to me, so he found me and took me home. If he hadn't come along when he did, I don't think I would be sitting here with you now."

"Bless you, Ronin," Greta said and touched his arm in gratitude. "But what is to be done?" she continued, looking into each of their faces. "What plan is there to claim your throne, Snow?"

"Claim my throne? I ... I don't think that is possible, Greta. The Contratulum are so strong, and they have the Power, how can I fight against them? I have recently learnt that Mirage has been spying on me when I believed myself alone, and we know they have spies everywhere."

"That odious toad," Greta declared fiercely. "Slithering and creeping about the palace. An ear to every door, and a finger in every pie. I told Raven to squash him before he got too powerful, but she was afraid to show our hand too soon. That if she removed the Contratulum's lackey they would know we were onto them."

"Then there is my aunt, Jay," Snow continued. "It was she who tried to have me killed, and my stepfather will certainly do nothing to save me."

"Weak and easily led imbeciles, the pair of them," Greta scoffed. "But Jay actually tried to have you killed? I knew she was a spiteful and jealous woman, but I never imagined she would stoop so low."

"She is with child," Snow explained. "Maybe she believes that with me out of the way, it could inherit the throne." Greta snorted in disgust. "She is also deeply envious of the ... high regard ... my stepfather holds me in." Greta frowned at Snow's hesitant voice, the embarrassment on her face, and her expression darkened.

"Hawk was always a pig of a man," she declared fiercely. "Many a time Raven had reason to order him to leave her maids alone. But to lust after his stepdaughter, his niece by marriage ..." She broke off and shook her head.

"You must claim your throne, Snow. Somehow, a way must be found for you to take what is rightfully yours. We cannot allow the Contratulum to gain complete power. If they did, it would mean an end to freedom in this kingdom. Somehow, they must be stopped.

After they had finished eating, believing that Arden deserved some time alone with his sister, Snow and Ronin excused themselves. Taking fresh cups of tea, they went out into the warm morning sunshine dappling Greta's verdant back garden.

Sitting on the bench and watching as Arden the cat rolled about in the grass and delicately licked his belly, Snow wondered how long they would be able to stay in this peaceful haven.

"What you said today about your Stepfather – about Hawk – and what you've said before about him. Was that all true?"

Snow looked up at Ronin's question. Shading her eyes from the glare of the sun, she studied his serious expression for a moment and then nodded.

"Yes, it's true. Once I achieved womanhood, he made it quite plain what he desired."

"Did he ...?" Ronin paused, and swallowed, his head turning away as if afraid to look at her. "Did he ever ...?"

"No," Snow replied resolutely. "The door to my chamber was always firmly locked and I kept the only key. He could knock and plead to be admitted as much as he liked, but I never let him in."

"He would do that?" Ronin turned shocked and disgusted eyes upon her. "By the gods, what kind of a monster is he?"

"He is no monster," Snow replied sadly. "He is a man, and as such is prey to his basest needs and desires. I truly believe he could not help himself."

"Not all men are like that."

"I know that now," she replied softly.

"I am not like that."

"I know."

The moment and the look stretched between them ...

"Snow," he began, then they were interrupted by Tibby bustling out with a basket upon her hip, and the moment was lost.

"Mistress has sent me to pick mushrooms from the forest to make soup for our midday repast," she explained, stooping to pet the cat which fawned without dignity over her feet. She turned her open, honest face up to them, the sun glinting off hair the same colour as the cat's fur.

"May I come with you?" Snow asked, abruptly needing time away from Ronin to consider all that had been said, and all that had been implied in that look. Her skin burnt uncomfortably beneath her chemise and the coolness of the forest was suddenly appealing.

Tibby shrugged. "If you like, Milady."

"Don't be too long," Ronin said, rising to stand beside her. "Stay close to Tibby. It would be easy to get lost in the forest. Oh, and Snow ..."

She was already following Tibby down the path and turned at his words.

"Yes?"

"Be careful."

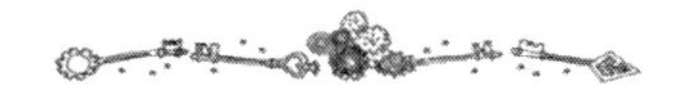

Wandering around the forest behind Tibby, Snow marvelled at how the girl seemed to know exactly which of the many identical tracks to take, realising she would be hopelessly lost in moments without her as a guide.

It was eerily quiet amongst the trees, apart from the cooing of woodpigeons and the soft soughing of the breeze amongst the branches. Sunlight flecked the forest floor with uneven confetti, and somewhere Snow could hear the muted babbling of a brook.

Finally, Tibby stopped at a tiny clearing where mushrooms sprouted in abundant profusion over the forest floor. Kneeling, she began to pick them. Delighted by the task, Snow knelt to pick, dropping them into Tibby's basket and realising how much she was enjoying the simplicity of the chore.

"Ooh, not that one, Milady." Tibby knocked the mushroom from her hand. "Look at the underside of the cap. See those red speckles? They mean it's a Nightshade mushroom and you mustn't eat them."

"It's poisonous? Would it kill me?"

"It would," Tibby agreed. "At the very least it'll give you a very bad bellyache, and you wouldn't want that."

"No," Snow agreed. "I wouldn't."

They picked on in silence, Snow making sure that each mushroom she dropped into the basket was creamy in colour and completely red-speckle free. Eventually, the basket was full, and the girls rose to their feet, Tibby viewing their harvest with satisfaction.

"That's a goodly lot, that is," she declared. "That'll make enough soup for us all, but we best be getting back so I can set it to cook."

"How long have you been with Greta?" Snow asked, following Tibby back along the path.

"The mistress? Oh, a fair, few years. My parents died of the sweating fever and there was no one to take care of me. Then the mistress took me in and trained me up to be her maid. Ever so grateful to her, I am. I don't know what would have become of me if she hadn't given me a home."

"That was kind of her," Snow murmured, as they reached the edge of the forest and let themselves back into the garden, where Tibby excused herself and disappeared into the kitchen to make the soup.

Wandering around the garden, Snow played with the cat as he shamelessly flirted with her in the sunshine, then sat once more on the bench and thought about things for a while. Through the open window above her head, she could hear the voices of the others and thought about joining them, but she was too comfortable in the sun to consider moving … and the sun was warm on her face … and her eyelids were so heavy …

Snow blinked awake at the sound of the gate latch and pulled herself up on the bench as Tibby let herself back into the garden.

"Tibby?" she murmured, rubbing sleep from her eyes. "I thought you were inside?"

"I was, Milady," Tibby replied. "But we were out of cream for the soup. I went to get some from our neighbour who owns a cow and barters with us for vegetables, herbs, and the mistress's lotion for rheumatism." She showed Snow the little blue and white jug in her hand. "Mistress always says that's the secret to a good mushroom soup, plenty of cream."

"I didn't see you go," Snow said, and Tibby's smile widened.

"Sleeping like a baby you were, Milady, so I crept by and you didn't stir."

"Oh," said Snow, feeling rather silly at being caught napping like an old woman.

Tibby grinned at her and bustled into the kitchen. A moment later her off-key singing floated out through the door. Snow listened in amusement to the tale of the trials the flighty maid put her staunch, would-be lover through before she would consider marrying him.

It was hot in the midday sun. Her eyelids prickled with tiredness, insisting that she sleep again. Arden the cat startled her by leaping onto the bench beside her and demanding attention. Letting her hands sink into his deep, warm fur, Snow was thrilled when he clambered into her lap and slowly blinked sleepy eyes at her.

Coming out into the garden to summon her in for luncheon, Ronin smiled at the pretty sight of the beautiful young woman fast asleep in the sun, the sleek length of the ginger tom curled up in her lap. He crouched before her, and the movement awoke Arden the cat. He blinked accusingly at Ronin, only slightly appeased by the friendly rub to the ears he received.

"Snow." Gently he shook her shoulder.

"Huh?"

"Tis time for luncheon."

"Hmm?" Slowly her eyelids fluttered open, and she looked at him, and he felt again that kick to the gut that those dark eyes always produced in him.

"Come," was all he said though. "Tis time for luncheon and the others are waiting. We have much to discuss and little time to waste."

Chapter Fourteen

The Red Wine Stain

As Tibby had promised, the mushroom soup was utterly delicious. Snow consumed two bowlfuls of the dark, creamy liquid flecked with fresh herbs from the garden, copying the men when they wiped thick crusty bread around their bowls to catch every drop. She wiped sticky fingers on her napkin and leaned back in replete satisfaction.

"You must come with us," Arden insisted.

"I will," Greta nodded in agreement. "But it will take me a few days to pack my belongings and say my goodbyes. This village has been kind to me, and I will miss my neighbours, and this cottage, sorely."

"What reason will you give for your departure?" Ronin asked.

"The truth – that my family wishes me to see out the rest of my days with them."

Ronin nodded and looked around the cluttered room. "I am unsure how we can transport all your belongings – certainly not in the skimmer. I am thinking it best if we three return, and then Arden can come back for you with the scoop. Although, in truth, even it cannot carry too much."

"Oh, I will not be bringing too much," Greta reassured him, "but I have a few precious things I cannot bear to part with. No, I must arrange for someone to take care of my cottage. A neighbour's son is to marry soon, and I know they face the prospect of living with his parents until they can build a home of their own. Mayhap, he will be amenable to taking on my cottage. And then there's Tibby. I must see that she is settled and content, for she is a dear child. I only wish I could bring her with me ... But no, tis best she stays with her own kind."

"I take it she has no idea ...?"

"That I am Dwarvian?" Greta finished Arden's sentence. "No, the child had her head stuffed with tales of how evil we were by her old great-grandmother. To discover that I am one of those monsters – no, I do not think she could accept that. It's best she stays behind, although I will miss her ..."

"Is it all right to clear the table now, mistress?"

Tibby's sudden arrival in the room made them all start and exchange glances. How long had she been there? How much had she heard? Yet the girl's face was calm, her ready grin as broad as ever when Greta replied.

"Yes, thank you Tibby, we have finished. The soup was excellent, my dear. Just the right consistency of cream."

“Thank you, mistress.” Tibby flushed with pleasure at the compliment.

“It was as well you went to fetch more cream,” Snow commented.

“More cream?” Greta frowned in confusion. “Did we use all the cream from yesterday then?”

“It was on the turn, mistress,” Tibby quickly replied, “so, I thought it best to get some fresh.”

“Of course.” Greta smiled at her servant fondly, as Tibby gathered up as many bowls as she could and left the room. Rising to her feet, Snow collected what remained and followed her to the kitchen. Tibby stood at the large, earthenware sink rolling up her sleeves. She jumped when Snow entered the room, hastily pushing her sleeves back down to her wrists.

“Oh, Milady,” she gasped, clutching her hand to her chest. “You gave me a terrible turn.”

“I’m sorry, Tibby,” Snow reassured her. “I was only trying to help. Is there anything I can do?”

“A lady like you? No, Milady.” Seemingly horrified at the thought of Snow sullying her hands with menial tasks, Tibby all but pushed her back out of the kitchen, and for good measure shut the door behind her.

“Snow?” Ronin was there with her cloak. “It is time to go. If we hurry and risk flying during daylight hours, then Arden can make a good start back before the sun sets. He may well be here by midday tomorrow.” This was to Greta, who nodded.

“I will be ready,” she looked at Arden and smiled. “I trust you have room in your cottage for one old lady and a cat?”

“Aye,” he agreed. “Although I’m not sure how Cesil will react to him.”

“Cesil?”

“A pig,” Arden explained, and Greta raised her brows but said nothing.

“Farewell, my darling Snow.” Greta gathered her up in a warm hug, which Snow fervently returned, realising how much she had missed the simple act of being held by another.

“We will see you again soon,” she murmured.

“You certainly will,” Greta agreed and glanced at Ronin.

“Keep them safe,” she ordered.

“I always do.”

Impatient for them to be on their way, Ronin led them back into the kitchen, where Tibby was now wiping up their soup bowls.

“Farewell, Tibby.” Snow hesitated long enough to smile a goodbye at the young girl.

"Farewell, Milady. I hope to see you again soon. Maybe next time I could take you to pick berries?"

"I would like that," Snow said, not having the heart to tell the girl that the likelihood was they would never see each other again.

"Snow!"

Ronin's impatient bellow from outside had her hurrying to follow, and they rushed over the grassland towards the forest, the coarse stubby stalks swishing under their feet. Ronin glanced at her as they reached the edge of the forest and Snow lingered, turning regretful eyes to the pretty abode they were leaving behind – probably forever.

"You seemed rather taken with the child?"

"I was. She is a dear girl, and I know she's going to be devastated when Greta leaves. Poor child, she has had an unfortunate life. What with losing both her parents when she was so young, and then, of course, being cursed with such an affliction."

"An affliction?"

"Yes."

"What affliction?" Arden asked, his keen eyes interested.

"When I went into the kitchen earlier, she was rolling up her sleeves to wash the dishes, and that's when I saw it."

"Saw what?"

"The poor child has a large birthmark all over one arm. It is truly grotesque. It is a livid red and looks like a ..." Snow gasped as realisation struck with the force of a hammer.

"Looks like a what?"

"A red wine stain!" she cried. Picking up her skirts, she ran for all she was worth back towards the cottage. Behind, she heard the confused shouts of the men, as her feet flew over the uneven ground as fast as she could go.

Bursting through the still-open door of the cottage she paused, her heart thumping madly as she glanced around the kitchen. There was no sign of Tibby, so she hastened to the sitting-room door.

There!

Silently creeping towards where Greta was bent over some book on the table. Snow saw the young girl raise a long, lethal-looking pair of scissors over her head and lunge towards the oblivious old woman.

"No!"

Snow's scream jerked Greta about as the scissors plunged, and instead of stabbing her back, they grazed down her shoulder. Crossing the room in one bound, Snow wrestled with the girl, who seemed to possess almost superhuman strength as she fought back.

The bloodstained scissors dropped to the ground as Ronin and Arden burst into the room. Ronin stunned the girl with a single punch, wrestling her off Snow and onto the floor. Snow staggered backwards, collapsing into a chair by the fire as Arden knelt by his sister.

"Greta?"

"I'm all right," she gasped, her hands clasped to her shoulder. "It's merely a scratch. But Tibby ..."

They all looked at the girl who was lying on the floor, thrashing violently, and growling under Ronin's restraining grasp.

"Why, Tibby?" Greta asked, slipping from her chair to kneel beside her maid. "Why would you try to kill me?"

"Filthy Dwarvian," Tibby snarled. Her eyes opened to reveal nothing but blackness staring back at them with evil intent. "You should all be wiped from the face of the earth. Filthy monsters."

"Oh, Tibby," Greta said sadly. "Not you too."

Tibby blinked. The blackness was gone, and the clear blue of the girl's eyes looked at them with confusion.

"Mistress?" she whimpered. "I'm so sorry, Mistress. They're in my head, they always have been. They told me if strangers ever came here, I was to let them know. So, I pretended we needed cream and I sent a message to tell them your family were here. They made me try to kill you. I'm pleased you stopped me. Even if you are Dwarvian, Mistress, you've been so good to me. I didn't want no harm to come to you."

She gasped with pain, and blood spurted from the corners of her eyes to run in rivulets over her freckled cheeks.

"Run, Mistress!" she screamed. "They're on their way. They'll soon be here. Run ..."

Blood gushed from her mouth. Tibby writhed in agony as more blood pooled in her eyes and streamed from her ears. Her back arched in a spasm of excruciating pain, and then she lay still.

Greta slapped a palm over her trembling mouth. "Tibby?"

Ronin felt for a pulse in the girl's neck, then sadly shook his head and closed the girl's eyes.

"We have to go," he ordered grimly. "Now."

"Ronin ..."

At Snow's hoarse whisper, his head snapped around to where she lay slumped in the chair, her hands clutched to her stomach.

"Snow?"

"I'm sorry ..." she said and held out her blood-drenched hands to him.

In one bound he was to her. His heart stopped at the sight of the gaping wound and the blood – by the gods so much blood – pooling onto her lap and around her hands as she tried to hold it in.

"I'm sorry," she whispered again. "She stabbed me. I'm sorry."

Stifling a curse, he grabbed the small cloth covering the table next to the chair and pressed it firmly to the wound. Then Greta and Arden were beside him.

"Quickly, get her into the kitchen," Greta ordered him.

Ronin swept Snow up into his arms, his heart hurting at the agonised cry she gave as he moved her. Her head fell limply against his shoulder, and he realised she had fainted.

"Onto the table. Undo her corset." Greta barked orders as she was pulling open cupboard doors and gathering an array of herbs. "Grind these to a paste," she told Arden, piling the herbs into a large pestle and mortar.

Quickly, he did as commanded, and Greta hurried to where Snow lay so still and white on the table. Blood was gushing from the wound and Ronin's face was as white as Snow's as he helplessly pressed down with the now soaked cloth, desperately trying to stem the flow.

Snatching scissors from the dresser, Greta cut away the red mass of Snow's chemise to reveal a gaping, ragged wound that pulsed red with every laboured breath Snow managed to draw.

"Do something," Ronin begged her. "She mustn't die. She can't!"

"It's bad," Greta told him. "The scissors were long, and they went deep. A wound like this ... I think it's beyond even my skills."

"Here." Arden thrust the mortar at her, and Greta placed it on the table beside Snow. Holding one hand over it she began to mutter incantations, her eyes squeezed shut with the intensity of the spell she was trying to cast.

Ronin opened his mouth to speak, but Arden put a hand over his and shook his head.

A green glow emanated from Greta's hand, which infused into the herbs and bound them into a thick, foul-smelling unguent.

"Wash the wound," she ordered. Arden snatched up the water pitcher from the side and soaked a dishtowel in it, hastily washing away as much of the blood as he could. As it began to pump again, Greta quickly slapped handfuls of the unguent over the wound. Smearing it all over, she kept going until the bowl was empty and the wound had stopped bleeding.

Releasing a shaky breath, Greta wiped her bloody hands on a cloth, then hurried to fetch a cotton pad and bandages from a drawer. Binding the wound tightly, she glanced up at Ronin, whose face was daring to show signs of hope.

"This is only a temporary measure," she warned. "It will stop the bleeding for a few hours, but the damage inside needs to be repaired, and that is beyond my skills as a healer."

"Grein," Arden exclaimed. "We need to get her back to Grein. He has the skill to heal her."

"But he's so far away. We won't make it in time."

"We won't, but you will," Arden said. "Take her and fly as fast as you can back to the others. The skimmer will be quicker carrying only two."

"But you, and Greta ..." Ronin began, clearly torn between what his heart was telling him and what he knew to be right.

"Will be right behind you. Get Snow to safety, then come back for us. Send out one of Kylah's toys to scout for our whereabouts. We will try to maintain a straight line between here and home, but we all need to leave."

"Yes, we do," Greta replied, bustling about the kitchen, and throwing supplies into a knapsack. "Tibby told them this morning that you were here, and there's a Contratulum outpost less than two hours' ride away. They could be here any minute, so we all need to leave. Now!" she snapped, as Ronin hesitated.

"Take Snow and go." Arden insisted. Ronin gripped him by the wrist and looked at him intently.

"I will return for you," he promised.

"The frick you will," Arden agreed.

Trying to be as gentle as he could, Ronin gathered up the still body of Snow into his arms and headed for the door.

"Hurry," Arden ordered Greta, and she held up a book before stuffing it into the already bulging knapsack.

"This is the last thing," she promised. "Do you recognise it?"

"Mother's spellbook," he gasped.

For a split second the siblings exchanged a look before Arden was snatching the bag from her.

"Come," he said, and they hurried from the cottage, following Ronin, who was already halfway to the forest's edge.

"Arden!" Greta called as they rushed down the garden path.

"What?" he called back over his shoulder.

"No, not you," she snapped. A blur of ginger fur streaked over the garden and leapt into Greta's arms. "Oh, this is not going to get confusing at all," she groaned, as they ran from the garden and started towards the forest.

Ronin had reached the treeline. He hesitated by the packs he and Arden had dropped when Snow had her moment of clarity earlier and dashed off back towards the cottage.

"Go." Arden waved him on. "We'll bring these."

Ronin nodded grimly and disappeared deeper into the forest. The others gathered up the packs and moved to within the trees.

Hearing shouts, they turned to see a legion of Contratulum soldiers moving through the hamlet. Villagers clustered on their doorsteps to see what all the fuss was about.

From their vantage point, Arden and Greta saw the commander of the legion bark something at a villager. Clearly terrified, the man pointed a trembling finger towards Greta's cottage, and as one the soldiers descended on it.

"Greta, we need to go." Arden pulled softly at his sister's arm and she turned to him, regretful tears glinting in her eyes.

"That was my home for so many years," she whispered. "I had it just as I liked it."

"I know." Briefly, he hugged her, then led her away into the forest. "But I have a cottage as nice as that one. Well, it maybe needs a woman's touch."

"Arden Turningleaf, please don't tell me as well as sharing your home with a pig, you also live like one?"

"No." He quailed under her stern enquiry. "Well, perhaps. It is the home of an old bachelor, but you will have free reign to do whatever you please to it."

"Good." She looked more cheerful, then glanced regretfully over her shoulder at the shouts behind them. A smell of smoke wafted through the trees and the shouting intensified.

"I think that's my home going up in flames," she said.

"It's in the past." Arden patted her on the arm. "Put it behind you and walk away. Come, we need to be gone from here before they start searching the forest."

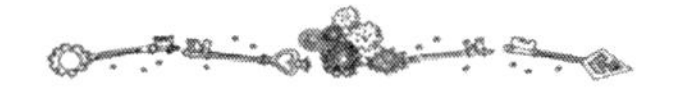

Reaching the skimmer, Ronin gently lay Snow on the ground and clambered in to collapse the middle seat. He figured she would be more comfortable lying down than bent in half, and he prayed Greta's spell would hold until he got her to Grein.

Getting Snow into the skimmer was awkward. His heart broke at her pained whimpers as he manhandled her up and over the side and laid her as gently as he could upon the seats.

“Hold on, Your Highness,” he whispered, brushing a strand of hair from her cheek, and arranging her arms by her side.

“Please, Snow. Please don’t die.”

She mumbled something but showed no signs of regaining consciousness. Given how much pain she must be in, Ronin thought that to be a good thing and scrambled hastily into his seat. Foregoing the pre-flight checks, he slammed the lever up and the blades whipped into life above his head. As soon as there was enough lift, he rose above the tree level and pointed the nose of the skimmer towards home.

“Hold on, Snow,” he muttered between clenched teeth and glanced over his shoulder at the woman lying as motionless as death behind him. To his relief, the bandage was still white, and he prayed to all the gods it would remain that way until he reached Grein.

At the sound of the skimmer’s engine, Arden and Greta paused and glanced at each other. Behind them, the shouts of the soldiers intensified. Wordlessly the pair melted away into the undergrowth. Arden the cat, who was draped around Greta’s neck, dug his claws in at the sudden change in direction, and Greta soothed him by stroking his front paws.

There was a loud intrusion into the peace of the forest. Men in Contratulum uniforms with its crest emblazoned across their tunics thundered by, not even glancing towards the shrubbery where the elderly siblings lay concealed. Patiently they waited until the whole legion had passed, before crawling out.

“Hopefully, examining the clearing will take them some time.” Arden breathed into Greta’s ear. “If we cross their path here and take a direct route that way, we should be long gone before they come back.”

Greta nodded. Hoisting Arden, the cat, more firmly onto her shoulders, she silently followed her brother across the faint track and into the undergrowth on the other side. Her attention was firmly on where she placed her feet, but her heart was far away. Soaring above the treetops in a desperate race to save the girl she loved like a daughter.

Chapter Fifteen

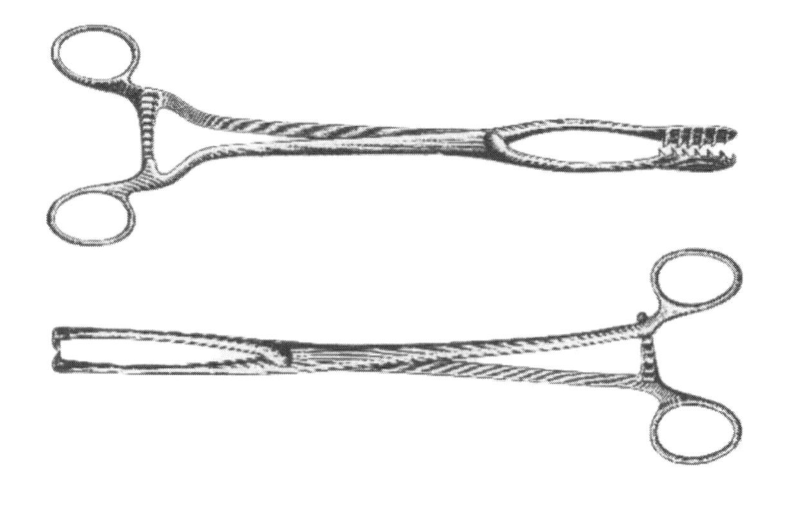

A Love Denied

She knew she should not worry – that Ronin was more than capable of looking after Arden and Snow – but still a niggle of unease plagued Fae all that night and into the next morning. Judging by the frown pulling at Kylah's normally smooth brow, Eli's unnatural silence, and the way Grein immediately disappeared back into his workshop after breakfast, that unease was shared by them all.

Left alone with Nylex when Kylah and Eli disappeared on an invented errand, Fae dropped a friendly hand onto his shoulder as he sat motionless and silent at the table. She raised her brows at his characteristic scowl, her hand tightening over the tension she felt beneath her palm.

"Try not to worry too much," she said, but the scowl deepened as he turned his gaze upon her in hostile frustration.

"I can't help it, Fae. This whole situation – the mission, her – it's all inviting them to find us. And when they do ..." his implication was clear.

Fae sighed and sat down beside him.

"I understand, Nylex. I really do. This must be stirring up old memories and regrets for you."

"Regrets?" His voice thick with bitterness, Nylex shrugged away from her well-meaning platitudes.

"It's because of me that our people were all but exterminated. My family ... yours ... everyone. I think I'm entitled to more than regrets about that."

"Nobody blames you, Nylex."

"I blame me!" he cried. "I should have been awake, but I fell asleep. I had been out drinking with my friends, so I fell asleep. If only I hadn't drunk so much. If only I'd been awake, I could have ..."

"What, Nylex?" Fae demanded. "What could you have done? There were too many of them. They had powerful airships, and weapons, the likes of which we had never seen before. There was no fighting them. We didn't stand a chance."

"I could have given them more warning," he insisted. "Perhaps those extra few minutes would have allowed more to escape. Our families ...."

"What happened was as fate intended," she told him. "Nothing you could have done would have made any difference."

He stared at her for a long, painful moment, then heaved a deep, shuddering gasp that shook his body with its intensity.

“It would have made a difference to me, Fae,” he replied quietly. “Perhaps, if I’d at least been able to try to save them, then I wouldn’t hate myself so much, and maybe ...”

His voice trailed away, and he gazed down at his hands. Unable to look at her for the condemnation he imagined he would see on her face.

“Maybe you would still love me?”

Fae asked the question into the silence. Unable to believe her courage in finally daring to name what lay between them. To remind him of all that they had been, and of all that they had lost.

“I never stopped loving you,” he insisted fiercely. “I stopped being worthy of you.”

“But I never thought that.” Tears sheening her eyes, Fae leant towards him and placed her small hand over his where it lay trembling on the table between them. “I never believed you unworthy of me, Nylex, and I never stopped loving you.”

“How can you love the person responsible for the deaths of almost everyone you ever knew and loved? Your friends, your parents ... How, Fae? Tell me how you can still love that man, after what he did.”

“Because the heart never forgets. How can you have forgotten that evening out by the lake when the moon rose so full above us it was as bright as day. When you took me in your arms and held me so tight, I felt we were one creature. And then you kissed me and asked me to be your bride, and even though we were so young, we knew it was right and true.

“And when I said yes – of course, I said yes, for had I not loved you since we were children - you trembled in my arms and told me we would be together forever. You promised to love and protect me until the day you died. Well, you’re still alive Nylex, and so am I, yet we’re not together and it breaks my heart more every day to see you so eaten up with bitterness and hatred.”

“I haven’t forgotten,” he told her. “But that man, the man who loved you without measure, he died that night. When the airships of the Contratulum rained down fire upon our village and burnt our people in their beds, he was destroyed as well.”

“Not destroyed. Not completely.” Fae wiped away the tears that spurted hotly onto her cheeks at his words. “I refuse to believe that he is lost forever.”

“But he is.” Nylex pulled his hand roughly away from hers. “Or at least is buried so deeply it makes no odds. I am sorry, Fae, I truly am. But you need to forget about me. Forget about what once was and make a new future for yourself.”

"There is no future for me that does not contain you, Nylex."

"You have seen that?" He looked at her intently. "You have seen a future where we are together?"

"No," she admitted reluctantly. "Not seen, as in a vision, but I feel it with every fibre of my being, that we are meant to be as one. Oh, Nylex, a love like ours can never die. It may be buried for a while or diverted down another path, but it can never be lost entirely."

For a moment she saw him waver. Her passionate entreaty penetrating the layers of dark self-loathing to strike a chord in the heart of the young man who had been hers so intrinsically, that the boundary where she ended, and he began, was forever blurred.

"Nylex, please," she sobbed, and then his arms were around her. For a moment – for one glorious moment – he allowed himself to forget, and their lips met. They were Fae and Nylex again, and she lived in the instant before abruptly it was over, and he was pulling away from her.

"No," was all he softly said, and her heart broke all over again.

"Nylex ..." she whispered.

"No, I'm sorry, Fae, but I can't."

"Nylex, please ..."

But he was halfway to the door, his back implacable, his intention to leave her clear – until her sharp cry of pain had him spinning around to find her clutching at her temples, her eyes clouded over with the white film of a vision.

"Fae!"

Swiftly, he caught her before her head could connect with the wood of the table.

"Fae?"

Cradling her to his chest, he felt the shudders that ripped through her slight frame, as her back arched against his chest. As taut as a bow, she strained further and further, until he feared she would snap her spine in two. Then she collapsed in his arms, struggling for breath, and clutching at her head.

"It's all right," he whispered, his large hands smoothing back her mussed-up hair. "I've got you, my love. You're safe, I've got you."

"Nylex?" she gasped, turning into his chest with a sob of relief.

"It's all right, you're back. What did you see?"

"I saw ... no, I felt ... Oh, the others, it's the others ..."

"What about them? Are they safe? Are they alive?"

His voice sharp with fear, he cupped her chin with one hand and turned her green gaze up to meet his own.

"Yes ... no ... I felt them all, they are alive ... but they are separated. Ronin and Snow are high up in the sky, and he is flying back as fast as he can ... Oh, so fast ... I can hear his heart beating. He is afraid of something. No, he is afraid *for* someone. It's Snow! Oh, Nylex, she's hurt. She's hurt so badly. Death sits upon her shoulder, but Ronin is pushing it away."

"What? Are you sure, Fae?"

"Yes, we must get Grein. He must prepare. Only he can save her. Only he can save Snow. Oh, Nylex. She mustn't die. She can't die. It would be the end of everything if she does."

Pushing the skimmer to its limits and beyond, Ronin continuously glanced over his shoulder to where Snow lay so still and pale. Pink was beginning to seep through the edges of the bandages. To fight down the rising wave of despair that threatened to engulf him, he spoke to her, pleading with her to fight it.

"Please, Snow," he begged. "Your Highness, please, stay with me. Try to fight it, Snow, and stay with me. We're almost home, we're almost there. Grein will help you, but you need to hold on a little longer, Snow. Just a little longer. Please, Snow, please, hold on."

Finally, he saw the clearing below him and the roof of his cottage, and he lined the skimmer up for the descent. Before the blades had even finished turning, he was scrambling from his seat, and then Nylex and Kylah were there with a makeshift stretcher ready and waiting.

"Fae," Nylex explained before he could say a word, and Ronin merely nodded. Scooping up Snow in his arms he gently lowered her over the edge and down onto the stretcher, following them as they rushed towards the cottage.

Inside, Fae was tending the fire, stoking it hotter and hotter, with Eli stacking logs in a pile beside it. They turned as the door opened and Snow was carried in.

"On the table," Grein ordered. Gently, they placed the stretcher on the long table and lifted her onto its cleared and scrubbed surface. Coming through the door, Ronin saw bowls standing ready on the side with strange instruments already soaking in alcohol.

"Nylex, Kylah, and Eli – I don't need you, so leave. Give me space to work," Grein ordered, and they left, taking the stretcher with them, Nylex's eyes meeting Fae's in a silent message of support.

"You!" Grein barked at Ronin. "Strip and wash. Make sure you scrub your hands in alcohol and then put on that robe."

Silently, Ronin moved to obey, his hands shaking with sudden exhaustion as he hung his coat on the peg by the door and stripped off his tunic and undershirt. Fae had already placed a pail of hot water and soap on the side for him, and he plunged his hands into the pail, lathering up the soap over his hands, arms, face, and neck.

Fae handed him a clean towel and he rubbed himself dry, before pushing his arms into the sleeves of the plain cotton robe she held out to him. Tying it at the back for him, Fae held the bottle of rubbing alcohol over his palms and at his nod dripped some into them. He winced as the stinging liquid found various cuts and grazes, and his eyes moved to the body of Snow lying on the table.

Grein was cutting away the clothing around the wound and gently removing the bandages and blood-soaked cotton pad. His eyebrows flew up at the green unguent beneath and he gingerly sniffed it.

"Who did this?" he demanded.

"Greta – Arden's sister. She said it would stop the bleeding for a while."

"It did," Grein agreed. "Clever. Right, let's see what we have." Blood spurted under his fingertips as he probed the wound, and he muttered to himself. Watching Snow, Ronin saw her eyelids flutter and her head thrash from side to side.

"She's coming to," he warned, and Grein glanced up in concern.

"Fae," he ordered, and Fae was instantly at Snow's side.

"Hush, now," she whispered, her hands poised on either side of Snow's head. "Sleep now," she suggested. "So sleepy. Sleep now." Obediently, Snow's eyes closed, and her breathing steadied as she slipped into the magic-induced slumber.

"That's better," Grein muttered, then looked up in annoyance. "Ye gods, it's so dark in here. I need more light."

Hurriedly, Ronin and Fae moved to light more lamps and candles, positioning them around the room until there were no shadows over Snow's body. Grein grunted in satisfaction.

Using a long-handled instrument, he clamped it inside the ragged red flesh and the bleeding abruptly stopped. Washing the wound with alcohol, Grein dabbed clean cotton into it until the area was clear of blood, then he pulled his magnifying goggles over his eyes and bent to examine it.

Ronin swallowed hard, wanting to avert his eyes but feeling it would be disloyal to Snow not to be with her every step of the way. Still, the sight of the jagged tear in her young, smooth, milk-white flesh was hard to look at, and a slight moan whispered through his lips.

Fae looked at him, her eyes sorrowful.

"It'll be all right," she murmured. "Grein will save her."

Ronin nodded but did not reply, watching as Grein picked a thin needle from one of the bowls standing on the side. Pulling out a length of finest thread, he peered at the needle and expertly threaded it, before leaning over the unconscious girl.

"Hold her completely still," he told them, and Ronin and Fae quickly took up their positions, Ronin holding her down by the shoulders, and Fae pressing down on her thighs.

"A vein is severed inside, so that needs to be stitched shut, and there is a tear in her stomach lining. Left unattended, that will cause her problems."

Time slowed to a standstill as he worked, his hands deft and steady as he confidently stitched her wounds. Once again, Ronin marvelled at the skill of the man. At his ability to work within a person's body to heal that which would normally kill.

Every now and then, Grein would pause and mutter something, his hands hovering over the wound. Ronin knew he was calling upon his magic, encouraging Snow's body to remember how it should be and to start to heal itself.

Finally, Grein stopped and doused the wound in alcohol again. Taking another needle from the bowl, he threaded it and neatly sewed the wound closed, the gaping gash reduced to a row of precise stitches that marred Snow's perfect creamy flesh.

"There." Grein stretched out his back and dropped the needle into the bowl. "It's done. The bleeding has been staunched and everything repaired. Fae, it's your turn now."

Fae nodded and took over his position. Gently, she passed her hands over the wound, muttering something under her breath.

"Yes," she agreed. "It is nicely done, Grein. Already her body moves to repair itself. A few days and it will not need your stitches, and by the time they dissolve all will be as it should be – maybe even stronger than before. I shall prepare her a poultice of healing herbs and they will help mend the skin and reduce the scar she will carry. Aside from that, a few days of rest and strengthening meals, and she should be fine." She smiled at Ronin as his face relaxed into a grimace of relief.

"You did well to get her here so quickly. And sending me a message so we could have all in readiness for you, well … that may have saved her life."

"I sent no message," Ronin said in confusion.

"Ah, but you did." Fae smiled. "Your pleas to Snow to hold on were so impassioned that I could not help but feel them too." Her smile broadened at Ronin's flush of embarrassment, then she moved to stand beside him at Snow's head. Gently running a hand through the inky black of the other girl's hair, her face softened.

"I, too, would hate to lose her," she said and placed her hand onto Ronin's sleeve. "She has become very dear to us both, has she not?"

"Aye." Ronin cleared his throat of the rough emotion in his tone. "She has."

After washing and pulling on clean clothes, Ronin and Grein were shooed from the cottage, and Kylah was summoned. Tenderly, the two women removed the tattered and bloodstained remnants of Snow's clothing, washed her body clean and gently dried and redressed her in a chemise taken from the chest of Lissa's old clothing.

Fae had glanced at Kylah at this point, but if the blonde woman was distressed at the sight of her lost love's clothes, she contained it well. Instead, her eyes were full of concern for Snow, and hands more used to tinkering with the innards of a machine were gentle as they helped Fae get Snow into the bed downstairs.

It had been decided, with no words being necessary, that even the thought of trying to manhandle Snow up the ladder to the loft room was impossible, so once again she was settled into Ronin's bed. Watching her sleep, Kylah awkwardly patted her on the hand.

"You'll be all right," she murmured.

Moving around the cottage, Kylah helped Fae gather up all the bloodstained clothing and cloths, which she took out to throw onto the campfire outside. Not wanting to disturb the delicate operation taking place in the cottage, Kylah had despatched Eli to check Ronin's traps. The two fine rabbits he found in them had been gutted and skinned by Nylex, then stewed in a pot hung over the fire, along with vegetables from Ronin's stores in the old stable.

A wonderful smell was emanating from the pot when Fae wearily sat down on the porch steps beside Ronin, thankfully accepting the glass of mead he handed her.

"How is Snow now?" he asked.

"Sleeping soundly," she replied and arched her back to relieve cramped muscles. "But it is a healthy, healing sleep and is what she needs for her body to repair itself." Looking around at the relieved faces of her family in the firelight, Fae had time to spare a thought for the missing member.

"But what of Arden?" she asked. "What happened? I gathered from what you said inside that you were successful in finding Arden's sister, but how did Snow come to be so badly injured?"

“Let us eat first,” Ronin said, “for it is a long tale and I am famished to the point of fainting myself. Once we have eaten, I will tell you all the story.”

They ate the meal in silence, their thoughts on their absent comrade and the sleeping girl inside, rather than the rabbit stew. Once finished, Fae gathered up their bowls and took them into the cottage, checking on Snow as she did. She was pleased to find that the girl’s breathing was steady and even, her pulse strong, and her skin cool to the touch.

Settling herself back onto the porch steps, she tucked her skirts under her knees and rested her cheek on her folded arms as she waited for Ronin to begin his tale. The fire warmed them, sending leaping flames of reflected light dancing in their eyes as Ronin told them everything that had occurred since they had waved goodbye the previous evening.

When he told of Tibby’s betrayal and demise, Fae’s eyes were warm with compassion, and she nodded when Ronin told her of the red wine stain the child had carried on her arm. She was thankful Arden’s sister was unharmed but was saddened that Snow had paid such a terrible price.

“Kylah – can you send one of your toys to find Arden and Greta tomorrow?” Ronin asked, and Kylah nodded, her eyes thoughtful.

“Yes, I have a bird automaton with me. It will do well enough. I will send it out at first light. It can carry a tracking device that Arden will know how to activate when it finds them. I can follow the signal in the skimmer and use it to guide them to me when I have landed as close to their location as possible.”

She paused, as though expecting him to protest when she nominated herself to go, but he merely nodded in agreement. She met Fae’s gaze, and the witch gently inclined her head towards the cottage. Kylah understood her meaning. Ronin wanted to stay close to Snow, to be there when she awoke. Wanted it so badly he was prepared to delegate responsibility to others.

“To think that Queen Raven was poisoned by Death’s Trumpet,” Grein mused.

“That is the one thing I do not understand,” Fae answered. “It was always my belief that the poison acted within minutes of being ingested, yet it took the Queen many hours to feel its effects, and a whole night before she succumbed to it.”

“It could have been that the poison was so diluted it took longer to act on her system,” Grein said. “Or perhaps between the apples being poisoned and the Queen biting into one it had rained, or there had been a heavy dewfall which washed away some of the toxins.”

"Maybe," Fae agreed. "I suppose we'll never know now."

"Indeed not," Grein agreed. "But it is a fascinating poison. To discover the antidote would indeed be an achievement."

"Well, when Arden and his sister arrive, perhaps you could discuss it with her," Ronin interjected, "for she seems to have more than a passing knowledge of the poison and possible treatments against it." He rose to feet and stretched in the firelight.

"Someone needs to sit by Snow tonight and ensure she does not suffer any ill effects from her misadventure. I will call you, Grein, if needed. I suggest we all get some sleep, for who knows what the morrow will bring."

He entered the cottage. Through the open door, they saw him drag his chair to the foot of the bed. It was clear that was where he intended to pass the night, and Kylah's eyes flew to Fae's in sudden understanding and concern.

It was a concern that Fae appreciated, and to a certain extent agreed with. For although her young, romantic heart thrilled to the notion of Ronin finding love after being so long alone, the fact remained that Snow was Princess Snow of the House White, the rightful heir to the throne, and leader of the kingdom. She was to be Queen, and queens did not marry penniless dispossessed leaders of a forbidden people.

Try as she might, Fae could see no outcome to this tale other than heartbreak and misery for one, or both, of them.

Chapter Sixteen

Between Reality and the Dreamworld

She was in darkness. A pitch blackness so absolute she could not see up from down. Then the veil lifted, and she was walking alone through a gloomy and menacing wood. Fear skittered down her spine and an intense pain lanced through her stomach. Putting her hands to her abdomen, they came away bloody, and Snow was afraid.

"Ronin?" she called, desperately wanting to find him. For him to hold her tightly and then take her home to their cottage in the woods. She did not care about the throne or being the queen – none of that seemed to matter anymore. Compared to never seeing him again it was inconsequential, of no substance. There was movement behind the trees and her breath caught.

"Ronin?" she called again, but the black shadow that stepped forth was not her kind-hearted Ronin with eyes that told her how much he cared. And at the sight of the dreaded long black locks and the mechanical eyepiece, her heart clenched with fear.

"Mirage?"

"Princess," he drawled. He smiled, but it was the smile of a wolf right before it devours its prey. "You're lost, Princess," he said. "So very lost. But have no fear, I am here to guide you home."

He gestured behind him to a tunnel twisting away through the bent and gnarled tree trunks. They dripped with a cankerous disease. Rotted and decomposing apples wept from their branches and things slithered over the mulched fruit remnants underfoot.

"This is the way home," he said, and Snow shrank back in horror.

"I'm not going anywhere with you," she stated. "And I am certainly not going into that foul place."

"Oh, but you will, Princess," he oozed. "Haven't you realised yet? You are dying. There is no hope for you. Even now you are bleeding deep inside, and no matter how hard your new friends try, they cannot save you. You belong to me now."

"No." Trembling with horror, still, she defied him, her chin rising in a flash of royal arrogance that had his eyes narrowing with anger.

"Always so proud," he murmured. "Yet you will succumb to me. You have no choice."

"Snow." At the much longed-for voice, Snow turned with a cry of joy, but Ronin was nowhere to be seen. "Snow." His voice came again. Hesitantly, she took a few steps away from Mirage and his words of death and despair.

"Ronin?" she cried. "Where are you? I can't see you."

"Hold on, Your Highness," he said. "Please, fight it and come back to me. Please, don't leave me, Snow."

"Never," she replied, scrambling faster and faster over the uneven ground towards his voice. Roots thrust themselves up to trip her, branches leaned over to snag at her hair and clothes, the wound in her stomach gaped even further and blood gushed down her legs. Sobbing, she kept going, pushing aside the branches, and ignoring the pain as she tried to reach his voice.

"Stay with me, Snow," he called again, and then she saw him. Standing at the edge of the forest on a high embankment with the pure, clean sunlight behind him. He held out a hand to her. Thankfully, she grasped it and he pulled her up and out of that dank and vile place.

Swinging her to safety behind him, he stepped forward. Drawing his large sword, he hacked at the twisted, grasping trees that shrieked and withered under the blade. Again, and again, he swung until all lay destroyed before him and there was only Mirage left.

"You shall not have her," Ronin stated, menacing the other man with his sword.

"Maybe not," smirked Mirage. "But neither shall you." In a whirl of black smoke, he was gone.

With a gasp of relief, Snow turned to Ronin, but he, too, was gone, and Fae stood in his place.

"Sleep now," Fae murmured. "You must sleep now."

Obediently, Snow sank into the sweet grasses and wildflowers of the meadow they stood in. Her eyes closed and she slept the deep and refreshing sleep of the innocent.

She awoke. For a moment all was confusion between reality and the dream world she had walked in. Blinking, she looked around. She was in Ronin's bed in the cottage. It was night, and firelight flickered over the already dearly familiar room. She was clean and dressed in a chemise that smelled of lavender.

Putting a hand under the covers to her stomach, she felt the lump of bandages, but there was no pain and Snow could sense that her body had been repaired. Swallowing back tears of relief, she looked up and there was Ronin.

He had pulled his chair to the very foot of the bed and was drowsing with his head propped up on one hand. He looked exhausted, his face falling into lines of weariness, but Snow had never seen a more welcome sight. For a while, she was content to simply watch him doze.

Then he must have sensed her gaze, for he opened his eyes and looked at her. "Snow?" he whispered.

"What happened?" she asked. "Where are Arden and Greta?"

"Still in the forest," he replied. "But I believe they are safe enough for now."

"Tibby stabbed me," she said slowly, trying to piece together her last memories. "And I remember falling into the chair and … she died, didn't she?"

"Yes," he said and shook his head sadly. "The poor child was under the mind control of the Contratulum and could not help what she did."

"I remember you picking me up, and then …" Snow frowned, and shook her head in exasperation. "Try as I might, I can remember nothing after that point."

"You fainted," he explained. "Greta managed to stop the bleeding for a while, but I had to get you back to Grein as quickly as possible. So, it was agreed that I should bring you in the skimmer, while Arden and Greta began the journey on foot. At first light, Kylah will send one of her devices to find them and take the skimmer to bring them back."

Snow nodded, then the tears she had been trying to hold back fought free and slipped down her cheeks. In an instant, Ronin left the chair and knelt beside her.

"Snow?" he whispered; his face concerned at her distress. "What is it? What's wrong?"

"I was so lost," she sobbed. "So alone and lost in the darkness, and I couldn't find my way. I couldn't find you, and I thought I had lost you too."

"Never," he promised her and gently took her hand in his. Clasping it to his heart, he smiled at her in the firelight. "You will never lose me, Snow. So long as you need me, I will always be here." Softly he tucked her hand back under the covers. "You need your rest, so sleep."

"Will you stay with me?" she asked, meaning forever.

"Of course," he said, meaning for the rest of the night.

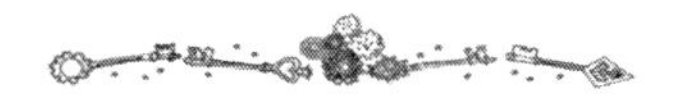

They travelled until it grew almost too dark to see, then made camp in a tiny clearing close to a pool fringed with wild garlic and ferns. Risking a small fire for warmth, they boiled the water to drink, not trusting the brackish green colour of the pool, and ate the cold leftovers from their packs.

After carrying him for a while, Greta had placed Arden the cat down on the ground and the ginger tom had meandered after them. Sometimes disappearing for half an hour or more, he always reappeared. Once he realised his sister seemed unconcerned, Arden stopped looking for his namesake.

They sat by the fire as night crept down on them, existence seeming to narrow until there was only them and the comforting anchor of their small fire. A rustle in the undergrowth had Arden tensing, then relaxing, as the small ginger form stepped forward with a water rat dangling from its jaws. Fixing its large topaz eyes unblinkingly on his for a second, the cat then crouched by the fire and crunched up its dinner, discarding the tail and a tiny green pebble, which Arden assumed was some internal organ of the rat's that the feline hadn't fancied eating.

"So, why did you call your cat Arden?" he asked. At its name, the cat glanced at him, before returning to his after-dinner ablutions.

"Why not?" Greta shrugged. "It is as good a name as any. And besides, when I spoke to him, I could imagine I was talking to you. I found him wandering in the forest the day after the news arrived of the massacre of our village. He comforted me a little in my grief."

"How did you find out?" Arden asked. "I would have imagined it was a secret known only to a few within the Contratulum."

"It was," Greta agreed. "But I have a few contacts at the palace and within the Contratulum itself. People who are loyal to the world Elgin and Raven built and wish to see a return to those days. There are more of them than you realise, Arden. And they are all merely waiting for Snow to attain the throne to reveal themselves."

"That is unlikely to happen now," he grunted. "If the child shows her face outside the forest she will be killed. You saw what happened back there. Contratulum spies could be anywhere. If it had not been for Fae's prophecy to beware of a red wine stain, then you would not be sitting here now."

"No, this Fae of yours sounds like a powerful prophetess."

"She is – and a witch and skilled healer. She comes from the Moonshadow family."

"Ah." Greta nodded knowledgeably. "Say no more. They always were more gifted than most."

"Yes. She even empowered a rose quartz with a concealment spell so that Mirage could no longer scry Snow and discover her whereabouts."

"That's a thought," Greta said and rummaged about in her knapsack. Taking out a wilted stem of green herb, she muttered some words of incantation about it, then stuffed the herb down her cleavage, much to Arden's amusement.

"Temporary concealment spell," she explained. "Mirage knows what I look like, so he might think to attempt to scry me. It's not as sophisticated or as powerful as the one I'm sure your Fae concocted, but it will serve its purpose until she can make me a better one."

"Will it prevent him from being able to scry you?"

"No, but the spell will allow him to see only what is in direct proximity to the herb."

"So, if Mirage tries to scry you, he'll only be able to see ..."

"Between my scraggy breosts, yes."

Arden let out a bark of laughter that had the cat startling and narrowing his eyes at him with a hiss of disapproval.

"Oh, Greta," he said, slapping his sister fondly on the knee. "I have missed you."

Awaking early the next morning, his back complaining painfully about a second night spent on the hard forest floor, Arden lay for a moment wondering what had roused him. There was a flutter and a commotion in the bushes by the edge of the clearing. Stiff back instantly forgotten, Arden rolled to his feet in one smooth movement and drew his dagger from his belt.

"Who's there?" he called. In her bedroll, Greta grunted in annoyance. There was another violent commotion, and a large bird erupted from the shrubbery with Arden the cat in hot pursuit. To his surprise, rather than fly away, the bird perched on a low branch and looked at him.

Opening its wings with a slight click and a whirr, Arden saw the cogs moving beneath its metal feathers and realised it was one of Kylah's devices. He held out his hand, and the bird alighted from the branch and landed on his wrist.

It was heavier than it looked, and Arden took a moment to appreciate the fine workings of its moving parts, the detailing around its eye and beak. Totally relaxed, the device surveyed him back. It opened and closed its eyes with a click, then delicately coughed up a diamond-shaped shiny metallic pebble into Arden's palm.

Recognising it for what it was, Arden gently pressed the button on the side of the small tracking device, then slipped it into his pocket. Even though it was not alive, he stroked the smoothness of the bird's head and back, and the bird preened into his palm, for all the world like a live pet bird.

Then it hopped back onto the low-hanging branch and surveyed him once more. A sudden streak of ginger fur, and the automaton was dangling in the clenched jaws of Arden the cat, who shook it by the wing, then yowled and dropped it. The cat wiped at its face with his paws, and Arden saw drops of blood on the cat's mouth, realising it had grazed itself on the serrated edges of the device's feathers.

"Serves you right, you cold-hearted beast, you." Greta was propped up on one elbow watching the proceedings, and at the sound of his owner's voice the cat trotted over to her, plainly looking for sympathy. Tutting, Greta examined her pet's mouth before pushing him away and scrambling to her feet.

"You'll be all right," she said, her attention focused on the clockwork bird. "Remarkable," she breathed. "A spy in the sky. For us, I am hoping?"

"Yes, this is Kylah's doing. She is a keen mechanic with way too much time on her hands. I believe that creating and tinkering with these toys keeps her sane."

"What did it give you?" Greta asked, and Arden fished the pebble from his pocket and showed it to her.

"A tracking device. I have activated it so the others will be able to locate us, but we should still keep walking – at least until we find a clearing large enough for the skimmer to land."

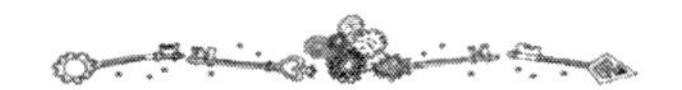

Drifting in and out of sleep, Snow was aware of the comings and goings of the others as they tiptoed about the cottage. Ronin was forcibly evicted from his chair by Grein, who muttered over the lines of tiredness that pulled at his friend's face, and the dark purple shadows under his eyes. Finally agreeing to go up to the attic to sleep, but only if he was called the instant the others returned, Ronin lingered by her bedside until she smiled at him and told him to rest and that she was fine.

She slept some more, waking when Eli dumped a jug of wildflowers by her bedside that cheered her spirits with their bright colours and sweet scent. Flushing at her croak of thanks, Eli stuffed his hands in his pockets and rocked awkwardly on his heels, until Fae gave him a task to do and he left.

Seemingly lost without Arden, Cesil moped about the cottage, getting in everyone's way, until Grein dragged him under Snow's bed and ordered him to "settle down" in such a stern voice, that the little pig immediately complied.

The day ticked by. Snow slept and healed and slept some more. At midday, Fae helped her to sit and spoon-fed her a thick broth made from rabbit, vegetables, and herbs. It nourished and satisfied, and Snow suspected a healing spell might have gone into its making, along with the fennel and parsley. After luncheon, she fell into a deep sleep that had the others in the cottage raising their eyebrows at each other in amusement at the soft whistling noises she emitted.

"I n-n-never thought that a p-p-princess would snore," Eli sniggered, and Fae slapped him lightly with a dishcloth.

Then, late afternoon, there was the commotion of Kylah landing the skimmer back in the clearing, and the relief at seeing the familiar face of Arden as he scrambled out and helped down his sister and Arden the cat. One of the two was distinctly unmoved by his adventure and stalked away as soon as Arden set him down on the grass.

Dog, who had been asleep under the porch, instantly awoke at the arrival of the feline and came prancing out, stiff-legged and barking, desperate to establish his position as top dog.

Arden the cat merely squatted on his haunches and licked at his front paw, until Dog stuck his snout aggressively in his face. Then several lightning-fast swats from the cat's claws sent Dog whimpering away to hide behind his master. Arden the cat then casually strolled into the cottage and settled by the fire, his lofty status at the top of the pack irrevocably settled to his satisfaction.

Greta was not quite so sanguine about the journey as her pet. Staggering to the ground as Arden and Kylah helped her out of the skimmer, she clutched at her chest theatrically.

"By the gods," she gasped. "I hope not to do *that* too often."

"Here, let me help you." Grein chivalrously offered her his hand and helped haul her to her feet, and Greta fluttered slightly at the unfamiliar male attention.

"Thank you," she said. "And you are ...?"

"Grein, madam."

"Ah, yes, the alchemist. Now, how is Snow? Did my potion halt the bleeding long enough?"

"It did, madam, and may I say how impressed I was by it? Could you tell me what was in it and which incantation you used?"

"Of course, of course." Greta beamed at him as she gathered up her belongings. "It will be such a refreshing change to talk to someone who understands such things."

"Likewise, madam." Grein gallantly offered her his arm, and Greta's fluttering increased.

"Oh, please, call me Greta," she insisted. "May I see Snow?" she asked, and Grein led her towards the cottage.

Kylah and Arden exchanged amused glances, then Arden gathered up the packs and Kylah barked at Eli to help her put away the skimmer.

That evening it rained, so they all crowded into the cottage to eat, perching where they could with plates of food balanced upon any surface they could find. Refreshed from her long sleep, Snow sat up in bed with a tray of dinner upon her lap, its enticing smell making her stomach rumble with such a healthy interest that Ronin, who was sitting in the chair by her bedside again, laughed at her embarrassed expression.

"It is good that you have an appetite," he said, and Snow shrugged sheepishly.

"I never used to get hungry before. But then nothing tasted as good as it does here. Meals were something to be endured. Most of the time, I had the maid bring a tray to my room and I would eat alone. But that was preferable to those occasions when I had to eat with Hawk and Jay. Then, it would be purgatory."

A shout of laughter erupted around the table at some mishap of Eli's, and even Nylex unbent enough to smile at the young lad's attempts to scrape up his peas from where they had shot all over the table.

"Mealtimes were never like this." Snow grinned at Ronin, who grinned back.

"I should hope not," he exclaimed. "I would imagine table manners played a much greater role in meals at the palace."

"No," protested Snow. "Well, yes, maybe – of course. But there was no laughter or fun when we ate. Just total silence in between Hawk's attempts to arouse my interest, and Jay's thinly disguised insults. Is it any wonder I preferred to eat in my room?"

"Well, when you are queen, you will be able to change all that," Ronin told her. "You can order music to be played, and amusements to be performed, and you will be able to invite all of your friends to attend to laugh, and chatter, to your heart's content."

"I have no friends," Snow replied sadly. "The only companionship I seek is right here in this room. So, Ronin, would you come to dinner at the palace?"

"If it is safe for us to do so, it would be my honour," he said.

"Besides," Snow continued. "I have decided I don't care about claiming the throne. I wish to stay here, with you all. I am happy here, and if you'd let me, I would love dearly to stay here ... with you."

She looked into his eyes, her meaning plain. The twin spots of colour high on her cheeks a testament to her nervousness.

"You do not mean that." Ronin's surprise was evident in his voice and expression, and an emboldened Snow took his hand in hers.

"Yes, I do. I can think of nothing I want more than to stay here for the rest of my days."

"But, your throne, your kingdom. What about your people?"

"What about them? Most of them don't care who sits on the throne. It barely impacts on their lives at all, so what difference does it make if it's me, or Jay, or her unborn child?"

"It makes a huge difference, child."

Engrossed in their conversation, they hadn't heard Greta join them, and they jumped, their hands falling apart onto the bedcovers.

"Why?" Snow asked. "Why will the people care who sits on the throne?"

"Because it will not be Jay, or Hawk, or even their unborn child who sits on it. Ultimately, it will be the Contratulum. Can you imagine what this land would be like if they had total and utter control over every man, woman, and child who lives within it?"

"But wouldn't they leave things as they are?"

"Leave things as they are?" Greta snorted in disgust. "You're a child, and innocent of the world, so your ignorance can be excused, but let me tell you what things would be like under the Contratulum. They would control every aspect of people's lives, from where they lived, to where they could travel, and whom they could marry. Any showing signs of magical abilities – and believe me, there are more than you think – would be found and either eliminated or pressganged into joining the Contratulum. War would immediately be declared on neighbouring kingdoms, merely to gain the natural resources they possess. After all, why barter and trade for things when you can merely conquer and own them outright?"

"But they would never be so foolish as to go up against armies mightier than anything the Contratulum itself might possess." Ronin twisted on his chair to look up at Greta where she stood, arms crossed over her chest in fierce denial.

"Oh, wouldn't they? Foolish boy!"

Snow smirked at the look on Ronin's face at being branded a boy – and a foolish one at that.

"Pah, what does it matter if the other armies are twice the size of their own or even ten times the size? What does the Contratulum possess that no other kingdom does?"

"Airships," Nylex ground out bitterly.

During Greta's tirade, the conversation around the table had ceased as all listened to her words.

"They have airships," Nylex said again. "And weapons that can rain down fire from the skies, incinerating everything it touches. No army could stand up against that, no matter how large."

"And as no other kingdom possesses airships, or even knows of their existence, then no kingdom stands a chance if the Contratulum chooses to invade them," Ronin interrupted.

Greta paused, and a smile spread across her face.

"No other kingdom? Really? Well, yes, I suppose you would think that. However, Raven had access to secret knowledge and that means that I know it too. There is someone else who has access to airships. Someone who is powerful and is no friend of the Contratulum."

"Who?" Ronin demanded, and the faces of the others turned towards Greta in stunned astonishment. "Who is this person you speak of?"

"I speak of none other than King Falcon of the House Avis, one of the most powerful and influential men in the world. He also happens to be my nephew, and your Grandfather, Snow, and I know he would be only too happy to help you claim your throne."

Chapter Seventeen

Built for Speed and Stealth

At Greta's words, pandemonium broke out in the room as everyone began speaking at once, all vying to voice their thoughts and opinions. Trying to be heard over the rabble, Arden finally lost his patience and banged heavily on the table with his tin mug.

"Silence!" he bellowed. Shocked, all faces turned towards him as he stared at Greta with the light of salvation in his eyes.

"He built them?" he whispered, and a grin broke out on his face.

"He built them," she replied, a corresponding grin spreading across her features.

"Enough of them?"

"My information is seven years out of date, but by now there should be more than enough."

"Wait, what are you saying?" Ronin looked at Arden in consternation. "Are you saying Falcon and the House Avis have airship technology? But that's impossible. None but Dwarvians, and now the Contratulum, have the knowledge or understanding of how to construct and fly airships."

"Nevertheless, he has them."

"But how did he come by such knowledge?"

"I gave it to him."

"You did?"

Snow, glancing from one to the other, realised by the horrified shock on Ronin's face that Arden had committed an unpardonable crime by allowing airship technology to fall into non-Dwarvian hands.

"Why?" Ronin continued, barely controlling his anger. "Why would you do such a thing?"

"For insurance against the knowledge somehow being lost. In case of just such a tragedy as occurred, and because I was advised, by someone I trusted implicitly, that it was crucial for me to give Falcon everything he needed to construct airships."

"Who? Who told you to betray our people and to violate our most sacred code?"

"I did." All eyes swivelled to focus on Fae, sitting calmly at the table. "I had a most powerful vision that it was of vital importance. I confided in Arden, knowing that he had the means to deliver the blueprints, and this he did."

"All right." Seeming to calm down at Fae's admission, Ronin rubbed a hand thoughtfully over his chin. "So, House Avis has airships. They have long been known to be sympathetic to our

Cause, and, of course, there is the blood connection through Queen Starling, but what does it mean for us?"

"Mean? It means, my boy, that at last there is hope. Real hope."

"Hope of what?"

"Hope of being victorious in our war against the Contratulum. Hope that we can still ensure Snow ascends to the throne in ten days. Hope for a better future for us all."

"War?" The word burst from Snow's lips and she stared at Arden in shock. "Go to war against the Contratulum? Is that possible? Would we stand a chance?"

"With the aid of House Avis, yes, we would outnumber the Contratulum and with airships of our own they would no longer have the advantage."

"But why would Falcon risk the lives of his own people to help us?" Nylex demanded.

"Look at her, just look at her." Arden waved a hand at Snow sitting up in bed, her raven-black hair startling against the stark white of the pillowcase and her chemise.

"Raven was always Falcon's favourite child. Her unexpected death hit him hard. If we go to him and tell him that the Contratulum murdered his daughter in cold blood. If he sees Snow – the dead spit of that beloved daughter – I honestly do not think he could refuse her anything. In fact, once he learns the truth of Raven's death, then I do not believe we could stop him from going to war against the Contratulum anyway."

"There's just one teeny, tiny problem," Nylex drawled sarcastically. "Even if we use every mode of transport we possess, the Kingdom of House Avis is still a week's journey. That doesn't leave us enough time to travel there, convince Falcon to help, and launch an offensive against the Contratulum – let alone win it, and install Snow on the throne."

Gloom descended on the room at his words, and the light dimmed in Arden's eyes.

"That is true," he admitted reluctantly. "I had not considered that."

"We cannot give up," Greta insisted. "There must be a way. There must!"

"There m-m-might be one way." Silent up until now, Eli finally spoke.

"Eli." Kylah's tone was one of warning, and Eli flushed at the threat it implied. He hesitated and looked at Kylah, then glanced at Snow and Arden. His expression was one of unfamiliar wisdom, and he turned to Kylah and placed a hand upon her arm.

"You have to t-t-tell them, Kylah. It's too imp-p-portant to keep secret any longer."

"Keep what secret?" Now Ronin's voice carried a threat as he turned on Kylah.

Flushing at being under such intense scrutiny, Kylah shrugged angrily. "All right," she snapped. "Lissa and I were working on a secret project together, and Eli was helping. We had almost finished – we had planned to reveal it the next day - when the attack happened. After that, I didn't have the heart for it anymore, so I sealed up the cavern we were working in and almost forgot about it, until now."

"Forgot about what?" Ronin demanded. "What were you and Lissa building, Kylah?"

"An accelerated motion mechanical air device."

"You mean ...?"

"A superfast airship, Ronin. We built a superfast airship."

The discussion lasted deep into the night before it was decided who was going and who was staying. Snow blinked awake in the chilly light of predawn to find Ronin crouched by her bedside, his eyes warm with affection.

"I only wanted to say goodbye," he whispered, and Snow struggled a hand from under the covers to grasp his.

"Be careful," she murmured.

"Always." His smile deepened. "If all goes to plan, we'll be back tomorrow." She nodded and squeezed his hand tighter. "Try to get some more sleep," he advised. But Snow knew sleep would be impossible until he, and the others, were back, with their mission safely accomplished.

Swirling his long leather coat about his shoulders, Ronin pulled on thick gauntlets as he strode out onto the porch to join the others. Already on their mechanical bicycle, its panniers loaded with supplies, and pulling down goggles over their sleep-deprived eyes, Kylah and Eli blinked at him in the gloom. His own mechanical bicycle awaited him, its panniers also bulging, and Nylex leaning against it. His eyes were hard and thoughtful as he watched Ronin approach.

"I still think this is utter madness," he muttered.

"Duly noted," Ronin replied, and swung a leg over the machine.

"Nylex, wait ..."

Nylex turned in surprise as Fae rushed from the cottage, a cloak wrapped around her chemise and her feet bare in the dew-soaked grass.

"Fae ...?" he began. She reached him. Standing on tiptoe she pulled his head to hers and planted a kiss of such passion upon his startled mouth, that Kylah and Ronin exchanged knowing looks, and Eli gawped in embarrassed wonder.

For a moment, Nylex forgot himself and his arms crept around her slender waist to pull her closer. Lifting her from the ground, he bent his head into her shoulder and sighed a heavy exhalation of reluctant regret. "Fae ..." he began again, his voice gentle.

"I only wanted to say goodbye," she whispered. "And to tell you to be careful."

"Aren't I always careful?"

"No." She slid back to the ground and cupped his face in her hands. "Not always, you're not. Come back safely. All of you." Still in his arms, she turned to smile at them. "Come back safely. We'll be waiting."

Drawing Nylex to her for one last, fierce hug, which he neither returned, nor rejected, she dashed back into the cottage, leaving the others taking deep breaths and looking at anything other than Nylex as he climbed onto the bicycle behind Ronin.

"Let's do this," Ronin said, snapping his goggles into place and kicking the machine into a throaty growl of life.

They travelled for several hours through the gloom of the forest as the sun crept over the horizon and spilt fingers of brightness over the ground. They used old half-remembered tracks and pathways, only occasionally having to stop and manhandle the bicycles over rougher patches.

It was mid-morning when the forest around them became achingly familiar and the trees thinned. Slowing his machine to a crawl, Ronin led the way through the final trunks. Abruptly the clearing was before them and the remains of their village lay visible as a stark reminder of all that had been lost.

Time and nature had softened the outlines, but still, the charred and blackened remnants of houses, workshops, and the school, could be made out under the gentle softening of ivy and brambles.

As one, they stopped and turned off their engines, the silence shocking after the constant roar. They lifted their goggles, looked, and remembered, each struggling with their own demons.

Ronin glanced at Nylex, concerned by his ashen complexion and the sudden hitch in his breathing. The young man shot him a look of such bitter shame, that Ronin almost regretted his decision to include him.

"We have to go on," Kylah said, pulling her goggles down and kicking her machine back into life. "Almost to the edge of the mountains."

Ronin glanced up to where the tree-hugged slopes of the Dwarvian mountain range could be seen reaching skyward over the treetops. Pulling his goggles back down and kicking his machine into life, he let Kylah take the lead and cautiously followed her through the remains of their past.

Beyond the village, she rode confidently for another hour, before pulling to a halt before a steep embankment of solid rock. Switching off her machine, she and Eli clambered off and removed their goggles. Walking over to the cliff face, they began brushing dirt from an area of ground located to the right of the escarpment.

"Here," Kylah murmured. "I thought it was here."

"What was here?" Ronin asked, as he and Nylex also climbed off their bicycle and joined the other two.

"I thought it was more t-t-this way," Eli said, and Kylah frowned.

"Maybe," she conceded, following the direction of his gesture. "Scuff up that earth, see if you can find it."

"Find what?" Ronin asked again. Ignoring him, Kylah knelt by Eli and pushed the dirt away with her hands.

"It was buried quite deep," she muttered. "But I think ... Ahh!"

At her cry of triumph, the others crowded around to see a dull metallic handle, which had been revealed by her excavations. Grasping it, she pulled with all her might, grunting in annoyance when it failed to budge.

"You try, Ronin," she ordered, wiping the dirt from her hands.

Bracing himself, Ronin grabbed the handle and pulled upwards. It resisted him, and he increased the pressure, feeling the muscles in his arms strain in protest. There was the sensation of something shifting beneath his palms. Abruptly the handle flew up, sending him sprawling onto his backside on the dusty ground.

There was a groaning and the sound of metal grinding on metal deep behind the cliff face. Taking the hand Nylex offered, Ronin scrambled back to his feet and dusted down the seat of his trousers, watching in fascination as a portion of the seemingly solid rock swung back to reveal an opening into the cliff wall.

"Hydraulics." Kylah shrugged at their looks. "With a little concealment spell thrown in for good measure."

Confidently, she led the way into the darkness, pausing to fumble around on the wall.

"There might be enough juice left to get the lights on," she murmured. There was a click and bright light splashed onto their faces. "Come on," she ordered.

Obediently, they followed her along the short rocky passage as it sloped down, then widened out into a monstrous cavern stretching up far away above their heads to disappear into shadow hundreds of feet above them.

Following Nylex, Ronin heard the young man let out a gasp as he stopped dead. Gently, Ronin pushed him forward, then saw for himself, and couldn't help the curse that erupted from his lips.

"What the frick ...? Kylah!"

"She's a beauty, isn't she?"

Beaming with pride, Kylah waited for him to comment, but Ronin was speechless.

Going further into the cavern, his professional eyes roamed in awe over the sleek lines and gleaming brass of the large airship that swung gently at tether in the huge, enclosed space of the cavern.

"She's more streamlined than usual," he finally murmured.

"Gives less wind resistance," Kylah told him. "We built her for speed and stealth. She's quieter and faster than anything we had before."

"Steam-powered?"

"Mostly, but there is a secondary engine to give an added boost. And see those adjustable fins on the side? They give her a much greater range of manoeuvrability."

"She's beautiful," he agreed, already hungry to captain her. To learn her quirks and foibles and make her his own.

"If we can get her to fly, she should get us to the Kingdom of House Avis in under two days."

"Really? That quickly?"

"*If* we can get her to fly?" Nylex broke in. "What do you mean, *if* we can get her to fly?"

"She hasn't been tested," Kylah told them. "She's perfect, in theory – but we never had the time for a test flight, so ..." She shrugged, and Ronin frowned.

"And we don't have the time now," he told them. "What do we need to do to get her flight-ready?"

"Right." A business-like Kylah ticked the chores off on her fingers. "Nylex, see about getting the generator back up and running, then I'll need you to help me fire the engines up. Ronin, you need to make this opening big enough to get her out, then get the bicycles and our belongings on board. Eli, you're with me."

Silently, the men hurried to obey her.

They toiled all afternoon until Kylah pronounced the ship as ready as it would ever be, and they stopped for the evening. Drained by the effort of magically enlarging the opening for the airship to pass through, Ronin sat on the ground by the small campfire Nylex had made.

He had thought to make a start back that evening, but it had taken longer than hoped before Kylah was satisfied with the ship – and then she had cautioned about conducting its maiden voyage in the dark. Reluctantly conceding to the sense in that, Ronin decided they would stay the night in the cavern, then start back at first light.

Watching as Eli bumbled about putting together a rough meal from the supplies they had brought, his eyes kept being drawn to the leviathan floating above them. Winching the bicycles up and onto its deck was an awkward and time-consuming task, yet he had been unable to resist taking a few precious moments to look around the ship.

With more space being devoted to its powerful engines, there was less living space. Ronin realised it would be a tight squeeze to fit nine humans, one dog, a pig, and one disdainful cat, plus supplies for two or three days on board. When he had called for volunteers to accompany him and Snow to the Kingdom of House Avis, every hand had shot up. Even Nylex, upon seeing Fae's hand firmly in the air, had reluctantly raised his own.

And so, they were all going, and Ronin wondered what reception this ragtag band of would-be rebels would receive from King Falcon.

"What's he like, Falcon?" Kylah asked, licking her fingers in satisfaction after polishing off a plateful of food almost as big as Eli's.

"I only know what Arden has told me," Ronin replied. "That he is a kind and fair man, but harsh to those who would harm his family or his people. They are a progressive kingdom, which is why I suppose Arden knew they would be able to interpret the blueprints he gave them. I know they share our views about the equal role that women should play in society – unlike that of the Contratulum, and through them, Hawk and Jay."

"I like him already," Kylah grinned and took a swig of ale.

"I still wish Arden had not done it," Nylex said, and Kylah looked at him curiously.

"Why?"

"Because I feel it dishonours the memory of our people and the strict code of no interaction with outsiders that we always lived by."

Kylah snorted. "Much good it did us."

"What do you mean?"

“Well, maybe, if we had not been so aloof and standoffish, when the Contratulum attacked our people a century ago, perhaps other kingdoms would have come to our aid. Instead, they believed the lies because they knew no better. And five years ago, if we had had such a powerful ally as House Avis, the Contratulum would never have dared to attack us.”

“It still seems disloyal,” Nylex grumbled. Kylah pulled herself upright and shot him a glance of such frustrated resentment that Ronin and Eli looked at her in surprise.

“No, I’ll tell you what’s disloyal and dishonourable, Nylex, and that’s the way you treat Fae.”

“What?” Shocked, the young man stared at her. “What do you mean – the way I treat Fae? I do not mistreat her.”

“No? She was the love of your life. You were to be married the next day. You were both fortunate enough to survive the attack and yet for five years, you have acted as though she means nothing to you. Hiding away in the forest, only meeting us if you have to.”

“I have my reasons,” he snapped. “And it is none of your business.”

“Yes, it is,” Kylah insisted. “Fae is my friend, my only female friend – apart from Snow. She is like a sister to me, so that makes it my business, and it makes my blood boil to see the callous disdain you have for her. She loves you, Nylex. Frick knows why, but she does. I don’t think she will ever stop loving you, and we all know you love her back just as much. Yet you’re not together. Why?”

“I … I can’t …” Nylex stuttered in speechless shock, his face flushed with affronted anger.

“You can’t? What kind of an answer is that?” Kylah was getting into her stride now, her face as red as his. “I lost my love that night, and most of my family – only Eli is left to me, and even he …” her voice trailed away, and there was a glint of tears in her eyes as she hugged Eli fiercely into her side. Ignoring his muffled protestations, she ruffled his hair, then let him go.

“Your love is still alive. Yet instead of honouring the memory of Lissa and the others who fought against the Contratulum airships long enough to give us a chance to escape, you instead smear dirt on their sacrifice. Do you honestly believe that Lissa would want you to punish yourself, and Fae, this way? It’s as if they died for nothing, Nylex, and it makes me sick!”

Springing to her feet, Kylah stalked away in the direction of the airship, her back a rigid declaration of her feelings. Hesitating for only a moment, Eli too scrambled to his feet and ran after her.

Ronin watched as the young lad reached his sister and put his arm around her. Leaning into the hug, Kylah murmured something into his hair and then they carried on towards the other side of the cavern together.

He glanced at Nylex. The other man's face was like stone. His eyes glimmered suspiciously, and he had clenched both his hands into tight fists. For a long moment, there was silence, then he looked at Ronin, his expression fierce.

"Is that what you believe? That I dishonour the dead? That I sully the memory of Lissa and all the others?"

Ronin hesitated. "I would not have put it in quite those words," he finally said. "But Kylah is right in that Lissa would not have wanted you and Fae to be apart this way, Nylex. She loved you both, and I know she was so happy when Fae asked her to be her maid of honour at your wedding. She would want you to be together, even if she can't be here to see it."

Nylex stared into the flames for a long time, then turned his face away from Ronin and lay down to sleep. Although Ronin knew from the stiffness of the young man's back and the shortness of his breath that it was not sleep that was claiming him, but sorrow and bitter tears of remorse.

Chapter Eighteen

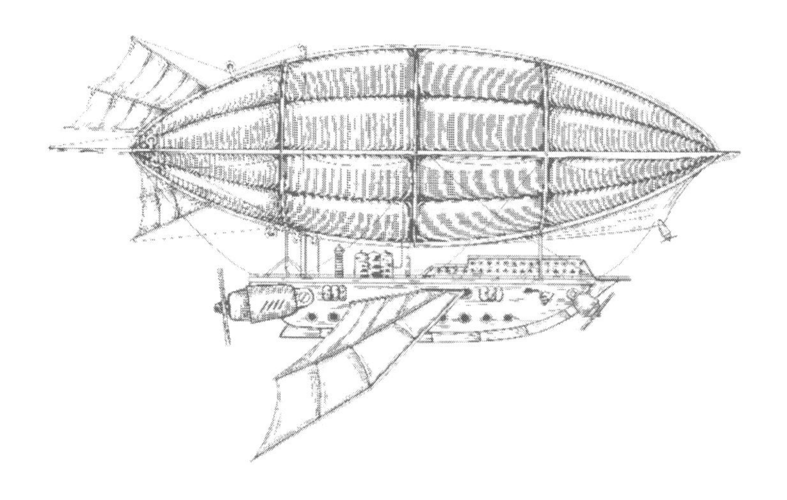

The Lissa

Ronin had told them – before he and the others departed – that they would leave for the Kingdom of House Avis the moment they returned with the airship, if they returned with it, although none dared voice that possibility. So, all that day they busied themselves with preparations.

As the cooking facilities on an airship tended to be basic, Fae explained to Snow, it was best if all the food they planned to take for the two-day journey was already cooked and only needed heating through. Lying in Ronin's bed, Snow watched the young witch bustle about the kitchen chopping, frying, roasting meats, and cooking a massive stew to reheat for dinner the following night.

Convincing Fae that she was well enough to get up, Snow was helped to the shower, where it was a relief to wash away the grime and sweat of the past two days. Watching the last vestiges of dried blood from her wound wash down the drain by her feet, Snow spent a few pleasant moments daydreaming of installing showers throughout the palace as soon as she was queen.

Tired out from the exertion, Snow was content to sit at the large table and chop and shred as Fae instructed, surprised by the vast quantities of food the other woman was preparing.

"We're a hungry bunch," Fae laughed. "And flying an airship is exhausting work. We'll need hearty sustenance, and besides, there's Eli ..." The two women exchanged glances and laughed, and the day passed companionably.

Later, Fae helped Snow to climb the ladder into the attic, leaving her with a knapsack and instructions to pack what clothes from Lissa's chest Snow thought she would need for a few days, and to call when she needed helping down.

Expecting not to be returning for a while, maybe never – again, none cared to voice this thought – Arden went out and pulled all Ronin's traps. Finding a rabbit in one, he brought it back to the cottage and sat on the porch steps to skin and gut it, ready for Fae to cook.

Watching him through the open door, Snow smiled as he threw the skin, bones, and guts to where Dog and Arden the cat were patiently seated by his feet. To her surprise, Dog stayed where he was until the ginger tom had delicately picked over the morsels and carried away the prime pieces for himself, leaving the rest in a pile. Greedily, the canine snatched up what was left and lay on his haunches snapping and gulping down the unexpected treat.

Grein was busy in his horseless carriage, aided by Greta, selecting what supplies they thought they might need, and making quite a sizeable pile in the centre of the clearing, ready to be loaded onto the airship. Then he and Arden carefully manoeuvred the carriage through the stable doors and down the ramp, to be safely hidden away until they returned.

They also searched the cottage for anything that needed to be concealed from prying eyes, or anything they believed might have value to Ronin. The chances of anyone stumbling upon the cottage were remote, Fae told Snow, yet still, the instinct for caution was too bone deep to ignore.

Finally, all was prepared. A pile of supplies sat in the middle of the clearing covered by a waterproof cloth, and baskets and packages of food and drink sat waiting in the kitchen. Sitting down to enjoy the rabbit that Fae had roasted with wild sweet potatoes, carrots, and onions, Snow looked around at their sober faces. She knew they were all thinking of the others, hoping that they had been successful and that they would return on the morrow.

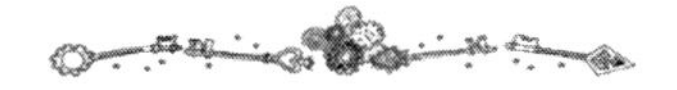

Dawn was poking its nose enquiringly through the considerably enlarged cavern entrance when Ronin reached the top of the rope ladder and swung his leg over the side of the ship. Taking a moment to run his hand appreciatively over the smoothly waxed railings, he walked to the bridge and gently placed his hands on the wheel.

A shock, like static electricity, flashed through his palms. Surprised, he let go. Taking a breath, he reached for it again. This time a warm wash of loving recognition swept over him.

Ronin ...

"Lissa?"

Gripping the wheel tightly, he searched for her with his mind. Knowing that when building the ship, Kylah and Lissa would have infused every rivet and bolt, every plank of wood and every yard of rope, with their magic, he closed his eyes and let his mind roam.

Everywhere, he sensed Kylah. Her strength and passion for her work had soaked through and through until the ship itself throbbed with pride and purpose, and then ... then he found her.

Lissa.

Her loyalty, her love, her nerves of steel, and her determination. It was there in every line of the ship. In the way it tugged at its tether, eager to be off into the wide blue yonder. In the way it reached for him, recognising him as her captain.

"Hello, ship," he murmured. Closing his eyes, he inhaled and could smell on the edge of his senses the poignant scent of lavender.

He smiled. Already he knew this was a good ship, true of line and swift of spirit. She would serve them well.

"Captain?"

He opened his eyes. Below him the others stood on the deck, their faces eager for the off, and sharing his sense of coming home. It had been too long since a Dwarvian had stood aboard an airship. Once, they had filled the skies with such mighty leviathans. Then the Contratulum had destroyed all who might build and fly them until only a pair had remained. Then even those two had been eliminated, and he had believed the age of flying to be at an end. That he would never again captain a ship.

But now, here he was, hands resting lightly on the wheel of a ship that had already claimed him as its own, and had pledged to serve him, heart, and soul.

"Captain," Kylah spoke again. In her hands, she held an iron plaque. "She needs a name, Captain."

An old tradition. The captain would always choose the name for his vessel. It was a sensitive and intuitive task, for it was believed the ship would live up to her name. But this time it was easy.

"The Lissa," he said.

Kylah swallowed and nodded, then held her hands over the plaque. For a moment she stood, head bowed in concentration, and all were silent. There were legends of ships rejecting their names, not feeling they were true reflections of the vessel's heart. Ronin had always believed them to be myths, but now he was not so sure.

Kylah removed her hands and held up the plaque for all to see. In curling script, so like Lissa's own hand, it was uncanny, the words ***The Lissa*** stood proudly embossed into the iron.

"Nylex, would you do the honours?"

Reverently, Nylex took it in his hands and crossed the deck to where grooves were already etched into the railing to take the plaque. Bowing his head almost as though at prayer, he carefully slotted the plaque into place. He stepped back so Kylah could run her fingers over the edges, welding the plate firmly to the ship's surface so it could never be removed.

"Ready for your word, Captain." Kylah stood to attention, with Nylex at her left shoulder and Eli at her right. Ronin smiled at his tiny crew.

"Let's take her out," he ordered.

"Eli, with me." Kylah and Eli vanished down the stairwell to the engine room below and minutes later there was the soft roar of combustion and the throb of kinetic energy beneath their feet.

“Nylex, trim the fins. It’s going to be a tight fit getting her out – we want to stay in one piece.”

“Aye, aye, Captain.” Nylex leapt to the controls and began cranking in the fins, which shuddered into place flush against the ship’s sides. Ronin nosed her forwards, and she gave a great lurch.

“Steady!” Kylah bellowed from below. “She’s sensitive, just a touch is all that’s needed. Pretend she’s a woman.”

Ignoring Nylex’s grin, Ronin tried again, this time almost operating by fingertip control. Quivering with anticipation, the ship eased forward, its responsiveness nearly intuitive – as if the ship were reading his mind.

“Take us home, Lissa,” he murmured.

Gently, he aimed for the cavern opening. Logically, he knew it would fit. But he also knew it would be tight. One miscalculation, one drift too far either way, and the ship would be losing its nice new paintwork on the rough stone.

Holding his breath, Ronin babied his ship through the opening, with Nylex poised to obey any commands he might give. Although he could feel the thrust of the powerful engines, there was barely any noise, and he thought how Kylah’s claim she was the stealthiest was probably true. He hoped her other claim – that ***The Lissa*** was the fastest – was also correct.

A second later they were out. Ronin eased back on the wheel to tilt her nose to the skies, and then they were up above the treetops. The sun was warm on his back and a breeze ruffled his hair.

Nylex gave a great whoop of delight and turned a face shining with excitement to Ronin. For an instant he saw the young man as he had once been – a handsome, joyful youngster – the boy Fae had been in love with – and he hoped that Nylex had finally turned a corner. That he could reach the understanding that punishing himself, and Fae, for his perceived mistakes of the past served no real purpose other than to cause misery and pain, where thankfulness should instead reside.

But he said nothing of this, instead sharing Nylex’s grin at the heady sensation of being airborne for the first time in five long years.

I was born for this, he realised. *And without it, I have only been half alive.* The idea of Snow being on board his ship crept across his mind, and his grin deepened into a warm smile.

“Let’s see how fast this lady can move,” he cried, and the ship gave a thrill of acknowledgement beneath him.

The waiting was agony. All was in readiness, and everything had been checked and double-checked. All had taken the chance to have one last shower, and all were now mooching about the cottage and clearing, finding non-important tasks to pass the time.

Snow was sitting at the table watching Greta as she ambled about the kitchen, wiping down already clean surfaces, and tutting at non-existent dust. Every now and then, she would glance in Snow's direction, as if words trembled on her lips but she was unsure whether to voice them or not.

Finally, she sighed and pulled out the chair opposite.

"What ails you, child?"

"Ails me? Why, nothing..."

"Come, this is me. I wiped your backside as a baby and smacked it when you told me lies about how many sugared plums you had stolen from the kitchen. You never could hide anything from me."

"It's just ..." Snow stopped and struggled to order her thoughts into some sort of cohesion. "All of this effort, all of this work to put me on the throne. Now, there is talk of war. I may be innocent and ignorant of the ways of the world, but I do know that war always means injury and loss of life. People will be killed, Greta, all for me. And what I'm wondering is..."

"Are you worth it?"

"Yes. I am completely untested as a monarch. I have never ruled. I have not even been trained how to be a queen. I'm scared that *if* Falcon agrees to help me, and *if* we are victorious, and *if* I claim my throne, that it all will have been for nought because I am not fit for the job."

"The very fact that you doubt your worthiness means you are already a far better monarch than most who have gone before you," Greta replied dryly. "Trust me, child. This is what you are meant to do. This is your destiny. This is what your parents always intended for you. It's the reason your mother stayed in the palace, even though she suspected they were onto her. You are Princess Snow, of the House White. You will be Queen Snow. And you will be a great and powerful ruler because you have a good and pure heart."

"What about if I don't want to be queen? What about if there are other ... things ... I wish to do with my life. If there is another path I wish to take?"

"Ronin?"

At Snow's guilty start, Greta's face softened, and she awkwardly patted the young woman's hand. "I may be old, Snow, but I'm not blind, and I'm certainly not stupid. I've seen the way he looks at you, and I've seen the way you look at him."

"Would it ever be allowed?" Snow whispered miserably.

"Who knows? But I do know you cannot place the love of one man above the love of an entire people. Every man, woman, and child in this kingdom, Snow, belongs to you. They are your people, and you are their queen. Their safety and happiness must always be paramount, over everything else – even over your own personal fulfilment."

"I know that, but I don't know what to do. How to act."

"You must decide now, child, what type of queen – what type of woman – you want to be, and then be her."

"Be like my mother, you mean?"

"No, I do not mean be a copy of your mother. What use would that be? No, I mean be the woman *you* want to be. Forget everything else. Listen to your heart and your instincts, and you won't go far wrong."

Snow fell silent, thinking about her words. Then the door burst open and Arden's excited face appeared in the opening.

"It's them! They're back!"

Excitedly, the women got to their feet and followed him outside to join Fae and Grein as they shaded their eyes against the sun and pointed into the sky. Following their gaze, Snow saw a black dot that was progressively getting bigger with each passing minute.

"It's fast," Grein murmured. "Very fast."

Snow couldn't tear her eyes away from the approaching shape, black against the sun, the vast balloon dwarfing the ship tethered firmly below it. How casually she had discussed airships with the others – never realising, never fully appreciating – that *this* was the reality. This skyborne behemoth. She tried to imagine a whole horizon full of them but couldn't. It was too much to even grasp the concept of one, let alone more.

All around her, the others were scurrying to gather their supplies. Greta and Fae rushing past her, ferrying out the packs and baskets of food it had taken a whole day to prepare. Sudden resolve flooded her body, and Snow clenched her fists as purpose ignited, and she strode back into the cottage.

"These are my things," she told Fae, gesturing to her knapsack on the side. "But there's something I've forgotten." And before the other woman could say anything, she had climbed up the ladder and vanished into the attic.

A journey that had taken them several hours the previous day had taken a mere twenty minutes in ***The Lissa***, and Ronin sensed the ship could do better. He had been holding her back, easing her into her maiden voyage, always on the alert for any problems or foibles that might affect performance or safety. But so far, he had found none. She was perfect.

As they hovered over the clearing, and Ronin saw the others scuttling about on the ground below, he eased down as low as he dared. He signalled to Kylah and Eli in the engine room that they were to turn off the engines.

Nylex threw down the ground anchor, and Arden and Grein activated the thick spurs which would fasten the ship securely to the ground and stop her drifting. Wanting a quick turnaround, Ronin ordered that the cargo cradle be lowered, and on the ground, the others hurried to load it.

Winching it back up, it arrived fully loaded, with Greta crouched in one corner, and Arden the cat perched coolly on the top of the supplies. Swiftly, Nylex, Kylah, and Eli helped Greta out, then unloaded the bags and packages, placing them carefully to one side to be sorted and stowed once they were underway again.

The next trip brought up the rest of Grein's supplies, Grein himself, and a wildly excited Dog, who barked furiously when Grein tossed him onto the deck. Charging around like a demented creature, Dog got thoroughly under everyone's feet, until Eli grabbed him by the collar, dragged him below deck, and shut the hatchway in his hairy face.

The next load was all the food, and Fae. Ronin noted with interest how Nylex hung awkwardly back, almost as if he were afraid to talk to her, or even look at her. If Fae noticed it herself, she gave no indication. Instead, she helped supervise the unloading of their essential food and drink supplies.

Next up was Arden, with Cesil, and the last few remaining packs.

"Where's Snow?" Ronin asked, his chest clutching with fear.

"She's coming," Arden reassured him, struggling to lift a reluctant and squealing Cesil onto the deck. Finally, being tempted on board by an apple Fae waved under his nose, he was helped the rest of the way by Arden's boot gently, but firmly, on his backside.

Again, the cargo cradle was let down and was winched back up carrying only Snow. She stood in the middle of the cradle, lightly holding onto the chain above her head for support, and her face was the first part of her he saw. He fell silent – they all did, as the cradle reached the deck and she stepped gracefully on board.

She was wearing Lissa's aviatrix outfit, the leather trousers moulding themselves snugly to long, shapely legs, and the corset accentuating her tiny waist. Long wrist bracers and a high leather neck brace were strapped over a pure white shirt, with a thick leather belt slung around her hips. Knee-high, well-worn leather boots completed the outfit. Her black hair was twisted into a thick knot on her head, held in place with goggles.

Her eyes met his.

He smiled, nodded his approval, and her face relaxed.

"Right, get that lot below decks and safely stowed," he ordered, and the others hurried to obey, although Fae lingered on deck for a moment, running her hands over the smooth wooden surfaces. Abruptly, she stopped. Her eyes flew to Ronin's in understanding, and a smile slipped onto her lips.

"Lissa," she whispered, then went to help the others.

Finding safe storage for all their supplies and strapping them securely down took the rest of the morning. As they gathered on deck to share a hasty luncheon, all were full of wonder and excitement about their new ship.

Looking around at their excited faces, and hearing their chatter, Snow marvelled at how easily they seemed able to put the uncertainty of the future from their minds and revel in the joy of the moment. Despite Arden and Greta's convictions, there was no guarantee that King Falcon would help them. Even if he did, the Contratulum would not be an easy foe to vanquish.

Her unease stayed with her for the rest of the day, even as she leaned on the railing and watched the great forest slip by below, enjoying the sensation of flying high with the birds. Helping whenever she was asked to, she still felt keenly her lack of experience, as the others all seemed to fall into natural tasks and positions on board the ship.

Grateful when Fae asked her to help prepare dinner, Snow relaxed during the meal, when they all sprawled on the deck under the stars and ate the delicious stew which she had watched Fae prepare the day before.

Gently ***The Lissa*** tugged at its mooring tether, which had been fired into a stout tree trunk, sharp barbs opening on impact and digging into the bark. It was so still and quiet, Snow could hear the treetops softly rustling in the light breeze, and the odd call of some nocturnal animal far below.

All too soon, though, the meal was over, and they were turning in for early nights, mindful there was another day of fast flying on the morrow. Settling down on the narrow bunk in the room she was sharing with Greta, Fae, and Kylah, Snow found herself unable to sleep, despite her physical exhaustion.

Softly, one by one, the others dropped into slumber. She smiled in the darkness at the nasal whistles of Greta, remembering how comforted she had been by that sound as a child because it meant Greta was in the next room, ready to soothe her at the first nightmare.

Seeking sleep, Snow closed her eyes and tried to force her mind to relax and go blank. Deliberately, she let go of all thought, all consciousness, until nothing remained but a smooth golden light.

Snow, a voice whispered. *Go to him, go to him now.*

Obediently, Snow slipped from the bunk and padded barefoot from the room. In the narrow passageway, she stopped, confused. But a light touch to the wooden wall of the ship and the way to go presented clearly in her mind. Quietly climbing the steep steps, she emerged onto the deck. A full moon hung like a bright shiny penny over to the east, and the night air was scented with the smell of fresh foliage and lavender.

The deck was smooth and cool beneath her bare feet. She walked swiftly to the bridge steps and climbed confidently up them. Some part of her knew that he would have taken first watch – that as Captain he would remain on deck, ever watchful in the dead of night, protecting his people from all that might harm them.

He was leaning on the railing and turned at her approach. In the bright glare of the moonlight, she saw the surprise on his face.

"Snow?"

Then she reached him, and her hands touched his face. Her breathing sharp and shallow, she crept into the safe harbour of his arms which instinctively enfolded her into a tight embrace, saying more than a thousand words ever could. Hearing his breathing hitch, she knew he felt it too, although his honourable intentions made him murmur a denial.

"No, Snow ..."

"Hush," she ordered and stopped his protest with a first kiss that quivered with the sweetness of new love – of first love, of forever love.

Powerless to fight against it any longer, he kissed her back.

Moving from his arms, she walked swiftly away and returned to her bunk, where she fell instantly into a deep and revitalising sleep to awaken in the morning with the whole encounter seeming like the sweetest of dreams. Wistfully, she accepted it as such, with a sigh of regret that it had not been real.

And all around her, the ship throbbed its approval.

Chapter Nineteen

The Kingdom of House Avis

All the next day, he observed her, unable to believe what had happened in the still watch of the night. Even more disbelieving that she could act as if nothing had occurred – that she could talk to him and look him in the eye with such an easy familiarity that he began to doubt his memory. But then his arms would remember what it had felt like to hold her, his senses humming with an intense recollection of that brief encounter under the moonlight. His lips throbbing with the desire to kiss her again.

She had kissed him as though she loved him, and at that moment he had known it to be the truth. But as the day wore on his faith wavered. As night once again crept over the deck, and they gathered for their evening meal, he had convinced himself that she had been sleepwalking, her mind unsettled by the unfamiliarity of being on board an airship. Perhaps she had roamed the deck in her sleep, and now had no memory of what she did, of what they ...

At this point, he would shy away from the memory and focus his attention on flying the ship. Marvelling at how responsive it was to the lightest of touches, he jealously guarded the wheel, unwilling to share her with any other.

That night passed uneventfully. If Snow once again roamed the ship in her sleep, she did not come to the bridge, and Ronin was unsure if he was relieved or disappointed.

The next morning dawned, sparkling and fresh. Ronin could tell by the sharp rise of the Dwarvian mountains to his left that they would soon be passing over the border between the Kingdom of House White and that of House Avis.

There was movement on the bridge steps, and Snow was before him, her face still soft from sleep and her hair mussed over her shoulders. She smiled at him, then glanced at the high mountain range that dominated the skyline.

"I never knew the mountains went so high," she said.

"They go much higher than that, Your Highness, but we shall soon be at the Avian Pass, so we will not have to climb so high." She nodded, then hesitated.

"Have you ever met him?"

"Who?"

"King Falcon. My grandfather."

"No, none except Arden have. He used to make the long journey to visit Greta at the palace before Raven married Elgin. Often, he would be gone for months – a year even. I do know he holds Falcon in very high regard." A cross breeze gusted. Instinctively Ronin eased the ship to face into it, before settling back on course. Curiously, Snow stepped closer and looked at the wheel.

"How do you know what to do? Did it take you long to learn?"

"My father was an aviator, so both Lissa and I learnt from childhood. But piloting an airship is not something that can merely be taught to anyone. You must have the heart for it – the instinct – if you like."

"Oh." Snow regarded the wheel with interest. "Do you think I could have the heart for it?"

"Come and try," he invited, and stepped back from the wheel, gesturing her towards it. Her face lighting up, she grasped the wheel tightly. "Gently," he cautioned. Placing his large hands over hers, he eased them back from the wood, waiting until they relaxed beneath his palms.

"Now, ease the wheel slightly to the right. It must only be the softest of movements for I have never known a ship to be as responsive as this one." Focusing intently, Snow did as he instructed, and the ship corrected its course minutely.

"I felt that," she murmured. "In my hands, and my feet."

"Good, that's good," he praised. He was achingly aware of her closeness, of her scent in his nostrils, of tendrils of her hair tickling his face. She leaned back into his chest and turned her head to look up at him, her eyes alight with excitement.

"Am I doing it?" she cried. "Am I flying the ship?"

"You are indeed," he confirmed, and she beamed with joy.

"Let me try alone," she ordered him.

Amused, he stepped away from her and leant on the railing, watching as she focused on the task at hand. Her hands were light on the wheel, her feet in Lissa's boots braced on the wooden planking. The well-worn leather of the trousers stretched over her trim backside as she relaxed into the task, and hastily he averted his eyes. A sudden gust caught them side-on, and he moved to take over, but she had already made the minute adjustment necessary to maintain their heading.

"How did you know to do that?" he asked.

"I'm not sure." Snow considered the matter, wrinkling her nose in thought. "It was like the ship told me what to do."

Ronin nodded, but stayed silent, thinking about his sister. About how she had taken great delight in meddling with his love life when she was alive and wondering if she was still such a meddler now that she was dead.

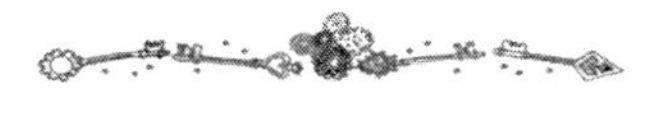

All morning, Snow stood at the wheel. Eventually, Ronin trusted her enough to catch a few winks of sleep himself below deck. Leaving her with firm instructions to call him the instant she had had enough, or if she ran into any difficulties, he was surprised to awaken from a two-hour nap feeling refreshed and alert.

Unsurprisingly, he had dreamt of Lissa and of one of the many times, he told her to cease interfering in his life. That if he wished to ask Maisie Greenblade to the dance, then that was his affair, not hers. Clearly, the memory resounded in his dream – Lissa standing before him, her face warm with a smug smile.

"You don't love her, Ronin," she replied. "So, don't waste the poor girl's time. Your heartmate isn't in the village, so there's no point encouraging any of the other girls either."

"Oh ho, so you're condemning me to a lonely bachelor life, are you?" he teased back.

"No, that's not what I said. I said your heartmate is not in the village, not that she isn't somewhere else. You simply haven't met her yet." Then she ran off before he could ask her what she meant.

Awaking to the scent of luncheon wafting into his eager nostrils, he sat on the edge of the bunk and rubbed a hand over his heavy eyes. He wondered about Lissa, about the ship, about Snow, and dreams in general. Stamping his feet back into his boots, he opened the cabin door as Nylex was about to knock on it.

"We're approaching the Pass," he said. "And Snow needs you."

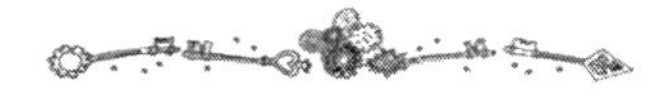

He took the bridge steps two at a time, and Snow looked up at his approach with relief on her face. "It started to get windy," she said, "and it's harder to control the ship."

"Aye," he agreed, taking over the wheel as she stepped gratefully away. "It's the crosswinds through the Pass. They'll be too strong for an inexperienced pilot to manage." Tuning himself back into the rhythm of the ship, he heard it creak in the breeze, its timbers flexing and contracting.

"Nylex." He ordered the young man who had followed him to the bridge. "Get ready to trim those fins on my command." Snatching the speaking tube from where it was attached to the rail in front of the wheel, he rang down to the engine room.

"Pass coming up," he told Kylah when she answered.

"Understood," she replied. He had always enjoyed flying with Kylah. An intuitive and experienced mechanic, none understood the workings of an airship better than she.

A throb beneath his feet told him that the vast coal-driven engine had been notched up a gear, giving the ship the power, it would need to hold true to its course in the powerful winds that gusted up here on the roof of the world. Winds that could rip a ship apart if it were being flown by an inexperienced or reckless crew.

"Here," he passed the tube to Snow. "Relay my orders as I give them." Looking thrilled and apprehensive at such an important role, she took the tube and braced herself against the railing.

"Slow to two knots," he ordered.

Quickly, Snow repeated his order to Eli, now positioned at the other end of the tube and poised to relay orders to Kylah who was busy with the engines. Snow knew both Grein and Arden would also be in the engine room, shovelling coal into the ever-hungry belly of the ship.

"Trim right fin," Ronin barked.

"Aye, aye, Captain." Nylex leapt to obey.

The ship slowed, turning onto a sharper heading towards the mountains. In the distance, Snow saw a deep, downwards V cutting into the jagged jaw of the mountain range. Like a missing tooth, it gaped an invitation, and Ronin lined the ship up to it.

Snow blinked, as the V appeared to flicker. It flickered in her vision again, and she realised there was a thick fog rolling down from the mountain peak, obliterating the pass from view.

"Ronin ..." she whimpered, but he had already seen.

"Frick," he muttered under his breath.

"Captain?" Nylex queried nervously.

"Trim left fin, quarter standing."

"Aye, aye, Captain."

"Slow to one knot," he barked at Snow, and she hastily relayed the order.

The ship slowed even more. Inch by painful inch, they crawled closer to the pass. The fog thickened, occasionally clearing enough so that Snow caught glimpses of the rough rock on either side of the pass. She swallowed.

From a distance, the pass had looked massive. Easily big enough for ***The Lissa*** to sail through. But as it grew ever nearer, she realised it was not as wide as she first imagined.

The fog thickened.

"Captain?" She heard the concern in Nylex's voice. "Captain – Ronin! The fog is too thick. It's too dangerous. We'll never make it."

For a moment Ronin hesitated, then his eyes met Snow's.

She knew she should be afraid, but she wasn't. Her chest heaved with exhilaration and her eyes sparkled with challenge as she met his gaze boldly.

"We're going through," Ronin declared.

"Are you mad?" Nylex snapped.

"Are you questioning your Captain's orders?" Ronin's voice was mild, but Snow heard the bite of steel beneath it. Nylex hesitated, then appeared to back down.

"No, Captain."

"Good. Now trim the right fin another quarter-point. Keep them tight, but ready to manoeuvre."

"Aye, aye, Captain."

"Slow to steady," he told Snow, and again she repeated the order.

The ship slowed until they were barely crawling forward, yet still, the pass approached, and then they were into the fog. Abruptly plunged into a wet, all-encompassing, cloud of white, Snow edged closer to Ronin, her excitement tinged with an edge of fear.

They were hardly moving now, creeping forward into this strange white world at a snail's pace. Briefly, the fog would wisp, and they would catch glimpses of the jagged edges of the pass.

Snow imagined the ship scraping along them, the giant balloon overhead being punctured, the ship hurtling to the ground. Herself, and Ronin, and everyone else on board, plunging to their certain deaths.

She sank onto the deck, clutching the speaking tube as if it were a lifeline, and glanced up at Ronin. Both feet planted firmly on the deck, he braced himself to hold the ship true to its heading. As he fought the buffeting winds that were now roaring through the pass, Snow saw his muscles bulge under the fabric of his shirt, all his energy being expended on keeping them on course.

Through a gap in the fog, she saw the taut face of Nylex. His features pinched with strain, he stood poised to leap to any orders his Captain might give.

Suddenly, the fog thinned, and the wind abated slightly. Then they were through, and the sun streamed down onto them, making their wet clothing steam in the sudden warmth.

Releasing a single hand from the wheel, Ronin fished his kerchief from his pocket and wiped it over a face glistening from the exertion. Catching Snow's eye, he winked at her and grinned.

"Now, that was exciting, wasn't it?"

"Very," she agreed.

"Fricking idiot!" Nylex snarled and stamped off the bridge.

“You weren’t afraid?” Ronin asked, and Snow considered his question.

“I was, and I wasn’t,” she finally said. “I was, because my head told me I should be and because I knew what would happen if we hit the sides. But then, I wasn’t, because my heart told me I was safe – that nothing was going to happen to me. And because it was the most intensely exciting thing I have ever done.”

“Aye,” Ronin nodded. “That’s how it is sometimes.”

For the rest of the morning, they flew towards the sun. Below them, the mountains rolled down into a vast hilly plain. Its lush greenness spoke of rich pasture, and Snow could even make out the small, moving dots of a vast herd of goats roaming the meadows.

“The Kingdom of House Avis is very blessed with its natural resources,” Ronin told her when she pointed them out to him. “They have fertile arable land, lush pasture for their stock, and rich deposits of minerals under the ground. Tis no wonder the Contratulum would invade if they could. But even without airship technology, Falcon would not surrender without a battle to the death.”

Snow nodded and leant over the railing, drawing in a deep lungful of crisp, mountain air. It was a beautiful day. Tiny white clouds scurried across a cerulean blue sky and the sun was warm on her face. She could be happy with this life, she decided and glanced furtively over her shoulder at Ronin. Very happy.

A black dot, way off in the distance caught her attention. Intrigued, she watched as it grew bigger and bigger until it was too big to be a bird. Besides, no bird she had ever seen could fly in such a straight line with no obvious signs of flapping wings. She blinked and rubbed at her eyes. If she didn’t know any better, she would have said that it looked like a …

“Ronin!”

“Yes?”

“Look, there. Isn’t that a skimmer of some kind?”

“What?” Following the direction of her pointed finger, he frowned. “Get Arden,” he ordered, and Snow hurried to obey. Locating the older man in the engine room, she gabbled out an explanation and saw the looks Arden and Kylah exchanged.

“Eli,” Kylah ordered, “maintain engine pressure. I want to see this too.”

Tumbling back up on deck, they saw that the black dot was much nearer now and was clearly a mechanical flying device. Sleeker looking than the skimmer, it stopped about three hundred feet from them and hung in the air. There was a whine, almost as if it was clearing its throat, then a voice boomed out, clear and perfectly audible, despite the distance.

"Unknown airship, you are in violation of Avian airspace. Please state your identity and purpose."

"By all the gods," Arden exclaimed. "How do we answer them? They'll never hear us all the way over there."

"Wait." Fae had appeared on the deck behind them. Quickly, she formed a tube with her hand in front of Arden's mouth. "Speak through this. I can project the words across the distance so the other pilot can hear them."

Looking vaguely silly, Arden crouched and placed his lips to Fae's hand. "Avian ship. We come in peace. We are a group of Dwarvian refugees who seek an audience with King Falcon. We have no weapons and bear you no ill will. Please, will you let us pass?"

There was a split second of silence, then the other ship gave a squawk of excitement. "Uncle Arden?! Is that you?"

"It might be," Arden blinked in surprise. "To whom am I speaking?"

"It's Robin! Follow me in. Stay exactly on my heading and I will guide you to a landing dock when we reach the palace. Oh, fricking hell! Gramps is going to pop a gasket when he sees you."

With that, the tiny ship turned in a tight circle that had Kylah whistling in admiration and set off the way it had come.

"Follow that ship," Arden told Ronin with a shrug. Taught with tension, they fell silent as Ronin moved to obey, and ***The Lissa*** moved onto its new heading, following the tiny skimmer as it hovered in mid-air, waiting for them.

"Uncle Arden?" Snow enquired, and Arden smiled at her.

"It's easier to wait until we land," he replied. "Then you will see for yourself."

Long minutes ticked by as the two ships flew deeper into the heart of the Kingdom of House Avis. Finally, they saw ahead of them a vast, craggy outcrop of rock and there, perched right at the top, was a splendid castle. Built partly into the rock itself, it loomed over the countryside below, its many towers and spires thrusting skywards.

"House Avis." Arden waved his hand towards it with pride. "Isn't it magnificent?"

"It's massive," Snow murmured. Suddenly she was afraid and glanced at Ronin apprehensively.

"It's all right," he said, seeming to instinctively understand her fears. "These are your family, Snow. They will not harm you, or any of us. They are good people."

The skimmer hovered over the castle and gave another squeak.

"There's a spare docking bay on the outer wall, Uncle Arden. Follow me down and pull up beside it. They are waiting to secure your tethers."

They rounded the corner of the vast castle and, as one, gasped in stunned astonishment. Airships! At least a dozen of them. All pulled up to a purpose-built aerial docking area with individual bays for each ship. They ringed almost three complete sides of the castle, and Snow's eyes widened with incredulity at the sight.

Kylah bolted from the deck, muttering something about not trusting Eli with the engines during such a delicate manoeuvre.

"Left fin retracted," Ronin snapped.

"Aye, aye, Captain," Shaking off his astonishment, Nylex leapt to obey.

"Slow to steady," Ronin barked at Snow. Hurriedly she grabbed the speaking tube and relayed his order. A moment later, ***The Lissa*** slowed and crept forward as Ronin delicately steered the ship towards an empty dock jutting out over the castle wall into the air. Slowly, inch by inch, he brought the ship alongside.

"Stop engines," he ordered when they were a few feet shy of the dock.

Snow relayed the order, wondering why he hadn't waited until they were closer. Then she realised, as the deck ceased to throb beneath her boots, but still, the ship moved, that Ronin had allowed for forward momentum. Gently, the ship nosed up to the dock and nestled up snugly alongside it.

"Release tethers," he ordered, and Nylex and Arden tossed the tethering lines over the side of the ship. Figures scurried to catch and secure the lines, pulling on them until the ship was tight against the dock, and Snow realised it would simply be a matter of climbing over the side to disembark.

The skimmer had landed on a large wooden platform constructed over the castle's vast open courtyard. A slight figure in flying leathers and goggles scrambled from the cockpit and exchanged a few words with the mechanics who swarmed over the small ship.

Running over a bridgeway that connected the central landing platform to the castle walls, the figure reached their dock as Ronin, Snow, and Arden climbed down onto its wooden surface.

"Uncle Arden!" The figure threw themself exuberantly into his arms.

"Robin?" Returning the hug, Arden drew back and looked the figure up and down. "Is it possible? Little Robin?"

"Well, it has been eight years, Uncle. Much has changed in that time."

"So, I see." Arden gestured to the mighty airships all around them.

The figure shrugged off their bulky leather jacket to reveal the unmistakable curves of a young woman, who then reached up and ripped off her goggles, unstrapped her flying helmet, and pulled it from her head.

Long, blonde hair tumbled over slender shoulders and Snow found herself face to face with a girl of about her age. Her merry blue eyes danced with amusement. Her lips were wide and full, with a broad smile revealing strong white teeth.

She looked Snow up and down, then quirked a brow at Arden.

"You bring company, Uncle?"

"I do indeed, Robin. May I introduce Princess Snow of the House White. Snow, this is Princess Robin of the House Avis, second in line to the throne and your first cousin."

"Hello, Cuz," Robin said.

Chapter Twenty

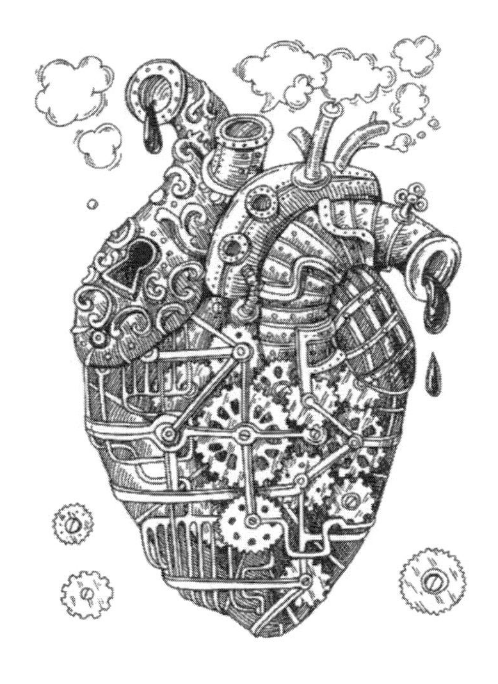

The Lost Boy

The message had stated that it was urgent, yet Slie had waited a day before responding. He was the Pontifex after all – head of the Contratulum, chief advisor to King Tanwyn, and mentor to the young Prince Elgin. He did not leap to a summons like a common servant, especially when it came from one as lowly as the matron of an orphanage in the poorest sector of the city.

Looking at her now as she bowed and scraped, wiping a grimy hand over her crusted nose, and then running it through the greying hair that hung in greasy, unwashed hanks about her skeletal face, an intense wave of distaste shuddered through him.

For two pins, he would have had her put out of her misery. Still, she had proven very useful in the past. Having access to a vast, ever-changing tide of children, she was advantageously placed to find those who were different to the others – those who were *special.*

He glanced at the two guards who accompanied him. Some twenty years previously he took them from this very same orphanage, from a life of poverty to – if not a better life – at least one that guaranteed the basic comforts. A life that offered enough food to grow strong, comradeship within their legion, a purpose to their lives, and, most crucially, reassurances that they were not freaks, but were indeed important.

Their faces remained blank. If they experienced any emotional resonance from being back within the four walls that had shaped their formative years, neither let that emotion so much as flicker across their countenance.

"You say the boy is approximately eight years of age?"

"Yes, Your Grace. There, or thereabouts. Of course, very few of these orphans know their history, so establishing an exact age, or even family background, is next to impossible."

"Of course." He waved away her apology. "You feel he may be worthy of my attention, though?"

"Yes, Your Grace." The woman paused, and a strange look flitted over her face. If Slie hadn't known better, he would have called it fear, but he knew this creature of old. Fear was not a familiar companion to her cruel and black heart, certainly not fear of a lowly, scraggly orphan of barely eight years. A whisper of interest flickered in his mind. Perhaps there was something here after all. Something out of the ordinary.

"What talents has he exhibited?"

"The usual, Your Grace. Knowledge of some events to come, predictions of bad weather, but there is more ..."

"Yes?"

"He can make the other boys do things."

"Things? What kind of things?"

"Whatever he wants them to do. Give him their food, their blankets, their places by the fire. And I can see they don't want to. He just makes them."

"How precisely does he do that?"

"I am unsure, Your Grace. He merely looks at you, and then you have an overwhelming urge to do whatever he suggests."

"You?" Pontifex Slie regarded her with surprise. "He can manipulate the mind of an adult. He has manipulated you?"

"Yes, Your Grace." Looking shamefaced, the woman wiped her hand over her nose again and surveyed it gloomily. Wiping it down her filthy skirt, she looked at him with a pleading expression. "Please, Your Grace, he's upsetting my establishment. Please take him away with you."

"Perhaps. I shall of course need to speak with him."

"Of course, Your Grace. Soon as I got word you were coming, I got him out of bed. He's waiting in my office." She gestured to the closed door behind her.

"I shall speak with him now," Slie declared, then raised a brow as the creature made a move as if to follow him. "Alone." The woman's face mottled an unbecoming shade of puce.

"Of course, Your Grace," she murmured. "I shall arrange some sustenance to be brought to you."

"Pray, do not worry yourself about that," he told her, suppressing a shudder at the thought of consuming anything touched by those hands. "Wait here."

This was to his entourage, who silently positioned themselves one either side of the door, as he quietly opened it and slipped inside. The boy was sitting at the matron's desk, shamelessly going through the drawers. At Slie's entrance, he glanced up, furtively stuffing paperwork back into a folder and slamming the drawer shut.

"Sorry, Sir," he muttered, but Slie waved away his apology.

"Find anything interesting in there, boy?" he asked. The boy shrugged, his eyes narrowing.

"Only that the old bitch is cheating the Royal Charitable Treasury. They pay her a lot more to feed us than she is spending on food. So, we get slop, and she pockets the difference."

"Indeed?" Feigning indifference, Slie made a mental note to inform the Treasury to decrease how much they paid the orphanage, and to maybe start demanding receipted proof of all expenditure.

"Now then, boy. I have come expressly to talk to you."

"Why?"

Pontifex Slie blinked. Normally the child he was questioning was humble to the point of terror. Fully cognisant of the elevated company they were in, it was sometimes all they could do to look at him, let alone answer back.

But then, as his eyes roamed over the scrawny lad facing him, he was beginning to realise that this boy was anything but normal. His hair was a mass of black, tightly kinked greasy knots which spoke of a Southern ingredient in his ancestry, as did his swarthy skin and hooded dark eyes. If anything, these traits should have marked him out as a target of bullying, yet the matron had claimed it was the other children who were afraid of him.

"What is your name, boy?"

"The others call me Mirage."

"Do they? And why is that?"

"Because I can make them see things that are not there. And because I can see things. If I stare into a mirror or a bowl of water, or any reflective surface, sometimes I can see what the others are doing in a different room."

Now the excitement did rise in Slie. The boy could scry. An unusual talent anyway, in one so young and untrained, it was practically unheard of. He must be a natural. At the thought, Slie's pulse quickened. There was no question about it now. The boy was coming with him.

"Mirage, how would you like to leave this place and come with me?"

"Where? To the palace?"

"No, not to the palace, to somewhere else ... Somewhere safe and private where you will be warm, well-fed, and clothed."

"Why?"

"Because you are very special, my boy. Very special indeed. Your skills elevate you far above most others, but they need to be honed. We will train you in how to control and manage them."

The boy considered for a moment; his head bent, studying his grimy bare feet. Strong white teeth worried at his thin bottom lip, and he flexed his surprisingly slender and long fingers together.

"All right," he replied, and Slie smiled at the naivety of the child imagining he had a choice. Still, it was always good if they came willingly. It made things ... easier.

"Splendid," was all he said, though. "Now, do you have any belongings to collect or goodbyes to say?"

"Nah, there's nothing here I want." The boy shrugged. "And no one who will care if I'm here or not."

“As you wish.” Slie opened the door and gestured the boy out into the dark hallway, where the two guards looked at the child dispassionately. “Once,” he told Mirage, “these men were lost boys here like you. Now they have a home, a family, and a purpose to their lives.”

“Is that what will happen to me?” Mirage asked, looking at the guards curiously as they fell silently into step behind them. “Will I become a soldier?”

“Oh, my dear boy,” Slie replied, sliding him a rare smile. “I think we can expect much greater things from you. Much greater.”

The years passed. Mirage fulfilled all Slie’s expectations – indeed he exceeded them in many ways. Discovering a keen intelligence, and a cunning brain beneath the grime and attitude, Slie revised his plans for the child and arranged for him to be extensively tutored.

Mirage proved himself an adept student who hungered for information to satisfy his ever-curious brain. When he came of age and put away his books of learning, Slie then took over his education. Wishing to hone himself a useful and loyal tool, he trained his protégé thoroughly in the arts of statesmanship, strategy, and political intrigue, until the lad could hold his own in any conversation.

Slie ensured he was well versed in the ways of the world, understanding all the intricate family connections and allegiances of all the Houses of the neighbouring kingdoms.

His background intrigued Slie, but dig as he might, no more could be discovered about the boy beyond his discovery on the orphanage steps as a malnourished and lice-ridden toddler. Where he had come from was up for speculation. Slie had his suspicions, but no proof on which to ground them.

Gradually, though, the lad became more to Slie than merely his latest protégé. The boy’s enquiring mind and his quick grasp of complex situations delighted the Pontifex, to the point where he began to regard Mirage with almost fondness. He enjoyed his company and the many hours they spent discussing the matters of court and the many intrigues of the Contratulum.

At twenty, Mirage was a tall and darkly handsome man, who set many a female heart aflutter when he walked through the city, and the Pontifex had come to regard him as the son he never had. He even toyed with the thought of grooming him to be his successor.

In turn, Mirage seemed to entertain a genuine fondness for his mentor, although Slie was never entirely sure what intentions were lurking within his heart. His inability to read the boy at all had come as a shock. When, after much testing, it was discovered that none could penetrate the barrier the boy had erected around his mind, the Pontifex was uncomfortably uncertain whether this was a useful gift or a dangerous security risk.

When the old King Tanwyn died, and his son, Elgin, inherited the throne, Slie felt an unmistakable lessening of his power over the monarch. Tanwyn had been of the old faith and believed totally in the need for the Contratulum. So long as Slie paid lip service to him, and appeared to be loyal, Tanwyn had left him alone to rule the Contratulum as he saw fit.

But Elgin was a different character altogether. Demanding to know what it was the Contratulum did, exactly, he seemed dissatisfied with the answers Slie provided to him, and the Pontifex was jolted from his complacency by a new broom of a king who was determined to sweep his kingdom clean.

Looking for a distraction, he planted the idea in the young king's head that a royal bride should be found, and quickly, to ensure that the succession was in order. Wanting to forge a strong, political alliance with their wealthy and powerful neighbours, House Avis, he arranged for the king and half the nobles at court to go on a grand tour to discover for themselves if the rumours of the beauty and grace of Princess Raven were true.

It was midnight. The corridors of the Contratulum were quieter than usual. Silently, the Pontifex moved over the plush carpet, trailed by Mirage. A prisoner they had been questioning had reputedly shown some interesting abilities, and Slie had determined to take over the interrogation himself.

Already, he was mentally rubbing his hands in anticipation of the deed. It had been too long since he had dirtied his own hands, and he had forgotten the rush of exhilaration the thought of inflicting pain on another always induced.

They reached the lower levels, where the cells holding the unfortunate souls who had come to the attention of the Contratulum languished in misery. Ignoring the moans and cries of the dispossessed, Slie gestured to Mirage to follow him down the central walkway to the interrogation unit placed at the end. A strategic positioning, as it meant prisoners would have to be dragged past their fellow inmates who would fall silent. Knowing full well where they were going, all knew their chances of returning were slim.

The prisoner didn't appear much at first glance. An emaciated and broken figure, he was draped over the wheel of extraction, his shallow pants of weary agony the only sound in the windowless room. Curiously, Mirage moved closer, stooping to examine the grey and haggard features of the man who had proved impossible for his interrogators to crack.

Dark, hooded eyes opened a slit to examine him, and a gleam of almost recognition flickered through them, triggering an answering echo of familiarity within Mirage. Yet, this man was a stranger to him – of that he was certain.

Noting the dark skin, and the black knotted mess of hair, he wondered whether there was a genetic link. This man certainly bore similar features to his own. Cautiously, Mirage sent feelers from his mind into the wretched creature's – and stepped back in surprise when from somewhere the man found the strength to fight back. Although weakened, his will was amazingly tenacious. Mirage pushed harder, determined to break through.

Stepping closer in fascination, Slie watched them silently battle. Beads of sweat dripped from the man's brow onto the blood-soaked straw below. There was one last gathering of the man's failing resources, and then Mirage was in and he saw ...

Everything.

A village, hidden somewhere deep within the forest – although without context it was impossible to know where. A man choosing to leave and seek a new life after the death of his wife, taking his young son with him.

An innocent, he had not known which areas of the city to avoid, and a vicious attack had left him near death and stripped of all he possessed in a dark alley. His child had fled the scene in terror, to be discovered by a soul possessing a rough, but kindly nature. They had dumped him on the orphanage steps and considered it their good deed done for the day.

For many months, the man lay in a coma in a paupers' hospice, until at last, he astounded his carers by arousing. At first disbelieving how long had elapsed, then frantic with fear for his son, he had searched for him, but never discovered his whereabouts. Eventually, he had resigned himself to his son's death and settled into a mean existence – barely surviving and drinking himself into forgetfulness whenever he had the funds.

Mirage staggered as this information slammed into his consciousness. This man was his father. He sought for a name but could only find one. Dwarvian. They were Dwarvian. An extinct and near-mythical race held in contemptuous fear for the dark arts they supposedly practised.

But there was more. Not drawing upon his magical talents for many years, the man had been surprised, when looking for work in an unfamiliar part of the city near the royal palace, to feel a keening in his mind that spoke of like calling to like.

Stunned, he had probed the surrounding buildings. Convinced he had discovered his long-lost son, he did not stop until soldiers from the Contratulum dragged him into their underground compound and threw him into a cell, where he had been ever since.

Realising that his life was forfeit, the man's only thought was to protect the identity of his son, and to stop the discovery that a whole village of his people still lived and thrived deep within the forest.

Where? Mirage demanded.

Will ... not ... the man's mind was almost burnt out under the strength of Mirage's, yet still, he clung to the need to protect.

You must. Mirage insisted. *They are my people, my birthright. I must find them.*

But the man must have sensed the duplicity behind his intent, for he gritted his teeth and scrambled to shore up his rapidly crumbling barricades.

Son, don't, please ...

But Mirage was remorseless and gathered all his reserves to deliver the final blow. He would obtain this information. He knew how valuable it would be to the Contratulum – to the Pontifex – to know where this last nest of vipers was to be found.

Abruptly, the man gave up, but Mirage's triumph was brief. Before he could extract the location, he became aware of another thought the man was trying to hold back. Following the thread of consciousness, Mirage realised the man was busy rearranging his body chemistry at a molecular level. Dismantling the walls dividing his cells, he was allowing dangerous elements that should never be in contact to mix. In short, he was turning his own body into a ...

Mirage's eyes flew open. The Pontifex was standing beside him, a hair's breadth away from the man. Desperately, Mirage shoved at him with all his might as the man exploded with all the force of a bomb. Shards of razor-sharp bone shattered from his destroyed torso at unbelievably high speeds, and with a force that would pulverise all that stood in their way.

Mirage was in the way.

“How is he?” Standing by the young man’s bedside, Slie asked the question of the doctor hovering beside him. Almost tenderly, he arranged the bedclothes neatly over Mirage’s bandaged torso, his gaze avoiding the shattered side of his face.

“He is alive,” the doctor told him, “and lucky to be so. We have removed shards of bone from all over his body. Much of the damage was superficial and will heal itself. That which was more serious we have managed to repair, and he will recover in time. However, there are two areas where it is beyond even my skills to mend him.”

“His eye and his heart,” Slie murmured.

“Yes,” the doctor confirmed. “We had to remove his right eye entirely. The retina had been so severely shredded by bone fragments that there was nothing left to save. The optical nerve remains intact, but there is nothing left to attach it to.”

Slie allowed himself a glance at Mirage’s previously handsome face. No maid would consider him handsome now.

“Being blind in one eye he could live with. After all, the other eye survived the blast and is unaffected. But the heart is another matter. Bone shards are embedded in one half of his heart. Every breath he manages to draw is weakening him further, and there is nothing we can do to save him. He needs a new heart, but of course, that is beyond current medical capabilities.”

“It may be beyond your medical capabilities, Doctor. But it is not beyond our mechanical ones.” Slie nodded at his chief mechanic as he slipped into the room, followed by a team of his most talented and trusted staff. “You may leave him to us now, Doctor.”

“But he is my patient,” the doctor objected. “I have a duty of care.”

“A duty which you have already informed me you will fail at,” Slie replied smoothly. “So, it is time for medicine to step aside and for technology to take over. Thank you, doctor, for your meticulous care of my protégé.”

“But ... I ...”

“You may see yourself out.”

Again, the doctor hesitated, his eyes moving between the prone figure on the bed, and the still figure of the Pontifex, who unblinkingly stared him down.

“Your Grace.” Realising that to protest any further, would be suicide, the doctor left the room. Slie looked at Duncan.

“Save him, if you can, Duncan.”

“You leave him to me, Your Grace. We will make him good as new. You’ll see, better than new he’ll be - better than new.”

In some ways, he was right. When Mirage finally regained his wits, he discovered he had survived, but that a price had been extracted for that miraculous event. His prosthetic eye was already attached to his optic nerve and sending information to his brain.

As for his heart, they had been able to save half of it. As Duncan had informed Slie, with no human component to his heart at all, who knew what senseless, unfeeling automaton they might create. Fully operational mechanical components had been intricately grafted onto it to heal his injuries.

It worked as well as the old, if not better. After his initial disgust at what had been done to him, and for the loss of his darkly handsome features, Mirage came to appreciate the sophistication of his new body parts.

One fear had been that without his eye, his ability to scry on others would be lost. Yet once he had recovered, Mirage was able to demonstrate to his own and Slie's satisfaction that his skill remained intact. This sparked a chain of experiments to investigate the theory that it was the brain that controlled this talent, and not necessarily the eye itself.

And so, he healed. And waited for the Pontifex to decide what role his alpha protégé should play. And then Elgin had died in a senseless, stupid hunting accident that had Mirage wondering, and resenting the implications if his suspicions were true.

If the Contratulum was behind the King's death, and he had not been aware of any such plan, then it meant that Slie still did not trust him. Although perhaps he was right not to.

Of the fact that the man was Dwarvian, Mirage had been fully forthcoming, enjoying the shocked look on Slie's face when he informed him of the existence of a whole village of Dwarvian survivors *somewhere* within the Great Forest.

Of the man's identity as his father, and therefore his own status as Dwarvian, Mirage remained silent. Unsure of how Slie would take the news, even conflicted as to his feelings about it, Mirage decided to keep those cards close to his chest for now.

The Princess Snow was born. For five years life passed uneventfully for the Royal House of White, apart from Raven's ill-advised marriage to Hawk. It was an attempt to consolidate ties of allegiance with House Avis, but it had backfired disastrously.

The Contratulum had previously been unaware of Hawk's predilections, and when Raven quickly banned him from her chambers and her life, one potential avenue for influence and control was closed.

So, they had Raven killed.

Almost shocked at the cavalier way they removed the anointed monarch, Mirage had watched as Hawk had been allowed to marry the Princes Jay, and at last, saw his opportunity. Persuading Slie that Jay should have an advisor – and what better person than himself – had been suspiciously easy. Mirage assumed that this had been Slie's plan all along.

So, he moved into the palace, and at last, he was on the path to fulfilling his destiny. Fully aware that the Contratulum had plans, the scope of which even he could only dimly guess at, Mirage was determined to be a part of those plans.

And all the time, he was aware of Princess Snow. As a child, then a youth, then a beautiful and poised young woman, who had the ability to resist his suggestions and withstand his manipulations.

As the day of her ascension to the throne grew ever closer, Mirage was aware of all the pieces of power moving into position. He knew the Contratulum planned to rule through Snow, believing her a quisling to be controlled. But he did not think they would find it that easy.

Then Snow had disappeared, thanks to that jealous bitch, Jay, and her petty concerns that the affections of her weak husband tended more towards his beautiful stepdaughter than his wife. And he discovered that the Contratulum had a backup plan all along. One that had shocked even him with its audacity.

As the days since Snow's disappearance ticked by, Mirage further realised a disquieting truth.

He missed her.

He missed their daily mental battles. The way her eyes would spark with quiet rebellion whenever he tried to bend her will to his. He missed her intelligence, her wit, her calm poise, and quiet dignity as she stepped through the mire of court life with a native skill that left him reluctantly admiring her.

The fact that he could no longer see her unsettled him more than he would have imagined. He realised how much he had relished those times he had observed her when she believed herself alone. Those peaceful evenings when she had relaxed in a bath or lain in her silken bed lost within the pages of a book, had been the nearest his tortured soul had ever come to peace.

He had fancied that somehow, she had sensed his presence and welcomed him, for at times her head would rise, and her beautiful eyes would look around her chambers as if searching for an intruder.

And now she was lost to him – lost to them all. And the Contratulum had had to revise its plans. Summoned at midnight by the Pontifex, he wondered as he left his weapons with the disdainful young prelate again and was granted admittance to Slie's office, whether he was finally going to be allowed to know what those plans were.

"Mirage," Slie said as he approached.

"Your Grace."

"It's happening, my boy. It's finally happening."

Palpable excitement had the Pontifex slipping into his long-abandoned pet name for Mirage.

"What is happening, Your Grace?"

"War, my boy, war. We are going to war!"

Chapter Twenty-One

The Court of King Falcon

Following a wildly excited Robin down long, echoing corridors towards the throne room, Snow was silent the whole way, listening to the other girl – her cousin – chatter to Arden.

Trying to fill him in on all that had occurred in the eight years since he had last visited them, her words tumbled over themselves until he laughingly raised a hand.

"Enough, Robin, enough. We will have plenty of time to talk later. First, we must see Falcon."

Snow's steps faltered at the name. King Falcon. Her grandfather. The most powerful man in the known world. What would he be like? What would he think of her? Would he agree to help her?

As if sensing her unease, Ronin moved to her side and briefly took her hand. "Don't worry," he murmured in her ear. "Falcon is a good man. All will be well."

Snow smiled at him and managed to squeeze his hand before he was pulling it from her grasp, and they swept through double doors into a vast chamber that seemed full of people.

As one, the group paused, drawing closer together, even the animals sensing the unease. Cesil shrank behind Arden's knee and the normally exuberant Dog was subdued. Snow looked around at all the strangers who turned to stare at this group of outlandish outcasts come amongst them. Arden the cat had elected to stay on the ship, and Greta informed them he would explore these new surroundings on his terms – almost as if she could read the feline's intentions.

Overwhelmed, Snow's eyes flew wildly about the room trying to take it all in. The rough magnificence of the walls, clearly hewn from the sheer rock of the outcrop the castle clung to. The wall of windows on one side appeared to open onto nothing but the sky. The richly dressed lords and ladies who stared curiously as their party made its way to the far end of the room, to where four thrones were placed upon a dais.

The two slightly smaller thrones had a man and a woman sitting in them, who looked so like Robin that Snow assumed they were her parents – Prince Peregrine and Princess Magpie. On the two larger thrones in the centre sat her grandparents – King Falcon and Queen Wren. Snow swallowed, and her steps slowed.

Falcon raised his head as they reached the dais and stopped before it. "Arden?" A delighted grin split his grizzled beard as he bounded from the throne like a boy and clasped Arden affectionately. "By all the gods, Arden! It has been too long. When intelligence reached us of the destruction of your village, we feared the worst. I am much relieved the information was false."

"Sadly, it was true, Falcon. We are all who are left."

"In truth, this is sad news." Falcon looked over their small party in shock, then his eyes lit upon Snow and widened. Nervously, she reached up and pulled the goggles from her head, allowing her long black hair to tumble down her back. Behind Falcon, she was aware of Queen Wren half rising from her throne.

"Raven?" The despairing, hopeful cry tore from a mother's throat.

"No." Falcon slowly shook his head. "Snow?"

"Grandfather?" she replied and was enfolded into his fierce hug.

"Welcome home, my child," he murmured, "welcome home."

There was to be a feast, Falcon declared. A feast to celebrate the homecoming of Princess Snow – the only child of their beloved Princess Raven. A hum of excitement rippled through the room at his words, and then Falcon was ordering that their party be taken to chambers to rest and refresh themselves.

Snow and Arden, he held back. Ronin flashed her a quick, reassuring smile as he followed the others from the throne room and Snow gave him a nervous grimace. For in truth, she would rather be going with them, than tell the rest of her family what had happened to her mother.

"Come." Falcon led them through a door behind the dais into a small and cosy room containing nothing but a large wooden table down the middle with chairs enough to seat twenty, and a sturdy sideboard bearing a tray of decanters and glasses.

"Here we can talk freely," he announced and gestured to them all to take chairs.

Quietly, Peregrine and Magpie poured glasses of rich red wine and began handing them out to the others. "Snow?" Prince Peregrine offered her a glass.

"Thank you, Your Highness," Snow murmured.

"Please, Uncle Perry will do," he said, his eyes twinkling kindly.

"And I'm Aunt Maggie," his wife informed her, then gathered her up in an impromptu hug. "Oh, you dear girl," she murmured. "You look so like your mother."

"She does indeed," boomed Falcon from the head of the table, then looked at his queen as she bent her head and dabbed at her eyes with a lace kerchief. "It's all right, my love," he said gruffly and patted her arm awkwardly.

"It's just – she looks so like her, Falcon," Wren whispered. "She looks so like our girl."

"I'm so sorry," Snow said. "I never meant to distress you by coming here."

"Oh, you darling girl," Wren exclaimed, smiling at her through a sheen of tears. "Nothing you could ever do would distress me. I am merely overcome that at last, you have come home to us. We were so worried when news reached us of your disappearance."

Arden raised his brows over his wine glass at Falcon. "It seems," he began slowly, "that your intelligence is better than our own?"

"Before she died," Falcon said, "Raven established a comprehensive network of spies within the palace and even some within the Contratulum itself. These operatives were made up of our people whom she had managed to place within the palace and others who believed in the new order that she and Elgin wished to bring to the Kingdom of House White. When she died, many of these operatives went dark, and we do not know if they were captured, or simply stopped reporting back because, without Raven, they had lost focus, however ..." he paused and grinned wryly at Arden.

"However, a few remain who still gather information for you?" Arden guessed.

"Correct. I suspect there are many more who are only waiting for Snow to ascend to the throne to make their allegiances known."

"And that is why we have travelled here," Arden replied.

"You require my assistance to help you claim the throne?" Falcon asked Snow, then smiled as her eyes widened at his perceptiveness.

"I guessed as much as soon as I saw you standing there." He sipped at his wine, thoughtfully.

"I do not dare return to the palace without a considerable force to back me," Snow explained. "The Contratulum planned to rule through me, to use me as their puppet, but I believe they had come to realise that would never happen. So now they would be quite happy if I were dead or discredited in some way. They could place Jay upon the throne, or at least declare her unborn child the future monarch." Snow bit her lip, unsure how to tell them the truth about their other daughter.

Falcon and Wren exchanged glances. "Spit it out, girl," Falcon barked. "We need to know it all if we're going to help you."

"Jay has never liked me – I think I reminded her too much of my mother – and as I attained womanhood, she hated me even more because her husband, Hawk, my stepfather he ... he ... made it clear where his preferences lay."

"I see." From his tight-lipped countenance, Snow realised he did.

"And when Jay saw a chance to remove me from Hawk's life … permanently … she took it."

Queen Wren placed her hand to her mouth, her eyes sad. "Jay was always a troubled child," she murmured. "She was so jealous of Raven, and always desired what her elder sister had. I think we have long known that Jay was as lost to us as Raven is."

"So, the Contratulum wants to control you, your aunt wants to kill you, and your stepfather wants to bed you. That about it?"

"That about sums it up," Arden hastily replied, as Snow's cheeks flamed, and she gawped at her outspoken grandfather.

"No wonder you came to us," Falcon drawled dryly, and his wife shushed him.

"You, poor child," she murmured, and rose and walked to Snow's chair. Placing a hand lightly on her granddaughter's shoulder, she smiled down at her. "You did the right thing, coming home to the family that loves you already."

"You don't know me," Snow whispered.

"You are Raven's daughter," Wren insisted. "And no child of hers could ever be unworthy of our love."

Across the table, Perry and Maggie smiled at her, their eyes warm. "My sister was a wonderful person," her uncle told her. "Her death affected us all greatly."

"And a fever, of all things," Maggie added. "Raven was always as healthy as a horse. We were surprised when we heard the news."

Snow's eyes brimmed again, and she looked up at her grandmother. Not wanting to be the one to tell them, but realising they deserved the truth. Something changed in Wren's expression. There was a hardening of the eyes and a tightening of the lips. For long moments she stared at Snow.

"How?" was all she finally said.

"They poisoned her," Snow said.

Wren's grip tightened on her shoulder. "Falcon!" The Queen's voice rang with steely authority as she looked along the table at her husband. "They murdered our daughter, and they have tried to murder our granddaughter. Are we going to let that go?"

"Of course not, my Queen." Falcon rose to his feet and raised his glass in Snow's direction. "I would like you all to raise a glass in a toast. To Queen Snow."

"To Queen Snow," the others chorused.

"Now, today you rest and recover," he ordered. "Tonight, we celebrate. And then tomorrow we draw up our plans."

Being shown to a simply furnished, but comfortable, set of rooms, Snow wearily pulled her boots from her aching feet and collapsed onto the bed. Her mind whirled with all that had happened that day, and she clasped a hand to her almost healed wound, which was throbbing from the exertion.

As she closed her eyes, the emotions that had threatened to overwhelm her all day arose unchecked, and Snow gasped out a sob. For the first time in years, she wept for the loss of her mother. For all that her mother had sought to achieve for her people, and for her life cut cruelly short.

She cried at the thought of the family she had newly acquired, and for the long, hard road that now lay before her. Snow was no innocent. She realised that once stepped upon, the path to the throne was one she could not deviate from until she was anointed queen or had perished in the attempt.

And lastly, she sobbed for herself. The quiet, simple life with Ronin that she had dared to dream was possible, now appeared heartbreakingly beyond her reach. She cried silently into her pillow until exhaustion claimed her, and she sank like a stone into the sweet oblivion of dreamless sleep.

Someone was knocking at her door. Someone persistent, who did not appear to be giving up and going away anytime soon. Grunting in confusion, Snow rolled over on the bed and clawed her way up from sleep, a muffled 'Huh?' being the best she could manage by way of reply.

Luckily, the person at the door interpreted that as an invitation to enter, because it burst open, and Robin bounced into the room in a swirl of vivid purple silk, long blonde curls, and a beaming smile.

"Good evening, Cuz," she trilled. "I thought I'd come and help you get ready for the feast."

"Feast?" Perplexed, Snow looked wildly around the room for some sort of timepiece. "Is it so very late?"

"Indeed, it is, sleepyhead. You've been asleep for simply hours. I wanted to wake you earlier, but Ma said I was to let you rest – that you must be exhausted after all you've been through." Robin rolled her eyes in exasperation. "But even she agreed that a mere hour before the feast you should be beginning to prepare, and then we thought you probably came so unprepared that you would have nothing to wear, so we went through our wardrobes and picked out a selection of gowns for you."

She waved her hands through the still-open door, and to Snow's astonishment, a pair of footmen wheeled in a dress rail from which billowed gowns of all shapes, colours, and styles. A trim lady's maid followed, carrying a tray on which rested an array of feminine necessities – ranging from hairbrushes to ribbons, to vials of perfume, and assorted jewellery which sparkled like stars in the dimly lit room.

"Now, why don't you go and take a shower, and then we can have fun dressing you up."

"A shower? You have showers?" Now interested, Snow pulled herself up in the bed and looked at Robin with eager anticipation.

"Well, duh, of course, we have showers, we're not animals." Robin paused and put her head on one side. "Although, to be fair, we've only had them for a few years. Uncle Arden told us about them the last time he visited and gave us the blueprints for how to build our airships. And of course, once our mechanics had learnt how to do that, completely replumbing the whole palace and installing showers was child's play. Every suite of rooms in the palace now has one – yours is through there."

She waved her hand towards a door in the corner of the room, and eagerly Snow slid off the bed to investigate. Opening the door, she found a small room with rocky walls. A huge bathtub, with clawed feet as large as her head, stood in the centre of the room, and mounted over the head of the tub was the instantly recognisable sight of a large, perforated disc.

"There are fresh towels on the side," Robin informed her, "and soap in the dish. Don't be too long, Cuz. I'm famished, and the smell of roasting hog has been driving me crazy all afternoon."

By the time Snow emerged from the bathroom, having scrubbed two days of airship journey from her body, the footmen had disappeared. The lady's maid was arranging items on the dressing table, all the lamps in the room had been lit, and Robin was sprawled in an armchair with a glass of wine.

"There you are," she exclaimed. "What an age you have been. Now, come and sit down and let Clara work her magic on you." She thrust a goblet of wine into Snow's hand, and Snow gratefully sipped at the rich, soothing liquid.

"Now then, Your Highness." Clara's deft hands removed the towel Snow had wrapped around her hair and ran her fingers expertly through the still-damp length.

"How would you like your hair?"

Snow hesitated, then glanced at Robin, who sat forward in interest. A smile spread across the other girl's face. "I know that look," she breathed. "What are you thinking?"

"I'm thinking," Snow began hesitantly, "that I want to impress. I want to look the part. I am asking your country to go to war for me, to support me in claiming my throne. People will most likely die to make me queen. So, I want to at least look as if I'm worth it."

"You want to look like a Queen?"

"Yes."

Robin glanced at Clara. "Think you can manage that, Clara?"

"Oh yes, Miss. I know I can." Snow was taken aback at the maid's familiarity, and some of what she was feeling must have shown on her face because Robin snorted with laughter.

"She thinks you are over-familiar, Clara."

"And I would agree with her, Miss," Clara responded with a cheeky grin.

"Nonsense. Clara is the same age as me, Snow. She has been with me since we were both children – first as a companion and then as my maid. Her family are wealthy merchants from the town. It would be the height of ridiculousness to expect her to constantly go around 'your highnessing' me. I tried to make her call me Robin like she used to, but in company, at least, she insists on calling me Miss."

"It's not that I meant any disrespect, Clara."

"None taken, Your Highness."

"But I think I am only beginning to realise how very different life is away from the palace – my palace. There things were very formal and staid. I did not trust, or even know very well, any of the palace staff, and I could not be sure they weren't spying on me for my aunt, or my stepfather, or perhaps for both. So, it seemed safer to remain aloof, and not encourage any overtures of friendship from anyone."

"That is very sad, Your Highness. That you had no one you could call friend and no one you could turn to in times of need or sadness."

Snow met Clara's eyes in the mirror and saw the genuine empathy and concern on the young girl's face.

"Oh, please," she said, taking a large swig of wine. "Call me Miss. Now, what do you plan to do with my hair?"

Running a finger nervously around his collar, which was a little higher and a lot tighter than he normally wore it, Ronin entered the large banqueting hall, vastly relieved to see Arden, Nylex, Grein, Eli, and Greta all standing by the large fireplace talking amongst themselves.

Weaving through the crowd towards them, Ronin was aware of the curious glances that came his way and reached the others with an audible sigh of relief. He felt uncomfortable, and out of place. After so many years of living simply within the forest, mostly alone, to be amongst so many strangers left him nervous, and achingly aware that this was not his world.

"Is everybody all right?" he asked in a low voice.

"They have been nothing but kind and considerate," Greta reassured him and stroked the full skirts of her new gown lovingly. "Nothing was too much trouble, and my room is extremely comfortable."

"Yes," Grein agreed. "My room is also very satisfactory."

"And dinner smells m-m-marvellous," Eli chimed in happily.

"A young lad and lass from the kitchen were even sent to take Cesil and Dog for some exercise and then to give them dinner and watch over them. They are certainly being very hospitable to us," Grein continued.

Ronin looked them over with a critical eye. All freshly washed and dressed in new apparel, they appeared happy and at ease.

"I cannot say too much," Arden muttered out of the corner of his mouth, "but it's good news. Falcon and the other royals have fully acknowledged Snow as the rightful heir to the throne of House White and have agreed to help her claim it."

"Good," Ronin murmured back. "That's good. Where is Snow?" he asked, his eyes scanning the crowded room for any sign of familiar raven black locks.

"She's not here yet," Nylex offered. "Neither is Kylah, nor Fae."

"They've just walked in," Greta told them, waving a hand in the air to attract the attention of the two women hovering nervously by the door. Thankfully, Kylah held up her hand in acknowledgement and she and Fae began to push their way through the crowd.

"By the gods," Grein spluttered, "Kylah's wearing a frock."

"So she is," Arden agreed.

Ronin looked again. It was true. Looking vaguely uncomfortable in it, and striding through the crowded room like a man, Kylah was clad in a full-skirted gown of rich blue which reflected into her eyes and made them an even deeper shade than usual.

"You look amazing," Ronin told Kylah.

"B-b-beautiful," Eli added. Kylah thumped him gently on the arm, then looked him over with a critical eye.

"You scrubbed up pretty nice yourself." Her eyes flicked over the rest of them. "You all did."

Ronin turned to Fae. Ravishingly pretty, in a gown of lightest pink which should have clashed with her auburn hair but didn't, she was looking at Nylex. He was staring at her with the look of a man who had been struck by lightning.

"Nylex?" from somewhere about her person, Fae produced a gorgeous lace fan, which she snapped open with a brisk flip of her wrist. Ronin wondered whether she had been taught by someone how to do that, or if it was a natural talent that all women were born with. She narrowed her eyes over the rim and stared challengingly at the speechless young man.

"You look beautiful," Nylex finally said, and Fae's expression softened. Stepping to his side, she placed a hand on his arm, then stroked the material of his shirt with an appreciative expression.

"Silk. Very nice," she murmured.

There was a rustle of interest, and a buzz of excited chatter as the doors were thrown open to their fullest width to admit the royal family. Foremost were King Falcon and Queen Wren, resplendent in their royal robes. Flanking them were Peregrine and Magpie on one side, and on the other stood Robin and Snow.

She stood tall. Her gown of finest white, trimmed with diamonds, hugged her slender form and crested to the floor in folds of silk and delicate lace. A diamond necklace was clasped around her long white throat, dazzling in its magnificence. Her lips pouted red, and her eyes were dark, glimmering pools in the candlelight.

But it was her hair that was her crowning glory. Swept upwards in layer upon layer of shimmering black, pearls glittered within its raven's wing depths, giving the illusion of a crown where none sat.

"Wonderful," Greta breathed, and Arden nodded in agreement.

"Truly, tonight she looks like the princess she is," he said.

"She doesn't look like our S-s-snow," Eli complained, and Ronin had to agree with him.

"No, she doesn't," Kylah said. "She looks like a queen."

And with her words, all the dreams that Ronin had dared to half believe in came crashing about his ears in shards of bitter reality and disappointment.

"That's because she *is* a queen," he murmured and turned to snatch a goblet of wine from a passing servant's tray and stalk away, his back stiff with unexpressed emotion. Leaving the others to exchange looks of sorrowful understanding.

Chapter Twenty-Two

Unsuitable Behaviour for a Princess

All evening she was achingly aware of him. Of the fact that he did not smile at her once. Did not catch her eye to reassure her. Did not even look her way. Instead, he sat with the others, far away on a different table, his attention mostly on their conversation, and he did not so much as glance her way once.

Miserably, Snow kept the sociable smile on her face, picked at the exquisite food laid before her, and sipped at the delicious, ruby-red wine, longing for the eating to be done so she could go and find him and discover what was wrong. Why he was ignoring her, and what could be done about it?

But when the banquet was over and the servants were clearing away their plates, Falcon gently took her arm and escorted her to meet the nobles of his court. Tall, stately men and beautiful women, spoke to her with deference, telling her how like her mother she was and pledging their allegiance to help her claim her throne.

Aware of what her Grandfather was doing, and not insensible to how crucial it was, Snow played her part. She talked and charmed and won them over so completely to her side, that not one of them could resist the appeal in her eyes when she spoke of her people abandoned to the merciless boot of the Contratulum.

Finally, it was done. She had spoken to all. With a whisper of approval in her ear, Falcon told her to find her friends and enjoy the rest of the evening. Gratefully, she curtseyed to him and moved sedately away through the revelling crowds. Resisting the urge to pick up her shimmering skirts and run to the far side of the room where she could make out the tops of their heads, she found herself humming under her breath to the lively jig a group of musicians were playing in the corner.

She reached their table, breathless with anticipation, but he was not there. Forcing her lungs to steady and not gulp for air, she accepted the glass of wine Arden passed her and glanced around with seeming casualness. “How is everyone?” she asked.

Fae and Kylah exchanged glances.

“He’s out on the balcony getting some air,” Fae told her, gesturing towards the wall of windows, all opened to their fullest to allow a cooling breeze into a room overheated from too many bodies.

Snow nodded at Fae in thanks for her understanding and moved swiftly away once more through the crowds. Inclining her head graciously to all who bowed and acknowledged her, she did not stop to exchange idle chit chat with any, and soon she was stepping out into the still evening air.

Pausing for a moment, she gripped the stone edge of the balustrade and took a deep, cleansing lungful of air to steady herself. Looking around, she spied a shadow at the far end of the balcony. Leaning on the balustrade, he had his back to her and appeared unaware of her presence.

Softly she walked towards him. Placing her wine goblet down, she rested her hands flat beside his and stood by him, the stone cold under her palms. He glanced at her, then glanced away. For a moment there was absolute silence between them, the only sound the muted hum of revelry drifting through the windows from the banqueting hall, and the soft chirp of night-time insects.

"I wish you would tell me what I have done to offend you."

"What?" At last, he turned to face her. "What do you mean?"

"For clearly, I have done something, for which I am truly sorry. But I am afraid I am at a loss as to what it is."

"Snow, you could never do anything to offend me." He seemed genuinely baffled and concerned by her statement. "Why do you believe you have?"

"Oh, maybe because ever since we got here you have ignored me. Not once did you look my way during dinner, and the moment you could you hid away out here. Was it to get away from me? One would presume so." To her horror, Snow heard a tremble in her voice and saw the stars above shimmer through a veil of barely held back tears.

"Snow, no, I ..." Ronin paused, then sighed. "All right, I could never lie to you. I have been avoiding you, but not because of any imagined slight on your part."

"Then I don't understand."

"It is because this is not my world, Snow. All of this." He gestured at the grandeur of the castle walls rising all around them and the sounds of the party behind them. "This is not where I belong. I will never fit in here. I belong in the forest, living quietly with my people."

"I want that too," Snow burst out. "To be back in the cottage, living simply with nature ... with you."

"But that can never be, Snow. You are a princess. If all goes well, you will soon be Queen Snow of the House White. Your feet are set on a path where I cannot follow you. It is your destiny to accomplish great things, and you cannot shackle yourself to a lowly woodsman. I would merely hold you back."

"But if our lives were different, if I were not a princess, if you were not 'just' a lowly woodsman – although I must tell you, Ronin, to me you are not that – would you want that life? That life with me?"

"You know the answer to that, Snow."

"Then, can we not ..."

"No, Snow. It would be too painful for us both. It is better to let things be. I am your friend and your champion. Tomorrow, or whenever Falcon calls upon me to do so, I shall pledge my allegiance to you and fight to my last breath to put you upon the throne. After that, if I am still alive, I shall return to my life within the forest, and hope that if you remember me at all, it is with fond regard."

"I could never forget you, Ronin." The words burst from her throat on a sob. "Don't you know how much I ..."

"Hush." He placed a finger to her lips. "Do not say things that cannot then be unsaid."

"Ronin."

"No, on this I am fixed, Snow. No matter what our feelings, this simply cannot be. It is best to end it now before you get hurt. Before I get hurt."

"I am already hurt," she cried, and his face darkened with regret.

"And for that, I am truly sorry." He stepped away from her and sketched an awkward bow in her direction. "Goodnight, Your Highness."

He walked away from her. Snow clutched the balustrade in disbelief, feeling her heart crack silently in half. Shaking with barely suppressed emotion, she fought to regain a modicum of control – enough to enable her to face the crowds inside and smile and lie and make any excuse to leave and gain the sanctuary of her room. Eventually, she drew herself up to her full height, threw back her wine in one restorative gulp, then glided back into the room.

And a quiet shadow detached itself from the gloom at the other end of the balcony. Gazing thoughtfully after the figure of her cousin as she wound her way through the crowds of revellers, Robin bit her lip in consternation.

Something would have to be done about this. Oh yes, indeed. Something *must* be done ...

The next morning, Snow was once again awoken by a pounding on her door. Groaning, she rolled over in bed and clutched her aching head. How much wine had she silently consumed upon reaching the haven of her room? Too much. Sitting at the dressing table, she had stared at her glittering reflection and realised the terrible mistake she had made.

She had wanted to look like a queen to convince the Avian nobles that she was worthy of their allegiance. Instead, all it had done was convince Ronin that he was unworthy of her. As the tears slipped silently down her cheeks, she had ripped at the pearls in her hair with hands that shook, scattering them over the table and onto the floor.

Struggling to free herself from the dress that now threatened to crush her ribcage into her heart, she shrieked with irritated rage as she stretched to reach the laces at her back. Defeated, she had yanked at the bellpull over the fireplace and paced in frustrated angst until Clara quietly tapped and let herself in.

"Miss?"

"Please, Clara, get me out of this ... thing ..." She slapped at the dress and Clara's brow wrinkled in consternation.

"You are unhappy with the dress, Miss? Do you wish to change it for something else?"

"No, the dress was beautiful – it is beautiful – but I need to get it off. I can't breathe and ..." To her horror, Snow's legs gave way and she dropped down onto the stool in front of the dressing table with a thump. "I have to get it off," she whispered miserably.

Softly, Clara crossed the room. Her hands patient, she worked at the knots Snow had managed to pull into the laces.

"There now, Miss," she crooned. "We'll soon have you out of this." Gently, she eased the dress down over Snow's shoulders and helped her to step out of it. "There's a nightgown hanging up behind the screen," she told her. "And when you've changed, I'll brush your hair ready for bed."

Grateful to be released and rubbing at her ribs where the stays had left deep grooves in her flesh, Snow slipped behind the screen and removed her chemise and undergarments. She pulled the loose, cool gown over her head. It slipped down to her ankles in a whisper of silken relief, and Snow rested her head against the edge of the screen for a moment.

Emerging from behind it, she discovered that Clara had tidied away all the pearls, hung up the dress, and lit several lanterns so the room was now bathed in a warm, golden glow.

"That's better, Miss," she said. "The dress was beautiful, but those stays can be a killer. I quite understand why you wished to be free of them."

Snow nodded, then sat again at the dressing table on the stool that Clara pulled out for her. Picking up the ornate silver hairbrush, which bore the phoenix crest of House Avis on the back, Clara began to gently stroke it through Snow's long hair. Over and over, down, and down, until Snow relaxed into the comforting rhythm and the tension in her shoulders dissolved into a heartbroken slump.

"There now, Miss," Clara soothed. "Doesn't that feel better?"

"Yes, thank you, Clara," Snow replied, then met the other girl's eyes in the mirror. "I don't suppose when this is all over and I'm queen, you would consider coming to House White to be my lady's maid?"

"Bless you, Miss, that's very kind of you. But I could never leave Miss Robin."

"You love her, don't you?"

"We love each other, Miss. She is closer to me than any sister ever could be. We have been together since we were children, watched out for one another, been there for each other throughout all our sorrows and joys, and always kept each other's secrets."

"And does Robin have many secrets?"

Clara's lips pursed into a mischievous grin. "A few," she admitted, and Snow smiled back.

"There now, Miss." Clara laid down the brush. "Is there anything else I can do for you? Anything you would like fetching?"

"No, that will be all for tonight. Thank you, Clara. It is very good of you to help me like this. It is good of Robin to spare you."

"That's all right, Miss. To be honest, Miss Robin doesn't take much in the way of looking after. Always been so independent, that one. Right from the start, Prince Peregrine and Princess Magpie insisted that she learnt how to carry out the tasks that those who care for her do. So, Miss Robin has been taught how to hem a dress, make a bed, clear out and lay a fire, care for her horse, and is a dab hand at pastry making."

"She is so lucky," Snow murmured. "I have been taught nothing. I am utterly useless." And she wondered if, when Ronin said he was unworthy of her, it was rather that she was unworthy of him.

"Oh, I wouldn't say that Miss. Haven't you got the entire court of House Avis to pledge to go to war for you? I'd say that's something."

"Yes, I've persuaded people to agree to die for me," Snow replied. "Some achievement."

"Oh, Miss," sighed Clara, and rested her hands gently on Snow's shoulders. "Try to get some sleep. Things will seem better in the morning, they always do."

"Thank you, Clara. Goodnight."

"Goodnight, Miss."

But after Clara had gone, suddenly wide awake, instead Snow had sat by the fire and drunk wine from the decanter that somebody had helpfully refilled in her absence. Staring into the flames, she wallowed in delicious self-pity, clutching the rose quartz pendant firmly in her hand.

When Clara had laced her into her dress earlier, she had attempted to remove the stone, and Snow had slapped her hand onto the crystal in sudden terror.

"Don't," she said. "I can never take it off – it's the only thing that stops the Contratulum from being able to see where I am."

"Then, in that case, keep it on," Robin nodded. "But it doesn't go with the rest of your outfit."

"I know," Snow agreed. "But I cannot remove it."

"You cannot remove the pendant, Miss, but can we replace the leather with a chain?" Clara suggested.

"I suppose that would be all right," Snow murmured, and Clara had fished amongst the jewellery until she had found a long, silver chain which she threaded through the hole in the top of the crystal. The chain was longer than the leather, so the stone had settled between her breasts, and Snow felt comforted by its familiar presence.

Then she had stared into the fire and thought about Ronin until finally, it occurred to her how pathetic she was being, and she went to bed in self-disgust.

In the bright glare of the early morning sun that bathed her room, Snow now bitterly regretted the previous night's indulgence. She blinked owlishly at the figure of her cousin standing in the doorway, dressed in what appeared to be male riding attire, and clutching a bundle of clothing.

Worse – she was smiling at the sight of Snow crumpled and smudged, still sprawled in bed.

"Oh, my," she murmured, then strode into the room. Lifting the empty decanter, she smirked at Snow. "Private party, was it?" She replaced it with a thump and jumped onto the bed, wringing a groan from her cousin as she tried to burrow her way back down under the covers.

"Go away, it's too early." Snow squeezed her eyes shut and wondered if she kept them closed for the time it took to count to one hundred, whether Robin would be gone when she opened them.

"Come on, Cuz. It is a beautiful morning, and it's going to be a lovely day. Pa and Gramps and all the nobles of the court are shut away making plans, and he told me to take you out and show you something of the kingdom until they send for you. So, I thought we could go for a ride. I take it you do know how to ride?"

"Of course, I know how to ride." Snow protested.

"Good," Robin retorted and dropped the bundle of clothing onto Snow's head. "So, get up, wash the wine from your brain, get dressed, and meet me downstairs in ten minutes. We'll grab something for breakfast, and then we'll go down to the stables."

And like a whirlwind, she breezed out of the room, leaving Snow with a hand over her eyes, wondering if she vomited onto Robin's shiny riding boots, whether she would accept that as an excuse not to go.

Probably not, Snow thought glumly and dragged herself out of bed to do as instructed.

Robin was right. It was a beautiful day. Clutching a hot buttered scone that Robin had informed her she had made herself that morning, Snow risked the occasional nibble and the food settled into her queasy gut. Following Robin out into the courtyard and through the archway that led to the stables, Snow surveyed the trim back view of her cousin and pulled at her britches to try and ease them away from her legs.

Snow couldn't tell whether Robin was significantly slighter than Snow was, this outfit was an old one that had fitted a thinner version of her cousin, or Snow's outfit had been taken in for some reason – but her riding attire seemed to fit her a great deal more snugly than Robin's did.

To her surprise, Snow realised she had finished her scone and that it, as well as the cup of tea her cousin had forced upon her, had helped to chase the last remnants of wine from her system. Taking a deep breath of the sweet, early morning air, Snow smiled with pleasure. Her heart might be broken, but she could still appreciate the beauty of the day.

They reached the stable block, where a groom awaited them, holding the reins of a pair of thoroughbred horses that pranced eagerly at their arrival. Sunlight glinted off their matching gleaming copper coats and they thrust their noses into Robin's chest as she approached them.

"Hey girls," she murmured lovingly. Fishing pieces of carrot from her britches pocket, she held them out to the mares, who nipped them daintily from her fingers. "This is Symphony, and this is Sonata," she told Snow.

Running her eyes appraisingly over their fluid lines, Snow stepped closer and ran her hands down Sonata's intelligent face.

"They're beautiful," she said.

"They are indeed," Robin agreed. "I thought you could take Sonata. She's more forgiving of beginners and will be kind to you. Symphony is a bit of a handful, she might ..."

Robin's voice trailed away, as Snow calmly swung herself up and into the saddle. Expertly adjusting her reins, she settled onto the horse with all the ease of one who belonged there.

Robin glanced at the smirking groom. "And perhaps you can handle a horse just fine," she finished. "Has the gentleman arrived already, Hobbs?"

"He has, Your Highness. He took Coaltar out into the paddock to get the feel of him."

"Excellent," replied Robin, swinging herself up into Symphony's saddle with a fluid ease that matched Snow's own. "We'll join him there."

"Join who?" Snow asked, moving to follow Robin. "Is someone else going on the ride with us?"

"Yes. I hope you don't mind?"

"Of course not," Snow replied. Although secretly she was a little put-out. She had looked forward to this ride as an opportunity to get to know her cousin better and to ask questions about her and the Kingdom. Now, it would be more awkward with a stranger present.

"Tell, me, Cuz," Robin began, as she and Symphony broke into a trot. "This Ronin, who seems to be the Dwarvians leader. Do you have any prior claim over him?"

"What?" Snow nudged Sonata to briskly move alongside Robin. "Ronin? No, I ... what do you mean?"

"I mean, are you and he lovers?"

"No! What makes you say such a thing? I'm a princess, and he's a ... he's a ..."

"Incredibly handsome and intriguing man. Oh, I do love them moody and broody. Course the ultimate in moody and broody is the gorgeous Nylex. But I get the distinct impression he belongs to that pretty, little witch friend of yours. And heaven knows, I have no desire to cross her. So, that leaves Ronin, although obviously, Cuz, if you have first dibs on him, then I'll stand back. Wouldn't want to step on anybody's toes, after all." She winked at Snow.

Snow took a deep breath, battling down the irresistible urge to shove her cousin off her horse. She forced a smile at Robin, who continued to leer in a manner most ... *male,* Snow decided irritably.

"No," she forced out through gritted teeth. "I have no prior claim to Ronin."

"Oh, good," Robin replied cheerfully. "Then you'll have no objection if I take him for myself."

She galloped away towards the familiar black-clad figure who was cantering easily around the paddock on a coal-black stallion.

Ten minutes into the ride, Snow had decided she hated her cousin with a passion, hated Ronin equally as much, and hated herself the most.

True, Robin had given her fair warning that she was going to take Ronin for herself, but did she have to be so blatant about it? And did she have to do it right under Snow's nose?

Watching as her cousin fluttered her eyelashes at Ronin, Snow ground her teeth together with annoyance. Robin simpered and flirted and laughed in a manner most unbecoming for a princess, she decided fiercely.

The track was only wide enough to ride two abreast, and *of course,* Robin arranged it so that she was riding beside Ronin. Snow was forced to lag miserably behind and watch as Robin leaned over from her saddle towards Ronin to whisper something to him that set him chuckling.

Logically, Snow knew they could not be laughing about her, but as Ronin looked down at Robin and answered back in a low voice, logic headed for the hills, and Snow seethed with silent fury.

When the steep track leading down from the castle levelled out and widened into a rolling plain, Snow had just about had enough. Leaning forward in her saddle, she touched her heels lightly to Sonata's willing flanks and the mare took off like a rocket.

Thundering past the startled pair, she ignored Robin's shout to slow down and wait for them and let the mare have her head. Oh, but it was glorious.

The freedom. The rush of the wind in her face. The sound of the hoofbeats pounding in time to her angry pulse.

The frick with him, she decided fiercely. The frick with them all. She was a princess, and she would not be treated like a village wench being toyed with by the local heartthrob.

Twin hoofbeats echoed to her right. Glancing over her shoulder she saw Ronin almost neck and neck with her. He caught her eye and grinned, urging his horse on.

He was racing her, she realised, and a wild whoop of exhilaration erupted from her throat. Sonata's ears flicked back, then her pace increased, and she stretched out her nose in determination not to let the black stallion have the day.

In the distance, Snow saw the glimmer of a river running through the meadow and realised it was the natural finishing line. Sonata seemed to come to the same conclusion and angled sharply to her left to run for a few yards alongside the bank until she came to halt, her head hanging and her sides heaving.

Dismounting, Snow looked up as Ronin thundered to a halt beside her and slid down from the frisky stallion, who nipped at Sonata's flank in annoyance at being beaten by her. Sonata showed him her teeth and he snorted his disapproval.

"I beat you," she said.

"You did indeed," he agreed.

They stared at one another. Snow was abruptly aware of her chest heaving with exertion under the tight corset. Briefly, his eyes flicked down over her body and away, a slight tinge of red touching his cheeks.

Suddenly, Snow was pleased that her outfit was so figure-hugging. Let him get an eyeful of what he was throwing away, she thought savagely.

He cleared his throat. "Snow ..." He stopped, coughed, tried again. "Snow ..."

And then Robin was there, pouting that they had raced off without her, and requesting that Ronin help her down – which he did, and then Robin practically fell against his chest with a squeal, so he had to catch her, and she clung onto him, and ... and ...

And Snow was back to hating them both and hating herself even more.

Chapter Twenty-Three

Be a Better Queen

They rode for a further hour, through lush pasture and rolling moors, dotted with small villages, peopled with cheerful residents who saluted Robin as soon as they saw her. Stopping to partake of tea and hot meat pasties in a tiny hamlet, Snow watched as Robin interacted with her people.

She was loved, Snow realised. All these people knew and loved their princess, would gladly go to war for her, and trusted that when the time came, she would ascend to the throne as their ruler. Snow thought about the people back home. They were her people, yet they barely knew her. Apart from state functions, even the nobles hardly ever saw her, and as for the common folk ... did they even know what she looked like?

She was ashamed that she had not been a better princess, and determined that should she be given the chance, she would be a better queen.

And all the time, Robin staked her claim on Ronin. To be fair to the man, he did nothing to encourage her. There were a couple of occasions when Snow was convinced a flash of annoyance briefly flared in his eyes, and once he bent a look of almost pleading upon her. But Snow ignored him. She ignored them both.

On the ride back to the palace, Robin's intentions towards Ronin became so blatant that, in the end, Snow allowed Sonata to fall back quite considerably so she would not be forced to listen to Robin's coos and simpers any longer.

Her temper rising every time she glanced at their backs – Robin so far twisted towards Ronin's it was a wonder she didn't unseat herself – Snow lagged further and further behind. By the time she entered the stable yard, she had lost sight of the pair of them.

Hobbs came running as she clattered over the cobblestones and took the reins as she dismounted. Snow wondered whether she should offer to help look after Sonata but following them into the stable she spied Symphony being cared for by another groom and no sign of Robin, so thought it best not to say anything.

"Where are the others?" she asked, and Hobbs threw her a grin over his shoulder as he led Sonata into her stall.

"Princess Robin went back to the castle, and the other gentleman is out in the paddock.

"Thank you, Hobbs."

"You're welcome, Your Highness. I trust you enjoyed your ride?"

"I did. Sonata is a magnificent animal."

"Aye, she is at that, Your Highness," Hobbs agreed, and patted the mare fondly on the neck as he unbuckled her saddle.

Leaving the stable, Snow hesitated. Was she angry enough to do something stupid? Something that could potentially backfire and cause her incredible embarrassment? Yes, she decided, she was. Marching out to the paddock, she saw him standing by the fence watching the horses that were busy eating the lush grass. At her thunderous approach, he turned, his face alarmed at her expression.

"Snow?" he questioned.

Then she was upon him. Grabbing his shirt, she yanked him to her and planted a fierce kiss of frustrated jealousy and resentment upon his startled mouth. Before he could react, she reared back and slapped him with all her might.

"How dare you flirt with my cousin like that! And in front of me. Have you no shame? How could you treat me like that? I thought ... Oh, it doesn't matter what I thought, because it was quite plainly all a lie. Well, I have had enough of being merely your plaything, so I will kindly ask you to refrain from treating me as such!"

And with that, she turned on her heel and marched away, her heart hammering in shock at what she had done, her lips tingling from the touch of his, and ... by all the gods, the palm of her hand was throbbing.

Footsteps pounded on the grass behind her. Then his hand was rough on her elbow pulling her back and spinning her around to face him. The mark of her hand stood out vividly on his cheek and his eyes were angry chips of ice.

"What the frick, Snow?! You are not just a plaything to me. You must know how I feel about you?"

"And how am I supposed to know that, when all morning you have been making it very clear how you feel about my cousin? Oh, Ronin ..." Snow adopted Robin's breathy simper perfectly. "Please could you help me down from my horse? Oh my, what big strong muscles you have." She stopped and glared at him.

"She's a princess. What was I supposed to do? Spit in her eye?"

"Yes!" Snow screamed back. "If it stopped her from taking you away from me." Her anger drained away at the ridiculousness of her words, and she began to tremble.

"Snow." His voice gentle, Ronin gathered her close and held her head to his chest. "No one is taking me away from you."

"But ... but ... the flirting ..."

"Was all flowing in one direction, and I must admit, I am surprised at the Princess Robin's behaviour this morning."

"Ronin?"

"Yes?"

"I will not ask you again, but please … will you kiss me once? I know and I understand everything you said to me last night, but please, just this once? I do not wish our only kiss to be one given by me in anger?"

"Are you not counting the one on board ***The Lissa*** then?"

"That was real?" Snow pulled back and stared up at him in shock.

"Well, it certainly seemed real to me, did it not to you?"

"I imagined it to be a dream – a beautiful dream."

"It was no dream."

Silently, Snow explored her hazy memory of the event. Trying to remember what it had felt like to be held by him. To know that he wanted her, to feel his lips on hers. Her eyes met his in shared recollection, and the hitch in his breathing told her he was remembering it too.

Slowly, her arms crept up about his neck. He did not resist, did not step away. Instead, his arms tightened around her waist. As if under another's control, his head bent to hers. She saw the glitter of his eyes right before she closed her own. Then the kiss was upon her and it was sweet and tender, and so loving.

He loved her. She could feel it from the top of her head right down to the tips of her toes. He loved her. But he was going to walk away from her because it was the honourable thing to do. Even if it ripped both their hearts from their chests, he was still going to leave her.

And then he did. And Snow was left alone, clutching her hand to her chest to still her heart's frenzied pounding, a tear scalding hot on her cheek as he walked away. He walked away, and he didn't look back. He turned the corner into the stable, and she could see him no more.

Snow took a deep breath. Then she clenched her fists and went to see her cousin to inform her that Ronin was out of bounds. That even though she could not be with him herself, she was damned if she would stand by and watch him be with anyone else.

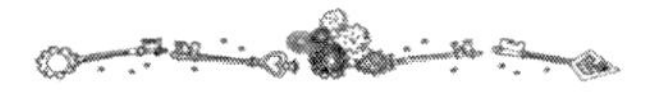

Without bothering to knock, Snow stormed into Robin's room to discover her cousin having her corset laced by Clara, and talking to two ladies-in-waiting, who were sprawled in an ungainly manner upon her bed.

At Snow's abrupt entry, all four women paused and turned to look at her. Snow hesitated, wondering if she should make her excuses and leave. But no – this had to be said, and she was determined to say it before her courage deserted her.

"Snow?"

"Robin, I would speak with you please."

"Of course." Robin gestured to a chair. "Sit down."

"I would speak with you, alone."

"I see." Robin raised a brow, then exchanged a glance with the two upon the bed. "Well, Clara you know, and these are my trusted ladies-in-waiting. I have no secrets from them. Whatever you need to discuss with me, can be spoken of in front of them."

"Very well. I have come to tell you that your behaviour towards Ronin is unacceptable."

"My behaviour?"

"Yes, your behaviour. This flirtation with him you have determined upon. It must cease. It is unseemly for one in your position to act in such a way, and I insist you refrain from behaving that way again towards him."

"Really?"

"Yes, really."

"And why, exactly, do you care how much I flirt with Ronin?"

"Of course, I do not care. But it is ..."

"Unseemly, yes, you said. But again, I ask, why do you care how I behave?"

"I don't care ... that is ..." Losing her composure under Robin's steady gaze and the interested faces of the other three girls, Snow reddened. "Leave him alone!" she angrily snapped. "For he is nobody else's, but mine."

"Yes!" Exuberantly, Robin slapped the palms of each of the girls on the bed.

"Told you it would work," one laughed.

"You did indeed, Franki. You are without a doubt, queen of the romantic plot."

"I still think giving her riding clothes that were too tight was inspired." The other girl lay back on the bed and chuckled at the thought.

"It was – and thank you, Clara, for taking in her britches so speedily."

"Clara?" Finally, Snow found her voice and stared at the maid in hurt bewilderment.

"Sorry, Miss." Clara flashed her an apologetic grin. "I only did as I was instructed." But from the gleam in her eye, Snow was in no doubt she had not only been a willing participant but had quite probably been the instigator of the prank.

"I don't understand." Snow sank onto a nearby chair in confusion. "For what possible reason did you tighten my britches?"

"Are you joking?" Robin laughed at her. "Did you not see the way his eyes nearly popped out of his head every time he looked at you? Oh, and when you raced away from us? That was perfect. We both had a wonderful view of your ..." Giving a snort of mirth, she cupped her hands in an imitation of Snow's backside.

"Of course, he chased after you. The poor man had no choice. But frick, did my arms hurt reining Symphony in. She so wanted to race as well. It was all I could do to hold her back."

"It was all a trick? A joke played at my expense?"

Beyond hurt, Snow stared at the cousin she had begun to love, unable to grasp that such a cruel prank had been performed on her. Robin stopped laughing and crouched before her.

"No, not a cruel trick, but a ruse. A necessary ruse to force you to admit how you feel about him."

"How I feel about him? But how do you know ...?"

"I was on the balcony last night. I did not mean to eavesdrop. I was waiting for him to leave so I could return to the party, but then you came out, and things got serious and then I couldn't leave, I was trapped there. So, I ..."

"Heard everything," Snow finished.

"Yes, I heard everything ... and I wanted to help. You both seemed so stubbornly determined not to be together when anyone with half an eye can see how much in love you are. So, I spoke to the girls about it, last night, and we came up with this plan. Oh, and that reminds me. May I introduce you to my ladies-in-waiting? The Lady Francesca di Salvio." The girl with the lighter brunette curls clambered off the bed and dipped into a perfect curtsey.

"And the Lady Teganna Consuella-Morwenna." The darker brunette also scrambled to her feet and curtseyed.

"Otherwise known as Franki and Tegan."

"Charmed to meet you," Snow murmured.

"But what we want to know," Tegan insisted, "is did it work? Did he kiss you?"

"I slapped him," Snow said, and Tegan's eyebrows shot up.

"Umm, that's not the outcome we were hoping for," Franki murmured.

"But first I kissed him," Snow admitted, and all four girls beamed.

"That's more like it, Miss," said Clara.

"But it was an angry kiss. A kiss of jealousy and rage."

"Oh, frick," muttered Robin.

"But then he told me no one could ever take him away from me."

"Oooh," breathed the others happily.

"And then we kissed each other."

“And how was that kiss?” Robin demanded.

“It was magical, beautiful, everything I had been dreaming of.”

“Ahh,” sighed the others.

“But then he told me goodbye, and he left me, and I know that it’s for good this time. His honour will allow him to do no more. He loves me, I am certain of that. But because I am to be queen and he considers himself nothing more than a lowly woodsman, he believes himself unworthy of me.”

“I see.” Clara having finished lacing her up, Robin sprawled into a chair and slung her legs over the arm in a very un-princess-like manner. “And you are going to go meekly along with that, are you?”

“What can I do?” Snow burst out miserably. “For he is right, it would never be allowed.”

“Allowed by whom?”

“I will be queen. It would not be allowed.”

“Well, you see now, Cuz, that’s the thing about being a queen. You can do what the frick you please and there’s nobody in the whole world who can stop you.”

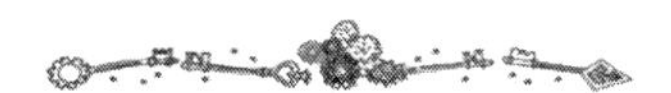

After she changed and had luncheon with Robin and her ladies, Snow gladly accepted the offer of a tour of the town in their company. She was eager to explore more of this kingdom, which was so radically different to her own, so when Robin linked arms with her, Snow flashed her an excited smile.

“Over the years, the town has crept further and further up the hill, so now it’s practically at the castle gates,” Robin told her.

Nodding, Snow looked around at the neat, trim houses which lined the road. Each one had been painted a different cheery colour, and window boxes and hanging baskets were festooned with bright flowering plants.

After a few minutes of walking, the four of them entered a large town square with a fountain in the centre. Glimmering in the strong afternoon sun, the water cascaded upwards in strong plumes before crashing down into a stone rimmed pool.

A small café had tables and chairs set out on the flagstones, and locals were sitting and enjoying beverages and cakes. Spotting Grein, Greta, Eli, and Kylah sitting at one of the tables, Snow greeted them with pleasure, smiling at the size of the piece of cake Eli was busy shovelling into his mouth.

“Where are the others?” she asked, and Kylah waved a hand towards the other side of the square.

“Nylex, Arden, and Fae are over there. Not sure where Ronin is.”

“He’s there,” Grein offered, and Snow turned her head to see Ronin stride into the square and join the others. Stooping to scratch Cesil under the chin, he fondled Dog when he jealously lolled against his leg and smiled at something Fae said to him.

Snow hesitated. She wanted to be with him but was unsure if she should intrude.

“We can wander over that way,” Robin murmured in her ear. “That’s the school they’re standing outside, and I wanted to show it to you anyway.”

Gratefully, Snow followed as Robin tugged on her arm and led her over to a large wooden building with a small fenced-in garden beside containing swings and a climbing frame. With Franki and Tegan following in their wake, the four women reached the small knot of chatting Dwarvians as if by accident and stopped to greet them.

“Uncle Arden,” Robin said. “Fancy meeting you here. Are you showing everyone around?”

“Well, I’m trying to,” Arden confessed. “But so much has changed since I was last here.”

“It has,” Robin replied proudly. “This whole section of town was practically rebuilt when we installed gas to most of the buildings.”

“Goodness me,” Arden exclaimed. “I never imagined how much further your engineers would go once they’d mastered airship technology.”

“Oh, there was no stopping them,” Robin laughed, then tugged on Snow’s arm. “Come on, I want to show you the school and introduce you to my old teacher.”

“You went to school here?” Unable to hide her astonishment, Snow looked from Robin to the humble building and back again.

“Well, of course, I went to school here,” Robin replied. “How else do you think I was educated?”

“By a governess or private tutor in the castle, maybe?” Snow murmured.

“But that’s ridiculous,” Robin laughed. “How would my people get to know me if I was stuck in the castle all day? How would I get to know the children, their parents, and how they lived if I was taught all by myself? No, all the children of the court nobility attend this school.”

Snow thought about her lonely lessons with a succession of sycophantic tutors and considered that maybe Robin’s way was better.

“But weren’t your parents afraid of assassination attempts if you were mingling with the people all the time?”

"Who on earth would want to assassinate me?" Robin exclaimed incredulously. "My people all love me, and they'd never want any harm to come to me."

Sadly, Snow nodded, wishing that she could say the same, but remained silent as she followed Robin into the building. Franki and Tegan trailed after them, chatting brightly to Fae who had tagged onto their group.

As they entered the large sunny room, the ring of children sitting on the floor all turned their heads as one to look at them. The schoolmistress rose from her chair, her kindly face wrinkling into new lines of welcome.

"Princess Robin," she said. "What a pleasant surprise."

"Sorry to interrupt, Miss Cooper," Robin replied. "But I wanted to show my cousin the school and introduce her to you and the children."

"The Princess Snow – of course, it would be our honour. Now then children, what do we say?"

"Good afternoon, Princess Snow," lisped fifteen small voices, and Snow smiled in delight.

"Good afternoon," she said.

"And good afternoon, Franki and Tegan. What fresh mischief have you two been up to lately?"

"Nothing," the girls protested in unison, then exchanged guilty glances. "Well, nothing much."

"Hmm," mused Miss Cooper, although her eyes were twinkling behind her spectacles.

"Only a flying visit, this time, Miss Cooper," Robin explained. "I want to show Snow over the town before it gets dark."

"Of course," said the schoolmistress. "Always a pleasure to see you, my dear."

"May I stay for a little longer?" Fae stepped out from behind the others and smiled at the children. Miss Cooper surveyed her with interest.

"You're one of the Dwarvian party, are you not?"

"Yes. My name is Fae."

"And I understand you've been dwelling in the Great Forest?"

"That's right."

"Well, we're about to have our nature talk, so maybe you could tell the children about the animals and plants that live there?"

"I would love to," Fae beamed happily and gracefully settled herself on the floor in the ring of children.

Saying their farewells, Snow followed the others back out into the town square, blinking in the strong glare of the sun made more powerful after their time spent in the shady schoolhouse.

"Now, then," Robin mused. "Where shall we go first?"

"The gardens?" Franki suggested.

"No, the library," Tegan insisted.

"There's time to do both," Robin promised.

By now they had reached the others, and Nylex looked beyond them with a frown on his face. "Where's Fae?"

"She stayed behind to talk to the children for a while," Snow explained, and he nodded.

"Fae loves children," he murmured.

Snow saw the interested glance that Robin shot his way, then the pointed look she exchanged with her ladies, and her heart sank a little. Hoping that they were not planning any matchmaking shenanigans on Fae's behalf, Snow decided to speak privately with them and advise them of the foolishness of such a thing. She had the feeling that any such meddling in his affairs would only anger Nylex and would not help Fae at all.

She opened her mouth to make a flippant comment designed to draw attention away from the young man when she became aware of a vibration beneath her feet.

"What's happening?" Ronin looked at Robin in alarm.

"Earth tremor," she replied. "Don't worry, they happen a lot. They're usually mild and are over in seconds."

Only slightly reassured by Robin's words, Snow braced herself against the wall of the nearest shop as the ground rumbled and groaned underneath them. Gradually, the motion ceased, and she relaxed, only to be knocked to the ground as it abruptly heaved and lurched violently beneath her.

"Snow!" Ronin cried and bent to help her up. "Are you hurt?"

"No," she gasped, wiping at her gown which was dusty from contact with the flagstones. "I'm fine, but that was ..."

Whatever she had been going to say was swallowed up by the sudden boom of an explosion behind them. Turning in shock, their eyes widened, and their jaws dropped in horror as the schoolhouse erupted into a sheer wall of flames that forced them back with the intensity of its heat.

Chapter Twenty-Four

The Flames of Passion

Frozen in the horror of the moment, Snow gripped Ronin's arm and held up her other hand to shield her face from the intense heat. Beside her, Robin staggered forward a few steps, only to be pulled back by Arden.

"Robin – no! The heat is too intense!" he cried.

"But the children!" she screamed. "Miss Cooper!"

"There's nothing you can do for them," he said. "No one could survive that."

All around them, people were running towards the schoolhouse, screaming, and crying out in horror. Snow saw several men attempt to enter the blazing building, only to be driven back by the inferno. Crying out the names of their children, women sobbed and clutched at one another, and tears sprang to Snow's eyes at the despair in their voices.

"Fae!" At Nylex's anguished shout, Snow remembered they had left her inside, happily talking to the children, and covered her mouth in dismay.

"Fae!" Bracing himself against the heat, it looked as though Nylex was fully prepared to throw himself into the burning building, and Ronin and Arden sprang forward and dragged him back.

"No, Nylex. You can't go in there."

"But Fae's in there."

"She's gone, Nylex." Ronin gripped the younger man by the arm and pulled him further away. "There's nothing you can do for her now. She's gone."

"No!" With a furious burst of strength, he shook them from him as if they were nothing and strode towards the flames. Ignoring the intense heat, he held out his hands and let out a growl of anger. For a moment, Snow wondered if he had lost his mind from shock, but then realised that something was happening to the flames.

Slowly, almost imperceptibly, they were growing less intense, less furious. His legs planted firmly on the ground, Nylex appeared to be forcing the flames down with the power of his magic. Sweat erupted on his brow, and from where she stood Snow could see the veins throbbing in his temples from the strain.

Frozen to the spot in stunned surprise, Ronin and Arden exchanged looks of astonishment, then as one stepped up to Nylex's side and placed their hands upon his shoulders.

"Take our strength," Ronin ordered.

Barely nodding his agreement, Nylex closed his eyes. Lines of strain streaked across his face and his lips drew back in a snarl of determined rage. Ronin and Arden swayed as light erupted from where their hands gripped Nylex's shoulders, and Snow could almost see them being drained of energy as Nylex drew upon every scrap they could spare.

And still, the flames grew less. Visibly diminishing with each painful beat of Nylex's broken heart, they dwindled and dwindled, until the fire was out, and black smoke belched from the schoolhouse doors and windows.

There was a second of stunned silence, then the townspeople rushed towards the schoolhouse, but Nylex beat them all to the door. Followed by Ronin and Arden, he stepped carefully into the smoking carcass of the building.

Snow began to cry. Not wanting to see the charred remains of her friend, and those innocent children she had spoken with only moments earlier, she turned her face away and wept in Robin's embrace.

"Nylex, stop." Ronin pulled the young man back. "Don't go in there. You don't want your last memory to be seeing her like that."

"Let me go, Ronin," Nylex's eyes were like chips of granite. "I have to see. I have to know."

Pulling aside the charred, fallen segments of the roof, they reached the centre of the building and saw ... Fae, kneeling with her arms outstretched, her eyes closed, her mouth screwed into a grimace of intense concentration. Around her huddled the bodies of the children and their teacher – alive. All alive, and untouched by the intense flames that had destroyed the building.

"Fae?" Quaking with shock and disbelief, Nylex clambered over fallen timbers to get to her, only to be brought up short by an invisible barrier.

"Fae!" he cried again, pounding his fists in mid-air. "Fae, you can let go now. The fire is out. Fae."

Slowly she opened her eyes and looked at him, their vivid green shocking in its intensity.

"Nylex?" she whispered. Her arms dropped and Nylex all but fell onto the group of children as the invisible wall lifted. "Nylex?"

Falling to his knees, he pulled her to him as she began to shake, tears streaming from her eyes.

"Are they safe?" she begged. "Are they all safe?"

"They're all safe," he reassured her, brushing the hair off her sweat-slicked forehead, and tenderly kissing her. "They're safe. I don't know what you did, but you kept them all safe long enough for me to put out the fire."

She nodded, then her eyes rolled back into her head and she fainted dead away in his arms.

Waiting outside the schoolhouse with the sobbing townspeople, Snow saw the tears rolling unashamedly down her cousin's cheeks. Impulsively she hugged her, extending her arms to include Franki and Tegan as they crept into the joint embrace. Shaking and crying, the four women gave comfort to one another, until a shout of joyful disbelief had them raising their heads to see ...

... Arden and Ronin, with a child on each hip, helping Miss Cooper over the fallen timbers of the destroyed schoolhouse and out into the square. People rushed forward, taking the children from them, snatching up other youngsters as they emerged. Tears of sorrow turned into sobs of stunned relief.

"She did it." The schoolmistress was babbling almost incoherently in shocked relief. "Her eyes went white, and she threw up a barrier around us as the building exploded. She saved us. She saved us all."

"Ronin?" Pulling free from the other women, Snow staggered over to him and clutched at his arms. "How ..." she cried. "How?"

"I don't know." He shook his head, then gestured behind him as Nylex carefully carried Fae from the still-smoking ruins. "Fae somehow managed to protect them long enough for Nylex to put out the fire and reach them."

"You didn't tell me Nylex could do that," Snow murmured.

"I didn't know Nylex *could* do that," Ronin exclaimed. "Frick, I don't think even *Nylex* knew he could do it, either."

By the time they arrived back in the castle, Fae had recovered and was walking slowly beside Nylex. Keeping his arm tight around her waist, he kept casting her sideways glances as if reassuring himself she was still there. Snow wanted to cry again at the look in his eyes each time they fell upon the petite form leaning heavily on his arm.

They walked so slowly that the news reached the court before they did, and when they entered the throne room it seemed the entire castle's population was crammed into its four walls.

An excited buzz erupted upon their arrival, and Falcon arose from his throne at their approach. Beside him, Queen Wren smiled tearfully down at Nylex and Fae as they bowed and curtseyed respectfully to the royal party.

"We owe you a debt that can never be repaid," Falcon began, emotion quivering in every word. "What you did today, what you both did ... you saved our children. How can that be rewarded? What prize or title can recompense such a deed? And yet, I will try. If there is anything – anything at all – that either of you desire or need, then name it, and it is yours."

There was a profound silence in the room at his words, and Nylex glanced down at Fae. Her face slack with exhaustion, she merely shook her head and buried it into his chest, as if absolving herself of any decision.

"Your Majesty," Nylex began. "There's nothing we need or want. We are happy that we were able to save the children and their teacher, and that is reward enough."

"Oh, come now," Falcon insisted. "There must be something?"

"No, nothing, except ..." Nylex hesitated, and Falcon pounced on his words like his namesake swooping down on his prey.

"Except what?" When Nylex remained silent, Falcon strode from the dais and faced them both, hands on hips, his bushy eyebrows beetling into a frown of frustration. "Come now, lad, spit it out. There's clearly something you want, so out with it."

"Well, Your Majesty, I was wondering if maybe you would ..."

"Yes?"

"If you could ..."

"What?"

"Marry me, Sire?"

At the titter that swept through the room, Nylex reddened.

"Marry you?" Falcon's brows shot up in amused surprise. "Well, flattered though I am, lad, I'm afraid I'm already taken."

"No, Sire ... I'm sorry, I meant ..." Looking down at Fae who had gone very still, Nylex gathered up both her hands in his and gazed into her face, oblivious to the interested stares of the onlookers.

"Fae, when the school went up in flames – when I thought I had lost you forever – it made me realise what a fool I've been. That even though our people are gone, we are still alive and not being together is making a mockery of those who sacrificed their lives so that we might live." Briefly, his gaze flickered up to find Kylah in the front row, her face still and serious. She nodded once, as if in approval.

"I've wasted so much time," Nylex continued, then to the thrilled delight of every woman present he dropped to one knee in front of Fae. Fumbling in his waistcoat pocket, he drew out a small ring and held it up to her.

"I don't want to waste another second of my life by not being with you, so I'm asking you, Fae Moonshadow – no, I'm begging you. Will you marry me?" The room held its breath as Fae looked down into his hopeful face, then glanced at the ring in confusion.

"But that's the ring you had made for our wedding. I thought ... I assumed it was lost in the attack?"

"I had it in my pocket that night," he explained. "And I have carried it over my heart ever since. Fae, my love, will you?"

"Yes," she replied simply, then dropped to her knees in front of him and fell into his arms. He gathered her to him in a kiss that went on forever as the room around them erupted into cheers and Falcon beamed in avuncular approval.

"Splendid," he boomed. "Only too honoured to marry you. You let me know the when, and the where, and I will endeavour to oblige."

"Here, tomorrow." Scrambling to his feet, Nylex helped Fae to hers and looked at Falcon intently. "War is coming, and the future is uncertain. We have wasted so much time, Your Majesty. We don't want to waste another second of it being apart."

"Well, much as I appreciate the sentiment, my lad, one day isn't enough to organise a wedding. There are things to arrange – frocks, and flowers ... cake, and ... and such things ..." Out of his depth, he glanced at his wife who was teary-eyed and clutching her hands to her heart at the romance of the moment.

"Tell him, my dear," he pleaded. "Tell him it's impossible."

"Let me do it, Gramps." The crowd parted as Robin and her ladies pushed their way through, followed by an excited Clara. "We can do it," she insisted. "I'm expert at arranging things – you know I am – and I can do this."

"Robin, it's a lot to undertake in less than a day, are you sure you could manage such a feat?"

"I'm sure, and I won't be doing it alone. Franki and Tegan will help, and Clara, and Mother ...?" There was a swirl of skirts as Princess Maggie swept down off the dais.

"Of course, I'll help."

"And I." Queen Wren eagerly joined the group, along with several ladies-in-waiting, all excitedly chattering.

"Please trust me." Robin looked earnestly at Fae and Nylex. "I can do this. I can make this the most beautiful wedding ever if you let me. You have to trust me."

Fae and Nylex exchanged glances and he shrugged.

"I just want to be married to you. I don't care about the rest."

Fae's eyes softened, and she nodded at Robin. "We trust you and thank you."

"Marvellous," Robin exclaimed. "Right!" All crisp professionalism, she swept into action like a commander marshalling her troops. "Mother, Grandmother, Ladies, come with me. Gramps, we'll be using your meeting room." Falcon threw up his hands in resigned agreement. "Uncle Arden, attend us please, I need your advice about Dwarvian weddings."

"And me." Snow stepped forward eagerly. "I wish to help too. What can I do?"

Robin thought for a second, then waved Clara towards her. "Go with Clara and Fae, think 'wedding dress'. Clara is a magician with a needle, but even she cannot conjure up a new gown in less than a day. Clara, you have full access to my wardrobes. Use whatever you need, whatever Fae likes, take any court seamstresses you need away from their other duties – only have the perfect gown ready by sunset tomorrow."

"Yes, Miss." Clara bobbed a quick curtsey.

"All right." Robin clapped her hands. "We have less than a day, so there is not a moment to waste. Come, ladies, we have the perfect wedding to arrange."

Exuding purpose, Robin and her battalion swept from the room in a swirl of silk and taffeta, with Arden trailing behind.

A sudden silence descended upon the throne room, abruptly shattered by Falcon's bellow.

"Jacobson!"

"Your Majesty?" A lean, hard-faced woman clad in the leathers of an engineer stepped from the crowd.

"I want to know why that schoolhouse exploded. I want it fully explained to my satisfaction, and then I want complete reassurances that nothing like this can ever happen again."

"Your Majesty." Jacobson gave a bow and turned to leave, only to be stopped by Kylah.

"Could you use an extra pair of hands?"

"That depends." Jacobson eyed her up and down critically. "You know your way around a toolkit?"

"You see that airship I came in on?"

"Yep, nice lines, good turn of speed as I understand it."

"I built her from scratch."

"Nice." Jacobson raised her brows, slowly nodding her head. "Fine, I can always do with an extra body on my team. Could be you'll be useful." The women left the room, and Falcon surveyed the remaining members of his court with his hands on his hips.

"It seems there is to be a wedding here tomorrow at sunset. Out of respect for our guests, and in recognition of all that they have done for us, I expect all who possibly can to attend."

Another buzz of excited chatter swept through the room.

"And I expect you all to act immediately on any orders issued by the Princess Robin – however bizarre they might be."

Snow passed a very pleasant afternoon with Fae and Clara, going through Robin's royal wardrobes – and of those of Maggie and Wren, who sent their own lady's maids up to them with instructions to assist in any way possible.

Pouring large glasses of wine for them both, Snow quickly realised her main role was to calm and reassure Fae, who had surprisingly collapsed into a fit of nerves upon reaching her chamber. She wondered whether Robin had realised this would occur and sent Snow along as the only female friend Fae had. Well, there was Kylah – but at the thought of Kylah having an opinion about laces, trimmings, and the subtle difference in shading between heavy cream and ivory in a gown, Snow's lips twitched.

Finally, a gown was selected, appropriate alterations were decided upon, Fae's measurements were taken, and accessories were chosen. Clara and the other lady's maids bustled off to the rooms of the court seamstresses, promising to have the gown back before luncheon the next day for a final fitting.

Seeing Fae's eyes droop with exhaustion from the excitement of the day, and the two glasses of wine she had consumed, Snow left her to take a nap before dinner and returned to her room to rest and select her outfit for the evening meal.

There she managed to unlace her gown and lie upon her bed thinking about the day's events. Mostly, she thought about the look on Nylex's face when he believed Fae to be dead. His realisation that he had run out of time, and he would never see her again.

Curling onto her side, Snow tucked a hand under her cheek and thought about Ronin. She believed she loved him, and she believed he loved her. But was it the kind of love that Nylex had for Fae, and that Fae had for him? Was it the kind that would endure under pressure? Was it the kind that would last? Pondering on this, she fell into a light sleep.

The kitchen staff had taken it upon themselves to prepare a betrothal supper for the young, newly engaged couple, and when Snow walked into the banqueting hall that evening, she found it beautifully dressed in fresh greenery and vibrant blooms, and twinkling lights sparkling at every level.

Feeling more confident than the night before, she chose to sit further down the table with her friends, rather than on the top table with the other nobility and squeezed into a space next to Greta.

The atmosphere was merry, and spirits were high. All around people chatted excitedly about the day's events and the wedding to come. The food was delicious, and the wine flowed freely. Snow laughed and talked with her friends, able to push to one side thoughts of the coming war, and a throne that must be claimed.

Amidst it all, Nylex and Fae were encased in their own bubble of private happiness. With eyes only for one another, oblivious to the looks and comments of those all around, they sat so close there was barely a whisper of space between them.

Snow watched them. Their love was now obvious for all to see. She thought about the five long years they had been apart – and yet still their love had endured. Inviolate and unbreakable, their hearts had remembered and kept the flame of passion burning – and now it was free to blaze as fiercely as the flames that consumed the schoolhouse.

She saw Nylex whisper something in Fae's ear that had the pretty witch dimpling a blushing smile at him, her hand tightening over his where it lay on the table. Softly, she placed her hand on his cheek and the look in her eyes promised a lifetime of love, only for him.

Snow swallowed back the envious longing that caused a lump to rise in her throat. She knew they were thinking ahead to tomorrow – to their wedding, and the night that would follow when they would finally be together in every way possible.

She glanced at Ronin and found his eyes fixed upon her face. For once, she didn't look away, but met his gaze boldly, her cheeks burning at the thoughts she was thinking. Unashamed of the desire that leapt in her breast for him.

He looked away first, and she bit her lip in frustration. Despite their kiss earlier that day, despite all that happened since, she knew he still held firm to his honourable intentions. That even if their love was true and sincere – or maybe *because* it was – he was still going to walk away from her once the war was won and the throne was hers.

Chapter Twenty-Five

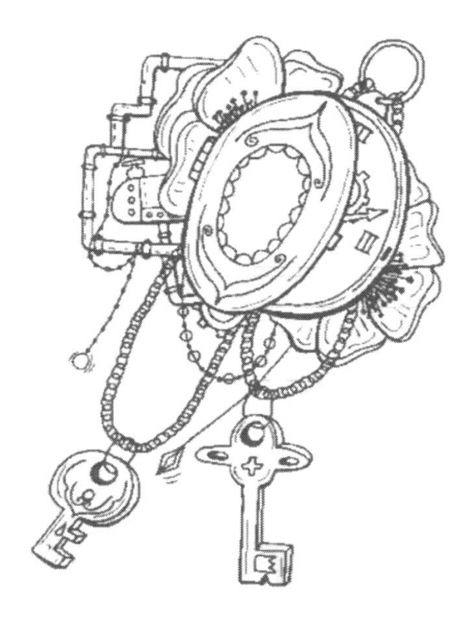

A Journal Full of Secrets

Next morning, Snow was woken early by a light tapping on the door. At her mumbled order to enter, it creaked open, and Fae stuck her head into the room.

Her eyes crinkled with kindly merriment at the sight of Snow struggling to sit up in bed, her hair mussed and her eyes squinting with sleep.

"I am sorry to awaken you so early, Snow. But I have a favour to request of you."

"Of course, what favour?" Snow asked.

Closing the door behind her, Fae pattered over the floor and clambered up onto the bed next to Snow.

"I was wondering if you would consider being my Maid of Honour?"

"Me?" Snow hitched herself up further on the bed and rubbed her eyes in surprise. "You want me to be your Maid of Honour?"

"Yes, I know we have not known each other very long, but I feel we have become very close, and I consider you one of my dearest friends."

Fae paused, then flashed a grin at Snow.

"I did ask Kylah as well, but the look of relief on her face when I said she didn't have to was comical."

"I can imagine." Snow grinned back. "Of course, I will, Fae. I would be honoured."

"Thank you, Snow. Clara will be along shortly to help you select a suitable gown. Choose whatever you think best. This wedding will be a simple affair, as there is no time for it to be anything else."

"Would you not rather wait? Do it properly once this is all over?"

"No." Fae considered the matter. "I have waited five long years for Nylex to come to his senses and lay down the burden of guilt that he insisted on carrying alone. I am not risking him having another change of heart," she smiled ruefully at Snow.

"And he is right that war is coming and that makes the future even more uncertain."

"Can you not tell what is going to happen? Can you see whether we live through this or not?"

"It does not work that way. Besides, I do not want fear of what might be to destroy my happiness in what is right now."

Fae planted a quick kiss on Snow's cheek then slid off the bed.

"I will see you later for our fittings – and thank you, Snow, for everything."

Downstairs, the castle hummed with frantic activity, and once breakfast was over, Snow found herself swept up into the whirlwind that was Robin's campaign.

Dashing about the castle with Franki and Tegan, she thoroughly enjoyed the frenzied busyness as they delivered messages, spoke to the musicians who were to play at the wedding, and chivvied the gardeners to deliver as much greenery and blooms as could be spared to the castle as soon as possible.

Leaving the others happily organising the construction of a bridal arch – apparently a crucial component of a Dwarvian wedding – Snow hurried to answer a summons from King Falcon to attend him in the meeting room as quickly as possible.

A man-at-arms was standing to attention outside the door as she approached, and Snow wondered whether she should tell him who she was. But before she even reached him, he was opening the door, announcing her arrival, and standing back so she could enter.

Inside, she found quite a crowd awaiting her. King Falcon and Prince Peregrine sat at either end of the long table, and, facing each other over the polished wooden surface were Arden, Grein, Greta, Ronin, Nylex, Kylah, and the chief engineer, Jacobson.

There were also other nobles, who Snow vaguely recognised as ones she had been introduced to, as well as several firm-jawed, and steely-eyed, commanders in uniform, both male and female.

Murmuring an apology for her tardiness, Snow slunk down into the one remaining empty chair, located between Ronin and Greta.

"Snow, thank you for joining us, my dear. I have asked you here because you alone among us are the only one with recent acquaintance with the key players in House White. Although we have received regular intelligence from our spies, it is patchy and fragmented, and cannot paint a whole picture."

"I see." Snow frowned at her hands clasped in her lap. "I'm not sure how useful I will be, Grandfather. As a woman, I was considerably sheltered from much that occurred at court – and of course, Pontifex Slie and Mirage were hardly going to share their plans or intentions with me."

"We understand that, but anything you can tell us may help. Any insights into the characters of these men could give us some clue as to their intentions. A war is waged by men, and it is only by understanding those men that we can gain a conclusion as swiftly and as painlessly as possible. Know thy enemy, Snow. It is an old but wise saying."

Taking a deep breath, Snow looked around at all those faces gazing expectantly back at her. She allowed herself a glance at

Ronin, and he smiled encouragingly at her, giving her the courage to draw back her shoulders and begin to speak.

Faltering at first, but then gaining confidence from the undivided attention all present gave her, she told them everything she could remember. Every comment she had heard, every action she had witnessed or heard tell of.

As she spoke, the royal scribe wrote down her words, occasionally interrupting her to request confirmation of what she had said. As she saw the pile of paper grow in front of him, she realised she had noticed more than she thought. That maybe, just maybe, she could be useful after all.

When she finally fell silent, her throat hoarse and her head pounding from the memories dredged from the darkest recesses of her mind, she gratefully sipped the water Ronin poured for her, and looked at her grandfather.

"There is no more. That is all I can recall that is of any import."

"It is well done," he told her gently. He turned to Greta. "What can you add to this, Aunt?"

"My intelligence is of course many years out of date," she warned. "But I will tell you what I know."

For an hour, Greta talked.

She told them of Elgin's growing suspicions of the underlying power the Contratulum was secretly amassing, of how he had shared this knowledge with his new bride, trusting in her sense and wisdom. Of how together they had planned to expose the Contratulum for the power-hungry and corrupt wielders of dark magic that they were.

Then Elgin had died – a stupid hunting accident that made no sense at all. Greta paused and looked steadily around the table. No sense at all, she explained, unless you *were* a power-hungry entity which would let nothing stand in the way of their plans.

Understanding her husband's death was not the accident it was claimed to be, Raven had bided her time.

Fearful for the child she carried, and for her own life, she acted the part of an ignorant and grieving woman. Wise, and capable of ruling the kingdom as regent for her baby daughter, she gave no hint that she was so much more than that.

Gradually, she built her network of informants and spies.

Slowly and carefully, she discovered who could be trusted and who could not. By planting seeds of rumour and lies, and seeing on whose lips they bore fruit, she weeded out the unreliable.

Over the five years following her husband's death, Queen Raven constructed an impressive web of contacts, agents, and methods of communication. Sending all the information she gathered back to the one person she trusted above all others – King Falcon, her father.

But then something went wrong.

Somehow, she was betrayed, and in an instant, the work of years came crashing down about her ears. The Contratulum grew wise to her schemes and plans, and so they removed her by means of a poisoned apple.

Falcon's face grew dark when Greta spoke of the last hours of Raven's life, of their fight to save her, and her despair when they realised it was to no avail.

Dabbing furiously at her eyes, Greta told of Raven's last meeting with her beloved daughter, and of her fear at leaving her behind to face the enemy who had murdered both her parents.

Her voice lowering to a husky whisper, Greta spoke of the vow that she had made to protect Snow to the best of her abilities. Here, she turned to take Snow's hand in hers.

"And I did try to do that, my child. You must believe I did my best. Even when they grew suspicious of me and sent me away, I tried to protect you by sending you a sprig of witch hazel every year, imbued with the most potent enchantments I could think of."

"I know you did." Snow squeezed her aunt's hand in return. "And you did save my life. Without your spells, Mirage would have broken my mind many years ago, and I wouldn't have had the courage to kill the guard who wanted to hurt me. Without your summoning spell, Ronin would never have found me and brought me home. And without your knowledge of medicinal herbs, I would have died before I reached Grein. Thank you, Aunt. You have more than fulfilled your vow to my mother."

"Bless you, child." Greta patted her hand, her eyes brimming over with thankful tears. "Bless you." Fumbling about her person for a kerchief, she gratefully took the one Grein gallantly offered her, blew her nose loudly, and handed it back to him.

"I only wish," she continued, "that Raven's journal had not been taken. If only we had that, then we would have access to all of her knowledge."

"Journal?" Falcon looked at her with interest. "Raven trusted her knowledge to a journal. What if it had been seized by the Contratulum?"

"Oh, it was," Greta informed him grimly. "After the funeral I searched for it, intending to place it far beyond their reach by sending it to you. But I was too late. Her chambers were stripped bare and its hiding place discovered."

"Then the Contratulum know everything that my mother knew?" Snow cried.

"No, child, your mother was too cunning for that. Everything was in the journal, yes, but it was protected by a powerful spell. None but those carrying her blood and possessing the key could open it. The Contratulum have the journal, yes, but much good it will do them. They cannot open it, and if they use too much force the journal is enchanted to ignite."

"Still, it would be very useful if the journal was in safe hands, would it not?" Falcon asked, exchanging a glance with Peregrine.

"Well, very useful, of course, but it is lost, so..."

Greta's voice trailed away as Peregrine unwrapped a large beautifully decorated leather-bound book and slid it up the table towards her.

"Oh, my ..." she gasped.

"Is this the journal?" Peregrine asked as Greta clutched at it in shock.

"Yes, this is it, but I don't understand. How did you come by it?"

"Three years ago, our operative within the Contratulum finally gained high enough status to have access to their workshops. He saw them working on the journal and recognised it as the one previously belonging to Queen Raven. Guessing its worth to be incalculable, and fearful if the Contratulum somehow gained admittance to it that his own and many other lives would be at risk, he arranged for a fire to break out in the workshop one night. In all the confusion, he managed to smuggle the journal out and send it to us."

"This is a miracle!" Greta exclaimed and hugged the book to her chest.

"But we still need the key," Snow cried. "Without the key, the journal is still inaccessible to us."

"Oh, child," Greta's eyes twinkled at Snow over the top of the book. "You have the key. You've had it all along."

"I have the key ...?" Snow stopped, then fumbled for her chatelaine. "Of course," she murmured, her mind flashing back to her mother's words. "Here."

She thrust the key at Greta who laid the book reverently, gently down on the table. Inserting the key into its lock, she eased it around.

All around the table leant forward and held their breath as the lock gave with a slight click and Greta opened the stiff leather cover, which creaked in protest.

Peering over the old woman's shoulder, Snow saw a page of neat handwriting and realised it must be her mother's.

Her heart trembled at the notion.

As if he could read her thoughts, Ronin softly brushed a hand over her arm.

"Remarkable," Falcon breathed. "To think that for all these years it has remained locked, guarding its secrets, waiting for the right person to reveal them to."

"Here."

Greta pushed the journal along the table towards the King.

"Take it. May it finally be the weapon that Raven always intended it to be."

"Oh, but ..." Snow began, then fell silent as Falcon turned his penetrating gaze upon her.

"I understand, Snow," he said. "And trust me, if there is ought in here intended for you, I shall ensure you see it."

"Thank you," she murmured.

"Now, then." Falcon looked around the table. "It is time to put all talk of war and intrigue to one side, for I believe there is a young man here who is about to discover the delights of being a husband."

Smirks and grins were bent Nylex's way, who reddened and smiled at the implication behind Falcon's teasing words.

"Your Majesty," he said.

"Let us reconvene this time tomorrow, and by then there will have been time to examine the contents of the journal and see if they can aid us in our endeavour. But in the meantime, we all have a wedding to attend, and a young couple to toast. I suggest we adjourn for now and prepare for what my granddaughter is insisting will be the most perfect of weddings."

Leaving the council room with the others, Snow was rushed at by Robin, who had a wild, slightly feral glint to her eye, and was apparently unaware that she was trailing a length of ribbon from the heel of her shoe.

"There you are," she exclaimed. "Go, hurry, Clara is waiting for you in your room with Fae. You need to help her get the bride ready, and you need to get ready yourself."

"But there's still plenty of time," Snow protested, as Robin grabbed her by the arm and dragged her towards the door. "There is at least an hour until sunset."

"And so much to do in that hour," Robin wailed. "I do not believe it is possible to achieve it all, but it must be done. So, you go and help the bride, and get ready yourself. I will send the bride's escort and the head groomsman up to escort you down in an hour."

"Oh?" exclaimed Snow with interest. "Who ...?"

"Go!" Robin demanded and pushed her towards the grand staircase. "No time for questions, just go."

Slightly afraid of the maniacal gleam in her cousin's eye, Snow went.

Upon entering her room, she discovered it to be a whirl of silk and satin, lace, and flowers. Fae sat calmly on a chair amidst the chaos, having her hair twisted upwards by Clara into an elaborate and beautiful hairstyle, while Franki and Tegan bounced around the room like enthusiastic puppies promised a walk.

"We thought it would be more fun to get ready here," Tegan explained upon seeing her.

"We have wine," Franki added, waving a bottle.

"So, I see," Snow replied in amusement. She met Fae's eyes in the mirror and smiled when the pretty witch rolled her eyes at her.

"What are you wearing?" Franki asked.

"This." Snow opened the wardrobe door to reveal her gown in all its splendour. Thinking it too fancy for a simple wedding, and not wanting to outshine Fae in any way, Snow had originally passed it over. But then Fae's eyes had lit up upon seeing it, and she had gently pulled it from the hanger and held it up to Snow.

"It's perfect," she had said. "Please wear it."

Now as the two girls oohed and aahed and rushed to stroke its shimmering gold perfection, Snow crossed over to Fae and lightly dropped a hand to her shoulder.

"How are you holding up?"

"I am holding up just fine," Fae replied, then took a deep breath. "I am getting married. I cannot believe it is finally happening. All these long, lonely years I never dared to hope that this day might come. Now it has, I intend to cherish every moment of it."

"Wine?" Franki offered and proffered the bottle again.

"Why not?" Fae laughed. "Wine for everyone – even you, Clara."

"No Miss. I couldn't."

"I insist, Clara. And as it's my wedding day you can deny me nothing."

Perching on a chair beside the dressing table, Snow sipped her wine and watched as Clara continued to work her magic on Fae's hair. Delicate flowers were threaded through the auburn tresses on skeins of silk that matched Fae's hair colour so precisely it looked as though the blooms were suspended there unaided.

"You look beautiful," Snow murmured, and Fae dimpled a smile over the rim of her glass.

"All brides are beautiful, Miss," Clara said slightly disapprovingly, then she unbent enough to smile at Fae's reflection. "But some are more beautiful than others."

"Robin said your escort and the head groomsman will come to take us to the wedding. Who did you choose to walk you down the aisle?"

"Arden, of course," Fae replied. "He is the closest thing to a father that I have. As to who the groomsman might be, I do not know who Nylex asked. Although I can guess."

And Snow should have guessed whom Nylex would ask to stand with him on his wedding day. When the knock came at the chamber door an hour later, and Franki and Tegan dashed to open it, she should have been expecting it to be Ronin standing tall beside Arden.

Promising to see them after the ceremony, Franki and Tegan sidled past the two men, pausing to glance up and down at Ronin's wedding finery and flash conspiratorial grins in Snow's direction.

"One moment," Clara insisted. She finished tying the laces on Fae's corset with an ornate bow, shook out her skirts, then stepped back for a last, critical look.

"You'll do, Miss," she said, dabbing at her suspiciously dewy eyes. She bobbed a quick curtsey and scurried from the room to take her place with the other servants, who had all been given leave to witness the ceremony.

"Will I do, Arden?" Fae asked as the men entered the room.

"Aye, lass," he cleared his throat and looked her up and down.

The gown was perfect. A rich creamy white that acted as a foil to her glowing auburn hair. The dress was simple, beyond the design of flowers woven into the fabric of the skirts. On the neckline of the corset was a row of silk flowers of cream and pale gold, which picked out the blooms sewn into her hair.

"You'll do," he said gruffly and held out his arm to her. "You'll do."

Snow handed Fae the bouquet of wildflowers that had been delivered to the castle earlier. A gift from Miss Cooper and the children, the card had read. Upon receiving it, Fae had been adamant that she would carry this simple memento of thanks and no other.

"Then take me to be married," Fae replied, placing her hand on his arm.

"It will be my honour." Arden smiled at the young woman he had long considered his daughter.

Elegantly, they swept from the room. Ronin smiled at Snow.

"You look lovely," he said. "I do like your dress."

Snow blushed and let her fingers brush lightly over the cloth-of-gold skirts of the ornate gown. Fearful the gown would overshadow the bride's simpler attire, she now realised that nothing she wore could ever compete with the glow on Fae's face and the brilliance of her smile.

"Snow," he began. "What happened earlier, in the council room, your mother's journal ..."

"Hush," she told him. "Not now, not here. There will be time enough tomorrow to discuss plans and strategies and warfare. Tonight, we are standing with our friends at their wedding. They have waited so long and suffered so much, that nothing can be allowed to mar this perfect moment for them. So, please, for one night, can we forget everything else?"

She smiled at him and took his hand.

"I want to witness my friends pledging their love for each other. I want to eat wonderful food, drink delicious wine, and laugh with my friends and newly found family. I want to dance the night away and forget, for now, that I am Princess Snow of House White, and that many will probably die to put me on a throne I don't particularly want but must claim for the sake of my people. So, I am asking you, Ronin. Can you forget with me?"

He hesitated, his eyes kindly as they lingered on her beautiful face, her dark eyes alive with warmth and hope. Then he smiled and held out an arm to her as Arden had to Fae.

"Yes," he agreed. "I can forget with you for one night, Snow."

Chapter Twenty-Six

A Night to Forget Everything

Reaching the great courtyard where the ceremony was to be held, Snow let out a gasp of delighted astonishment. Although she had watched the courtyard being arranged under Robin's critical supervision, to see it now in all its completed splendour was a magnificent sight.

With the going down of the sun and the gathering gloom, the rows of twinkling lights strung overhead had been lit, and their soft glow illuminated the happy faces of the assembled guests.

The potted trees which lined the perimeter were strung with coloured lanterns that glowed in the twilight. As many rows of chairs as possible had been squeezed in to accommodate all those gathered to witness the wedding of the pair of Dwarvians. Garlands of flowers looped from chair-to-chair culminating in great falls of sweet-smelling blooms at each row's end.

At the head of the aisle, a dais had been constructed, upon which a graceful arch of foliage and flowers made a focal point. Under the arch, Nylex paced nervously, and Falcon stood ready to unite the pair in his official capacity as monarch.

Arden and Fae were waiting inside the vast doors of the great banqueting hall which opened onto the courtyard. The hall, as well, had been magnificently decorated, its long tables laid ready for the sumptuous feast which would be served upon completion of the ceremony.

"There you are," Robin exclaimed, appearing from nowhere and fussing about Snow's gown, shaking out the skirts and straightening the laces on her gold-embroidered corset.

"I'll signal the musicians to start, then give me a moment to reach my seat before proceeding." She paused before Fae and took a deep breath.

"It's all perfect," the young bride assured her. "It all looks so beautiful and so magical. Thank you, Robin. Thank you for all your hard work."

"You're welcome. It was the least I could do. Right. You ready to do this?"

"I have been ready for this moment all of my life," Fae told her.

Robin squeezed Fae's hand, nodded at Snow, then slipped out of the doors.

A second later they heard the lilting refrain of what Snow had been told was a traditional Dwarvian wedding tune, which the musicians had hastily learnt that day.

"Shall we?" Arden asked, gesturing towards the doors.

"Yes," Fae replied calmly, placing her hand on his arm.

Snow had never been to a wedding before. Having no preconceptions, she was utterly charmed by the beauty and quiet simplicity of the occasion. Escorted down the aisle by Arden, Fae had eyes only for the tall, dark man awaiting her under the arch.

His gaze never left hers. Handsome in borrowed finery, the look on his face when he saw Fae coming towards him made Snow swallow down a lump of pure, painful emotion. Unable to stop herself, she glanced at Ronin.

Their eyes clashed. He felt it too – she knew he did. For a moment, she allowed a wild dart of hope to pierce her heart. Somehow, she had to make him understand that a world without him in it, was a world she did not want. Robin's words echoed through her mind – *that's the thing about being a queen, you can do whatever you want* – But could she? Could she defy all convention and do what *she* wanted?

Maybe. But that was a concern for the future, and as Fae had said, why let fears for the future destroy her happiness right now? He had promised her tonight. Snow fully intended to make good use of that time to make it as hard as possible for him to walk away from her.

His voice kind and gruff, Falcon spoke the ancient words of the binding ceremony. Words that, once spoken, could never be undone except by death. Listening to the beautiful vows being exchanged by Nylex and Fae, Snow allowed herself wonderful daydreams of what-ifs and maybes.

Then the ceremony was over, and they were filing back into the banqueting hall to enjoy the wonderful feast the kitchen staff had spent the last twenty-four hours preparing. As the Maid of Honour, Snow had a seat at the top table, and as the Groomsman, so did Ronin.

Never had Snow enjoyed a meal more. Surrounded by the laughter and easy talk of her friends, she bloomed with happiness, and her smile gladdened all who saw it. Picking up on her mood, and maybe remembering his promise, Ronin too cast his usual taciturn manner aside to tease and joke with her.

Dinner over, the guests wandered back out to the courtyard. In their absence, servants had toiled to move all the chairs to the edges to create a large area for dancing. As the wedding party emerged into the balmy glow of the evening, the musicians struck up a gay, lilting refrain that had Fae turning to Nylex in delight and pulling him into the centre of the floor.

Laughingly protesting about two left feet, he still placed one hand lightly about her waist and took her right hand in his. As he spun

Fae around in a complete circle under his arm, her skirts whirled, and she threw back her head in a happy laugh.

The musicians picked up the pace, and the couple spun around the floor as the onlookers clapped and cheered. To Snow's delight, on the upward sweep of the fiddles, Nylex clasped Fae around the waist and lifted her off her feet, spinning around to set her gently back down and rush breathlessly back into the dance.

"That looks like fun," Robin exclaimed beside them and grasped Arden by the hand. "Please tell me you know how to do this, Uncle?"

"Of course," he replied. "It's a traditional Dwarvian dance played at every wedding, so I ..."

"Good," she cried and pulled him onto the floor.

Then Franki was dancing with a delightedly blushing Eli, and Tegan had pulled a mildly protesting Grein after them. Bowing formally to an overwhelmed Greta, Prince Peregrine escorted her onto the dance floor. One by one, other couples joined them, quickly learning the simple steps until the dance floor was filled with whoops and hollers as the men swept the women off their feet in swirls of skirts and petticoats.

Galloping madly past her, Robin sent Snow a meaningful look as her eyes darted in Ronin's direction. Snow hesitated. Did she dare? Then she remembered her promise to herself to forget all constraints and duties that night, and merely live in the moment.

"Do you know this dance?" she asked Ronin.

"Yes."

"Then teach it to me," she ordered and pulled him onto the floor.

The dance was repetitive and easy. Snow quickly picked it up as Ronin's firm hand on her waist guided her through the steps. Laughing and whooping when he swept her up, she beamed with delighted joy, and he smiled back, enjoying her uncomplicated merriment.

On and on the musicians played, seeming to understand that none wanted the dance to end too soon. As she was whirled past with Ronin, Snow saw King Falcon and Queen Wren performing a more sedate version of the dance.

Out of the corner of her eye, she saw Kylah and the chief engineer, Jacobson, sitting at a table on the side of the dance floor. They were talking to one another intently, and the next time Snow was whirled about by Ronin she saw Jacobson lay a hand over Kylah's, and she wondered.

When the dance finally ended with a resounding wail of the fiddles, all were invigorated and ready to dance all night. Caught up in the atmosphere created by sparkling lights, the scent of blossom from the trees, and the full-bodied wine being circulated by the servants, the guests eagerly swept into the next dance, which was a more sedate waltz.

Held firmly in Ronin's arms, Snow let out a heady sigh of complete happiness and briefly rested her cheek on his chest.

"Are you having a good time?" he murmured.

"Yes, the best time. I wish we could stay like this forever."

"Your wish is my command, Highness. This night will last for as long as you desire it to, and the dawn will never come."

"Oh, how I wish that were true."

"I wish it was in my power to give you all that you desire, Snow."

"But it is," she replied, and looked up into his face, shocked by her boldness.

"Snow ..." he whispered. The teasing light faded in his eyes to be replaced by a longing so intense it burnt right down to her bones.

"Walk with me," she gently commanded. "I need some air." Realising how ridiculous a statement that was – after all, they were already outside – she nevertheless tugged gently at his hand and led him from the dance floor. She pushed their way through the masses who ringed the courtyard, laughing and talking, goblets of wine and ale clasped in their hands, and he followed her without protest.

Crossing the banqueting hall – now deserted except for servants scurrying about clearing away the remnants of the feast – she led him out onto the balcony which hung over the sheer drop down to the valley floor below.

Twinkling lights had been strung here as well, and the scent of night-flowering jasmine was heavy on the evening air as they reached the balustrade, stopping to lean on it and simply gaze out into the night. Silence fell between them. Now that she had achieved her goal of getting him alone, Snow had no idea how to proceed. She felt awkward and ill at ease.

There was a rustle in the shrubbery at the far end of the balcony, and Arden the cat emerged. His eyes glinting in the gloom, he surveyed them over the dangling body of the snake he was clutching in his jaws.

"Oh, my," Snow exclaimed. "He caught a snake?"

"He did," Ronin grinned. "But he had better not let Kylah see it. She's petrified of the things."

"She is?" Snow raised a brow at him. "That is surprising. I always believed her scared of nothing."

"Don't be fooled by her tough exterior. Inside, Kylah is as soft as the rest of us, and there is much that she fears."

"Such as?"

"Snakes. That she won't always be there to protect Eli. That she will never again find a love like the one she shared with Lissa."

"Did that not concern you?"

"What?"

"Well, because they were both women."

"No. Why should it have done? Lissa was a grown woman and free to love wherever she chose."

"It is frowned upon in my kingdom. I do not believe it ever happens there."

"Oh, Snow," he laughed at her naivety. "Trust me, it happens. And why not? Love is love, and it comes in many shapes and sizes."

"I suppose so," she said, then smiled at him. "Is this yet one more thing on the list of changes I must make when I become queen?"

"Maybe," he agreed. Silence fell between them again, but this time it was a companionable one, as both reflected on private thoughts.

"Ronin."

"Yes?"

"May I talk with you?"

"Talk with me?" He looked puzzled. "But is that not what we have been doing?"

"No, not really. There are things I wish to say. Things that I know you believe would be better left unsaid, and maybe that is the wisest course of action. But tonight is not a night for wisdom. Tonight is a night for sharing what is in my heart."

"Snow ..."

"No, please let me finish. You promised me tonight, Ronin – one night. That is all I am asking of you. War is coming. We both know it is inevitable. And with war comes pain and misery and death. You could die. I could die. This might be the last time we are ever able to be together like this, as friends. For we are friends, are we not?"

"Yes," he said, and his hand was warm on hers. "The best of friends."

"And maybe more?"

"Maybe," he reluctantly agreed. "But as I have said before, Snow, I cannot live in your world and you cannot live in mine. So, whatever our feelings are, friendship is all that can ever lie between us."

"So, you have said," she shrugged irritably. "But for tonight, I wish us to put all that to one side. Did you see the look on Nylex's face when he thought Fae was dead? That he had lost her forever, and never had a chance to tell her what was in his heart."

"Yes, I did."

"Well, I do not wish to look in the mirror and see that look on my own face."

"What are you saying, Snow?"

"I am saying that I love you Ronin. I do not know how and when it exactly came upon me, I only know it to be the truth. I love you. There can be no other for me. And I understand you think I am too young to be so sure. That I am inexperienced in the ways of the world and of men, and maybe you are right. But I can only state what I feel in my heart right now, at this moment, and that is that I love you Ronin – with every fibre of my being, I love you."

"Snow, it cannot be, you know this."

"No, I do not know it. I only know that you think it, which is probably the same thing. But for tonight, Ronin, just for tonight, can you not put aside your doubts and worries, and tell me what is in your heart? I will live on those words for the rest of my life if I must, but we are going into war, and our lives may not be as long as we think."

He turned away from her and braced his hands on the balustrade. Looking up at the moon shining serenely above them, he took a deep breath, then looked at where she stood, gazing quietly back at him. Something changed in his eyes, and he raised a hand to her cheek, cupping it in his warm palm, he bent into her.

"For tonight. For tonight only, I will be honest with you, Snow. I will allow myself to open up and tell you what is in my heart. But this can only be for tonight, for on the morrow we must become different people. War is coming, and you are right, our futures will be uncertain. You are also right in that should anything happen to you, and I did not take this chance to be with you, then I would regret it for the rest of my days."

Tears pricked at her eyes and she rubbed her cheek into his palm, feeling the rasp of his calloused hand against her soft skin.

"I love you, Snow. I love the Snow that got covered in dirt cleaning a room for the very first time. The Snow who greedily ate all the blackberries. The Snow who loves dogs, and dancing, and listening to stories. The Snow who swallowed down her fear and flew for the very first time. The Snow who is kind and loves her friends and family. And most of all, I love the Snow who dressed in leathers and learnt how to fly my ship. That's the Snow I love."

"You do love me," she whispered.

"I love that Snow," he corrected. "The Snow I cannot love is the Princess Snow. The Snow who can command an entire kingdom to go to war for her. The Snow who has the most powerful king in the world for a grandfather. The Snow who has had to negotiate her way through the political intrigues and machinations of the royal houses.

And most of all, I cannot love the Snow who will become Queen Snow, my sovereign, to whom I must swear allegiance."

"But she is one and the same."

"Not to me, she isn't."

"For tonight then," she replied, her heart cracking at his words. "For one night, can we just pretend? Can we make believe that we are simply normal people attending the wedding of our dearest friends? Can we dance and drink and laugh and be together? That is all I want from you, Ronin. Just for tonight, can I be your Snow?"

"Yes," he briefly closed his eyes. "For one night you can be my Snow."

"Then kiss me," she murmured. "Kiss me the way you would kiss the Snow you love."

Gently, he took her into his arms and looked down into her face. The moonlight glittered in the depths of her dark eyes as he bent his head to hers. Then his lips brushed softly over hers and he felt her quiver in anticipation.

It was his undoing.

Crushing her to his chest, his hands plunged into the silken mass of her hair, and his mouth took what she was offering.

It was a kiss that exceeded all that had gone before. The desperate kiss of lovers who knew they were soon to be parted forever. It was a kiss that cried for the love that it contained – a love that simply could not be.

The next morning, Snow was awakened by the sound of shouting far below in the courtyard, and the tramp of booted feet on the flagstones. Confused, she sat up in bed and listened.

It had been late when Ronin finally escorted her to her door, and she remembered the way he looked at her. As if he were committing her to memory. As if he expected never to see her again.

Her emotions swirling, for a wild moment, Snow wanted to pull him into the room after her and forget all that she was and all she must become, just to be with him in every way possible. But she knew she could not – that she must not. Ronin had made his feelings clear, and she could not ask him to besmirch his honour.

There was time for one last look that said everything, then he opened her door and pushed her gently inside. Snow stood, her forehead to the cool wood of the door, and placed her palm flat beside her. On the other side of the door, she sensed Ronin do the same, then she heard his footsteps walking away.

Snow swallowed down the tears of regret. Kicking off her shoes, she took her aching feet to bed – only wishing her aching heart could so easily be soothed.

In the cold light of the early morning, Snow hung her head at the memory, and a moment later there was an urgent knock at the door. At her bid to enter, a maid stuck her head into the room.

"Yes?"

"Begging your pardon, Your Highness, but King Falcon requests your presence immediately in the council room."

"What is it? What has happened?"

"I don't know, Your Highness. I only know a message arrived early this morning and now the whole castle is in an uproar with soldiers and commanders all over the place."

"Is it war? Is it already upon us?"

"I don't know, Miss." The maid trembled with fear and Snow didn't correct her breach of etiquette. "I'm sure I don't know anything other than the King wishes to see you now."

"Then help me into my gown," Snow ordered, throwing back the bedclothes. Her head spun slightly as she stood up.

"Yes, Miss." The maid rushed to obey. Snow hastily pulled yesterday's gown off the screen where it had been thrown, stepping into it, and turning so the maid could help her with the corset and lace her up.

Hurrying downstairs, a scant ten minutes later, Snow saw servants scurrying about in a panic, and heard the bellow of shouted orders in the courtyard outside, where the remnants of the wedding were still in evidence.

Entering the throne room, she pushed her way through the crowds of nobles who huddled in gaggles, urgently conferring with one another. By their general state of dishevelment, Snow concluded they, too, had been roused from their beds unexpectedly early.

She reached the council chamber. Two men-at-arms opened the doors, and she hurried inside, stopping short at the sight of Falcon leaning over the table on which a large map had been spread. On the faces of all within the room, she saw grim despair and knew what she feared was the truth.

"What's happened?" she cried. "Is this ..."

"War?" Falcon answered. "Yes, although I am confused by the manner of its beginning."

"Why?" she asked. "What has occurred?"

"There's been an attack. Almost an entire village has been massacred."

"No." She sank into a nearby chair, her lungs struggling for air under her stays. "I am so sorry. Which of your villages was it?"

"That's the whole crux of the matter," Falcon barked. "It wasn't a House Avis village."

"Then I don't understand," Snow murmured. "If not House Avis, then whose?"

"House White. Late last night, soldiers wearing the House Avis insignia attacked the village of Arrowford, just over the border into the Kingdom of House White. They laid waste to it, killing almost every man, woman, and child."

"But that makes no sense," Snow gasped. "Why would the Contratulum attack their own people? It makes no sense at all."

"It makes perfect sense." Ronin pushed through the crowds to face the king. "They wanted to start a war with you, but they knew their people would never countenance an outright act of aggression on the part of House White. So, what's the one thing they needed?"

"A motive," Falcon ground out.

"And now that House Avis has apparently attacked first, a motive is the very thing they have."

Chapter Twenty-Seven

Articles of War

Hurling all his weapons into the basket without being reminded, Mirage waited impatiently for the young prelate to activate the lever and open the door into Slie's office. Marching furiously across the darkened room, for once he spared no thought as to the dimensions of the chamber, nor of what could be lying in the shadows beyond.

Reaching the desk where the Pontifex sat calmly looking at some papers, Mirage did not wait to be invited to speak. Instead, he slapped both his hands down on the table and leant aggressively forward to snarl one word into Slie's face.

"Why?"

The Pontifex looked at him. Brows raised, he continued to stare Mirage down in a silence laden with his power and absolute right of supremacy. Against his will, Mirage felt his eyes lower, and his shoulders relax.

Finally, Mirage stepped away from the desk, his arms dropping to his sides in defeat and an angry flush rising on his cheeks. Even though he had won, and he knew it, Slie continued to stare until at last Mirage sank into the other chair and waited.

"My dear boy." The sarcasm was ripe on the word 'boy'. "Something appears to be vexing you?"

"I have heard the news."

"And what news would that be?"

"Arrowford."

"Ah, yes. A regrettable necessity."

"Almost every soul within the village was butchered. By our troops!"

"Come, come. Do not behave as though you are appalled by such an act. We both know you are capable of far worse."

"But these were our people. They were innocent."

"There are no innocents in war – you should know that. As to them being our people, they were merely fodder. Convenient props in the charade that had to be acted out."

"Charade? What charade?"

"Think about it calmly, boy. We needed a reason to go to war against House Avis, we now have a reason, the unwarranted, brutal attack upon an innocent village by the vicious troops of House Avis."

"But they were our men."

"Yes, but the people do not know that. The soldiers were wearing the House Avis insignia, ergo, they were Avian troops."

Mirage stared at him. Aghast at the calculated coldness of the scheme, and reluctantly admiring the sheer brilliance behind it, his mind raced as it grasped the implications.

"So, has House Avis responded?"

"Not yet, the news will barely have had time to reach them."

"Why was I not informed of this plan?"

"It was of the utmost secrecy. Only those who absolutely had to knew of it, and even they were only informed at the last minute. Believe me, I wanted to tell you, but it was decided the risk was too great."

Slie's eyes would not meet his and Mirage knew this to be a lie. Even though Slie paid lip service to the Council of the Elders, it was no secret that he held all the reins of power within his fleshy hands. If Slie had wished him to be informed of the planned attack, then no contradictory bleating by any Elder would have stopped him.

No, Mirage was not informed because Slie did not wish him to be. Not for the first time, Mirage wearily wondered how much more he had to do before Slie would trust him. How many other body parts did he have to sacrifice?

"When we attack one of their villages in retaliation to their supposed attack, with what force can we then expect House Avis to respond?" he asked, and Slie's eyes gleamed at the question.

"Considerable," he purred, steepling his fingers and looking at Mirage over them with intense satisfaction. "But of course, it matters not the might of their army, for whatever the size it will pale into insignificance once we show our hand, and finally reveal what it is we have been working on all these years."

"The airships," Mirage murmured.

"The airships indeed," Slie agreed.

"And the coronation? That is a mere five days away. Am I allowed to ask how plans are progressing on that?"

"Ah – now there I do have some interesting news for you. As you are aware, we have – or should I say had – a spy within the old lady's household – she who was nurse to the princess."

"Had?" Mirage picked up on the word instantly. "Your spy is dead?"

"Yes. Sadly, her brain suffered irrevocable damage when ordered to kill her mistress."

"Why did you do that? I thought the old lady harmless and of no interest? I am astonished at how long you kept the spy in place, considering how many years the old lady has lived blamelessly to the point of boredom?"

"Everyone has the potential to be of interest, my dear boy, and sometimes it is the longest game that produces the most surprising results. The child spy reported to us that her mistress had a group of visitors. Strangers who had appeared out of nowhere from the Great Forest."

"Really?" Mirage leaned forward in interest. "Did she say who they were?"

"Well, the old lady told her they were her family, which is curious. As you know, the nurse came with Raven from House Avis when she married Elgin, so that would make her Avian, and any family she might have, Avian as well."

"And were they?"

"Were they what?"

"Avian!" Mirage knew that the Pontifex was deliberately doling out the information in the meanest portions possible, enjoying the power being the one with the knowledge gave him.

"No, they turned out to be something much more interesting."

"Which was?"

"Well, my dear boy." Leaning back in his chair, the Pontifex selected a large orange from the bowl to his right, picked up a knife from his desk and slowly began to pare the peel away from it. "We activated the remote viewing device we had put in the child's brain when she was a youngster, and the order was relayed that she was to kill her mistress."

"Why? Why kill the old lady? Surely bringing her in for interrogation would have been more sensible?"

Slie let a long sliver of peel drop to the polished wood of his desk. "That would have been my decision as well, but the commander in charge of the outpost near Thornfield was not as level-headed as you and I. He overstepped his authority and gave the order that the old lady should be disposed of, without waiting for my orders – a decision he has come to bitterly regret."

Slie paused as the last curl of peel dropped to the desk, then dug his large fingers into either side of the orange. Juice squirted as the fruit was torn apart, segment by segment, and fed into Slie's fleshy red mouth.

Patiently, Mirage waited. Almost amused by the little games Slie liked to play, he wondered exactly when he had learnt to see right through them. As if disappointed at Mirage's lack of response, Slie seemed to lose his enjoyment of the sport and wiped his mouth and fingers on a snowy white napkin.

"Yes, that unfortunate commander now has a very long time to reflect on his actions. A very long time indeed."

Not dead then, Mirage thought, but probably wishing he were. The oubliettes under the castle were dark and deep, not many emerged once banished to them.

"However, here is where it gets interesting. The child was stopped from carrying out her orders by intervention from a very unexpected source."

"What?"

"It would be more apt to enquire, 'who'?"

"Very well, who?"

"Why, none other than our missing princess."

"Snow? Snow was at Thornfield?"

"In the flesh, as it were."

Mirage sat back in stunned bemusement, his mind racing at the news. Snow was alive – or had been a few days ago. Alive! Surprised at how much this news pleased him, Mirage kept these feelings far from his features and raised a brow at the Pontifex.

"My, that is ... unexpected."

"Isn't it just? But it gets better. The child overheard them talking, and the two men who had arrived with Snow were none other than Dwarvians – as, it appears – so too was her old nursemaid."

"Dwarvians?!"

This time Mirage could not contain his surprise. His mind raced back to that long-ago encounter with his father in the dungeons far below his feet. Feeling a twinge in his heart at the memory, he angrily shut it down.

"But I believed we had eradicated that problem forever?"

"So, did I, my dear boy, so did I. But it appears a few survived. Not many, as I understand it, but still, a few. Truly, these people must be kin to cockroaches. Their survival capabilities are beyond astonishing."

"So – Snow was found by this band of Dwarvians hiding within the forest, and they took her to her old nurse? But why? Why risk her life for the sake of a sentimental visit with a woman she has not seen in years?"

"That I cannot answer."

"Snow is no fool, she would have known the risk she was taking. If she went to see the old woman then it was for a reason – an important reason."

"It may be a moot point," Slie continued. "I told you that the child was stopped from killing her mistress. Well – it was Snow who intervened, and during the struggle, she was stabbed herself."

"Snow was killed?"

"No – I said Snow was stabbed. Inconveniently, our spy died of a severe conflict within her brain before we could establish whether the princess was killed or not. For all we know, she has since died of her injuries."

"I see." Mirage considered the information calmly, the mechanical half of his heart labouring to keep up with the wildly pumping human half. "So, it would appear Snow has enlisted the aid of these Dwarvians. Yet why would they help her?"

"Why indeed? One can only surmise that they, too, are playing a long game. Tell me, who is the one person who could help shake off their pariah status and live their lives without fear?"

"Queen Snow," Mirage muttered. "If they have aided her, then maybe it was in return for her promise to help them in exchange."

"Precisely. Now – on their own, a handful of pathetic Dwarvians would be no threat. But allied with a princess who is part of the most powerful family in the known world, what do you believe their next move will be?"

Mirage thought about Snow's family – her pathetic letch of a stepfather and a spiteful aunt who had already made one attempt on her life. She could look for no help there. But, further back along her familial tree ...

"Falcon," he said slowly. "She'd go to Falcon. He is the obvious choice. As her grandfather, he would be honour-bound to offer her sanctuary at the very least."

"And at the very most?"

"He would help her ascend to her throne. It would be in his own best interests to ensure that it is a grateful granddaughter who wears the crown – not an estranged and bitter daughter such as Jay, nor a weak fool like Hawk, and certainly not if he suspected they were merely our puppets."

"Exactly." Slie leant back in his chair and smiled as if Mirage were a child who had completed a complicated mathematical equation. "For all we know, the princess may already be in House Avis."

"That's not possible." Mirage shook his head. "It's simply too long a journey on foot. Why to travel there from Thornfield would take a good week of hard walking – maybe longer, as the princess is not used to such exertions."

"That's if they are on foot."

Again, Mirage stared at the Pontifex as his mind digested the older man's words, picked out the sense of them, and realised, as always, that Slie was one step ahead of them all.

"You think they may still have airship technology?"

“I am uncertain as to whether they possess an actual airship, but when the legion sent to Thornfield explored the immediate forest beside it, they reported hearing a strange sound, like a roaring. Yet when they reached the place the noise had come from, they found only an empty clearing. However, the sharp-eyed second-in-command discovered this lying on the ground.”

Slie pulled an object wrapped in paper from his desk drawer and laid it down in front of Mirage.

“He showed his commanding officer, who dismissed his find as being valueless. The second-in-command disagreed and dispatched his find back to me. This second-in-command has since had the singular good fortune to be promoted to commander of the legion, following the sudden and inexplicable disappearance of its previous commander.”

Slie smiled widely, showing all his teeth in a wolfish grin. Mirage wished he hadn’t and bent his attention upon the item. Slowly, Slie unwrapped it and removed a frond of dark green fern which he passed over to Mirage.

Confused, Mirage examined the fragment of wilting plant, finding nothing of interest until his fingers slipped on something black and smooth on its stem. Puzzled, he looked at his fingers, now coated with a sticky substance.

“Oil,” he exclaimed, and his eyes met the Pontifex’s in instant comprehension. “So,” he began slowly. “Even if they do not possess an actual airship – which presumably they do not because even a half-blind idiot could not have failed to see an airship hovering above the forest – then they have a mechanical device of some description which enabled them to escape our soldiers.”

“And such a device could conceivably have been used to transport the princess to House Avis a great deal quicker than on foot.”

“If she is still alive.”

“If she is still alive,” Slie conceded. “Interesting, is it not?”

“Very,” Mirage agreed. “But what implications does this have for the plan?”

“Played correctly, this knowledge could add fuel to our people’s hatred of the Avians. For not only did they launch a vicious and completely unprovoked attack upon an innocent village, but foul spies, who had penetrated the very heart of the palace, kidnapped our beloved princess when she was on her way to visit her sick old nurse.”

“That could work,” Mirage mused. “It would provide an adequate reason for an insurgency deep into House Avis territory.”

“Not only that, but when we reveal our armada of airships, the people will be only too grateful that we have such a powerful means of fighting back and attempting to rescue the Princess Snow. They will not think to question precisely how and where we achieved such knowledge.”

“And are we going to rescue her?” Mirage casually enquired.

“Oh, yes,” Slie assured him. “After all, we still require her to claim the throne, so that the Contratulum can then control her – or quietly dispose of her – immediately upon her being crowned queen.”

“And if Snow is dead, or we do not recover her in time?”

“It matters not – we will merely use her doppelganger.”

“Without Snow’s heart, will it pass the test of the Crown of Purity?” Mirage enquired.

“That antiquated device.” Slie shrugged irritably. “That shall be one of the first things we change when we have power. But it is an interesting question – will an absence of heart be enough to fool the Crown that our princess is free of all malicious intentions?”

“And if it isn’t?”

“Then Snow White will be declared unfit to rule, and the Contratulum shall move to crown either Princess Jay or her unborn child in Snow’s stead.”

Mirage sat back and stared at the Pontifex in reluctant admiration. Whether the real Snow was crowned and then controlled, discredited, or assassinated and replaced – or her clockwork counterpart crowned in her place – the days of the Royal House of White were numbered.

Chapter Twenty-Eight

On Matters of Love and War

All that day, preparations for war surged ahead. The castle rang to the sound of shouts and the marching of boots on flagstones, as troops were summoned, provisioned, and ordered to report to their airships.

Every time Snow caught sight of those monstrous leviathans tugging at their mooring ropes in the morning breeze, she imagined them filling the skies with the sounds and sights of battle. Adrift and not knowing what task she should be performing; Snow roamed the castle getting underfoot until Robin found her and suggested she offer her services in the hospital that was being prepared in the lesser-used west wing of the castle.

Snow looked at her cousin. Dressed in flying leathers, with her hair tightly scraped back into a blonde plait and a lethal-looking weapon strapped to her hip, she no longer looked like the madcap, fun-seeking princess Snow had come to know and love over the past three days. She looked like a warrior – almost as if she were going into battle herself.

"But of course, I am." Robin frowned at her in confusion. "I have command of ***The Thrush***. What did you think? That I would sit at home and sew whilst sending my people into battle?"

"But you're a woman."

"So? Honestly, Snow, Kingdom House White is positively in the dark ages when it comes to your attitudes towards women. It's as if it hasn't evolved at all in the past century."

"I don't believe it has," Snow replied sadly. "I think the Contratulum has deliberately stifled the country's development, wanting all the power for themselves, I believe they have stunted the nation's natural growth."

"Yet another good reason why they should be stopped," Robin told her, then turned as her ladies-in-waiting hurried down the passageway towards them.

"Robin, we have to go," Franki said, and Snow gawped in astonishment. Gone was the pair of flighty, pretty girls who liked nice clothes, dancing, and wine. In their place stood a pair of steely-eyed soldiers in flying leathers, also toting impressive weapons.

"***The Thrush*** is loaded and ready to cast off," Tegan said. "We're merely awaiting the Captain's inspection."

"You're going as well?" Snow asked.

"Where I go, they go," Robin told her. "You are looking at my second-in-command." Franki bowed. "And my Communications Officer." Tegan flashed her a grin. "We've been training all of our lives for this moment. Nothing would keep us here. Not when there's a war to be won."

"Please, take care," Snow begged.

"Don't worry, Cuz." Robin clapped a hand to her shoulder. "We'll win your throne for you."

They left, in a rustle of leather and a jingle of metal. Watching them go, Snow had never felt so useless in her life, so went in search of the hospital. There, the castle healers were arranging the placing of beds and surgical equipment, supervised by Grein, who had offered his services and Greta, who had also volunteered to do what she could. Surprised not to see Fae there, Snow enquired about the new bride.

"She's out in the courtyard saying her farewells," Greta told her, and her eyes crinkled in sympathy. "It's so hard for them. Not married even a day and already being separated."

"Separated?" Snow stuttered. "What do you mean?"

"Well, both Nylex and Ronin have been sworn into the Avian Forces. They're leaving this morning on one of the airships."

"What? No, but that's ... no ..."

Gathering up her skirts, Snow bolted from the room, hurtling down the corridors with her heart pounding fit to burst. Would he leave without saying goodbye? If he thought it best for her – yes, he would, her head told her.

The courtyard was packed with a confusing melee of soldiers bidding goodbye to loved ones, servants loading provisions onto cradles ready to be hoisted up to the docking platforms high above, and commanders barking orders as their troops assembled into legions ready to board the airships.

She saw Nylex and Fae in each other's arms. For a moment she ached for them, but then she was by them and searching for a familiar tall, dark figure. She couldn't see him anywhere, and she leant on a wall in breathless frustration. Glancing up at the airships, she wondered if maybe he was already on one, and groaned in despair. He couldn't be gone already. He just couldn't be.

"Snow?"

She spun around and peered into the shadowy gloom of the cloister. There was movement, and Ronin stepped into the light. Dressed in the uniform of an Avian soldier, he had a sword on one hip and a gun on the other. Grim-faced at the thought of what was to come, still, his eyes were soft upon her.

"Ronin," she gasped and threw herself into his arms. "I thought you'd gone without saying goodbye."

"Never," he murmured. "I was coming to look for you."

"I'm so afraid," she whispered. "And I'm so angry at myself for being afraid. And I feel so useless. Robin and her ladies are going to fight – she is commanding her own airship. And you and Nylex are going. Grein and Fae will be helping in the hospital – even Greta has an important task to do. But I have nothing. I am nothing."

"Snow." Gently he stroked the hair from her face. "You are everything. Without you, there would be no point to this war, and no hope of something better for our people. You are our hope, Snow. Our hope of a better future."

"I don't want you to go," she said miserably. "I don't want to lose you."

"Snow, we agreed, one night. That was all it could ever be."

"Oh, the frick with that!" she burst out angrily, and he blinked at her language. "I'm greedy. One night is not enough. It will never be enough. I want a whole lifetime with you, Ronin." She pulled him to her and kissed him as if her life depended on it.

Looking slightly dazed, when at last she let him go, he turned as a voice rang out from the courtyard ordering all troops to report to their ships.

"I have to go," he murmured reluctantly.

"I know."

"I love you," he said, and she smiled through the tears.

"I know that too," she replied with a teasing shrug, and he laughed. "Come back to me," she ordered.

He threw her a smart salute. "Is that an order from my queen?"

"It is an order from your Snow. Come back to me Ronin, or nothing will ever mean anything again."

The voice bellowed again. There was time for one last, hasty kiss that tasted of desperation and loss, and then he was gone, and she was alone. Bracing herself against the wall, she breathed deeply, trying to hold back the tears. Then Fae found her and held her, and the two women cried together for the men they had sent away to war.

Glad to discover he was assigned to ***The Kittiwake*** with Nylex, Ronin spotted another familiar face as they went below decks to stow their kitbags under their assigned hammocks – that of Jacobson, the chief engineer. She grinned at them both and shook their hands.

"Welcome aboard," she said.

They thanked her, and Ronin looked about the cramped room.

"She looks a fine vessel," he said, and Jacobson beamed with maternal pride.

“She is at that. Helped build her myself. Course, she’s not as slick and speedy as ***The Lissa,*** but she’s built for combat. She has twenty cannons, swivel-mounted for aerial and ground attack. And she’s a sturdy mare. It would take several direct hits to bring her down.”

“You haven’t seen what the Contratulum has,” Nylex muttered, and Jacobson frowned.

“No, you’re right, we haven’t. I heard about what happened to your people, and I’m sorry, but at least this is your chance to get your revenge.”

Ronin nodded but thought how revenge was a poor exchange for the life of his sister and all the other men, women, and children who had been lost. Thinking of children, he looked at Jacobson with interest.

“Did you ever find out what caused the explosion in the schoolhouse?”

“Yes, the earth tremor knocked a pipe coupling loose, and then a spark must have ignited the gas. Kylah and I fixed it, and she put some sort of magic into the iron to make it flexible enough to bend with stress should another tremor occur.”

“That’s good. I’m glad Kylah was able to help.”

“Yes, she’s something, that Kylah. Really something ...”

The chief engineer’s voice trailed away, and she reddened under their stares.

“Right, well, better get to the engine room. This bird won’t fly herself. Maybe catch you around later.”

She hurried away through the crowds of embarking soldiers, leaving Ronin and Nylex exchanging grins.

“So,” Ronin began companionably, as they finished putting away their belongings in the nailed-down trunks located under each hammock. “How are you enjoying married life so far?”

“Oh, it’s great,” Nylex drawled sarcastically, looking around the crowded quarters, then his expression sobered.

“It was so hard,” he confided quietly. “Leaving her, it was so hard.”

“Do you regret getting married so quickly? Do you wish you’d waited?”

“No.” Nylex’s reply was swift and certain. “No, I’m glad we didn’t wait. Whatever happens, at least we had last night.”

“Aye,” Ronin agreed. “At least there was last night.”

Fae had gone to the hospital, promising to send for Snow should they need her. Neither woman wanted to state the obvious – that this wouldn't be until the hospital began to fill with the hurt and the dying.

Wandering past the throne room, Snow saw Falcon comforting Wren as she wept in his arms. Lingering in the doorway, Snow wondered whether she should say something or simply keep walking when Wren spotted her and held out her arms. Desperate for a hug, Snow dashed across the floor and threw herself into her grandmother's embrace.

"Oh, Snow," Wren sobbed. "All those young people going into battle. Peregrine and Robin, and those two young ladies of hers. And your friends, Ronin and Nylex – and he only married last night – and I am so worried for all of them."

"I know," Snow murmured. "I'm worried too, and I wish I could do more to help."

"You can," Falcon told her. "We haven't had time to read all of your mother's journal, so maybe you could come and help me. We need to find out who her contacts were, whether they are still our allies, or have been captured or turned by the Contratulum."

"Of course," Snow cried, her spirits jumping at the thought of doing something to help, something that would make her feel useful.

"I'll leave you two to it," Wren said, then smiled at Snow. "Keep an old lady company at luncheon?" she asked, and Snow nodded.

"I'd be happy to, and you're not old," she hastily tacked on. Wren dimpled her pleasure, then glided elegantly from the room.

"Come," Falcon said and led her to the council room. Settling her at one end of the table, he slid the journal and a stack of blank paper and pens towards her. "Jot down anything you think may be relevant," he ordered. Then he moved to the other end, where Arden and others awaited him with maps and battle plans.

For two hours, Snow poured over the journal. As she carefully scrutinised every line of her mother's neat, rounded handwriting, it was almost as if Raven was talking to her, and Snow felt a pang of longing and a great wave of hatred towards the Contratulum. They had taken both her parents away from her, and now they would kill or manipulate her if they could. They had to be stopped.

She thought of all those soldiers on their way to her Kingdom, ready to fight for her and claim her throne. She thought of all the injuries and deaths that would probably happen, the innocent blood that would be on the Contratulum's hands.

Pausing only to sip at the water that someone had thoughtfully placed by her elbow, Snow jotted down names and passwords, surprised at how many there were. She was surprised how many she recognised as court officials, servants, or members of the royal guard. Some were even in the Contratulum's legions. One, by the name of Barnabus, had been high up in the ranks. She figured by now, if he wasn't dead, he would be a second-in-command – maybe even a commander. He could be useful, and she underlined his name thoughtfully.

One of Raven's contacts fascinated her. Unusually, Raven had written down almost his entire backstory. A youngster living rough on the streets – she had found him when he tried to pick her pocket on one of her furtive undercover visits to the town.

She had given him money and food, and each time she came back he would seem to sense her presence and find her. At first, Raven wrote, it was clearly for the scraps of food she brought him and the few shillings she would give him. But then he started bringing her snippets of information that he had overheard, transactions he had witnessed, and for two years he acted as her eyes and ears in parts of the city where she could not go.

Then one day he vanished. At first, she was not too concerned, but as the days turned to a week, Raven grew afraid her young friend had fallen victim to the vicious underbelly of the city. The life of a street child could be short and brutal, with none to care or intervene if they were in trouble.

Discreetly, she put out feelers and offered a reward for any news of him. A few days later, she received intelligence that a boy matching his description was in the paupers' hospital. Raven sent Greta to check out the lead, and she returned some hours later with a grim expression. She had found him, lying on a filthy pallet in his own waste in a room crowded with the sick and the dying.

He was delirious, she told Raven, and running a temperature. He had not eaten or drunk for days, and he was not expected to last the night. Horrified, Raven sent men she trusted to retrieve him and take him to a safe house hidden within the city.

Taking nourishing food and medical supplies, she and Greta slipped from the palace at dusk and sat by the boy's bedside all night. Cleaning him, dripping fresh water into his parched lips, and helping to prepare healing potions infused with the strongest spells Greta knew, Raven fought death all night for the young lad's soul.

Watching as Greta forced potions down the boy's reluctant throat every hour, on the hour, Raven merely nodded when she told her the boy had magic of his own. Faint, and not particularly powerful, nevertheless it was there and fighting to keep him alive.

Raven had already suspected as much. The boy was either incredibly lucky or blessed with pre-knowledge of which situations to run from, and which could be advantageous. As she held his hand and spoke softly to him, begging him to remain and to fight the infection, she thought of her little girl, safely asleep in her pretty bedroom in the palace.

Come daybreak, the boy's fever broke, and he opened his eyes to find his beloved lady smiling at him. Fully aware of all she had done for him, he burst into tears of gratitude and swore that from that day on he was hers to command. That whatever he could do to aid her cause, he would.

This was a vow he was to more than fulfil when the Contratulum detected his magical abilities and enlisted him into their service. Risking discovery, he met with Raven in secret and promised that from his position within the enemy's stronghold he would gather whatever information he could and send it to her.

Six months later, Raven was dead.

Snow looked up from the journal and drew a deep, shaky breath. The story of the young street boy had touched her deeply. Almost feeling he was her shadow brother, Snow wondered what had happened to him after his queen had died.

Greta paused by her chair, her eyebrows raising at the look on Snow's face. She glanced over Snow's shoulder and read the last lines of the journal.

"Yes – the boy," she murmured. "I remember him."

"What happened to him?" Snow asked.

"I can only tell you a little more of his story," Greta warned. She settled into the chair beside Snow's, and her eyes grew dim with the memories of those long-ago, dark days after Raven had died.

"He waited until the day of Raven's funeral – Slie had pronounced it a day of national mourning for the whole city ..." Greta's mouth twisted with disgust at the hypocrisy.

"The young man managed to bribe my chambermaid with a shilling to pass me a note. She was too young and silly to give it much thought, and she dropped the note onto my dinner tray that evening."

"What did the note say?" Snow asked.

"He wanted to meet. I managed to slip out of the palace later that evening and meet him in a safe place. I'll never forget his face when I told him ..."

"Told him what?" Snow urged when Greta fell silent.

"Told him how your mother died. It was then I realised how much she had meant to him. That the mission – her mission – was the only thing that mattered to him." Greta shook her head.

"His face ... I could see it in his eyes. The devastation and the rage. I watched as it grew into an all-encompassing hatred of the Contratulum and all it stood for. He made an ardent vow to me, to continue the work Raven had started. I told him that our only hope now was to hang on until the Princess Snow – until you – attained the crown. That you were a good and noble child, Raven's daughter to the core. That I would continue to build on the foundations Raven had laid with you, and we just had to be patient."

Greta gave Snow a sad smile as her mind wandered back to those long-ago days of despair and betrayal.

"For a few more years he passed any scraps of information he gathered directly to me until the Contratulum became aware of how much influence I had over you and sent me into exile. There were other operatives within the city, and before I left, I managed to give him names and the password that must be given or received. I told him they could pass anything he gave them directly to House Avis – to your grandfather. Falcon was the most powerful man in the world, I knew he would help when the time was right.

"What happened then?" Snow asked, and Greta shrugged.

"That, I cannot tell you," she said.

"I can," boomed a voice behind them. Unseen by the two women, Falcon had stood and listened as Greta told her tale.

"He is one of our most valuable and most strategically placed operatives. I can tell you the rest of his story." Falcon smiled at Greta. "He bided his time. Rising through the ranks, he was the perfect apprentice, and then a hardworking young prelate. He became secretary to Pontifex Slie."

Falcon rested a hand on Snow's shoulder.

"But all the time, I think he was waiting. Waiting for you, Snow – the daughter his queen had loved so much – to grow to maturity, and then attain the throne." Snow swallowed at the thought.

"He eavesdropped on conversations between Slie and Mirage. He intercepted messages and passed any information he gathered onto us. It was he who saved Raven's journal and sent it to us. And it was he who sent us word of your possible demise. We hoped and prayed it was not true. For if you were dead, then it would all have been for nought."

The day dragged. At nightfall, a message was received that House White had officially declared war on House Avis in direct response to their cowardly, and unprovoked, attack on the village of Arrowford. And for the kidnapping of the Princess Snow.

At this, Falcon's brows rose so far, they practically met his hair, and he exchanged a long hard look with Arden. "Does this mean they know Snow is here?"

"I think it means they suspect. If they were gathering intelligence through the child Tibby, then they know Snow was alive a week ago in Thornfield. It's not too big a jump for them to assume she would come here to seek sanctuary and aid."

"It gives their people yet another reason to rise up against us," Falcon mused. "Clever, very clever."

"Slie is clever," Snow interjected. "Do not underestimate him. He is one of the most cunning and manipulative men I have ever met, and I think he possesses levels of the Power far beyond that of Mirage."

"You know this for sure?" Arden asked, and Snow bit her lip in thought.

"There was always something about him – something dark and dead behind his eyes. I believe Slie sold his soul to the darkness many years ago, and now there is nothing left inside him but rot and corruption."

"That makes him even more dangerous than we thought," Arden said, and looked at Falcon in concern. "What have we sent our people into? What have we done?"

"We have done what we had to," Falcon declared firmly, then looked at Snow. "Have you found anything useful?"

"Yes, there are more allies in House White than we suspected. Although of course, I do not know who is dead or alive, or who is still on our side. And there is one line that my mother wrote over, and over, again. I believe it was a secret code or password, or maybe a rallying call."

"What is it?"

Snow rested her hands thoughtfully on her mother's journal.

"It doesn't only snow in winter."

Chapter Twenty-Nine

It Doesn't Only Snow in Winter

Another day dawned, and with it came devastating news. The small hamlet of Wingham, just over the border into the Kingdom of House Avis, had been attacked with the loss of three hundred men, women, and children. The precious few survivors told a frightening story of an airship that loomed over the horizon at dawn before any were about and rained down fire upon the village.

"It's gone, Your Majesty," sobbed a young shepherd lad who had been tending his flocks up on the hillside and had witnessed the entire event. "It's all gone!"

Stoney faced, Falcon ordered that the survivors be taken to the hospital and treated for their injuries, given a hot meal, and be found beds. Then he paced angrily about the council room.

"We need to know where they will attack next," he stormed. "Our airships are on their way, but without knowing where to go we will be forced to stretch our ships too thinly."

"I wish ..." Snow began, then stopped, uncertain if what she was about to say was ridiculous or not.

"You wish what, Snow?" Arden asked gently.

"I wish it were possible to contact our spy within the Contratulum. The communication seems to only flow one way – towards us – and it is so frustrating that we cannot get a message to him. Surely, he is in a prime position to find out their plans. Then at least we could be waiting for them when they attacked."

Falcon stopped pacing and stared at her. Running his fingers through his hair until it stood on end, he turned on his advisors, who shuffled awkwardly and glanced at one another.

"Is it possible?" he demanded.

"There might be a way, Your Majesty," they finally admitted.

"A way? What way?" Falcon pounced on them, and Snow swore she saw them visibly flinch away from him.

"Two years ago, when the young man attained a level of confidence within the Contratulum and began to be truly useful, he sent a message. He asked whether we had a discreet listening device he could plant in Slie's office. He requested, if such a device existed, that we send it to him so he could eavesdrop on his master's private conversations. He requested it be left with the landlord of a tavern in a rather less salubrious part of town. This was done. Two weeks later, intelligence of a highly intimate nature began to make its way to us, so it was assumed he had not only retrieved the device but had been successful in planting it."

"So, if you left him a message with this landlord, there is a chance he might get it?" Snow demanded in excitement.

"It is possible," the advisor said. "But we do not know if he regularly attends this tavern, or if it was merely a one-time arrangement to receive the device."

"It's worth a try," Falcon decided and snapped his fingers at his advisors. "Prepare a message, use the code assigned to him and tell him we need him to try and gather information about where the Contratulum plan to attack next."

"But Grandfather," Snow protested. "It will take weeks for a message to get to the city, and possibly many more weeks before he collects it – if indeed he ever does. By then, the Contratulum could have attacked every single village and town in the kingdom."

Falcon looked at her, then he glanced at his advisors.

"No, Your Majesty," one of them said. "It is too risky to show her."

"She is my granddaughter," Falcon retorted. "She is Princess Snow of the House White and these are not only our people she is trying to save but her own as well. If you cannot trust her, then you cannot trust me either."

"Trust me about what?" Snow demanded in bewilderment.

"Snow," Falcon put his hands on her shoulders. "What I am about to show you must travel no further than these four walls. And that goes for you too, Arden." Behind him, the advisors threw up their hands in despair.

"You know that anything you choose to share with me will remain a secret," Arden remarked mildly.

"And I," Snow agreed.

"Then come with me," Falcon said and lead them to where a large tapestry hung on the end wall. Moving it to one side, he revealed a door, which he pushed open and gestured them through. Exchanging glances, Arden and Snow followed him, and the tapestry dropped behind them.

They found themselves in a large room, at the centre of which was a huge, low table containing the biggest map Snow had ever seen. All the kingdoms were represented, with name tags showing where the towns and villages were located.

Her mouth gaping, Snow moved closer. There was the Kingdom of House Avis as a bird would truly see it, with the castle marked. On the border, a red cross had been drawn over the hamlet of Wingham, and a little further into the Kingdom of House White, she saw a similar cross over the village of Arrowford.

Fascinated, Snow looked for and found her own palace, then her eyes moved to the coastline and traced it down to where her kingdom bordered that of House Coral, and then the wild southern lands beyond which were ruled by no royal house but were a jumble of small principalities and unclaimed territory.

To the north was the mountainous kingdom of House Ursa, it's land one of cold and almost year-round ice. Snow had heard tell of how hardy the people of this kingdom were. Out in the sea were all the small islands that together made up the kingdom of House Narwhale. Her eyes flicked up to meet those of Arden who was also gazing at the map in disbelief, then to those of her grandfather, who was silently watching their reaction.

"This is extraordinary," she murmured. "I have never seen anything like it."

"With the airships, we have been able to expand our knowledge of our world and map even the most inaccessible portions of it. But this is not what I wanted you to see. Here," he gestured towards a raised walkway which ringed three sides of the room, reached by a shallow flight of steps on either side.

Rows of chairs were arranged around each wall, at which sat men and women with strange-looking devices covering their ears – like the goggles she had worn in the skimmer, Snow thought – but covering the ears instead of the eyes.

"What are those devices they are working at?" Arden asked. Snow followed as he and Falcon climbed the steps to stand on the walkway behind a young woman, who completely ignored them. Her attention was on the device in front of her, and Snow wondered whether she had even heard them come up behind her, so thick and all-encompassing was the contraption covering her ears.

"This," Falcon began proudly, "is the most remarkable thing that our mechanics have invented so far. More incredible than the airship, and just as useful. It is a remote wireless communication device. Every airship is equipped with one, and has a communications officer fully trained in how to use it."

Snow remembered Robin telling her that Tegan was her Communications Officer. At the time, she had assumed it meant communication with the rest of the crew, or perhaps signalling to other ships, not that it meant ... what did it mean, exactly?

"Yes, but what does it do?" Arden asked the question for her.

"Our mechanics have discovered that it is possible to send messages through the air using these devices – messages which can then be received by another device elsewhere."

"What? But ... but ... that is amazing," Arden exclaimed. "What is the range?"

"I am unsure of the exact distance, but we have many of these devices hidden in your kingdom, Snow. It is how we can send and receive messages to and from our operatives almost immediately."

"Then can you not use one of these ... wireless devices ... to send a message to the spy within the Contratulum?" Snow asked.

"Unfortunately, no. Although there is a wireless hidden in a safe house within the city, unless he were to go to that location it is impossible to get a message to him. There is no way any of our operatives can get into the Contratulum's base of operations – not with any hope of surviving."

"I see." Snow looked around at the dozen men and women all sitting at their devices. "So, all these people are in communication right now with your armada of airships?"

"They are," Falcon agreed. "We can get almost instantaneous messages to them and receive regular progress reports from them." Snow fell silent, looking at the devices in wonder. The fact that Ronin could be so easily contacted was strangely comforting, even though she knew she could not ask to speak to him herself.

"Remarkable," Arden murmured, looking thunderstruck at the revelation. "Absolutely remarkable."

"I'm sure you appreciate this must be kept strictly secret. If the Contratulum were to discover we possessed such technology ..."

Both Arden and Snow hurriedly gave their reassurances again, then Falcon escorted them from the room, and they went their separate ways. Falcon to meet with his advisors, Arden to see if he could offer his services in the hospital wing, and Snow to keep her luncheon appointment with her grandmother.

It was strange being on an airship that was crowded to the gunnels again. It felt even stranger for Ronin not to be its captain. When he and Nylex went back on deck to assist with casting off, it was to find Prince Peregrine at the wheel dressed in the leathers of a captain.

Seeing them, he threw them a hurried smile then went back to the delicate process of manoeuvring ***The Kittiwake*** away from the dock. This was made more complex by the fact that eleven other huge airships were also intent on doing the same thing.

Jumping to obey the second-in-command's bellowed orders, Ronin admired the skill of Peregrine as he managed the wheel, edging his ship away from the castle wall and up into the sky. The man knew what he was about, and Ronin relaxed slightly.

Having confidence in one's captain was a crucial factor for the crew of an airship. Watching the way this crew worked as a well-oiled, cohesive unit, Ronin realised they had flown together regularly enough to be able to anticipate their captain's orders even before they were given.

They flew for half a day before the border between the kingdoms of House Avis and House White approached, and Ronin wondered where they would go now. Giving the order to cast anchor for the night, Peregrine strode from the deck and the crew settled down into spending the night hovering on the Avian border.

Soon the good honest smell of dinner cooking wafted onto the deck and the crew visibly relaxed. Packs of playing cards were produced, and the soft strains of a fiddle being played somewhere drifted across the gathering groups of men and women.

In the distance, Ronin could see the other airships had also dropped their ground anchors. He remembered Snow saying that Princess Robin had command of her own ship, and he wondered which one it was.

Snow.

For the first time since casting off, he allowed himself to think about her. He tried to imagine what she must be doing now. Perhaps eating dinner with her grandparents and the others. He hoped she and Fae were a comfort to one another, and he cast a glance to where Nylex was leaning against the railing staring out over the darkening land below.

Appreciating how hard it must be to be separated from his bride of only a few hours, especially after the five wasted years that lay behind them, he crossed to stand companionably beside him. Nylex glanced at him, then glanced away. But Ronin knew he was aware of the silent support he was offering and was grateful for it.

And far away in the city Snow had once called her own, a young man sat in a tavern and nursed an ale. Supposedly, he was on the hunt for people gifted with magic. It was an assignment that had suited him well over the past two years, allowing him to venture outside the Contratulum's stronghold and conduct any business of his own without arousing suspicion.

Distasteful although he found his task, he was wise enough to know he had to be successful at it more times than not, or else questions would be asked, and he might fall under unwanted scrutiny. So, he found the Contratulum enough recruits to satisfy them but was picky about who he chose.

That young brawler of a man was heading for a probable early death in some knife fight, he reasoned, and had a chance of a better life in the legions of the Contratulum. A newly orphaned child would be dead, or worse, within a week if left on the streets, and he considered it a mercy to take them in. But that young woman looking forward to her wedding and a life of normality? Her he would pass by.

He knew it was a far from perfect scheme, but for the sake of his own protection and the cause he fought for, it was an easy decision to make. Nothing could come between him and the goal Raven had set for him. The fact that it seemed so attainable now only made him more determined to succeed.

He finished his ale and furtively stretched out his mind to search for any scrap of magic within the other patrons. There, that man in the corner playing cards with his friends. As he watched, the man won another hand to the groans of his companions. There was a reason he was so 'lucky', and his flicker of precognitive magic could be useful to the Contratulum. Taking him in would add to his cover as the perfect, ambitious prelate heading for the top.

Going up to the bar, he slid his now empty glass towards the surly faced landlord, who glanced at him. Taking a jug of ale from under the bar to fill it up, he said casually, "Will that be all? The wife has made some right tasty meat pies if you're hungry."

"No, thank you, just the ale is fine," the young man shook his head.

"Powerful cold night out there," the landlord said, and the young man wondered at his uncharacteristic chattiness before an idea occurred and he glanced up to find the landlord staring at him.

"It is," the young man agreed slowly. "It feels almost cold enough to snow."

"Maybe," the landlord shrugged and looked him straight in the eye. "After all, it doesn't only snow in winter."

The young man's heart stood still.

"Maybe I will have one of those meat pies after all," he said, placing a handful of coins on the bar. The landlord's eyes flicked down and spotted the glint of gold under the baser metal of the shillings. Swiftly, the coins were scooped and pocketed as he placed the now foaming glass of ale on the counter.

"You sit yourself down, and I'll have one brought over to you."

Silently, the young man took his ale and returned to his table. Although he had used the landlord before to receive an important package for him, it had been a one-off transaction based on the fact that the sour-faced man valued money over any degree of curiosity as to what was in the package. But now ... the young man glanced up and briefly caught the man's eye. He had known the password. Did that mean there were more sympathisers in the city than he imagined?

The note was wrapped tightly in a twist of oilskin in the very heart of the pie. Even though he was expecting something of the sort, he almost choked on it and coughed it up into his napkin as though it were a gristly bit of meat.

Slyly pocketing it, he burned to read what it said but forced himself to calmly finish his pie and his ale. Before leaving, he nodded a casual farewell to the landlord and walked slowly back to the Contratulum's base. Once inside, he reported his findings to his superior and gave a full description of the card-playing man to two guards, who were then dispatched to collect him.

"Well done," his superior clapped him amiably on the shoulder. "Now, go and wash the smell of the tavern off you. I know how distasteful an assignment this must be for you, having to go outside and mingle with the likes of them, but it's worth it. The recruits you bring into the fold are usually exactly what we are looking for. I honestly don't know how you manage it."

"Just lucky, I suppose." The young man summoned up an earnest, wide-eyed smile, then left to do as ordered. Only when he was alone in his room, with a chair propped against the door, did he take out the package. The note had been protected from the filling of the pie, and he read the single sentence it contained - so used to his code he did not have to think about translating it. Then he sat back on the bed and considered what it said.

They wished to know where the Contratulum would strike next. He thought about the question. Although the listening device in the Pontifex's office had yielded much that was useful, all the important discussions took place within the chamber of the Council of Elders, deep within the complex. It would have been impossible to plant the device there, so he had had to be content with the scraps of information he gained from the meetings between Slie and Mirage.

A way must be found to gain this knowledge. Still thinking about it, he methodically chewed and swallowed the scrap of paper, then burnt the oilskin wrapper in his candle until it was reduced to ash, which he also swallowed with a mouthful of water. A way must be found, but he was at a loss as to how.

All the next day, Snow went through her mother's journal again. Her admiration of the methodical way Raven had run her underground resistance movement grew page by page, and she wished that the queen had lived long enough for Snow to know her as an adult.

And through all the schemes, and maps, and charts, and reports, ran the same phrase over, and over, again – it doesn't only snow in winter. Eventually, Snow came to realise that it was a greeting used to establish kinship and could be used as a warning.

She read a report written by her mother of how an operative had met with a spy within one of the Contratulum legions. Instead of the correct phrase, the man had said, 'It only snows in winter', and the operative knew that the man had been compromised.

Aware it was probably a trap, the operative paused only to dispatch the man – who had simply stood and allowed it to happen – then fled down the dark alleyways of the city, hearing sounds of pursuit behind him. Only his superior knowledge of the terrain allowed the operative to escape capture, and Raven concluded by writing that the loss of the spy was a great shame.

Here, Snow paused in her reading. There was a splotch over the last word as if water had been spilt before the ink had dried. Running her finger softly over it, Snow realised it was a teardrop. Raven had cried over the death of the spy.

It made her mother seem achingly close, and Snow was pleased that she had not been hardened by her work – that the loss of every life under her charge mattered.

She closed the journal, her mind so lost in those long-ago days that it took a moment to comprehend that all around her voices were being raised.

Confused, she pushed back her chair and stood.

"What is it?" she cried. "What has happened?"

"Airships spotted over the Great Forest, heading to Larkhaven."

Falcon paused by her side. His face was as black as thunder.

"Larkhaven!" Snow exclaimed in shock.

Larkhaven was no mere hamlet or even a village. A bustling metropolis containing some ten thousand souls, it was the largest town in the Kingdom of House Avis, and the heart of its trading and banking empire.

Located at the southernmost tip of the kingdom, it was strategically placed for trading with the kingdoms of House White and House Coral and even had dealings with the southern states. An attack on it would be devastating for House Avis.

At the thought of all those people at the mercy of great airships, Snow clutched at her heart which thumped within her chest.

"The armada?" she cried. "Can they reach it in time?"

"Messages have been sent, and they are setting out at their fastest speed. It will be a close-run thing, but at top speed, they might make it in time. They must make it in time. If we lose Larkhaven ..."

Falcon didn't need to finish because Snow knew what he was thinking. Lose Larkhaven, and that would be the war lost before it had begun.

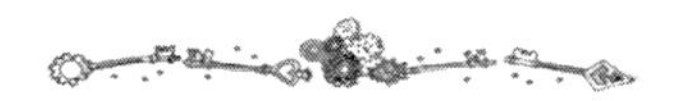

The young man chewed the problem over for most of the next day as he went about his usual duties, but by the early evening, he was no closer to finding a solution. Sitting at his desk outside the Pontifex's office, he calmly finished writing his report of the previous evening's recruiting mission, but all the time his mind was busy contriving and discarding one plan after another.

There was only so much he had access to. Although he was in the higher levels of prelateship and trusted to a degree, gaining knowledge of that nature required a far greater clearance than he currently had.

His thoughts were interrupted as the door to the office opened and the bulky figure of Slie appeared before him.

"Clear the supper things from my desk," he ordered. "I shall be back presently."

Bowing his head in acquiescence, the young man entered the darkened room and made his way to the desk in the only square of illumination it contained. As Mirage had done many times before him, he wondered as to the exact dimensions of the room, and what lurked in the darkness beyond the light.

Taking the tray, he loaded it with the remains of the Pontifex's supper. Wiping crumbs from the desk, he picked up the paperwork, which was also adorned with the detritus of a meal sloppily eaten and tapped it to dislodge the crumbs onto the plate.

Glancing at the paperwork, his hand slowed and then stopped. A quick look over his shoulder reassured him that he was still alone. Swiftly his eyes scanned the information, his heart missing a beat at its significance. There was to be another attack at dusk the next day.

Quickly, he searched for the name of the target. Featherwell, a small village in the north of the Kingdom of House Avis. Rearranging the paperwork exactly as he had found it, he took up the tray and was leaving the room as the Pontifex returned.

"I am retiring for the evening, so will have no further use of you tonight," Slie told him, and the young man inclined his head.

"Very well, Your Grace."

He took the tray to the kitchen and informed them that the Pontifex would not require anything further that evening, then slowly made his way to his room.

As the clocks struck midnight some two hours later, a shadow slipped noiselessly from a little-used side entrance off the kitchen. Making his way swiftly through the back alleys of the city, he paused before a doorway concealed in deepest shadow.

He knocked softly, once. Waited a moment, then repeated the knock. A small hatchway slid back in the door and eyes glinted at him in the darkness.

"Who comes knocking at my door on such a cold night?"

"It doesn't only snow in winter."

There was a pause, then a hand came through the hatchway and the young man slipped a tightly folded note into it.

"Be sure this is sent immediately," he murmured. "It's of vital importance."

In the shadows, he saw the nod of a head, and then the hatchway slammed shut and he was left alone in the gloom of the ill-smelling alleyway. Hoping that the information could be of some use, he made his way silently back to slip unnoticed into his room.

Relieved to have survived another day undiscovered, his pulse thrummed at the thought that things were beginning to happen and that soon – so very soon – his mission would be accomplished. That he might finally sleep at night without the dark dreams that gnawed on his sanity and would not let him be.

Chapter Thirty

An Urgent Mission

Before dawn the next day, a servant pounded on Snow's door to inform her that King Falcon wanted to see her immediately in the council room. Struggling from bed, she took a moment to dash some water over her face and run a comb through her hair. Clambering back into the dress she had wearily stepped from scant hours before, she attempted to fasten the laces of the corset as she hurried down the deserted corridors.

Spying Arden entering the throne room before her, she hailed him, and he waited as she panted up to him.

"What's happened?" she gasped, and he shook his head.

"I know no more than you," he replied, then finished fastening the laces for her as they approached the council room doors. Nodding her thanks, Snow ran a shaking hand through her hair as the man-at-arms threw open the doors for them and they entered a scene of chaos.

Falcon was pacing the floor, a piece of paper clenched in his fist, which he occasionally stopped to wave furiously at his advisors who were clutched in a huddle around the far end of the table.

"What has occurred?" Arden demanded, approaching the King.

"We have had a message from the spy within the Contratulum with the name of the next village – which they plan to attack at dusk tonight."

"Which village?"

"Featherwell."

"No." Arden sank into a chair and looked at Falcon with shattered eyes.

"Featherwell?" Snow desperately tried to remember her geography. Wasn't it north of here? Almost as far north as you could go, whilst their airships were now as far south as ... In an instant, she grasped the problem.

"There's no time ..." she muttered. "There's no time for the airships to turn around and reach Featherwell before the attack – and besides, they will probably all be needed to defend Larkhaven."

"There are over three hundred souls in Featherwell," Falcon said. "And no way to warn them. With all our airships heading to Larkhaven, even if we were to send a message, they would be too late by the time they'd turned around and gone north."

"There must be something we can do," Arden insisted. "Some way to warn them. Do you not have one of your miraculous wireless devices in the village? Could we not send them a message?"

“No – the devices are so scarce they were placed in key locations only. A small farming community in the north of the kingdom … it was never imagined they would need one.”

“Then there is truly nothing to be done?” Arden put his head in his hands. “All those people. They will be sitting ducks to a Contratulum airship.”

“We must go and rescue them,” Snow declared, and her grandfather stared at her in despair.

“Our whole fleet is on its way to Larkhaven. We have a few skimmers left, but they don’t have the speed of an airship, and would never reach the village on time.”

“There is an airship left,” Snow exclaimed. “***The Lissa***. She’s the fastest airship ever built. She could make it to the village on time.”

“She’s right,” Arden excitedly agreed. “She could easily make it to Featherwell long before dusk if we set off immediately.”

“And what would you do when you got there?” Falcon asked. “She has no weapons, no means of engaging with the Contratulum, and there’s no time to fit her with any.”

“Then we won’t fight,” Snow said. “We simply get the villagers on board and make a run for it back here.”

“Could the ship hold that many?” Falcon looked at Arden who considered the matter.

“It would be tight,” he finally said, “but it could be done.”

“It is a good plan,” Falcon reluctantly conceded. “Apart from one fatal flaw. We have no one to pilot her, no engineers to work the engine, no crew to man the decks. All our aviators left with the fleet. A few deckhands are waiting to help dock any ships that come back, but none of them is trained to fly an airship. There is no one who could captain her.”

“Yes, there is,” Snow said. “There’s me.” Silence fell over the room as every man present turned to look at her.

“Don’t be ridiculous, my dear,” Falcon began gently. “I know you want to help, but you are not trained to fly an airship.”

“I flew her a lot of the way here,” Snow insisted. “Ronin taught me. The ship accepted me, and even helped me.” Falcon raised his brows at this, then looked at Arden for confirmation.

“It’s true,” Arden agreed. “Snow did fly her part of the way here. And Featherwell is on a direct line from here. No mountains or seas to traverse, it’s meadowland all the way.”

“That may be so,” Falcon reluctantly conceded. “But you have no engineer, no crew.”

“Yes, we do – Kylah,” Snow cried. “She built the ship from the ground up, so there’s not an inch of her she doesn’t know intimately.

She could probably fly it herself singlehandedly. Then there's Eli – he helps Kylah, and Grein knows how to crew, and Fae, and ..."

"And me." Arden slapped his knee with excitement. "Damn it, Falcon, it could work. If you lend us those few deckhands you mentioned and we leave now, we could get there and evacuate the villagers before the Contratulum's ships arrive."

Falcon hesitated, looking at his granddaughter.

"I can do this," she stated with quiet conviction. "This is my chance to be useful. All those people are going to war on my behalf – it made me feel so useless. Well, this is my chance to make a difference. To actually help."

Silence stretched in the room as Falcon considered her, then glanced at Arden. Behind him, the advisors appeared to hold their breath. Falcon sighed and ran his fingers through his hair.

"Don't tell your grandmother," he muttered, and Snow knew she had won.

"There's not a moment to lose," Arden insisted. "If we are to reach the village and evacuate everyone before the Contratulum arrives, then we need to leave immediately."

"Fetch the others," Snow told him. "I need to change. I'll meet you at ***The Lissa***."

She had worried, despite her reassuring words to Falcon, that once stood behind the wheel of ***The Lissa*** again, she would not remember anything that Ronin taught her. That this grand plan of hers would be over before it even began.

Standing on the deck less than an hour later, she lightly took hold of the wheel and the ship shivered. An intense vibration, it travelled upwards through her palms and into her spine.

"Lissa," she murmured. "We need your help now more than ever. We have to fly like the wind if we're to save all those poor people." As if in response, the ship tugged persistently at her mooring.

"Release mooring ropes," Snow ordered.

"Aye, aye, Captain," Arden grinned, as he and a deckhand hurried to obey. The ropes safely stowed, the ship nosed away from the dock and Snow gently tipped the wheel to guide it forwards.

"Ahead slow," she ordered, and Fae – standing beside her with the speaking tube – quickly relayed the order to Kylah in the engine room. Almost immediately, the ship began to creep forward, and Snow instinctively adjusted the heading to take them out.

Once clear of the docking bay, she turned the ship to face the direction the deckhand on compass duty indicated, and when they were a safe distance from the castle, ordered full speed ahead. The ship bucked beneath her feet, like a thoroughbred anticipating a race, and then they were off.

Oh, the exhilaration! That rush of power controlling the mighty airship gave her. Snow grinned in pure delight, and beside her Fae caught onto her mood and grinned back. Fae looked trim in borrowed leathers, but Snow saw the sadness in the other girl's eyes and took a second to appreciate how hard it must have been for Fae to send Nylex off to war after such a short time together.

They flew hard for several hours until the land dipped down into a series of shallow valleys, and Arden went below decks to relieve Grein who had been hard at work shovelling coal. Grein then came to relieve Fae on the speaking tube, so she could prepare a hasty luncheon for them all, to be eaten at their posts.

Snow glanced at the alchemist. He appeared deep in thought, and when he caught her surveying him quizzically, he rubbed a hand over his stubbled chin and smiled sadly at her.

"Is everything all right, Grein?" she asked.

"Yes. It's been a long time since I crewed on an airship, and it reminds me of when my brother and I were stokers together."

"Your brother? I didn't know you had a brother."

"Well, I don't anymore," he replied, and Snow could have kicked herself for her tactlessness.

"I'm sorry," she said. "I suppose he died in the attack like everyone else?"

"No, he left long before that. His wife died and he sunk into a great depression. Nothing could convince him that life was still worth living without her. As the weeks went by, he became more and more dissatisfied with our lives. It fitted no man, he used to say, to have to hide away in the middle of a forest, fearful for his life and those of his friends and family. I knew he was unhappy, but I didn't think he would ever act on it, until one day he was gone."

"Gone where?"

"I know not. He and my young nephew simply vanished. They took a boat and left the village in the middle of the night. Of course, we searched for them, but there was no trace of them – until months later the wreckage of the boat was discovered many miles downstream. My brother couldn't swim, and my nephew was only a small child – so, I do not think they could have survived."

"I am so sorry, Grein, that's awful. To lose them like that ... to never know what happened to them. I can't imagine how you must feel."

"It was a very long time ago." Grein shrugged in resignation. "It has been a while since the thought of my brother crossed my mind, and I only hope he found the peace he was looking for. My nephew would have been a grown man by now … and it is such a waste." He shook his head. "Such a waste."

Snow nodded sadly, her heart aching for the alchemist as he hunched his shoulders and turned away from her. Then Fae arrived with hot drinks and a luncheon of bread, cheese, and fruit to be consumed one-handed as Snow flew the ship ever onwards.

The further north they flew, the colder it became, and as they approached a deep fold in the land where the village was located, a thick fog swirled around the ship. Snow ordered a dead stop.

"Featherwell directly below us," the deckhand assured her, and Snow peered uncertainly over the side.

"This fog is so thick a blind man would struggle to find his own backside," Arden muttered grumpily, and Snow looked at him.

"What should I do?" she asked.

"Send down an advance party?" he suggested. "I'll go if you like. I'll take Grein and one of the deckhands with me, and we'll make first contact with the villagers."

"I'll come with you," Fae offered. "They'll be scared and concerned. Perhaps seeing a woman with you might help allay their fears, and the village women might be more prepared to listen to me."

"All right," Snow agreed. "If you think that's for the best."

"You get the ship turned around and ready for a speedy exit. It's gone midday already, and we need to be loaded and away before dusk," Arden advised.

The cradle was hastily swung over the edge. Arden, Grein, and one of the deckhands clambered aboard, and Arden gave Fae a hand to climb in. She smiled reassuringly as the cradle began to lower.

"See you soon," she called to Snow, then the fog swirled around them and they disappeared into the murk.

It felt as if they were gone for ages. Trying to quell the apprehension that was crawling along her spine, Snow busied herself with slowly manoeuvring the ship, relying solely on the shouted directions of the deckhand with the compass, until they were pointed in the opposite direction, and all was ready for the villagers to come on board.

Time dragged by and still, they did not come. Snow was considering whether to order another landing party to go and look for them, or even go herself when the bell on the cradle rope clanged, and she let out a heavy sigh of relief.

The cradle had come down in the village square. Clambering from it, Fae shivered as water droplets settled on her face and hair. She looked at the dense white wall which pushed against them. The fog was thicker than it had been above, and her vision was restricted to a mere couple of feet all around.

"I don't like this," she murmured. "I don't like this at all."

"It's a real pea-souper, isn't it?" Grein replied. "Let's find the villagers as quickly as possible so we can all get out of here."

"Yes, but where is everyone?" Fae asked. They wandered through the narrow streets of the village, but the place looked deserted.

"Inside?" he suggested. "I wouldn't want to be out in this."

"Maybe," she agreed, but something was bothering her. Reaching out with her mind, she tried to sense the presence of the villagers who must be there somewhere. After all, a population of three hundred was a lot of people to be kept hidden and quiet.

"I can't feel them," she said.

"Feel who?"

"The villagers – I can't feel them at all. It's this wretched fog. It's restricting my magic somehow, almost as if ..." She gasped with sudden horrified realisation.

"What's wrong?"

"The fog – it's not natural. It's been created by magic." Its sticky tendrils clutched at her mind, trying to trick her, disorientate her.

"It's a trap!" she cried. "We have to get back to the ship now."

Quickly, they ran through the eerily silent streets to where they had left the cradle, only to find it gone. Looking at one another in a shared second of panic, they glanced up at the sound of weapons fire, and the angry shouts of battle that came from above.

"The ship is under attack!" Arden cried.

Then they all jumped back as a body hurtled down out of the fog to hit the flagstones with a sickening thud.

Snow watched as the cradle was winched up in response to the bell, wondering if it would just be their people, or whether they had managed to convince the villagers to evacuate already. Even though they had a signed order direct from the king, she had anticipated it would take longer than this to persuade the villagers of the danger of the situation.

There was a loud bang. The deckhand who had reached out to guide the cradle into place cried out and fell to the planking, and then the ship was swarming with guards wearing the uniform of the Contratulum.

Crying out in anger, the other deckhand raised his weapon, and the leader of the invaders casually gunned him down where he stood.

"Throw that overboard," he ordered his men, and Snow gripped the wheel in horror as two guards grabbed the unfortunate man writhing on the deck in agony and tossed him screaming over the side.

The leader, clad in the uniform of a Contratulum commander, strode over to her and ripped her flying helmet from her head. As her raven-black hair tumbled over her shoulders, a cunning smile spread across his face.

"Well, well. Look what we have here. I never thought to capture such a prize and I know the Pontifex will be very pleased to see you indeed." He tapped his cheek with the barrel of his weapon, and a cold smile spread across his face. "Now then, Your Highness, tell your people to stand down or else things will get very ugly, very quickly."

Icy cold fear gripped Snow's heart. She knew from the look in his eyes that this man wouldn't hesitate to kill everyone on board if she didn't do as he ordered.

Hurrying to the crumpled body, Fae turned it over to discover it was one of the deckhands with a gaping gunshot wound in his stomach. Relieved it wasn't Snow, or Kylah, or Eli, she was still appalled that anyone had met such a horrific end and looked up at Grein and Arden in white-faced shock.

"What's happened?" she whispered. "Who's attacked the ship?"

"The Contratulum," said a voice from the whiteness.

Jumping to her feet, Fae backed away with the two men. The fog was clearing, she realised. The buildings around them were becoming solid, and her heart clenched at the Contratulum troops that encircled them, weapons trained at their hearts.

"Who are you?" Arden demanded bravely. "What do you want with us?"

"That depends," the apparent leader spoke again. A tall man in the middle years of his life, he had an open, kindly face and the mad thought dashed through Fae's mind that he didn't look like a cold-blooded killer.

"On what?"

"On what you are doing here, so far north, where the wind is bitter, the winters long, and the snow deep."

Arden stared at the man, an odd expression crossing his face. "Isn't it the wrong time of year for snow?" he tentatively enquired.

"It doesn't only snow in winter," the man replied, and Arden's face sagged with relief. Still, he surveyed the men and their weapons warily.

"It's all right," the man reassured him. "These are all my men, true to the cause – to the memory of Queen Raven, and the hope of Princess Snow. I am Barnabus, commander of this legion. Or rather, I was, until that evil toad, Mirage, recommend I be replaced by my weasel of a second, Heyes."

"What happened here?" Arden demanded, and Barnabus shook his head.

"A trap. I only know that Slie laid out false information as bait, and then waited to see which fish tugged at the line. I fear one of your operatives within the Contratulum will be in danger because of it, but there is nothing we can do about that now. My men and I wish to defect to your side and serve Princess Snow – and aid her to claim the throne as the only true and rightful heir.

By now the fog had cleared, and Fae glanced up into the clear blue sky above them. Shading her eyes against the brilliant sun she squinted into the glare.

"The ship has gone," she cried, and Grein and Arden looked up in concern.

"Heyes was ordered to capture it and take it back to the capital," Barnabus told them. "I am truly sorry for your people left aboard, but if they cooperate then they will most likely be placed in the interrogation cells. They can be released when the Princess is crowned."

"You don't understand." Fae cried in anguish. "Snow is on that ship."

"Frick!" Barnabus looked up into the now empty sky, his face falling into an expression of utter despair. "If the Contratulum has her, it is truly the end for us all."

Chapter Thirty-One

The Trickster at Work

They approached Larkhaven at full steam and arrived late in the afternoon. Below them the busy town went about its business, apparently unfazed by the arrival of a dozen fully armed airships which hovered above them, blocking out the light. Working on deck, Ronin continually glanced east, expecting to see the airships of the Contratulum heave into sight any moment, but the skies remained empty.

An hour passed, then another, during which time the crew went from taut battle readiness to an uneasy tension, muttering amongst themselves and shifting with anticipation.

Watching Peregrine, Ronin saw him confer in a low voice with his second-in-command, who then issued a chain of orders setting the crew to work on maintenance and cleaning. Designed to keep them busy and stop them from fretting, this strategy had Ronin's quiet approval.

Looking around, Peregrine caught his eye and motioned him over. With Nylex following, the two men hurried to where Peregrine stood by the wheel.

"Come with me," he ordered, and led them from the deck, down the stairs and into a small cabin, in which a young woman in flying leathers was sitting at some sort of contraption. It was like nothing Ronin had ever seen before, and he looked at it with interest.

"What is it?" he asked. Peregrine hesitated, then seemed to decide to tell them.

"It's a wireless device for sending messages over very long distances."

Ronin and Nylex exchanged shocked glances.

"That's incredible," Nylex exclaimed. "How great a distance?"

"We have yet to determine the exact range," Peregrine replied, then glanced down at the young woman who had turned to them and was eyeing Nylex with interest.

"Have a break now, Mabel," Peregrine told her. With obvious reluctance, she took some sort of mechanical earmuffs from her head, dropped them onto the table, and flounced from the room.

"You're a married man now, Nylex." Peregrine gently chided him with a grin. "You shouldn't be noticing the young women anymore."

"What?" Nylex looked startled. "Who? What? I never ..."

"I am but jesting with you," Peregrine clapped him on the shoulder, then the smile dropped from his face and he eyed them both with a serious expression. "Are either of you beginning to wonder whether the information we received might have been false?"

"What do you mean?" Ronin asked in alarm.

"They should be here by now," Peregrine said. "In faith, the whole way here I was imagining arriving too late and finding Larkhaven in flames. But this silence, this absence of them ... my senses are telling me something is amiss." He paused as if considering something. "As you know, I have Dwarvian blood in me from my grandmother, Queen Starling. Sometimes, I know things before they have happened. I have an intense feeling when something is not right, and I've been feeling this all the way here."

Interesting, Ronin thought. Diluted as it was, it appeared that Dwarvian magic still ran in Peregrine's bloodline, and he wondered whether Snow had indeed inherited any powers.

Snow.

The thought of her made his sense of disquiet rise. Although he knew her to be safe back at the castle, far away from all of this, he still felt a vague sensation of unease.

"What are you saying?" Nylex demanded. "Do you believe this to be a trap of some kind?"

"I am unsure," Peregrine confessed. "In faith, it may merely be my imagination. But something feels wrong. I wished to seek your opinion. It is well known that some Dwarvians possess the skill of prophecy, and I wanted to ask if either of you were blessed with such a gift."

"No," Ronin shook his head. "I am afraid that's not the direction my talents lie."

"Nor mine," admitted Nylex. "That is more the province of my wife." He reddened a little over the word. "She is the one gifted – or perhaps – cursed, with the magic of foreseeing."

"I see." Peregrine's face fell.

"But why not contact the castle on this wireless device contraption and ask her if she has experienced any visions or images about this?" Nylex continued, and Peregrine's face brightened again.

"Excellent suggestion," he said.

"Do you wish me to go and find the operator for you?" Ronin asked, but Peregrine was already fiddling with knobs and levers and turning dials.

"No need," he said. "I have been trained in its basic use. Enough to contact the castle and speak to my father, at any rate."

Watching in fascination as the prince began speaking into a round, dish-like device mounted on the end of a joystick rather like the one that controlled the skimmer, Ronin marvelled at how far the Avians had advanced technologically in such a short space of time.

Peregrine spoke quickly to the voice at the other end. Minutes later, Falcon's familiar tone was booming into the small room – so clear, it was as if he was standing there with him.

"Remarkable." Nylex shook his head in wonder. "Truly remarkable."

Peregrine voiced his concerns to his father and requested that Fae be sent for, so they could ask if she had sensed anything out of the ordinary concerning their mission.

"Afraid that's out of the question," Falcon said. "She's not in the castle anymore."

"What?" Beside him, Nylex tensed in concern. "What do you mean, she's not in the castle. Where has she gone?"

"She's gone with Snow and the others to evacuate the village of Featherwell. Our operative in the Contratulum managed to get a message to us that it was to be attacked at dusk tonight, so they've gone to get the villagers out before the troops get there."

"But how could they possibly get there in time?" Peregrine demanded. "It's several days journey on horseback, and a day's journey by airship – even supposing they had one."

"They do have one," Falcon said. "They took ***The Lissa.*** Kylah was sure they could reach the village with time to spare to evacuate all its people and bring them back here to safety."

"Who piloted her?" Ronin demanded, although he already knew.

"Snow did. She said you taught her how to fly the ship. She seemed pretty confident."

That sense of unease was rising. Beside him, he could feel Nylex tensing and knew he was feeling it too. Both their women were missing, gone on a dangerous-sounding mission to rescue a far-away village.

"Was there time to equip ***The Lissa*** with a wireless?" Peregrine enquired.

"No, nor cannons. But they were not anticipating any trouble. It is to be a rescue mission only. Why the concern? Do you believe something is wrong?"

"Where are the Contratulum airships?" Peregrine demanded. "If they are not here, where are they? And why pick a small village to attack so far north of here? It makes no sense."

"Maybe the information that they were to attack Larkhaven was to distract us from their real plan," Nylex mused.

"Whatever that is," Peregrine muttered.

"Are you concerned Snow and the others may be in danger?" Falcon asked. Ronin heard the concern in his voice and realised how fond the king had become of his granddaughter in the few days he had known her.

"Divide and conquer," Nylex said, and the other two men looked at him.

"What did you say?" Peregrine asked.

"Divide and conquer," Nylex said again. His eyes were glittering intensely, and Ronin realised the trickster in him was once again coming to the fore. Buried and unneeded for five long years, that part of Nylex that was cunning and intuitive was re-emerging, as concern for his wife forced him to embrace once again all that was sly and clever about himself.

"Let's think it through," Nylex said and paced about the small room. "What do we know about the Pontifex Slie?"

"Snow said he was cunning and manipulative. That he was one of the cleverest men she had ever known, and that he had sold his soul to the Power long ago." Falcon's voice boomed loud and clear through the wireless,

"Right." Nylex tapped his finger to his cheek thinking. Ronin watched in fascination. He had forgotten what it was like to watch Nylex pick through a puzzle or a conundrum.

"Think on this," Nylex demanded and looked at Ronin. "They had a spy in Greta's household – the serving maid?"

"Yes."

"And she had been in place for years, so clearly Slie understands about playing the long game. What about if before she died, the girl described Snow to them."

"She had reported to the local Contratulum outpost that we were there," Ronin agreed. "And even an idiot would recognise Snow from a description, I mean she's ... well, she's ..."

"Quite." Nylex agreed wryly and saved Ronin the awkwardness of saying in front of Snow's uncle how beautiful he thought she was.

"So, they knew Snow was in Thornfield. The soldiers were right behind you when you took off in the skimmer. Is it possible they caught a glimpse of it? Or maybe heard the sound of the engine and surmised that you had a flying machine of some kind?"

"It's possible," Ronin agreed.

"So, they know Snow has access to a mechanical flying device, although they don't know what it is. They only know it is not an airship, because – let's face it – there's no way they wouldn't have spotted that hanging over the forest. They try to put themselves in Snow's shoes. Where would she go? Who would she turn to for help?"

"Me," Falcon helpfully inserted.

“That’s correct. You, Your Majesty. They will assume she has the means to get there quicker than on foot. They don’t know yet that the Avians have airship technology.”

“Are you sure about that?” Peregrine asked anxiously.

“I don’t think they would have openly declared war on one of the most powerful Houses in the world, without being very confident you had no hope of defeating them,” Nylex replied, and Peregrine nodded thoughtfully.

“So, they plant false information – either through one of your operatives that they have corrupted or merely by making sure it is leaked somehow – that their intended target is Larkhaven, the largest town in the kingdom. They knew you would instantly despatch all the forces you have to march to its defence.”

“As we did,” Falcon agreed.

“And Featherwell?” Ronin asked. “What part does that play in this little charade of Slie’s?”

“I’m not sure,” Nylex frowned. “On the surface, it doesn’t appear to play any part. Other than being at the opposite end of the kingdom from Larkhaven, it bears no comparison, so why ...”

“Perhaps that’s it,” Ronin suggested. “Perhaps its distance from here is why it was selected?”

“Maybe,” Nylex agreed. “Maybe Slie wasn’t sure who the traitor in the Contratulum was, so he set two false trails to opposite ends of the kingdom, hoping that one, at least, would be successful.”

“So, Snow and the others could be walking into a trap?” Ronin demanded, and Nylex looked at him with frightened eyes.

“I believe they are, but that’s not Slie’s main objective. He has got far bigger fish than that to fry. After all, he had no way of knowing that Snow herself would go to Featherwell. No, we need to think bigger – much bigger. Slie will not want this war to drag on for too long. He wants a quick, sharp victory.”

“But surely he would have achieved that by destroying Larkhaven?” Peregrine insisted. “After all, it’s the most important place in the kingdom.”

“No, it’s not,” Nylex said quietly.

There was silence in the cabin for the split second it took for his words to sink into the brains of the other men. Then Peregrine’s face blanched white and he grabbed the speaking device.

“Father!” he shouted. “They’re coming for you. They could be upon you at any moment. You must prepare as best you can for an attack. We are leaving now, but it will still be over a day before we can reach you.”

"We'll hold out until you get here," Falcon promised him, but there was fear behind his words, and Ronin wondered if they were more to reassure himself than them.

Quickly, Peregrine leapt from his seat and yanked the cabin door open. "Mabel!" he yelled when he spotted the figure of the wireless operator leaning against the wall talking to a deckhand. "Get in here now."

"Captain?" she asked, scuttling into the cabin, and looking at them with frightened eyes.

"Get onto the fleet immediately. Tell all captains to prepare for instant departure."

"What heading shall I give them, Captain?"

"Home! Tell them we are heading for the castle at top speed. As soon as we are underway, tell them that I want a private conversation with all captains. And it is to be strictly private. Then send for me when all are sitting by their wirelesses."

"Yes, Captain." Mabel dropped into her seat and pulled the headpiece back over her ears. Twisting the dials and levers, she began speaking urgently into the device as Peregrine pushed Ronin and Nylex from the cabin and set off for the deck at a run.

"Prepare for instant departure," he yelled at his second-in-command as they emerged back on deck.

"Aye, aye, Captain!" the man cried and instantly, organised chaos ensued as deckhands rushed to obey his orders.

Helping to crank the rudder, Ronin saw the rest of the fleet beginning to turn. Like a huge pod of sky whales, they sluggishly rotated, figures scurrying about their decks and swarming up ropes to begin the long journey home.

"Will we make it on time?" he muttered to Nylex, as the young man bent beside him to coil a rope.

"I don't know." He looked up at Ronin with concern etching lines across his face. "I just don't know. I hope so, but I'm afraid we will be too late."

"How much could the castle take? If they get there before we do, how much of the Contratulum's firepower could it withstand?"

"I don't know, not much, I ..." Nylex's eyes were haunted as long-suppressed memories bubbled to the surface. "You weren't there, Ronin. You didn't see what those airships were capable of. It was like red-hot lava raining down from the sky." He paused and shook his head in despair.

"I don't think anything could hold out for long against that."

Chapter Thirty-Two

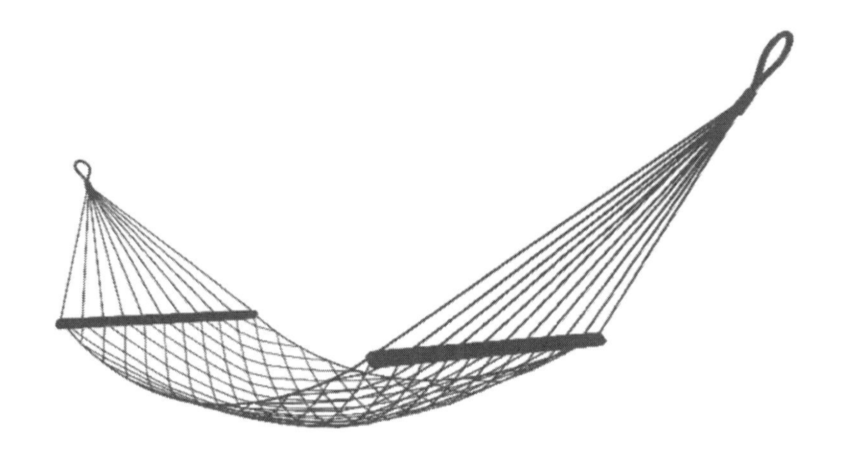

Plans Gone Awry

One of the soldiers seized her by the wrist and pulled her roughly away from the wheel, another taking control of the ship. Beneath Snow's feet, ***The Lissa*** shuddered in protest, but the man's grip was brutally strong, and the ship had no choice but to submit.

Trying not to slip in the blood oozing from the body of the first deckhand they had shot dead, which was lying by the cradle, Snow tilted her chin higher under the Commander's sardonic gaze. She would not let them see how scared she was. She was a princess – it was time she started acting like one.

"Take your hands off me," she hissed. The soldier gripping her wrist instinctively let go, glancing at his superior in mortification. To Snow's surprise, the man's grin merely widened, and he caught up her hand in his.

"Your Highness," he said, and pressed a firm kiss to the back of her hand. Snow shuddered at the rasp of his dry lips over her skin and snatched her hand away. "I am Commander Heyes," he continued. "And I owe you my sincerest gratitude. Because of you, I am going to be well rewarded. Slie was certainly not expecting Snow White herself to take the bait, but I know how delighted he will be to see you. I might even get a transfer away from this frozen hellhole to the city, where the real action is. So, for that, I do indeed thank you, Your Highness."

He executed a mock bow, and distaste crawled down Snow's spine. Then he raised his weapon and gestured to the steps leading below deck.

"After you, Your Highness."

Keeping her back ramrod-stiff, Snow went slowly down the steps, her skin prickling when he followed her. His boots echoing on the wooden planking, he pushed her before him to the engine room, where Kylah turned as they entered.

"What's going on ...?" she began, then her eyes widened in shock at the sight of Heyes behind Snow. His weapon moved to cover them all as Eli scurried to his sister's side. His boyish face twisted with incomprehension, he looked at Snow in alarm.

"S-s-snow?" he stuttered.

"Oh, S-s-snow," mocked Heyes, and Snow wanted to kill him herself.

"Shut the frick up!" Kylah yelled, and an ugly look crossed the man's face. Shoving Snow forward so violently that she stumbled into Kylah's arms, he backed away out of the room.

"Now you stay here, Your Highness, and tell your crew that there's been a slight change in plans. Convince them that it will be in their best interests to keep quiet, behave themselves, and keep shovelling the coal. It's a long journey back to the city, so we might as well all try to get along."

He slammed the door behind him and left Snow facing Kylah and Eli in despair.

"What's happened?" Kylah asked and shook Snow slightly. "Snow? Who the hell is he? What's going on? And where are the others?"

"Contratulum. We've been boarded by the Contratulum. That's Heyes, the commander of the legion. They killed two of the deckhands, and Fae and the others have been left down in the village."

"Are they all right?" Kylah demanded as Eli whimpered in distress. Snow shook her head. Completely dazed by the speed with which everything had happened, she was having trouble focusing on anything.

"Snow?"

"What?"

"Snow!"

"Sorry, I can't ... I don't know ..." Snow's voice wobbled into silence as she began to shake.

"Princess Snow of House White!" Kylah roared. "You will not fall apart. Not now. Not Ever! Your people need you to hold it together. Do you understand?"

"Y-y-yes, but ..."

"No buts!" Kylah shook her again. "I asked: do you understand, Your Highness?"

"Yes." Snow took a deep breath and drew herself upright. "Yes, Kylah, I understand. I'm sorry. I'm all right now."

"Good." Kylah looked at her, then surprised them both by pulling Snow to her in a fierce hug. "Now," she continued, "tell us everything that's happened, and let's see what can be done about it."

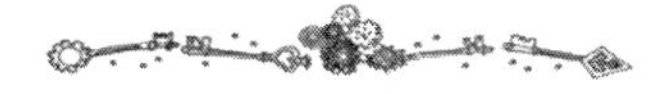

Onward raced the fleet of mighty airships. Keeping up the desperate pace, all around them the crew scrabbled to constantly trim the sails, adjust the fins, and anticipate their captain's orders before he gave them.

Taking their turn at shovelling coal, Ronin and Nylex stripped off their tunics and strained their backs and arms as they bent, shovelled, and threw the coal into the hot and hungry mouth of the furnace. To maintain such speeds, a constant supply of fuel was needed, and there could be no let-up – no decrease in the fire which raged and consumed all it was given.

After three hours of intense and backbreaking work, two fresh crew members came to relieve them, and they were sent to snatch an hour's precious rest. Staggering into the galley, their muscles screaming in protest and their skin glistening through its dusty black coating, they secured a bowl of broth each from the tight-lipped and stressed cook, and inhaled it sitting at the long wooden table.

Looking at the exhausted, silent people crowded around them, Ronin knew they couldn't keep up this breakneck pace for long. Yet he could also sense the resolve in every man and woman on board.

After Peregrine's hasty briefing of the captains of the other ships, it had been decided to be completely honest with the crews. Shock had reverberated through them at the news that their home was under threat – that even now the ferocious death machines of the Contratulum could be heaving over the horizon ready to unleash torrents of flaming death onto the castle and town below.

Determination replaced the shock and, without being asked, every crewmember on every ship set to work with steely resolution. They would make it in time, and they would defeat the enemy fleet. Any other outcome was unthinkable.

Given a few scoops of water in a bucket, Ronin and Nylex scraped the coal dust off themselves as best they could, then went to rest in their hammocks. Although physically drained, his mind would not switch off, and Ronin found himself unable to stop thinking about Snow. Was she safe? Had she managed to successfully evacuate the village? Was she even now on her way back to the castle, unsuspecting of what she was taking ***The Lissa*** into?

"Where do you think they are?" Nylex's voice intruded quietly into his thoughts.

"I don't know," Ronin muttered. "Safe, I hope."

"Maybe it was a good thing they went on this hare-brained mission. If it means they're not at the castle when ..." His voice trailed away, and Ronin silently finished the sentence in his head.

"Maybe," he agreed.

There was a long silence as both men swung gently in their hammocks to the perpetual forward motion of the ship. Ronin knew he would be unable to sleep, though, and suspected Nylex was as wakeful as he.

"You love her, don't you?" Again, Nylex broke into his thoughts.

“Who?”

“Snow. You love her, don’t you?”

Ronin remained silent, unsure of the best way to respond.

“You don’t have to answer. It’s obvious to anyone with eyes that you do. And it’s equally obvious how much she loves you in return. I think when you first met and it looked as if she could never return to her life as a princess, that you thought it might be possible for you to be together. But now all this has happened, now that she is Princess Snow again – soon to be Queen Snow – I think you’ve resigned yourself to let her go.”

“It’s better that way,” Ronin finally replied, and below him, Nylex sighed.

“Better for who? I don’t think it’s better for her, and I sure as frick don’t think it’s better for you.”

“It’s complicated, Nylex,” Ronin protested, and Nylex gave a tired snort.

“It’s only as complicated as you let it be, Ronin, and I should know. All those years I wasted believing I couldn't be with Fae when all the time the only thing stopping me was me.”

“This is different.”

“No, it isn’t. Not really. I don’t want you to feel the way I did when I thought Fae was dead and I hadn’t moved heaven and earth to be with her. Going into that schoolhouse, expecting to find her charred body, it was as if I had died too. We got lucky, that time, but it taught me not to take anything for granted – and that you need to seize every moment as if it were your last.”

At Nylex’s words, a memory crept into Ronin’s mind of warm arms and soft skin against his own, of sighs and whispers, and kisses as sweet as honey. Of a night that he had wished could last forever. Was he prepared to leave it at that?

“She’s going to be the queen,” he hissed fiercely. “There will be no room in her world for a penniless outcast. What can I possibly hope to give her?”

“Oh, I don’t know – maybe loyalty, and friendship, and companionship,” Nylex replied casually. “Maybe the security of having a partner who will always have her back, and always be on her side. And maybe – just maybe, you know – spending the rest of her life with the man who loves her and whom she loves back. But you’re right, that’s nothing at all,” he finished sarcastically.

Ronin lay silently rocking in his hammock, thinking of what Nylex had said. Then he thought again about Snow. Casting his eyes out of the porthole he saw stars twinkling in the darkened sky, and far away the lights bobbing on another ship. It had been decided to fly all through the night, and the ships had drawn further apart to avoid the risk of an accidental collision in the dark.

"Is it close to dawn, do you think?" he asked, and Nylex shifted in his hammock beneath him.

"Must be, it feels as if this night has lasted forever."

"Then the girls should be back with ***The Lissa*** by now. I want to know they made it back safely."

"Perhaps I could go and see if Mabel is on duty and ask her if there's been any news?" Nylex offered, and Ronin rolled to his side and peered down at the young man.

"I wouldn't want you to risk your virtue," he teased, and Nylex gave him a tight smile in return.

"Oh, there's no fear of that. Fae is the only one there has ever been in my life, and she is all I want forever. But, if a smile and a flirt will get us the news we want, then I'll stain my virtue just a little."

Ronin raised his brows, but nodded, and swung down from his hammock when Nylex scrambled from his. Following the young man down the crowded passageways, he paused outside the wireless room, and Nylex tapped softly on the door. Obeying the summons to enter, he looked at Ronin then slipped inside the cabin. Ronin leant on the wall to patiently wait.

Ten minutes later, Nylex emerged back into the passage, his face drawn into a tight knot of concern.

"So, how much of your virtue did you have to sacrifice?" Ronin asked.

"None of it," Nylex replied. "I told her the truth, that my bride of one night has gone on a dangerous mission and I am worried sick about her. Turns out, young Mabel has a romantic soul and was only too happy to put my mind at rest, so she had a little chat with her friend manning the receiving device in the castle and asked if ***The Lissa*** was back yet."

"And is it?"

"No, no sign of it. Of course, that's probably because Snow has stopped somewhere for the night. After all, she's not an experienced pilot and might not have wanted to fly in the dark."

"Maybe," Ronin agreed, but then he thought about Snow and an airship full of frightened villagers. With no food, no drink, and no medical supplies on board, and with the villagers being able to bring only what they could reasonably carry, he suspected Snow would have wanted to get them back to the castle as quickly as possible. Thinking about her brave stubbornness, he didn't believe a little bit of darkness would have stopped her either.

"She also told Mabel that the castle is in an uproar, preparing for the attack. That Falcon has ordered every able-bodied person to man the cannons upon the castle roof, and that Queen Wren and Princess Magpie are organising the evacuation of the children, and all who cannot fight, out of the castle."

"Good," said Ronin, and rubbed a hand wearily over his face. "Come on," he said. "Let's get back to work." The two men turned to go as the cabin door flew open behind them and a terrified Mabel barged into them in her haste to get out.

"What is it?" Nylex cried, steadying the girl as she fell onto them.

"I have to get to the Captain," she gasped.

"What's happened?" asked Ronin.

"We're too late! They're there! The Contratulum airships have reached the castle and opened fire on it. We're too late!"

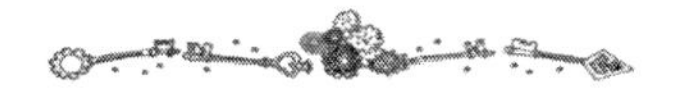

There was an airship hidden over the brow of the hill, Barnabus told them. Heyes had been only too happy to snatch all the glory of seizing the unexpected prize of ***The Lissa***, leaving his newly demoted previous Commander to clear the village and secure the landing party.

What about the fog? Fae asked, and Barnabus' lip had curled in distaste. They had a weather talker amongst them, he explained, and the Dwarvians had nodded. Such magic had occurred from time to time in their people as well. The ability to control the weather could be a useful talent when employed for the benefit of all, but Fae recalled the foul and sticky touch of dark magic in the fog and shuddered at the memory.

Leading the way out of the village, Barnabus again offered the services of himself and his men. Events were coming to a head, he explained. What with Snow's coronation a mere two days away, the Contratulum could no longer hide in the shadows but must show their hand – whatever it might be.

"We would be grateful of a lift back to the castle of House Avis," Arden requested, and Barnabus nodded. Devastated by the loss of Snow, the Commander seemed adrift, uncertain of what the future held for him and his men.

Cresting the hill, they discovered the airship hovering where Barnabus had said it would be, along with a large group of frightened men, women, and children huddled together, guarded by four soldiers with weapons trained on them. Upon seeing their leader, the men put up their arms and told the villagers they were free to go.

Quickly, the people scrambled to their feet, gathering up their children and hurrying away over the hill, casting curious glances at the Dwarvians as they went by. Fae smiled reassuringly at them, hoping they would quickly recover from their frightening experience.

"What's happened, Sir?" one of the soldiers asked as they approached.

"Change of plan, I'm afraid," Barnabus told them. "The Princess Snow has been captured by Heyes who even now will be taking her back to Slie."

The faces of the troops fell, and they cast desperate glances at one another.

"What are your orders, Sir?"

Fae was impressed at the loyalty Barnabus could command. For one wild moment thought that if this had turned out differently, she would be personally recommending him to Snow as the man fit to command her army.

"We will be taking these people back to House Avis, then we will be heading back to the city at speed to mount a seek and rescue mission."

"Rescue?" Arden looked startled. "You think to rescue Snow?"

"But of course," Barnabus replied in surprise. "It is unthinkable that we will not attempt to rescue the Princess from the clutches of Slie and Mirage. I shudder to think what those two will have planned for her."

"You'll never succeed, man!" Grein cried. "Not against the Contratulum. You will be vastly outmanned and outgunned."

"That may be so," Barnabus agreed grimly. "But it is all we can do now."

"You won't succeed alone," Arden stated with undoubting certainty. "But ..." he continued as Barnabus opened his mouth to protest, "you might succeed with some help."

"Help from whom?"

"King Falcon, Snow's grandfather, will be very keen to rescue his granddaughter."

"Any troops he would be prepared to spare us would be very gratefully accepted," Barnabus replied thoughtfully.

"But there is only so much space on our ship, and we cannot wait for ground troops. Speed is of the essence. It wants but two days until the coronation, and whatever Slie has planned for the princess it will happen before then – it must. And besides," he continued, "there is no doubt that this is a hopeless mission, so we cannot ask others to join us, for it will undoubtedly end in death for us all."

"Not necessarily," Arden said, and a grin crossed his face. "Tell me, Commander Barnabus, what would you say if I told you that I know of a dozen heavily armed airships, manned with experienced crews, who would be prepared to come with you to the city?"

Barnabus stared at him for long seconds, then a flicker appeared in his eyes and a smile quirked the corner of his tired mouth.

"I would say," he began, "that it would mean there's hope for us all."

Once onboard the airship, Fae quietly excused herself and slipped away to the galley. Surveying the supplies, she rolled her sleeves up and began preparing an enormous pot of beef and vegetable stew. Guessing that all must be hungry, she determined to ensure that every man had at least one hearty meal before departing for House White to attempt to rescue Snow.

Snow.

Pausing in the act of peeling a potato, Fae wiped a single tear from her cheek with her elbow and wondered how Snow, and Kylah, and Eli were faring.

Hoping beyond hope that they were unharmed, Fae wished her magic would allow her to somehow reassure them that help was coming and that they only needed to hold on until then.

But her magic had not been very forthcoming the last few days. Since the incident in the schoolhouse, she had not had any visions or flashes of pre-knowledge at all.

Well, all except one intensely private revelation that she had received that morning.

At the wonder of it, her lips curled into a smile and she gently placed a hand upon her abdomen.

Then the smile slipped as she thought about Nylex and wondered where he was.

"Stay safe, my love," she whispered, scraping the chopped potatoes into the bubbling savoury liquid.

"Stay safe, and please come back to me. Come back to us."

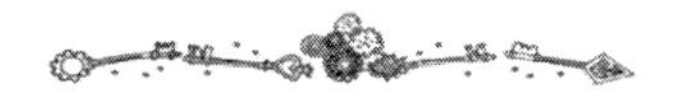

The commandeered Contratulum airship ***The Revenge*** was fast and deadly. Bristling with cannons, and weapons that could drop vats of liquid fire onto their victims below, it flew through the gathering dusk heading for the castle. The plan was to reach it as quickly as possible, meet with Falcon and tell him what had happened. Arden had no doubt he would then immediately order his fleet of airships to head for House White, and that Barnabus and his men would join them.

Exactly how Falcon would pass such orders to his fleet, Arden kept to himself and Barnabus did not enquire, assuming that the fleet was still at the castle.

The Revenge had been stripped of the insignia identifying it as a Contratulum airship, and Arden hoped it would be enough to at least delay Falcon from opening fire on them.

Gratefully, all accepted the heaped bowls of delicious hot stew when Fae appeared with trayfuls, and silently handed them around. They ate as night fell in a swirl of black velvet, in which the stars shone with icy brightness.

Taking his turn to shovel coal with the others, Arden thought about Snow in the hands of the Contratulum and shuddered. He worried about Kylah and Eli as well. The Pontifex presumably needed Snow if he wished to gain control of the kingdom, but he did not need the others, and Arden feared for their safety.

On and on they flew, as fast as they dared in the darkness until the first faint flush of dawn appeared on the horizon and the land below changed into rich pastureland dotted with flocks of sheep and goats.

Having caught some sleep in one of the empty cabins, Fae wandered up onto the deck to join Arden by the railings. Clutching a blanket around herself as a defence against the chill morning air, she tucked an arm through his and leant against him.

"Almost there," he told her, looking down fondly at the auburn head on his shoulder.

"Good," she murmured.

"When we reach the castle, Fae, you are to stay there. Do not think to go with them to House White. I know you are worried about Snow and the others, and you want to help, but you must stay where it is safe. You are no warrior."

"Neither are you."

"I know. That is why I will be staying behind with you. Mayhap, I can be of some use to Falcon in an advisory capacity. Grein will stay behind as well, he is too valued as a surgeon to risk sending into battle."

"I had planned to stay behind anyway," Fae reassured him. Then she bit her lip and looked out over the dawn-kissed landscape beneath them.

"I no longer have only myself to consider," she said, and Arden nodded in agreement.

"Yes, consider Nylex. He would want to know that you are safe."

"Nylex, yes ... also ... I am with child, Arden."

Arden stared down at the young woman who flushed prettily and gave him a small smile, her palm resting lightly on her middle.

"With child?"

"Yes, but please do not tell anyone yet. I do not wish Nylex to know until this is all over."

A loud boom echoed across the horizon, quickly followed by another, and there were shouts and the sounds of running feet as the soldiers rushed to the cannons placed along the edge of the ship.

"What is it? What's happening?" Arden cried, and a young soldier hurriedly swinging the cannon next to them to face over the railing paused to look at them in concern.

"Cannon fire up ahead!"

"The castle!" Fae cried. "The Contratulum must be attacking the castle."

"Aye," Arden agreed grimly. "With our ships too far away to be of any use."

Chapter Thirty-Three

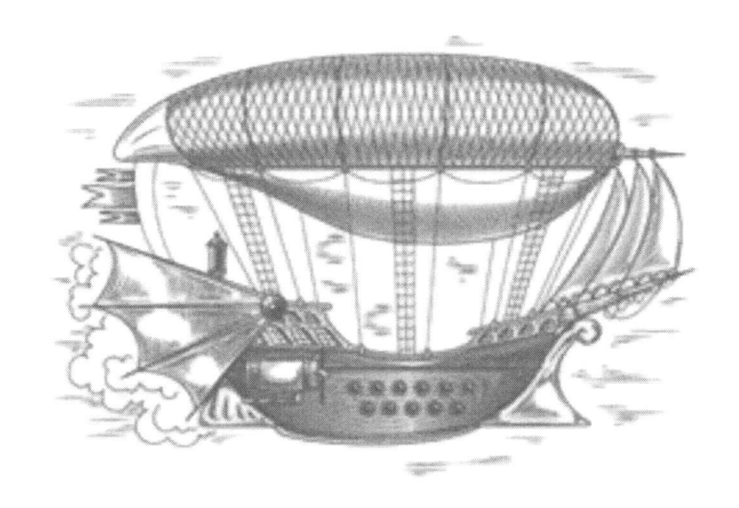

The Battle for the Castle

All through the night they flew. As the first faint flushes of dawn approached, Ronin paused to glance over the railing at the now visible landscape below them and realised that the castle could not be too far ahead. All the ships tightened into formation at the coming of the light, and he could see crewmembers scurrying about on the decks of the ships closest to them.

They rounded the final outcropping of the foothills of the Dwarvian mountain range, and there, in the distance, was the craggy peak with the castle atop and the town clinging to its side.

"Enemy ahead!" screamed the lookout.

Shading his eyes against the glare of the sun, Ronin saw, to his horror, four black shapes of the Contratulum airships looming like shadows of death over the castle and firing mercilessly down onto its exposed walls.

There was a muffled boom as a cannon fired back from the castle roof, and one of the airships flinched as it was hit. Yet if it was damaged, it was minimal, and in retaliation, he saw a glowing stream of liquid fire pour down onto the castle.

"Hard about!" yelled Peregrine, and Ronin hurried with the others to heave the fins around and set their ships on a course towards the enemy.

All around him he could see the other ships manoeuvring into position. The Contratulum airships were heavily outnumbered, but they were bigger, with more cannons – and those frightening weapons that spat fire hot enough to melt the flesh from a man's body.

He saw a part of the castle's battlements explode outwards from a direct cannon hit and waited for the Avian ships to commence firing their cannons – but they were still too far away. Plus, he realised they needed to go around the castle – not wishing to risk hitting it with their own cannon fire.

"Look at that ship!" Nylex cried beside him. "What's it doing?"

Ronin looked where he pointed. A fifth ship had appeared on the other side of the Contratulum airships. Stripped of all identifying colours or insignia, it loomed like an avenging angel, and to the astonishment of all, commenced firing its weapons at the enemy ships.

"What the ...?"

Ronin looked to where Peregrine was clutching the wheel in bewilderment, his eyes wide with shock at the sight.

"Is it ours?" Ronin shouted, and Peregrine shook his head.

"No, I don't know who it belongs to, nor where it came from."

"Who cares?" Nylex cried. "They are attacking the Contratulum ships, so that makes them our allies."

With ***The Kittiwake*** in the lead, half of the Avian ships rounded the east side of the castle and commenced firing upon the nearest ship. On the far west side of the castle, ***The Thrush*** was doing the same with the other half of the fleet.

The noise was indescribable. Cannon after cannon, both friend and foe, were fired in a cacophony of sound that rendered all deaf to anything but the sounds of battle.

Hauling on a rope and fighting to keep the ship steady against the backlash of constant cannon fire, Ronin saw one of the Contratulum's ships go down in a blaze of flames to crash into the rocky side of the cliff far below the castle.

A ragged cheer went up on his ship and it swung to go after the next airship that was still blasting the castle. With ***The Sparrowhawk*** close on their port side, ***The Kittiwake*** unmercifully blasted shot after shot into them, until a lucky cannonball ripped through the huge balloon above, and the Contratulum's ship listed dangerously to one side.

Ronin saw crewmembers sliding over the railings of the enemy ship to fall shrieking into the void below. Then the ship itself keeled over in mid-air and plunged almost gracefully down, flames licking at its sides until a huge explosion ripped through its midsection, wrenching the ship in half as it plummeted down to join its fellow ship at the bottom of the valley.

On the other side of the castle, ***The Thrush*** and the other Avian ships had succeeded in destroying one of the Contratulum's ships, and the other was still being mercilessly pounded by the unknown vessel.

The Contratulum's ship broke off engagement. Turning ponderously, it headed for the gap to the right of the rogue airship, and with a surprising turn of speed, shot through and away before ***The Kittiwake*** could reach it.

Wondering whether Peregrine would order them to pursue it, Ronin glanced around the deck and became aware of how much damage they had sustained themselves.

All about him, people lay groaning in bloodied heaps. Gaping holes in the deck had scattered vicious splinters of wood far and wide, and becoming aware of a pain in his abdomen, Ronin looked down to discover a long rent in his tunic and a raw scratch bisecting his belly.

"Ronin?" He turned to find a white-faced Nylex beside him clutching onto the railing for support. "Could you possibly pull this out for me?" he asked and turned to show Ronin a foot-long shard of wood sticking into his back.

Sucking in a gasp of concern, Ronin examined the wound.

"If I pull this out," he said, "it's going to start bleeding. Best to wait until we get to a healer."

Nylex nodded, then looked about them. "Is everyone all right? Did we lose any of our ships?"

"No, we seem to all be intact, although I would imagine they are damaged as well."

"That rogue ship is still there." Nylex nodded his head towards the unknown ship drawing in closer to the docking area of the castle.

"Wait a minute," he exclaimed, squinting to see as the ships drew closer together. "Isn't that Arden?"

"What, where?"

"On the strange ship? There, standing on the deck waving at us? And, oh by all the gods, that's Fae beside him."

"Can you see Snow and the others?"

"No. Oh wait – there's Grein, but I can't see Snow, or Kylah and Eli. Perhaps they're below decks."

Impatiently, Ronin waited as ***The Kittiwake*** limped into the dock beside the other ship. Having been at the forefront of the battle, she had been pounded more than most and was badly listing to her port side.

Ronin doubted that the ship would be fit for another battle any time soon, and he wondered where the rest of the Contratulum fleet was. Surely four ships were not the extent of it.

On the damaged dock, people scurried to secure the mooring ropes. As he helped Nylex over the railing and onto the solid planks below, Ronin was aware of the rogue ship being secured in the dock beside them.

"It's all right," he heard Arden bellowing, as Avian troops poured onto the dock and aimed their weapons at the grim-faced soldiers behind Arden. "They're on our side and we need to speak to King Falcon immediately."

"Nylex!"

Fae had clambered off the other ship and spotted them. Her smile of delighted welcome changed into a gasp of dismay as she spotted her husband's injury, and she rushed to his side.

"I'm all right," he promised her and attempted to prove it by gathering her to him in a passionate kiss of welcome, that had all the crewmembers clambering off ***The Kittiwake*** behind them letting out a ragged cheer of approval.

Grein and Arden reached their side, leading what looked to be a legion of Contratulum soldiers.

"Grein, help me," Fae begged, as she slipped her shoulder under the white-faced Nylex's arm to support him.

To Ronin's concern, blood was beginning to stream down the young man's back, and Grein tutted as he peered at it.

"To the hospital with you," he commanded. "Come along."

He pushed Ronin out of the way and took his place under Nylex's arm. Slowly, he and Fae moved away, supporting a shaky Nylex between them.

"Ronin, come with us," Arden ordered. "We need to report to Falcon immediately, and I think you're going to want to hear what we have to say."

"I will," he murmured distractedly, busily scanning the ships and docks for the familiar sight of long, raven black hair and a beautiful smile.

"Where is she?" he said, turning on Arden in despair. "Where is she?!" he shouted when Arden didn't answer.

Arden silently looked at him, and Ronin knew. He just knew.

"How?" he demanded, his legs beginning to shake beneath him. "How did she die?"

"Oh, she's not dead," Arden quickly reassured him. "Ronin, Snow isn't dead, but if we don't act quickly, she soon will be."

"Then I don't understand," he cried in anguish. "Where is she?"

"The Contratulum took her," Arden said, his face reflecting his dismay. "They took her, and the others, and she'll be halfway back to the city by now. Back to Slie and Mirage."

His mind could not process it. As he hurried behind Arden and the commander of the Contratulum soldiers, who apparently had defected to their side, and had secretly been on it the whole time, his brain repeated the words over, and over, again.

She was taken – gone. On her way to the very people who wished her harm.

He remembered her saying how war was coming, and either of them could die. He had assumed it would be him – had never imagined it could be her.

They won't kill her, Arden had promised. They needed her until after the coronation, at least, so they would keep her alive until then. But the coronation was only one day away. They were running out of time.

At the thought of Snow in the hands of Mirage, a moan of despair escaped his lips. She must be so afraid – so terrified of what they would do to her.

And what about Kylah and Eli? As Arden had said, they needed Snow alive for now, but they did not need them.

All around him he could see the damage that the castle had sustained during the attack. Great piles of masonry lay collapsed and shattered. The banqueting hall doors had been blown out into the corridor, and through the gap, as they hurried by, he could see a hole in the ceiling.

The castle's people fared little better. Many were nursing injuries or helping others to the hospital wing. Covered in a layer of dust and a coating of blood, they were unrecognisable from the happy and beautiful people who had attended the wedding two days previously.

Would it have been better, he thought, if he had listened to Snow, and granted her wish to stay hidden in the forest with him for the rest of their days? They could even have been married by now, joined forever by ancient words of binding power.

At the thought of them living peacefully and happily in his cottage, meeting up with the others, raising children together, lying still and quiet in his bed listening to the rain pounding on the roof and talking in the firelight, he wanted to fall to his knees and sob with despair.

He should have said yes to her – at least then she would be with him. She would be safe. After all, who cared who sat on the throne? But he knew that Snow cared. That she could never have abandoned her people to the mercies of the Contratulum.

This road was one they had always been bound to take, and perhaps this was the ending fate intended for them all along.

They reached the throne room, where King Falcon and Queen Wren awaited them. His eyes narrowing in incredulous suspicion when he spotted the Contratulum commander, Falcon looked to Arden for an explanation.

Succinctly and clearly, Arden told all.

At the news that Snow had been captured and taken back to the city, Wren gave a great cry of anguish and sat heavily on her throne. Falcon's face darkened, and his eyes glinted with barely contained rage.

"Your Majesty." Barnabus bowed his head and spoke for the first time. "My ship received minimal damage. My men and I are ready to leave immediately to attempt to rescue the Princess."

"What is your name, Sir?" Falcon demanded, pacing down from the dais to stand before the commander.

"Barnabus, Your Majesty."

Meeting Falcon's gaze with a coolly collected stare of his own, Barnabus did not waver, although he must have been apprehensive. Surrounded by Avian troops who would kill him and his men at a single command from Falcon, how could he be otherwise? Yet if he was, he did not show it.

"Barnabus?"

"Yes, Your Majesty."

"My daughter, Queen Raven, spoke highly in her journal of an operative of hers called Barnabus. Might that be you?"

"Yes, Your Majesty. I had the great honour of meeting the Queen on a few occasions. She was a powerful force for good – one that has been sorely missed."

Falcon merely nodded, then turned to Arden and clasped him on the shoulder.

"What do you think of this hare-brained scheme of his to go to the city to try and rescue Snow?"

"I do not see that we have any choice in the matter," Arden replied. "We cannot leave her in the hands of the Contratulum. Not just because she is Snow, but because she is the rightful heir to the throne. If they manage to break her – make her their puppet – then there will be nothing they cannot do. They will rule the Kingdom of House White through her, and nobody will be safe from their greedy intentions."

"She is Princess Snow of the House White and my granddaughter!" Falcon roared. "They will never be able to break her."

"With all due respect, Your Majesty," Barnabus interjected. "You do not know what they will do to her. They have the foulest black Powers to call upon, as well as such subtle instruments of torture that none could hold out for long against them. Certainly not a frightened young girl."

Ronin didn't think he'd made a sound, but he must have, for Falcon turned to look at him.

"Your Majesty," Ronin began. "If this man is going to rescue Snow, then I am going with him."

Barnabus looked him up and down.

"I could do with all the able-bodied warriors I can get," he said. "And you look as if you know how to handle yourself in a fight."

"You are conscripted in my army," Falcon reminded him. "You go only if I give you permission to go."

"I am aware of that, Your Majesty," Ronin replied. "However, I am going. We cannot leave Snow there. I am going to find her, with or without your permission."

Falcon's brows beetled together, and he looked about to argue when a soft voice from behind stopped him in his tracks.

"No, Falcon, wait."

Queen Wren arose from her throne and gracefully descended the steps. Ignoring the bows of the men around her, she paced over to Ronin and put a hand to his cheek.

"Tell me, Ronin, why would you defy the word of a king to go after my granddaughter?"

"Because I have to," he whispered brokenly. "Because she's my Snow and I have to try to save her or die in the attempt."

Wren nodded, then turned to her husband, who was looking confused.

"But Wren ..." he began, and she gently put a finger to his lips.

"You must let him go," she said. "And I will explain it to you later."

"If he's going, then so am I," said a voice from the doorway, and Robin stood there with her ladies flanking her on either side. "***The Thrush*** is relatively undamaged. She merely needs to take on more fuel, and she will be ready to go."

"And I will go as well." Prince Peregrine strode into the room. "Unfortunately, ***The Kittiwake*** is in no fit state to go. Unless another ship can be found for me, I shall be crewing for my daughter, but I am determined to go."

"Fine." Falcon threw up his hands in despair. "Why don't we pack a picnic, and all go, make it a real family affair."

"Gramps – Snow *is* family," Robin insisted. "And we are the only family she has left." Did her eyes flick to Ronin? He could have sworn that they twinkled at him.

"And we simply can't leave Snow in the hands of those people."

"Oh, my old friend," Falcon sighed and looked at Arden. "If I had known what trouble you would drag on your heels when you first arrived at my door, I might not have let you in."

"Yes, you would have," Arden replied. "Because she is Raven's daughter to the core, and you will do anything within your power to save her."

In the end, nine out of the twelve airships were deemed flight and battle-ready. Removing the injured, and refuelling and provisioning the ships, took time, as did deciding how the vessels were to be manned. The captain of ***The Merlin*** had been seriously injured in battle, so Prince Peregrine took her place, taking many of his original crew with him to replace those from ***The Merlin*** who had been injured or killed.

Jacobson, the chief engineer, upon hearing of the capture of Snow, Kylah, and Eli, had also immediately volunteered to go, and the room was found for her on board Robin's ship ***The Thrush.***

Ronin was going with Barnabus. He had seen the light of determination in the man's eyes when he spoke of rescuing Snow and decided his best chance of reaching her was with the commander. Also, he figured that a Contratulum ship probably stood more chance of getting close to the palace before anyone realised it was fighting for House Avis.

Despite his protests, he was ordered to the hospital to get his wound seen to, where he was issued with a fresh set of clothing. Removing his tunic, he sat on the bed and fretted impatiently whilst Grein examined him.

"A scratch," he pronounced. "But a deep one, and it could get infected."

"I'm still going." Ronin insisted.

"I never said you couldn't. I merely said it could get infected. Here," he slapped a pot of ointment into his hand, "put this on and try to keep it clean. But I'll want to see you when you get back."

On the other bed, Fae was sewing closed the wound on Nylex's back. Her fingers deft as she pulled the stitches tight, she finished and dropped a kiss onto the back of his neck.

"A few days rest and you'll be fine," she said, handing him a clean tunic.

"There is no time to rest," he told her, pulling it over his head with a wince and doing up the buttons. "The fleet is leaving within the hour, and I shall be going with it."

Fae's face crumpled and she turned away, a hand to her mouth in distress.

"Would you stay if I asked you to?" she whispered.

"I can't," he said and held her close. "You know I can't. I must go. Not only to rescue Snow but Kylah and Eli as well. They're family, Fae – they're the only family we have."

"Family?"

For a moment, Fae looked on the verge of saying something, then she nodded through her tears.

"I know," she murmured. "But please, be careful and come back to us."

"I will," he promised, and Ronin turned away as they kissed like lovers who expect never to see each other again.

"Is there an extra berth available on your ship?" Nylex asked, and Ronin nodded.

"Please look after him," Fae hugged Ronin so tightly he could feel the pounding of her heart.

"I will," he promised.

"And bring her home. Bring them all home."

"That's the plan," he tried to joke. She smiled, but it didn't reach her eyes.

As Fae watched them go, Grein looked at her curiously.

"Why didn't you tell him?"

"Tell him what?"

"About the baby."

"How did you ...?"

"It's my job to know. So, why didn't you tell him? It would have given him something to live for?"

"Maybe." Fae turned sorrowful eyes on him. "Or it might have given him something worth dying for."

Chapter Thirty-Four

Prisoners of the Contratulum

Left alone in the engine room, Snow tried to help by shovelling coal, but quickly realised the limits of her physical endurance. Unable to keep the furnace as hot as it needed to be, Snow felt the speed diminish until at last, ***The Lissa*** was barely crawling along, and Heyes himself came to shout at them to go faster.

Fearless, Kylah stood up to him and yelled back that if he wanted more speed, then he had to supply more manpower because a skinny lad and a useless namby-pamby princess simply weren't enough.

Heyes fumed and blustered, but then stomped away and a few minutes later four burly soldiers entered the room. Thankful, Snow relinquished her shovel and stepped back, wiping the coal dust from her face, and arching her spine to relieve the cramping pain. One of the soldiers looked up and down her body and exchanged a grin with his fellows.

"See this, lads? It's been a long time since I've come across such a pretty little piece of arse." To Snow's horror, he pulled her close to him and cupped her backside with his large hand.

"Let me go!" she demanded, but he laughed in her face and toyed with the lacings of her corset.

"How about me and you go somewhere where you can show me how nice you can be to me?"

"S-s-snow." stuttered Eli and tried to pull the man off her.

"Sort him," the man ordered, and one of the others shoved Eli violently back into Kylah, who caught him and pushed him behind her.

"You do realise who she is, don't you?" she enquired casually.

"Princess Snow, yeah – what of it. She's a woman, and I know what women are good for."

"She's the Princess yes – but the Pontifex needs her alive to crown her as his puppet queen."

"So? I'm not going to kill her – just show her what it's like to be with a real man." He leered into Snow's face and groped at her breasts through the thick leather corset.

"Tell me, Princess," Kylah continued casually. "I once heard a tale about the crown they use during the coronation ceremony – the Crown of Purity, is it? That it can tell if someone is pure or not?"

"Yes," stammered Snow, cringing away from the foul breath, and even fouler touch, of the man. "The Crown of Purity is placed upon the heir apparent, and it glows white if they are pure of heart."

"And what happens if it doesn't glow white?"

"The crown rejects the heir, and they cannot be named monarch."

"So, if you've been soiled by this filthy pig, what will happen to the Pontifex's grand plan to make you his puppet queen?"

Snow stared at Kylah for a split second, then in a blinding flash, understood Kylah's ploy. Clinging to the hope that these men were too ignorant to know how the crown functioned, she followed Kylah's lead.

"It won't work," she gasped.

"And what will the Pontifex do to that man, and to any who helped him?" Kylah asked, and looked at the soldiers one by one. They shifted uneasily and exchanged terrified glances. They knew only too well what would happen to them should they be stupid enough to upset one of the Pontifex's plans.

"Come on, man," one of his comrades seized him by the arm and pulled him from Snow. "It's not worth all of us being killed, or worse, for the sake of a fumble with a bit of skirt."

For a moment it looked as if the man was going to ignore them, for his arm tightened around Snow's waist and he sniffed at her exposed neck. Then he pushed her away in disgust.

"You're too skinny to give a man a good ride anyway," he growled and snatched up the shovel. The others also picked up shovels and began to scrape up the coal, throwing it into the furnace as Kylah and Eli came over to where Snow was trembling in shocked disgust.

"Why don't you two go and get some sleep. It's been a long day, and heaven only knows when you'll next get the chance."

"But Kylah," Snow whispered. "We can't leave you here with them."

"I'll be all right," Kylah assured her. "Go on now, the pair of you, get some rest."

With teams of soldiers shovelling coal in shifts, ***The Lissa*** raced through the skies, and it wasn't long before the towers of the capital city and the palace could be seen on the horizon. Ordering a bucket of hot water be brought to her, Heyes gave orders that Snow was to wash. He wanted her to look her best when he dragged her before the Pontifex to claim his reward for the unexpected prize.

Grateful for the hot water, if not for the reason behind it, Snow quickly washed the bits of her she could reach and pulled her hair over her shoulder to plait it neatly. Securing it with a piece of string she found on the floor, she took a deep breath, then sank onto one of the bunks.

Still shaking from the feel of the man's hands roaming over her body, knowing how differently the encounter could have ended were it not for Kylah's cool head and quick wits, Snow swallowed down the acrid bile that bubbled into the back of her throat.

"No," she whispered fiercely to herself. "You will not fall apart, Princess Snow. You will put this in a box, and you will not look at it until this is all over. You have more important things to worry about." Drawing one shaky breath after another, Snow peered miserably from the porthole.

It was over. All their grand plans for war and revolution were over. Once she was in Slie's hands, he had won. Determined to hold out for as long as possible, Snow was also sensible of the fact that she probably would not be able to withstand torture for long.

She shivered at the thought of Slie's darkness slipping into her mind and stripping away her willpower – until she was no longer herself but instead was a tool for them to use as they will.

Thoughtfully, she opened her chatelaine and took out the tiny scrap of witch hazel. She sniffed at it, catching the faintest suggestion of a scent, and wondered whether the magic it contained was strong enough to help her against the combined might of the Contratulum.

Afraid they would take the chatelaine away from her, she tucked the yellow sprig inside her corset, next to where the rose quartz lay warm between her breasts.

On a whim, Snow drew the pendant out and pressed the stone to her hot forehead. Closing her eyes, Snow thought about Ronin.

She wondered where he was, and if he had heard about her capture yet. Squeezing her eyes even tighter shut to stop any tears from escaping, she clutched the crystal and thought about how he must feel, knowing she was lost to him forever.

Ronin!

Desperately, she let her consciousness roam free of her body. She pictured him in her mind, her heart giving a miserable lurch at the thought of never seeing him again. Around her, the ship shuddered in sympathy.

Ronin.

Was that her, or ***The Lissa***? With her mind connected to the quick, lively sentience of the ship, Snow was unsure where she ended, and the ship began.

Ronin! Find me! Find us! Hurry, before it is too late.

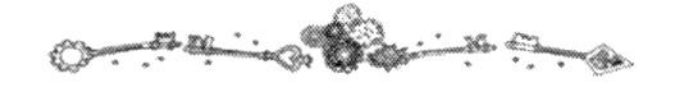

Exhausted after two days with next to no sleep, Ronin didn't argue when Barnabus ordered him and Nylex to get some rest and take the last watch. Stumbling downstairs into the hold, he fell into the nearest hammock and an instant and deep sleep.

Annoyed when he awoke before his watch began, he turned onto his back and stared into the darkness. Around him came the soft, rhythmic creak of the ship as it powered through the sky, and the mumbled snores of the other sleeping men.

Trying to force himself back to sleep, he froze as a voice whispered into his brain. Insidious and insistent, the tendril twined through his mind.

Ronin!

"What?" he asked, wondering whether Nylex sleeping in the hammock above had spoken. But all around him in the hold was stillness and the sound of men sleeping.

Ronin.

Lissa? he thought incredulously. *Is that you?*

Ronin! Find me! Find us! Hurry, before it is too late.

Snow?

But there was silence. The voice did not come again, and Ronin was left wondering if he had merely imagined it.

They were marched to the palace dungeons to await orders from Heyes to take them to the Pontifex. Unwilling to relinquish the shock value of exactly who his prisoners were, Hayes swore his men to secrecy and merely requested an audience with the Pontifex to brief him on what happened at Featherwell.

He was told he would have to wait. Pontifex Slie was meeting with the Council of Elders and would see him later.

Muttering with discontent, Heyes had personally taken them down the long flights of steps to the grim and cheerless holding cells and shoved them into one.

Lingering to press an unwanted kiss onto Snow's hand, he threw orders at the gaoler that they were to be given food and water immediately and then left in a flurry of cloak, his boots ringing on the flagstone floor.

Grateful to still be together, Snow looked around their new quarters with a shudder. All of her life she had lived in the sumptuous palace above, with no idea there were dungeons far below her feet that poor unfortunate souls were kept in.

“We need to do something, and we need to do it fast,” Kylah muttered, casting a glance over her shoulder at the gaoler as he shouted something at one of the other prisoners.

Shaking, the poor wretch handed back his food bowl with his meal half-eaten. As they watched, the gaoler thumped his obese backside down at the table and proceeded to slurp the food into his cavernous mouth.

“Yes, but what?” Snow murmured.

“I don’t know, but once Slie sees you it’s all over.”

“L-l-ook,” Eli interrupted. “He’s taking away all their food and only letting them eat half of it. That’s t-t-terrible.”

His mind fixated on the indignity of having half your dinner removed, Eli seemed blissfully ignorant of the bigger picture, and Kylah rolled her eyes at Snow.

“We have to get out of here, that’s the first thing.”

Thoughtfully, Snow looked at the iron bars and the solid lock on the door, and a memory stirred. Excitedly, she looked at Kylah.

“Ronin told me you can bend iron to your will. Could you do anything about that lock?”

“Probably.” Kylah glanced over her shoulder. “But then there would still be old greedy gutbucket out there and his big fricking gun to deal with.”

“He’s t-t-taken away half of all of their dinners.” Eli hissed furiously.

“Yes, I know, Eli, it’s terrible,” Kylah agreed soothingly.

An idea formed in Snow’s mind.

“Eli, could you bring a plant here?”

“P-p-probably,” he said.

“What are you thinking, Snow?”

“There’s a mushroom – it’s creamy white on top but has red speckles underneath. Do you know of it?”

“The Nightshade? Yes, I k-k-know of it. But why do you want it? You can’t eat it, it’s p-p-poisonous.”

“I know why she wants it,” Kylah told him and looked at Snow in admiration. “Clever. Very clever. Just do it, Eli.”

Eli closed his eyes and cupped his hands together, and when he opened them, the mushroom lay in his palms. Creamy white in the gloom of the cell, it looked innocuous, and Snow hoped it was as deadly as Tibby had said.

Burying it under the straw in the corner, they sat on the bench and waited for their promised meal to be brought to them.

They didn’t have to wait long.

There was a knock at the door and the gaoler grumbled and heaved his bulk from the chair. Opening the door, he took a tray from a servant, who cast him a nervous glance and fled as quickly as possible.

Sniffing in anticipation at the food, he wiped his greasy chops with one meaty hand and brought the tray over to the cell.

"Only eats half, little people," he told them, passing the bowls through the slot. "You only gets to eat half, then you gives the other half to Cradoc and he eats the rest. That way you gets to not be thumped, and Cradoc gets his din-dins."

Looking at the bowls of slop in distaste, Snow only managed a few spoonful's before she placed the bowl down on the bench beside her, pulling a face at Kylah, who only managed a bite more than her.

"Not exactly up to Fae's standards, is it?" she muttered, and Snow ruefully shook her head.

Eli slurped at his for a bit longer before even he screwed his nose up in distaste and pushed away his bowl with a lot more than half left.

"Not n-n-nice," he pronounced sadly.

"Quickly, now," Kylah muttered and moved to block the gaoler's view of Snow as she fished the mushroom out from under the straw, brushed it clean, then crumbled it into the slop. Breaking it up into tiny pieces, she stirred it well in.

She hoped it wouldn't make it taste so bad that even the gaoler wouldn't eat enough of it.

"All finished with your nice din-dins?" the gaoler asked and waggled his hand through the bars. "Gives them to me. Gives them to me now."

Eli passed the bowls through to him, and they silently sat on the bench and watched as he tipped everything that was left into one bowl and hungrily consumed the lot.

Belching and wiping at his greasy mouth with a filthy rag, he patted his stomach in contentment and beamed benevolently at them through the bars.

"You won't be so fussy after a while, little people. You'll nom nom up your nice din-dins once you've been in here a while."

Time ticked by and nothing happened.

Desperately, they exchanged glances. Snow wondered if perhaps there hadn't been enough of the mushroom to affect the corpulent creature, or perhaps the rumours of its toxicity had been exaggerated.

Then the gaoler shifted uncomfortably in his chair and clutched at his gut. A film of sweat broke out on his bald head. A loud expulsion erupted from his nether regions and he groaned in agony. Wrinkling their noses at the foul odour, they waited in anticipation as he cursed and grabbed at his stomach.

"What's wrong with Cradoc?" he cried, as another explosion of odour and sound burst from him and he cried out in pain.

"Help me!" he screamed, and Snow hoped nobody was in earshot. By now realising something was happening to their greedy gaoler, the other prisoners crowded to the fronts of their cells. Clutching the bars, they watched in horrified fascination as he began to heave and gasp, grabbing at his throat as if he couldn't breathe.

He rolled sideways. The chair broke beneath his not inconsiderable bulk as he crashed to the floor and bucked in agony. His eyes rolled towards them, and Snow felt a moment of acute pity at his obvious terror, before hardening her heart.

One last gasp for air. One last volcanic eruption from his trousers. Then Cradoc lay still, his eyes wide and staring.

"Finally," Kylah muttered and pressed her hands over the lock. Closing her eyes in concentration, she carefully manipulated its internal workings with her mind until ... click! The lock sprang open and they were free.

Grabbing Cradoc's gun from where it lay by the bulk of his body, Kylah checked it over with a grin of satisfaction.

"Nice," she murmured and beckoned the others to follow her towards the door.

"Wait!" One of the prisoners called after them, and Snow paused to look back at him. "Please," he begged. "You can't leave us like this."

Snow hesitated.

"Snow, come on." Kylah hissed from the doorway.

"Please," the man begged again. "It doesn't only snow in winter."

Snow's eyes flew wide, and she stared at him in shock.

"It doesn't only snow in winter," he said again, "Your Highness."

Swiftly, Snow snatched up the keys from Cradoc's body and tossed them to him through the bars. He caught them in one hand and quickly fitted them to the lock.

"Go!" he told her when she hesitated. "You must go. I will release the others."

"Thank you," she murmured, then turned and fled after Kylah and Eli.

Silently, they crept up the dank and winding stairway, figuring they needed to go up before they could get out. They didn't have a plan beyond staying undetected and getting out of the palace. Seeing the grim expression on Kylah's face, and the way she held her weapon ready, Snow was pleased that the other woman was there. Selfish though it might be, Snow was desperately glad she wasn't alone.

Reaching an iron door at the top of the stairs, Kylah creaked it slowly open and peered through. Creeping into the empty corridor, she motioned them to follow her. Unfamiliar with this part of the palace, Snow had only shrugged helplessly when Kylah asked her which way they should go, and so they chose a direction at random.

Hearing voices coming their way, they flattened themselves into an alcove as a gaggle of servants hurried past, carrying what looked like armfuls of silver bunting. Chatting excitedly amongst themselves, the group never even glanced in their direction. Once they had passed, Kylah beckoned them back out.

"What was that they were carrying?" she muttered.

"It's the decorative bunting that is used for festivals," Snow replied. "Although why they would be ... oh, the coronation. They must be getting ready for the coronation."

"Won't be much of a coronation with you supposedly a prisoner of House Avis," Kylah drawled, and Snow frowned in confusion.

"No, maybe the people don't know I'm no longer in the palace," she said.

"Or maybe Slie knows you're back," Kylah replied, and Snow's heart gave a terrified thump.

Chapter Thirty-Five

A Surplus of Escape Plans

The Contratulum airship was faster than those of the Avians, and they soon left the rest of the fleet behind. This was no bad thing, as the plan was to get as close to the palace as possible without arousing suspicion. To this end, all the Contratulum colours and insignia had been reinstalled on the ship.

Haunted by the voice he had heard in the night, Ronin silently urged the ship on faster and faster, convinced that they were running out of time. Every time he imagined Snow at the mercy of Slie and Mirage, his jaw tightened, and he vowed to himself that if they had harmed one hair on her head, he would kill them.

He heard the murmurings of the men around him and realised that they did not expect to live out the day. Working alongside them, his admiration of Barnabus and the loyalty he installed in his men grew. Finally, the Commander summoned him and Nylex to his cabin, where a plan of the palace was spread out over a table.

"I've been thinking how best to go about this." Barnabus wearily rubbed a hand over his face, and Ronin wondered how much sleep he had got if any at all. "I think we should be able to get into the palace without any suspicion. Nobody knows that our allegiances lie elsewhere, and Heyes will be too excited about presenting his prize to the Pontifex to spare a thought for us."

Ronin nodded in agreement and looked at the plans with interest.

"Until now, the Contratulum have hidden their airships in vast caverns beneath the palace, but since the declaration of war upon House Avis, they have created docks up on the palace battlements. We will dock there. We have spare uniforms for you and Nylex, so we should be able to enter the palace without being challenged."

"And what then?" Nylex asked. Barnabus shrugged.

"I have no idea where they will be holding the princess and the others. Logic says in the Contratulum dungeons far below the palace, in which case it will be almost impossible to get to them. But there is a chance they are holding her in the palace dungeons, or even in the palace itself, in preparation for the coronation."

"They won't have broken her that quickly," Ronin stated.

"You don't realise what they are capable of." Barnabus looked at him in pity. "I have seen grown men destroyed after a few moments alone with Slie. I don't know what power he possesses, but I've seen its effects. I'm telling you a young girl like the princess, no matter how strong you believe her to be, doesn't stand a chance."

"You don't know Snow," Ronin stated firmly.

"No, I don't," Barnabus looked at him. "I only knew her mother. If she is one quarter the character of Raven, then maybe you are right. Maybe she will be able to hold out until we can reach her."

"She will," Ronin reassured him. "She has to, so she will."

They edged into a dock high up on the battlements of the palace as dawn was beginning to break. It was the day of Snow's coronation, Ronin realised. The day that everything had been building up to. By the time the sun set that evening everything would be over – one way or another.

He wasn't afraid to die. If that was the price demanded for saving Snow, then it was one he would gladly pay. But he did want to see her one last time. To know that she was safe. That she had been crowned as queen and could go forth and rule her people in kindness and wisdom. Yes, he would die happy knowing that.

He and Nylex changed into the uniforms of Contratulum soldiers. With their long hair tucked into their collars, and the helmets pulled low over their faces, none would recognise them as being anything but firm-jawed soldiers back from a mission – maybe in the palace to provide extra security for the coronation.

There was a soft bump as the ship docked, and Ronin held his breath, but no shout of challenge came.

"Right," said Barnabus, and pulled his helmet on. "No point hanging around here, I suppose."

In tight formation, they marched from the ship and onto the dock. His eyes looking everywhere at once, Ronin saw airships – lots of airships – straining at mooring ropes in the early morning breeze. He counted at least a dozen and exchanged a quick despairing glance with Nylex marching next to him.

So many ships. More than they had imagined. They outnumbered the Avian fleet, and Ronin hoped that the element of surprise would work in the Avian's favour. Then he heard an almost imperceptible gasp from Nylex, and the young man poked him in the ribs. Following his gaze, Ronin saw ***The Lissa*** bobbing gently above them. They were here. *She* was here. Somewhere in the palace, Snow was waiting for him to rescue her. He squared his shoulders, his resolve newly fired, and saw the matching excitement in Nylex's eyes.

They marched down the ramp and into the palace. The wide stone passageway was crammed with soldiers and Ronin relaxed slightly. Amongst so many, they blended in, and his hopes began to rise that this crazy plan might succeed.

The Pontifex was having an eventful day. It had begun with the acknowledgement that without the real princess, they would have to proceed using her clockwork counterpart. It was an imperfect solution, but the Pontifex was sanguine about its chances of success.

People expected to see the princess, and that is what they would see. If she appeared a little characterless, a little wooden in her movements, then people would put it down to nerves.

Rumours had already been spread throughout the palace amongst the servants about how sick with nerves the young princess was – positively prostrate with fear, they muttered sympathetically, as they hurried about their duties.

Considering how things had turned out, it was for the best that he had not released the news of the princess's kidnap. Keeping it close to his chest like a much-needed ace in the hand, Slie had waited to see how the people would react to the shock of the airships first.

Then that newly appointed commander from the north, Heyes, had arrived back at the palace and demanded to see him. Having despatched him to wait in the godforsaken hellhole of Featherwell, to see if anyone nibbled at the bait he had left out, Slie had not expected anything to come from that particular trail of breadcrumbs, so his eyes narrowed in suspicious disbelief when the man finally gained admittance to his office.

Puffed up with obvious pride, the man had barely gone through the courtesies of greeting before blabbering out the unexpected news that Snow White herself had come to the village.

At first, Slie was dubious, but, as Heyes described the long raven-black hair and the outstanding beauty of the woman he had captured, flutters of excitement palpitated Slie's frozen heart.

"And where is she now?" he demanded.

"She, and the pair of Dwarvians we captured with her, are in the palace dungeons."

"What?!"

Slie looked at Mirage who had been listening to the report with a sceptical look. "Fetch her to me now," he ordered. Mirage nodded and made to exit the room. "Wait!"

Mirage turned at the command.

"First, bring me the prelate who is on duty outside." A terrible smile spread across the Pontifex's face and he steepled his fingers in satisfaction. "Now I know which of my little fishes nibbled at my bait, I intend to make sure he never does so again."

Mirage strode to the door and flung it open, staring out into the corridor at the now-abandoned table, and the inkpot that had been inadvertently knocked over in its occupant's obvious haste to be gone from there.

"He's gone," he informed Slie, and the smile deepened.

"So, he wishes to make things more interesting, does he? Well, I suppose I should have expected nothing less. Fetch more guards! The hunt is afoot."

He should have known it would end this way. Sitting at his desk outside the Pontifex's office, the young man had discreetly listened to Slie's meeting with Mirage and the northern commander, Heyes. The device that enabled him to pick up the words spoken within the room was concealed within the lining of his hood, and he was well used to listening intently whilst appearing to be working.

He had only scant seconds to recover from the shock of hearing that the Princess had been captured and was even now in the palace dungeons when he heard Slie order Mirage fetch him from his post at the door.

Desperately, he jumped to his feet, knocking over the inkpot in his haste, his heart furiously pounding. *Run*, his brain ordered, and without thought, his body jumped to obey. Quickly, he hurried down the corridor and up the stairs that led to the upper levels, where there was a concealed way to enter the palace.

Few knew of this entrance. Even Mirage himself had always been forced to use the city entrance like everyone else, but the young man had made it his business to find out everything about the complex in which he was, to all intents and purposes, a prisoner.

One particularly wet and filthy evening, he had been surprised to see Slie arrive in his rooms clad only in indoor clothes, and dry as a bone. Determined to find out how, when the Pontifex left to return to the palace and his duties there as advisor to the princess, he carefully shadowed him.

Slie had slipped up a little-used staircase leading only to storerooms, then entered a room where extra clothing was stored. The young man had waited patiently outside for an hour, before realising that the Pontifex wasn't coming back out. Ripping a hole in his robe, he entered with the ready excuse of wishing to replace it but quickly found it not to be necessary, for the room was empty.

Searching intently, his diligence was at last rewarded when his probing hands discovered a crack in the wall, through which a whisper of air was trickling. Feeling all around, he happened upon a depression in one of the stones and pressed it. Silent as the grave, the door swung open to reveal a stone-flagged passage leading away into what he assumed was the servants' section of the palace.

Now he made it to the room unseen and took precious seconds to shed his prelate's robe and bundle it with a jumble of clothes in the corner. Hoping that his simple tunic and leggings would help him blend in with the palace servants, he slipped out of the Contratulum complex and into the palace for the first time in his life.

His heart thumped with the nearness of his escape, and his mind burned with the zeal of his new mission – to reach the dungeons before Mirage did and save Princess Snow.

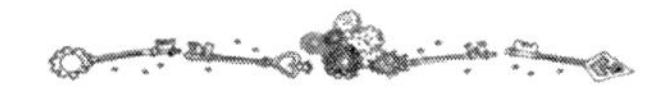

The servants' entrance to the palace was tantalisingly within their reach – only another corridor to go – when they turned a corner and realised their luck had run out. Mirage was coming towards them at the head of a group of guards. Snow's eyes met his and she saw his one human eye widen in stunned recognition.

"Run!" she cried, turning, and pushing the others before her.

Pelting down the corridor, with the sounds of pursuit hot on their heels, Snow's brain raced trying to remember where the nearest safe exit from the palace could be found. The gardens – of course!

"This way!" she cried, and veered left into a passageway that would take them to the orangery, and then out through the double glass doors into the gardens. From there they could escape into the maze – many long hours spent exploring it as a child meant Snow could lead the way to the other side blindfolded. There they could force their way through the hedge, and through the woodland garden, to make their escape into the city beyond.

Trusting her completely, Kylah and Eli fell into step behind her as they pounded along the corridor and raced up the wide stone steps to the orangery. Snow skidded to a halt in petrified horror. An entire legion of guards was marching along the corridor towards them.

She dithered for a second, then realised they had no choice. She led the way up the next flight of stairs, hoping against hope they could find somewhere to hide until the guards had gone by, and they could then find a way back down to one of the exits.

Ronin couldn't believe it. They had marched down endless flights of stairs to reach the palace dungeons – the first place they should look for Snow and the others, Barnabus had said. They turned a corner into a wide, well-lit corridor that ran alongside some sort of glasshouse in which orange trees in pots were releasing their sweet smell into the morning air. There was a flash of movement at the other end, and Snow, Kylah, and Eli erupted into view.

Before anything could be said or done, they turned and dashed up the nearby stairs.

"Was that ...?" Barnabus asked.

"Yes," snapped Ronin.

"Didn't think it would be this easy," the commander admitted with a grin as they shifted into a brisk trot and set off in pursuit. As they reached the bottom of the stairs, another group of soldiers rounded the corner at speed with Mirage at their head.

It had to be Mirage. Snow's description had been too precise for it to be any other. Besides, there was something about the man that made Ronin's hackles rise. He oozed coldness from every pore, his one black eye glittering with the thrill of the chase.

"You men, with us." Mirage snapped the order, and Barnabus nodded to his men to obey. For a moment, Ronin wondered why he didn't signal his men to open fire on Mirage and his guards – after all, they outnumbered them two to one – but he saw the sense of the Commander's decision to keep their cover for a little longer.

The less attention they drew to themselves the better, and if there was a chance to rescue Snow and the others without it turning into a pitched battle, then Barnabus was wise to take it.

Up the stairs they ran, the sounds of pursuit behind them. Snow cursed their bad luck at running into that legion of soldiers and tried to think about where they were going. At the top of the stairs the corridor branched off in two directions and Snow took the right. This led to a wide stone bridge stretching high over the vast central courtyard. Beyond, Snow knew she would find the servants' stairs, leading back down to the exits. If they could only reach it, then they would stand a chance of escaping from the palace.

"Look," Kylah grunted, running easily beside her, still clutching the gun she had taken from the gaoler. "Up there."

Snow looked up, realising that it was growing darker. Far above them, a ceiling of ornately patterned glass stretched up into a dome, which usually let light shine down onto the courtyard far below, but now great black shadows were looming where the makeshift docks and the airship fleet of the Contratulum were located.

"What are they?" she cried, and Kylah shook her head.

"They look like ..." she began. An explosion ripped through the palace, shaking the bridge beneath their feet.

"The palace is under attack?" Snow screamed in disbelief, gripping the edge of the stone balustrade to steady herself.

"Not the palace, the airships!" Kylah shouted back. "It must be House Avis. They've come to rescue you. We need to get to the roof so they can airlift us off. How do we get up there?"

"Servant's stairs, over there," Snow yelled. "They go up as well as down. Come on." With renewed hope and energy, they started to run again as the soldiers erupted onto the bridge behind them.

"Stop them!" Mirage bellowed, and the soldier beside him raised his weapon and loosed off a shot that had Snow and the others diving for cover.

"Don't be a fricking fool!" Mirage smacked the weapon down. "You might hit the Princess. Get after them."

"Go!" Kylah gasped, staggering to her feet, and raising her weapon. "I'll hold them off and catch up." She let off a couple of wild shots into the group of soldiers, hitting one and causing the others to flatten themselves.

Unable to call out to her for fear of drawing attention to themselves, Ronin, Nylex, Barnabus and his men drew back off the bridge. Afraid that in her enthusiasm Kylah could well hit them, they crouched behind the balustrade and the flimsy cover it provided.

Uncertain what to do, Snow and Eli reached the end of the bridge and stumbled onto the covered balcony on the other side. They hesitated, looking at Kylah as she walked backwards, firing at Mirage and his soldiers – who brought up their weapons to fire back. Now that Snow was not next to the mad-eyed blonde woman with the gun, Mirage had no scruples about aiming at her.

"Shoot the bitch," he ordered, and his men opened fire.

The bridge shuddered again as more cannon fire was loosed on the airships above, and Barnabus looked up in concern.

"If they hit one of the engines, we could be in trouble being right underneath," he murmured.

A second later, the glass ceiling shattered into a million shards of crystal as an airship plunged straight through it with all its cannons still firing and exploded into a massive fireball above them. Kylah started to run for the other side, but it was too late. The bridge detonated under her feet as a dozen cannonballs impacted at short range and blew the bridge sky high.

Chapter Thirty-Six

After the Fall

There was a roaring in her ears and her lungs were constricted, as if someone were kneeling on her chest. She was lying flat on her back. When had she fallen over? Snow tried to move, but her limbs refused to obey her orders.

Eli was kneeling over her, shaking her, and pulling at her arm. He was shouting something. At least, his mouth was moving, but she couldn't hear his words. She blinked. Grit was in her eyes and up her nose. She could taste it in her mouth.

Shakily she put a hand to her face. It came away covered with white dust and Snow realised she was looking up at a hole in the roof of the balcony above her. There were flames somewhere off to the side, she could feel their heat on her face.

Slowly, she struggled to sit up, with Eli pulling and shouting at her. Then her ears popped, and with a great roar, sound rushed in to fill the silence.

"Snow. Get up! The b-b-bridge collapsed, and I can't see Kylah!"

"Huh? Kylah?"

"The bridge collapsed when she was s-s-still on it."

Snow shook her head, desperately trying to gather her scattered wits. What had happened? Staggering to her feet, she looked around. Eli was right. The bridge had collapsed and there was no sign of Kylah.

"Kylah?" She crawled to the edge of the damaged balcony and peered over. Below she could see a great mound of shattered masonry and wreckage. Small fires were burning all over the heaps of splintered wood and there were shapes ... dead bodies ... she realised with a clutch of horror. There were dead bodies down there.

Looking up, she saw that a Contratulum airship had crashed through the great atrium window above and caught in the opening. Flames still gushed from it, and ropes and the wreckage of the ship itself dangled precariously in the vast open space above.

"Kylah?" she called over the precipice, but nothing moved below except the leaping flames and the gentle fall of powdered masonry raining down over everything.

"S-s-snow?" Eli crawled up beside her, his face twisted with fear. "Snow, where's Kylah?"

"I don't know, Eli," she sobbed. "I think she fell - when the bridge collapsed. I think she's down there."

"B-b-but there are only dead people down there," he said, and Snow's heart broke at the bewildered expression he wore.

"I know," she whispered, then hugged the young man to her as his face twisted and he began to cry. *Look after Eli.* She could almost hear Kylah bark the order at her. Snow knew that would be Kylah's wish, for her to look after her baby brother.

"Eli, we have to keep moving." She tried to pull him to his feet.

"Kylah," he cried. "We can't leave her!"

"We have to," Snow told him. "We have to go. The last thing Kylah would want is for you to be captured. We must get up onto the roof and hope one of the airships can pick us up. Or maybe we can reach ***The Lissa***. Eli, could you fly her?"

"Without Kylah?" he seemed shocked at the suggestion.

"Yes? Could you at least move the ship? Get us away from the city?"

"I don't ... I don't think so ... Kylah never lets me touch the controls ..."

"You've watched her do it, though – and you were training to be an airship pilot, Eli."

"But that was b-b-before." he cried. "That was before this!" He stuck his head angrily.

For a second Snow was stunned into silence. It had never occurred to her that Eli realised what had happened to him – what he had lost. That somewhere within his sweet and simple mind, a spark of the sharp and intelligent person he had been still lingered.

"Eli," she said quietly. "I know you can do this." Cupping his face in her hands, she looked him in the eyes. "I have faith in you, and I know you can do this." She pressed a soft kiss to his shocked mouth, and a deep flush stained his cheeks. Then he straightened his spine and considered for a moment.

"I guess I could t-t-try," he said.

"Good." Snow looked at the devastation all around. "We need to keep going up. Come on." With one last glance over the edge, she led him to where she hoped the servants' stairs were still intact.

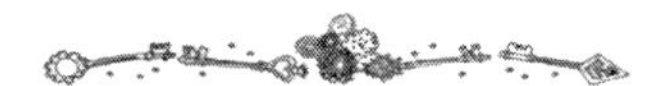

Protected though they had been in their position crouched behind the balustrade, Ronin and Nylex had been knocked sideways and left stunned and deafened by the explosion. Pulling himself up, Ronin was shocked to see the bridge had completely collapsed and looked desperately over at the other side.

Had they reached it safely? Was Snow still alive? Or was she buried under that ten-foot pile of masonry down there?

"Look!" Nylex pulled at his arm and pointed. "There's Snow and Eli."

They were scrambling over fallen debris and disappeared up another stairway as Ronin heaved himself to his feet and bellowed "Snow!" at the top of his lungs. They didn't stop. He realised there was no way she would have heard him over the roar of the flames above, the creak of falling wood, and the rumble of settling masonry.

"They were heading up," Nylex said. "They must be trying to get to the roof. At least, I saw Snow and Eli. I didn't see Kylah ..." His voice trailed away, and they looked at the devastation below.

"What happened to Mirage and his men?" Barnabus got shakily to his feet, dusting himself down and looking at the remains of the bridge.

"They must be down there," Ronin replied, and Barnabus raised an eyebrow and nodded.

"What's the plan now?" he asked.

"I'm going after Snow," Ronin said. "It looks like they're heading up to the roof. At least we no longer have Mirage to worry about, but Slie is still in the palace somewhere."

"How will we get across?" Nylex asked.

"If we go back down the stairs we came up," Barnabus interrupted, "they will lead us to the courtyard. Cross over and there will be stairs going up. If we keep going, we should catch up with them eventually."

As they spoke, he was rallying his men and checking for injuries. Remarkably, aside from cuts and bruises they were all unharmed, and fell into formation, following Barnabus as he led them back to the stairs.

Quickly, they hurried down and into the great courtyard. At ground level, the devastation was even more acute. They were forced to slow their pace as they picked their way over great chunks of smashed stonework, and twisted spars and planks from the airship, precariously dangling high above them.

All around were shouts and screams as people rushed into the courtyard, crying out in horror at the scene of carnage, and hurrying to the aid of those injured. Ronin felt guilty for not stopping to help. Looking at Nylex and Barnabus, he knew they felt the same, but Snow was more important. They had to find her before Slie did.

So, they kept going, and then halfway across the courtyard, they ran into Heyes and his men coming the other way. They might have got away with it. More concerned with what had happened, he barely glanced at them. They kept their heads down and hurried past him until his voice snagged at them.

"Hey there, you men. Come back and help us look for survivors." Barnabus kept moving. "Stop! I gave you a direct order. Come back here."

They stopped and slowly turned to face Heyes, who was surveying them with an annoyed expression that changed to one of puzzlement.

"Barnabus?" he asked. "What the frick are you doing here? You better have a damned good reason for abandoning your post."

"Oh, I do, Sir," Barnabus assured him, raising his gun, and firing at him.

Heyes dived to the ground, yelling to his men to open fire as Barnabus and his men took cover behind piles of masonry and began firing back.

"Go!" Barnabus barked at Ronin. "We'll hold them off. Find the princess and get her to safety. That's all that's important now."

"Get to the roof if you can," Ronin told him, unshouldering his weapon, and firing off a round. "We'll meet you there."

Barnabus nodded, as he and his men lay down a ferocious barrage of covering fire, which had Heyes and his men ducking down in a sudden panic. Ronin and Nylex sprinted towards the far door and shot through into the corridor beyond.

"Stairs? Where?" Ronin gasped, and Nylex gestured to his right.

"There!"

Up and up, they ran, occasionally meeting the odd terrified servant scuttling down, who ignored them due to their uniforms. They met a group of soldiers hurrying down. Pressing themselves flat against the wall, Ronin and Nylex tucked their heads down as the men pushed past them, then continued up the stairs until they burst out through a door onto the roof.

Frantically, they looked about. In the skies above them, a battle was raging as the Contratulum airships – sluggish to respond to the surprise attack of House Avis – were beginning to fight back. The roar of cannons was deafening, and the two men crouched and covered their ears. The docks were empty, except for ***The Lissa*** and ***The Revenge*** still bobbing on their mooring ropes.

"Do you think they're on board?" Nylex asked, gesturing towards the Dwarvian vessel.

Ronin hesitated. All his senses were pulling him back down the stairs, telling him that somehow, he had missed her. He was positive that Snow was still somewhere in the palace, and he wondered if it was the spell on the witch hazel that was calling to him, or something else.

"I don't know," he admitted. "I think she may be still in the palace, but I suppose they may be on board. Why don't you go and check it out and I'll double back – see if I can pick up their trail again."

"If they're not there, should I come and look for you?"

"No, we could miss each other, and then I'd have to come and look for you as well. Stay on board but keep an eye out for Barnabus and his men. If they make it back to the roof, then tell them to take off. There's no point them risking being accidentally fired on by House Avis in the belief they are Contratulum."

"Right," Nylex nodded, then his face fell. "Ronin, Kylah's still down there ..."

"I know. But there's nothing we can do about it now. Kylah would be the first to tell us to save Snow and Eli before worrying about retrieving her body."

He clasped Nylex's arm briefly, then turned and pounded back down the stairs, wondering where Snow was and hoping he found her before anyone else did.

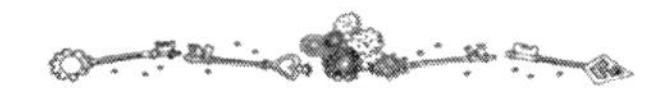

They had narrowly missed running straight into a large group of soldiers coming full pelt down the stairs. Snow had grasped Eli by the hand and pulled him back, only to hear more footsteps coming up the stone stairs behind them.

Panicking, Snow yanked Eli through a door to their left and they found themselves in the sumptuously carpeted wing where the royal bedchambers were. Walking slowly along the deserted corridor, Snow wondered where everyone was. Were they all over at the cathedral for the coronation, or had the palace been evacuated due to the battle?

She paused and listened. Only the dullest of thuds could be heard through the thick stone walls.

"Where are we?" Eli whispered.

"Near my bedchambers," she whispered back.

"Are we going to hide in there?" he asked, and Snow considered the question. She had the only key to the room so knew they would be safe and secure. Glancing at Eli, then down at herself, she realised it might be the perfect opportunity to wash the dust from their hands and faces, and maybe change their clothes so they didn't stick out so much.

A familiar voice echoed down the corridor and Snow flattened herself to the wall, pulling Eli with her. Sidling along, she peered around the corner. Slie was coming out of her room. He was locking the door behind him and giving the key to the soldier standing on guard.

"No one is to enter this room except me," he ordered, "until I send my guard along to escort the princess to the cathedral."

"Yes, Your Grace." The guard pocketed the key.

Slie oozed his way down the corridor away from them, leaving Snow's brain racing. How could the princess be escorted to the cathedral when the princess was out here? She peeked around the corner at the door again. A bright, shiny lock screamed its newness, and she realised the old one must have been removed, so her key was now useless.

As she looked at it, an urgent conviction arose that she *had* to get inside that room. That the answer to everything was in there. But how was she to get the key?

"Eli," she muttered in his ear. "This is what we need to do."

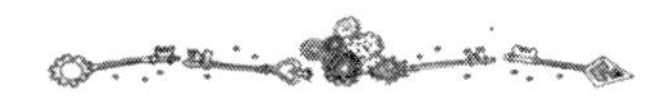

Shifting from foot to foot, the guard wondered how much longer the escort would be. Standing outside a locked chamber door wasn't his idea of fun, even if it were guarding the princess, and he wanted to join his comrades in the cathedral on crowd control, which would be a lot more interesting.

There was a soft cry, and a thud further along the corridor and he looked up, his attention caught. At the corner, he could see the outline of a body lying on the ground. It looked like a servant, and he wondered if one had fainted or fallen ill.

He hesitated. His orders were to guard the door – but seriously, who would try to get to the princess – and he did have the only key.

"Hello," he called out. "Are you all right?"

The figure on the floor let out a groan and clutched at its stomach. Cautiously, the guard walked along the thickly carpeted hall and bent over the young lad who was lying there. He didn't look so good, it had to be said. The guard was wondering if whatever had caused his skin to go so white was contagious, when a flicker of movement caught his eye and he looked up.

"Sorry," said the Princess, and hit him over the head with the large marble bust of a famous general that had been standing on the nearby windowsill. The guard collapsed onto Eli with a loud thud and Snow winced, wondering if she had hit him too hard.

"Aggh, g-g-get off me," Eli moaned. Snow helped to roll the guard off him and pulled the young lad to his feet.

"Well done, Eli," she praised, and Eli blushed. "Is he still alive?" she asked anxiously, and Eli felt for a pulse.

"Yes, he's alive. But I think he'll p-p-probably have a headache when he wakes up."

"Good. Right, let's get him inside."

She fumbled in the guard's pocket for a key as Eli lifted the man over his shoulder and staggered towards the door. Unlocking it, she anxiously gestured him inside then shut and locked it behind them.

"S-s-snow," Eli stuttered in bewilderment, and Snow turned ... to see herself.

At first, terrified and jumping at every encounter, the young man quickly realised that everyone was so busy they had no time to notice anything – least of all an extra body lurking about the servants' quarters.

Dodging into the first door he came to, he found a well-stocked pantry and purloined one of the aprons hanging on hooks along the wall and snatched up a wooden tray. Piling it with drinking goblets, he hurried about the corridors looking like just another harried servant with too many chores on coronation day.

When the first explosion sounded, he was looking for a way to the dungeons and braced himself against the wall as the noise vibrated down through the stone. Curiously, he peered through the archway to his right and saw a vast courtyard with a fountain sparkling in its centre, and benches and statues dotted around its wide-open expanse.

The sound of gunfire made him look up. To his stunned astonishment, he saw her. It *had* to be her. Even from a distance, he could see her long, black hair as she ran across the stone bridge which spanned the courtyard. There was such a look of her mother about her, that he knew she was Princess Snow, Raven's child.

She was running with two others, and Mirage and a large legion of Contratulum soldiers were chasing them. One of them fired his weapon at her and the young man's heart stopped. But they missed. She and the lad reached the other side safely, while the other woman stood her ground and fired indiscriminately at the soldiers.

Then the bridge exploded. He was knocked to the ground. Where he lay for long moments, trying to decide whether he was still alive, or not. Crawling to his knees, he staggered to the archway and peered upwards, hoping against hope she had survived.

There! She and the lad were peering over the edge – obviously looking for the woman. He watched as Snow held the lad's face, then pulled him away towards the stairs. Quickly, he clambered over the fallen masonry into the courtyard.

Looking around, he saw no sign of Mirage and the soldiers who had been on the bridge with him. Good – maybe that problem had taken care of itself. But the other legion had now emerged into the courtyard and were running towards the stairs as well. Then they were confronted by a different legion and before he could fathom out what was happening, a barrage of weapons fire sent him tumbling for cover behind a pile of masonry.

He peered over the edge of his hiding place in confusion. Why were the Contratulum soldiers firing on one another? As he watched, two soldiers from the first group sprinted away and out through the door, exiting the courtyard.

Keeping low, the young man worked his way around the vast pile of fallen masonry and piles of wood. Small fires were flickering, and he averted his eyes from the bodies he encountered – servants, lords, and ladies who had had the great misfortune to be in the courtyard when the bridge collapsed on top of them.

He was almost at the door when a faint groan stopped him in his tracks. Lying partially buried under a pile of splintered decking lay the woman who had been with Princess Snow. The man hesitated. Sense told him to leave, but then that whisper of magic that had guided him his whole life, telling him which decisions were wrong and which were right, tickled at his mind.

Help her.

He had never known it to guide him amiss, so he knelt beside her and began pulling the debris from her body. She should be dead. The height she had fallen from – she should be dead. But by pure luck, she had fallen onto one of the many potted shrubs that were placed around the courtyard and it had taken the brunt of her fall.

She groaned again, and her eyelids fluttered open.

"Who …?" she gasped and fumbled for the gun she still clutched.

"It's all right," he told her. "I am an ally and I want to help you."

"Snow and Eli?"

"The princess and the boy escaped, but two soldiers are chasing them. We must hurry before they catch them."

The woman nodded and began helping to toss aside wood and stone. He was impressed by her strength and wondered what her function was with the princess. A bodyguard maybe? It seemed likely and made his decision to help her make more sense.

“Which way?” she asked when he had finally freed her and helped her scramble to her feet. Coated from head to foot in a fine white powder, she was also covered in blood, which she seemed intent on ignoring, so he did too.

“Over there,” he motioned to the archway leading from the courtyard and she glanced at the gunfight that was still happening in the far corner.

“What gives?”

“I do not know. They simply began shooting at one another.”

Kylah thought about it for a second, then shrugged, and slung her weapon over her shoulder.

“Let’s go.”

Quickly, they crouched and ran, behind the pile of masonry beneath the balcony and out through the doors. And behind them, unnoticed by Heyes and his men, or by Barnabus and his, there was a disturbance in the pile of rubble as a hand clawed its way out.

Chapter Thirty-Seven

A Mirror Image Princess

It was like looking in a mirror. Such an exact copy of her, that for one mad second, Snow wondered whether a full-length mirror had been placed in her room. But no, this thing sitting in a chair and coolly studying them was no reflection.

Fascinated, Snow padded over the thick carpet of her receiving chamber and paced about the creature. It *was* her, down to the smallest detail – but a much cleaner and more grandly dressed version of her. Attired in a beautiful white lace gown, with its hair rippling in a gleaming, jet-black curtain down its back, it looked the way Snow might after a shower and a full week of undisturbed sleep.

It occurred to her that the gown it was wearing was the one the court dressmakers had been working on for her coronation. Surely, Slie had not planned to somehow crown this doll in her absence. As like her as it looked, it would not stand up to close examination.

With a grunt, Eli heaved the body of the guard down onto the floor and stood beside her, staring at her doppelganger with interest.

"It looks exactly like you, S-s-snow. Why would they want another Princess Snow?" As if responding to his words, the creature turned its head to look at him.

"Good morning," it said, in Snow's voice. "I hope you are well this morning. I am fine and looking forward to my coronation."

"It talks?" Snow jumped back in alarm, and Eli knelt beside the thing running his hands over the side of its face.

"It's an automaton," he told her. "I can feel the hum of its motor beneath the skin."

"Like the things Kylah makes?"

"Yes, b-b-but she's never made anything on this scale. It's incredible."

"Thank you," replied the automaton, giving Eli a dazzling smile.

"Is it alive?" Snow gasped and Eli shook his head.

"I think it's been p-p-programmed to respond to questions, but it can't think or act on its own accord."

"They must be planning to crown it in my place," Snow said, her mind dashing through all the implications and consequences. "With this thing on the throne they could rule the kingdom."

"B-b-but it's just a mindless puppet," Eli protested, his face wrinkling with confusion. "They wouldn't be able to fool people for very long."

"Long enough for it to make rules giving the Contratulum ultimate power?"

"Oh, I didn't think of that." Eli's face fell. "What should we do now, Snow?"

Snow stared at the creature, who stared back, then beamed a radiant smile – more disturbing for being her smile. Her smile ... an idea flickered.

"Help me get it into the bedroom," she ordered. Eli gripped its arm, then jumped as the thing rose gracefully to its feet and glided into the bedroom. Snow noticed a hesitation in the way it walked – a slight hitch to its gait as it stopped in the middle of the room and turned to face them.

"I am happy to comply," it said. "Please tell me if there are any more instructions you wish me to obey."

"Take off your clothes," Snow ordered. Obediently, the doll began to unlace its gown.

"Snow?"

"Go and swap clothes with the guard, Eli."

"Why?"

"Because you and I are going to a coronation."

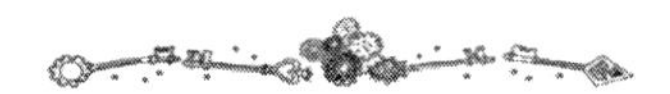

The woman was hurt – he could see that. Badly hurt. But she kept going, and his admiration of her grew. As they went up the stairs her pace grew slower, though, until eventually she paused and braced herself against the wall. He looked at her in alarm. Her breathing was shallow, and her skin had taken on a waxy pale sheen. Struggling to breathe, she looked at him in grim determination.

"Are you injured?" he asked.

"I'm not sure," she said. "My stomach hurts."

"Show me," he ordered. She eased up the edge of her flying leathers and pulled aside the undershirt to reveal a vast, livid purple bruise that spread across her whole abdomen. He had seen such bruising before, on the bodies of those the Contratulum had broken under torture. It indicated that the person was bleeding severely inside, and none that he knew of had ever survived such a thing.

She was dying. As she silently surveyed the bruise, then rearranged her clothes, he suspected she realised it as well.

"We were trying to reach the roof," was all she said though. "House Avis is attacking the Contratulum airships, so we were going to try and either get to our ship, ***The Lissa*** – if it's still there and still in one piece – or attract the attention of one of the Avian ships and get them to pick us up."

"Do you think the princess is sticking to that plan?"

"Yes. I know her priority will be to look after Eli. I would imagine they believe I'm dead, so I know that's what Snow will do."

"How can you be sure?"

"Because Snow knows it would be my wish that she gets my brother to safety."

He fell silent, thinking about a princess who would put the needs of a lowly boy before her own. A frisson of excitement arose at this first proof that she *was* the princess he had been promised by Greta all those years ago. That his whole life spent in service to Raven and her memory had not been in vain.

They kept going, up and up. Occasionally they passed servants hurrying down who ignored them in their haste. Eventually, they reached the roof and entered a world of noise and violence. Most of the Contratulum airships were airborne now and the battle had drifted to the left of the palace.

Kylah tried to count the enemy ships. There were at least ten left against the eight Avian ships. One had gone down into the palace and another was listing to its starboard side in the sky. Flames licked at it hungrily and the crew was swarming over it like ants defending their nest.

To her relief, ***The Lissa*** was still tied at its mooring, next to the only Contratulum ship in dock. Called ***The Revenge,*** it looked deserted. Stopping to catch her breath again, Kylah then hobbled after the strange young man who had rescued her and claimed to be on their side.

"Kylah!"

To Kylah's huge relief, Nylex was clambering onto the dock from ***The Lissa***. He caught her in a hug that had her choking back a cry of pain.

"Are you all right? We thought you were dead. Have you seen Snow and Eli?"

"They're not with you?" Her voice sharp with concern, Kylah ignored his first question to focus on what was important.

"No, they're not on board. Ronin felt certain Snow was still in the palace, so he has gone to look for them. He told me to wait here."

"What about Fae, Arden, and Grein?"

"They're all right. They're safe back at the castle."

"How ...? Never mind, that's not important right now. We need to find Snow."

"You are not strong enough to go back down those stairs." The young man spoke for the first time and Nylex eyed him with suspicion.

"Who's this?"

"Oh, a friend," Kylah casually replied. "He dug me out of the rubble and helped me get here."

"Are you injured?" Nylex asked in concern.

"Think I might have a few broken ribs or something." Kylah dismissed his concerns with a sharp sideways glance at the young man. He understood that she did not wish her friend to know the true extent of her wounds and respected her for it.

"I will return to the palace and look for the princess," the young man said.

"I'll come with you," Kylah insisted.

"No, you will only slow me down and draw attention to us."

"But you're not even armed," she protested. "Here," she thrust her weapon at him. "Take this."

"No servant would carry such a weapon," he pushed it away. "The soldiers would stop me immediately."

"Then take this," said Nylex, unstrapping the knife sheath from his thigh and handing it to him.

Drawing the wickedly long knife from the sheath, the young man balanced it in his hand, feeling its weight and approving of the way it fitted his palm exactly. Quickly tying the sheath around his thigh, he pulled his tunic down over it, nodding his satisfaction that it concealed the weapon entirely.

"Look." Kylah glared at him. "Don't be a hero or try anything stupid. Find Snow and Eli and bring them here as quickly as possible. We'll get the ship ready to go as soon as you get back."

He nodded. Quickly, he ran to the door and set off down the stairs to search for his princess.

After sending a legion of his most loyal guards to fetch the princess and escort her to the cathedral for the coronation, the Pontifex paused to don his most elegant robes. Image was everything, and he was relying on the sheer grandeur of the occasion to mask any inadequacies in the performance of his mechanical princess.

She only needed to last through the coronation ceremony itself. Slie had persuaded the minister into trimming all the fat from it to make it as short as possible. The poor Princess Snow was sick with nerves, he had told the minister and trickled a whisper of the Power into the man's head so that he believed it was all his own idea.

By the time, this necessary farce was over, Mirage would have taken the real princess down to Duncan and his team of technicians. They were awaiting her in the workshop, ready to extract her heart.

This would make their clockwork princess so real, the Contratulum would be able to rule through her for many months – before the heart deteriorated to the point it was no longer functioning.

But by then, the puppet would have served its purpose and handed all the power of the crown over to the Contratulum. The people of the kingdom would then be under the control of a new regime, without a single shot having to be fired.

Slie smirked at the thought of all his plans coming together so neatly. It was a shame the real princess was not under their control and so could not be crowned. But, having her contained and ready to donate her heart was the next best thing. Snow had played so conveniently into his hands it was as if she was complicit in them.

He glanced at his pocket watch. He should be making his way to the cathedral. After all, it wouldn't do for the most important man in the kingdom to be late to the coronation. He stretched into his Power and found it glorious. Soon, everything for which he had planned, schemed, and sacrificed would be within his grasp.

He opened his chamber door, and Mirage fell onto him. Wheezing with pain, he clutched at Slie's velvet robe, leaving a smear of white powder across the front of it.

Alarmed, Slie dragged him into the room and deposited him none too gently into the nearest chair.

"Report!" he barked, as Mirage's eye glazed over, and he looked about to pass out. "Report!" he screamed again. The familiar command snapped Mirage back into himself. He straightened in the chair and took a deep breath.

"Snow and the Dwarvians have escaped from the dungeons. I was pursuing them across the courtyard bridge when House Avis launched an attack on our airships. At least one has been destroyed – it crashed through the glass ceiling of the courtyard and its cannons exploded the bridge whilst I and my men were on it. All of them were killed. I was lucky to escape relatively unscathed, although I was buried, and had to dig my way out."

"The princess?"

"Dead, I think. I am unsure. There was no obvious sign of her in the courtyard, but there are many dead, and many bodies still under the debris."

Slie cursed under his breath. Once again, his plans had suffered a blow.

"Despatch men to dig for survivors, but do not tell them there's a chance she's there. How goes the battle?"

"Badly. They have no more airships than us and theirs are generally smaller, but they are nimble and have greater manoeuvrability, and their crews fight as if they are possessed."

"They must not be allowed to be victorious."

"But what can we do about it?"

"Have they finished installing the cannon on the tower?"

"Yes, it was completed two days ago."

"Then send men up there and tell them to start firing at the Avians."

"But Your Grace – its aiming mechanism has yet to be calibrated. There is a chance they could inadvertently hit one of our ships."

"It matters not. Give the order."

"Yes, Your Grace."

"Oh, and Mirage?"

"Yes, Your Grace?"

"Launch ***The Dreadnought***!"

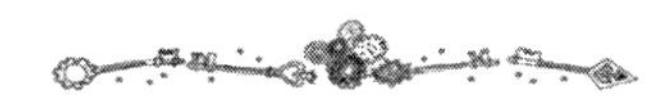

Somehow, he had missed them again. Not coming across them on the upper reaches of the stairs, Ronin felt confident Snow wouldn't have gone all the way back down to the courtyard, so began searching the silent and oddly deserted corridors that the staircase opened onto.

Floor after floor and room after opulent room, he searched. The palace appeared deserted. He wondered if all the nobility were already in the cathedral waiting to see their princess being crowned. They were going to wait a long time, he thought grimly.

Another sumptuous corridor stretched eerily silent and empty before him, and the thick carpet muffled his footsteps. Hearing voices as he approached a corner, he pressed himself against the wall.

Something crunched underfoot. Looking down, he saw the remains of a marble bust lying in fragments on the floor, then peered cautiously around the corner. A legion of Contratulum soldiers was approaching a pair of ornate doors, outside which a young guard stood with his helmet pulled down over his face.

"Unlock the door," the Commander of the legion ordered, and the young guard hurriedly pulled a key from his tunic and unlocked the doors. Standing back, he allowed the Commander to enter.

A moment later, Ronin had to stop himself from calling out when the man re-emerged from the room behind Snow.

Her face perfectly calm, she seemed unharmed, and he drank in the sight of her. Looking beautifully radiant in a dazzling white lace gown, she regally inclined her head when all the soldiers went down on one knee to her.

Puzzled, he watched as she walked off down the corridor at the head of the legion. The young soldier who had been guarding her door fell into step behind the others.

Giving them a moment to pull ahead, Ronin crept down the corridor behind them. Wherever Snow was going, he would follow. Sensible of the fact he was outmanned eight to one, he decided to bide his time, and wait for the right opportunity to rescue Snow.

Preparing ***The Lissa*** for a speedy exit, Kylah was relieved Nylex was there to shovel coal into the furnace. She knew that if she tried, she would collapse on the engine room floor. Busying herself with cogs and dials, she set the backup generator running to supply power to the engines, pull them away from the dock, and get them airborne.

Emerging back on deck with Nylex, she was aware of the pitched battle raging in the distance. Kylah worried about all the people they knew on the ships of House Avis, risking their lives to save Snow and see her crowned queen.

All this for one young girl, Kylah thought. Was it worth it?

Yes.

"What did you say?"

Nylex looked up at her question and frowned. "Nothing. I didn't say anything," he looked over at the battle and frowned. "I wish there was something we could do to help them."

"So, do I," said Kylah. "But we don't have any weapons."

"They seem to be holding their own."

"House Avis built smaller, more compact ships," Kylah told him. "The Contratulum's are bigger and faster over long distances, but they're more cumbersome and are difficult to turn quickly. Look, the Avian ships are dancing around them."

Nylex nodded, then they both ducked and clutched their ears as a loud boom echoed out over the castle walls and an Avian ship lurched to one side. Watching in horror, they saw it slip further and further until it was plummeting down to land with a soul-splintering crash in the city below. Fire erupted from the impact.

"What the frick was that?" Nylex shouted.

"A giant cannon! Look, up there." Kylah pointed up to the highest tower of the palace, where the gleaming black snout of the biggest cannon she had ever seen was visible over the battlements.

The gun shouted again, but this time it sailed between an Avian and a Contratulum ship, causing minimal damage to both. Again, and again, the cannon fired, randomly hitting both its own ships and those of House Avis.

"What's the matter with them?" Nylex cried. "They don't seem to care who they hit."

"Aiming mechanism hasn't been calibrated properly," Kylah said. "They're having to fire and hope."

"Well, even if they are missing our ships more times than they're hitting them, they're still doing enough damage. We have to stop them."

"How? We have no weapons?"

"If you can get me up there," Nylex snapped, "I can stop them."

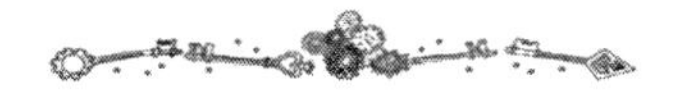

Following Snow and the soldiers at a discreet distance, Ronin's attention was drawn to the young soldier marching at the back of the others. He didn't seem to be a very good soldier – always on the wrong foot compared to all the others. His uniform looked baggy as if it were meant for a bigger frame.

Watching as he clutched at his britches for the fourth time, as if scared they were going to slither down around his ankles, Ronin had a wild idea it was Eli. Something about the way this soldier was bumbling along reminded him so much of the young lad that he knew he was right.

The soldiers marched from the palace and onto the royal promenade. Ronin would have expected it to be crowded with people, come to see their princess crowned. But barricades and more soldiers were holding back what few there were, and high above them the sounds of a pitched aerial battle could be heard.

He glanced up, wondering who was winning. Wondering how Nylex was, and whether Barnabus and his men had managed to get away. He hoped so. In the short time, he had spent with the commander, he had grown to trust and respect the man enormously.

They reached the cathedral. The guards waiting there bowed to Snow and opened the giant double doors for her to enter. Silently catching up behind them, Ronin kept his head down - merely another helmeted soldier in a sea of others pushing their way forward into the cathedral to form a solid rank of burly helmeted men at the back.

Slipping behind a pillar, he worked his way forward until he was standing beside Eli, then turned to stare intently at him. For long moments, he watched the boy fidget in his uniform. Looking miserable and apprehensive, Eli kept his eyes on the long aisle, which Snow was currently pacing along until finally, the weight of Ronin's gaze penetrated, and he turned to look.

His eyes widened with glee and he opened his mouth, but Ronin quickly put his fingers to his lips and gave a slight shake of the head. Eli shut his mouth and glanced around at the soldiers, then back at Ronin in an unmistakable 'what do I do?' movement.

Ronin gently beckoned. Eli slowly took a sidestep, then another, and another, until he was standing next to Ronin. Staring straight ahead, they melted unobtrusively backwards through the lines of soldiers, until nothing but the solid wall of the cathedral was at their backs.

Looking around, Ronin spotted a small door set into the right-hand wall and nodded towards it. Eli blinked his acknowledgement and they oozed quietly along the back wall until they reached the door. Quietly trying it, Ronin was relieved to find it was unlocked and cracked it open enough for them both to slip through.

Holding it ajar for a moment, Ronin watched to see if any had noticed. But all eyes were on the spectacle taking place at the front of the cathedral, and none had been interested in the antics of two lowly foot soldiers.

He softly closed the door, and Eli launched himself at him. Gently, Ronin soothed the shaking and terrified young boy. Knowing it would be pointless to bombard him with questions, Ronin waited until Eli had calmed enough to pull away and remove his helmet.

"Eli, what's happened? Why are you dressed like a Contratulum soldier and why is Snow currently being crowned?"

"I don't know. She hit the soldier and then told me to put his clothes on. She took the clothes off the other one and said that this was her chance to get crowned right under the Contratulum's nose because they wouldn't know it was her. They'd think it was the other Snow, the doll one."

"What other Snow? Eli, you're not making any sense."

"I want to go home. I don't want to be at war anymore, I just want to go home and for things to go back to the way they were."

"I know, Eli, and we will go home soon. If Snow is crowned, then it will all be over. We'll have won."

"But what about Kylah?"

"I'm so sorry, Eli."

"Is she d-d-dead?"

"She fell a long way, Eli. She would have been buried under all that rubble when the bridge exploded."

"I don't want Kylah to be dead, and I want to go home."

"I know, Eli, and we will. But first, we must help Snow. It's what Kylah would have wanted, isn't it? For us to look after Snow?"

Eli rubbed at his eyes and kicked truculently at a nearby stool.

"Don't know," he muttered.

"Eli?"

"Suppose." The young lad reluctantly conceded. "But how can we help Snow when we're in here and she's out there?"

Good question, Ronin thought, and looked about the room they were in. Long and narrow, he could see it ran alongside the entire length of the cathedral and was plainly used for storage – perhaps for all the extra chairs they had had to put out to seat the nobility who were attending the coronation.

A few yards down, a narrow flight of steps ran up to another level, where an open-sided stone balcony lined with many decorative pillars flanked the main body of the cathedral.

"Up there," Ronin said and led a reluctant Eli to the steps. "Now keep behind the pillars, keep your head down, and keep quiet." Eli nodded and silently followed him up the steps.

Sheltering behind the first large pillar, Ronin risked a glance out over the congregation to the aisle where Snow was still slowly making her way to the dais at the top.

Hold on Snow, he thought. *Hold on a little longer. If you can manage to be pronounced queen, then this will all have been worth it.*

To his horror, he saw Slie step forward from the shadows at the back of the dais to stand at the top of the steps. Watching Snow process down the aisle towards him, he merely waited for her, a sly smile playing about his features, and a palpable air of intent hovering over him like a bad odour.

Ronin's head snapped between the corpulent figure of the Pontifex, and that of the slender young woman in white slowly pacing towards him.

Every instinct in Ronin's body was screaming that something was wrong, but he was powerless to do anything other than watch Snow walk towards her fate.

Chapter Thirty-Eight

Long Live the Queen!

Slowly, she told herself. Pace slowly. One foot precisely after the other. Control your breathing. Ye gods, did this aisle ever end? It felt as if she had been walking down it forever. Calm now, Snow. Breathe slowly. You're almost there.

At the end of the aisle was an enormous dais spanning the entire width of the cathedral. It was reached by a shallow flight of steps, and as Snow approached them, a figure loomed at the top.

Pontifex Slie.

Snow's heart clutched with fear. Somehow, she had to convince him that she was that thing in her room – that puppet princess they wished to crown in her stead. She reached the bottom step and stopped. Surveying the stairs as if unfamiliar with such a concept, she cocked her head to one side, blinked, then carefully held up the front of her skirts and began to climb.

Making her movements a little awkward and jerky, she remembered to blink less often, the way the automaton had. But all the time, Slie's gaze was upon her and she fought her rising panic. Wanting to do nothing more than run, she gained the top step and let her skirts drop back into place.

Slie stepped up to her and gave an obsequious bow that oozed insincerity. Shuddering inside, Snow schooled her features into a politely blank expression. When he gave her his arm, she gently placed her fingers on it and allowed him to lead her to the waiting minister and the throne.

Over to the left, she could see her aunt, Princess Jay, and her stepfather, Prince Hawk, sitting with the other senior nobles of the court. Hawk smirked at her, and the tip of his tongue flicked out like a reptile to moisten his thin lips. Suppressing a shudder, Snow looked over the head of her aunt as if she weren't there, but she could feel the hatred burning behind her aunt's placid gaze. The fury barely contained in her bunched fists, which lay on the scarcely showing bulge in her midriff.

As she had been instructed in countless lessons over the past six months, Snow knelt on the gold-embroidered cushion that awaited her, and the minister smiled gently down at her.

"My child," he said fondly. Snow blinked and formed her lips into a mechanical smile that she did not allow to reach her eyes.

"My lord," she murmured.

Facing the packed cathedral, the minister raised his hands over Snow's head and launched into the coronation ascension speech – but a vastly abridged version to the one Snow was familiar with. Slie must have ordered it trimmed, she realised. Afraid that the illusion of his toy princess wouldn't last the whole hour-long version, he must have somehow coerced the minister into cutting it in half.

Keeping her position, even though her knees were beginning to ache, Snow did not move so much as a muscle as the speech finally ended. Leaning down, the minister put his hands on her elbows. He helped her to rise and lead her to the throne.

Turning gracefully to face the congregation, Snow took one precise step backwards and settled herself onto the throne. She smoothed her skirts down, placed her hands on the arms of the throne, and stared forward as the minister held the Crown of Purity above her head.

Speaking aloud the ancient words of power, he reverently lowered the crown, and all within the cathedral leaned forward, holding their collective breaths. This was the most crucial part of the ceremony. If the sacred crown did not deem the heir worthy of the throne, then it would remain as a plain metal crown, and the monarch would be rejected as unfit to rule.

There was a split second of doubt, then the crown blazed forth in a blast of pure crystal white light that bombarded the vision of all who looked upon it. Dazzling in the reflected glow, Snow slowly stood and paced to the front of the dais. Standing tall so that all could see her, she held out her hands, palms up, to indicate her readiness to serve her people.

"You see before you, Queen Snow of House White. Long may she reign," bellowed the minister.

All surged to their feet to cry out as one.

"We pledge our allegiance to the Queen. Long live the Queen! Long live the Queen! Long live the Queen!"

Trumpets sounded. And dimly, from far away, Snow was sure she heard an explosion. Briefly, the thought of the battle being fought high above their heads flashed through her mind, and she wondered how the Avians were faring.

The Avians were faring very badly. As were the Contratulum airships. Firing indiscriminately, the giant cannon seemed hell-bent on destroying both fleets, and Nylex waited impatiently as Kylah eased them out of the docks and up into the sky above the castle.

As he shared his plan with Kylah, she looked at him as if he were mad – and perhaps he was. But if she could think of a better plan, she chose not to voice it, and instead frowned as she ran through it in her mind.

"How are you going to get away, though, Nylex? Without a way to do that it's nothing more than a suicide plan."

"I know. I found these below decks." He held up Fae's wings, and Kylah's frown deepened.

"But they were built for Fae's weight. I doubt they could lift you very far."

"They don't have to lift me," he told her. "They only have to let me down gently."

She nodded, seeing the sense of what he was saying, then clutched at her stomach as if in pain, a sheen of sweat breaking out on her forehead.

"Are you all right?" Nylex asked in concern.

"I'm fine," she snapped. "Let's get on with this hare-brained scheme then, if you're determined to do it."

"See you afterwards," he said. They looked awkwardly at one another. Aware this could be the last time they ever spoke. She was reluctant to let him go but could think of nothing to say to him.

"I'm glad about you and Fae," she finally said.

"So, am I."

"And I'm sorry."

"What for?"

"For those things, I said to you, back in the cave when we went to get the ship. I didn't mean them."

"Yes, you did, but it's all right. They were words that needed to be said, and words I needed to hear. They helped me to see how foolish I was being – that true love like the kind between me and Fae, and the kind you and Lissa shared, doesn't come along every day. When it does, you should cherish it."

"Yes," Kylah said. "You should."

"Oh, and Kylah?"

"Yes?"

"Don't bother coming back for me. You get out of here."

"But how will you ...?"

"I'll get on board ***The Revenge***. Someone has to let Ronin and the others know what's happened."

She nodded in agreement. Strapping the wings on, Nylex clambered into the cradle, where carefully filled glass jars of oil were already securely wedged into the corner. Holding onto the edge, he smiled a grim smile of goodbye at Kylah as she swung the cradle over the side of ***The Lissa*** and lowered it until it was hanging down under the ship.

She painstakingly climbed the steps to the wheel and gripped the smooth wood. The pain she had managed to hide from Nylex was threatening to engulf her, and she took deep, steadying breaths to push the blackness away for a little longer.

"Come on, my darling girl," she murmured. "Let's get this party started."

Beneath her touch, ***The Lissa*** shivered as if in agreement, the wheel trembling under her palms. Kylah closed her eyes. The sweet fragrance of lavender was all around, and it felt as if Lissa had placed her hands over Kylah's and gently kissed her cheek.

She was Queen. Snow gazed out over the heads of the cheering congregation and fought to keep the emotion from her face. She was Queen now, and there was nothing Slie could do to change that. The temptation to denounce him here and now was too strong. As the crowd fell silent, awaiting her inauguration speech, Snow knew she was going to deviate from the carefully rehearsed text written for her by Slie.

"My people," she began, then stopped and swallowed. "My people," she started again. "I stand before you as your rightfully anointed queen, the only child and heir of King Elgin. You have waited many long years for me to ascend the throne, and this was a day that many feared would never come … as did I, and with good reason."

Stepping closer to the edge of the dais, Snow abandoned all pretence and looked out at her people. They gazed back at her, and she wondered how truly loyal to the throne they were. Or whether years of corruption in the court of Hawk and Jay had blunted their sensibilities and made them only too happy to submit to the rule of the Contratulum.

"You may not be aware, but far above us, a great battle is raging between the miraculous flying machines of House Avis and the Contratulum. You have been told that we are at war with House Avis. That they viciously attacked us first, and the butchery we then levied on one of their villages was justified. This was a lie."

There was a fluttering and muttering in the congregation. Out of the corner of her eye, Snow saw Slie rising to his feet, comprehension creeping across his face.

"House Avis are not our enemy. They are our allies in the fight against an enemy which has been here all along. Slithering in the shadows like a serpent, our enemy has manipulated and indulged in the use of the Power to gather control for themselves."

The fluttering became gasps. People looked at one another, and furious whispering broke out.

"So, I call upon you, my dear people. Will you rise up with me and drive the evil that is the Contratulum from our land? Will you help me build the world my parents dreamt of, and bring House Snow out of the darkness and into the light? With your trust in me, I can make this a kingdom to rival any other and ensure we all have a life of peace and plenty. So, I ask again. Are you with me?"

There was a split second of silence, then a young nobleman arose.

"I am with you, my Queen," he cried, and looked around him. "Long live the Queen!" he shouted, and a few voices joined with him – but most people were looking confused and scared. Mumbling to each other, they stayed seated, and Snow's heart sank.

Then Slie was behind her, flanked by his men, and Snow struggled as his fleshy hand closed around her elbow in a vicelike grip that made her cry out in pain.

"Let me go," she screamed, but he was too strong, and yanked her back into the arms of his men.

"Get her out of here," he hissed. "Take her to my office and wait there for me."

Almost lifted off her feet, Snow was hustled to the back of the dais and down the steps to the rear entrance of the cathedral, kicking and screaming as the men roughly dragged her with them.

"Wait." It was Hawk. "Snow, my dear child, you are unwell. It is the stress of the coronation. She doesn't know what she's saying. Let me take her to her chambers, where she can lie down and rest." His hands were all over her, besmirching the pure white lace of her gown and sending shudders of disgust roiling through her stomach.

"Get off me!" she screamed. "I am the Queen, and you shall never touch me again."

"But Snow," he began, pulling her to him in an embrace.

Gathering all her strength, Snow brought her knee up in a woman's age-old defence, and Hawk dropped like a stone. Chuckles rippled through the soldiers, and maybe one or two of them glanced at her in admiration, but their hands were still like steel as they carried out Slie's orders.

"Defend the Queen!" she heard the cry of her champion behind her, then the clash of steel on steel as she was dragged from the cathedral, and Contratulum soldiers waded in to perform a spot of crowd control.

Ronin watched her coronation with an overwhelming sense of pride. Against all the odds, and despite numerous crippling setbacks, Snow had been crowned. Now the undisputed reigning monarch, she was Queen Snow of House White, and none could take that title away from her.

Then she gave her speech. Below him, Ronin watched the crowd. Would they rise up with her? Would they follow her into battle against the Contratulum?

His heart had leapt in hope when the young nobleman had jumped to his feet, but as the rest of the congregation stayed stubbornly in their seats, he realised she was asking too much. Events had turned too quickly for most to follow, leaving them confused and conflicted.

Slie made his move, and Ronin had to watch as Snow was dragged from the dais. Furious at seeing her so roughly treated in the brutish grip of Slie's henchmen, he silently cheered as Snow showed her mettle by dropping Hawk where he stood.

"Good girl," he muttered.

"Ronin." Eli pulled desperately at his sleeve. "They've got Snow. What are we going to do? Are we going to attack them?"

"No, Eli, we'd be cut down before we got anywhere near her. What good would we be to Snow then? We're going to follow them and await a chance to rescue her."

Easing back into the shadows, they climbed down into the storage area and ran silently along to the end. As he hoped, there was a small wooden door leading to the outside with the key in it. Ronin eased it around and opened the door a crack. Peering through, he was in time to see Snow being dragged past by the soldiers.

"Let me go!" he heard her scream. "I am your queen and I order you to let me go."

"You may be the queen," one of them retorted. "But you're not the one who pays our wages – and to be honest, sweetling, I'm more afraid of the Pontifex than I am of any girl, queen or no queen."

At that Snow fell silent, probably realising that to protest anymore was futile, and she would be better off saving her strength.

Giving them a minute's head start, Ronin slipped through the door and beckoned Eli to follow.

Outside, he quickly realised that whilst they had been in the cathedral something momentous had happened. All around people were frantically running, and in the distance, he could hear screams and shouts.

"What's happened?" he asked an old woman hobbling in the opposite direction as fast as her legs and her stick could take her.

"One of those blasted airships came down on the city," she cried, the rank smell of fear hanging about her frail form. "The city's on fire. Best you go and help, both of you!" she ordered, and Ronin realised she thought they were soldiers of the Contratulum.

"Ronin?"

"It's all right, Eli. We need to find Snow. That's the most important thing for us to do now."

"B-b-but if it's one of the airships of House Avis then maybe we can help."

"If they've crashed, Eli, then I'm afraid they are probably beyond anyone's help, and we need to find Snow before anything happens to her."

"Why? What will they do to her, Ronin?"

Eli's voice trembled with fear, but Ronin didn't answer him, too afraid of the images arising in his head to be of any comfort to the boy.

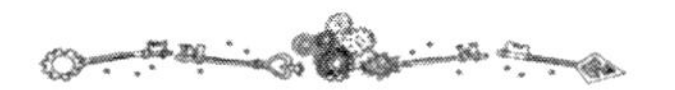

Crouched in the bottom of the cradle, Nylex braced himself as it swung madly from side to side. They had counted how long it took to reload the cannon between each blast, and Kylah had only two minutes to get him up to the battlements and move away before they could reload and blast ***The Lissa*** out of the sky.

He raised his head and glanced over the side. He was almost on top of the tower – close enough to see the shocked faces of the soldiers as they looked up at this weird contraption that was plummeting like a stone towards them.

Crying out in fear, and convinced it was going to hit them, they ducked, cowering in the bottom of the cannon pit as Nylex stood up in the cradle with the bottles of oil clasped to his chest.

Steadying himself against the side, he waited until he was almost on top of them before throwing the jars of oil down one after the other. They smashed on the stones, their sticky black contents oozing out.

Scrambling onto the side of the cradle, he held onto the chain overhead until it swung back over the cannon pit. The men were scrambling to their feet and wiping in confusion at the black liquid that was clinging to everything.

Then he leapt down, landing on the parapet, and holding up the last jar of oil. This one had an oil-soaked rag stuffed into the neck. Baffled, the men stared at him.

Nylex grinned back at them. He clicked his fingers to produce a spark of fire which he used to light the rag, and then tossed the bottle to explode at their feet.

"Boom!"

Praying to whatever gods might be listening, he opened Fae's wings, slapped the control on his chest to activate the motor, and fell backwards off the parapet.

The tower exploded in a fireball that tore at his clothes with hot, hungry breath as he plummeted downwards towards the docks on the castle roof.

As he hoped, despite his weight, the wings did slow his descent, but he crashed to the hard stones in a jarring thud that knocked the breath from his body and ripped the wings from his back.

Ruefully, he surveyed the twisted strips of metal and hoped his wife would be so relieved about getting her husband back, she wouldn't fuss too much about her destroyed wings.

Struggling to his feet with a groan, he looked for ***The Lissa***, and with relief saw it heading away from the scene of the battle. Then he set off at a jog towards ***The Revenge***, hoping against hope that Barnabus, or Ronin, or Snow, or Eli – or anyone friendly really would come along quickly so they could join the battle and help the Avians defeat the Contratulum.

On board ***The Thrush***, Princess Robin stared at her second-in-command, Franki, as that blasted cannon that had been ripping shreds out of them, exploded in a fireball which billowed out from the castle and took down almost the entire tower with it.

"What do you suppose ...?" Franki began.

"Who cares!" screamed Robin. "Hard about, aim cannons. Fire as soon as a Contratulum ship is in range."

On their port side, ***The Cormorant*** exploded in a wave of violence which ripped at ***The Thrush*** and sent her spinning out of control. Fighting with the wheel, Robin's muscles strained as she pulled with all her might and managed to bring the ship around.

"Robin! Look!" Franki screamed and pointed behind them.

Robin turned to look, and then wished she hadn't.

Huge. It was huge and black and menacing. The largest airship she had ever seen was bearing down on them from nowhere.

It had no balloon, nor sails, to aim for. Instead, multiple blades – like those on a skimmer but much, much larger – whirred noisily above its long, sleek, metal-plated body.

Cannons bristled all along its length – cannons currently aimed at them. Robin clutched at the wheel as her crew cried out in terror, many of them dropping to their knees and entreating whatever deity they worshipped to save them.

"I have an urgent message from Prince Peregrine," Tegan erupted onto the deck, then skidded to a halt and stared at the apparition, her jaw gaping in fear.

"What the frick is that?" she gasped.

"The message?" Robin snapped. "What's the message?"

"Retreat!" Tegan cried. "He's ordered everyone to retreat."

Chapter Thirty-Nine

A Battle of Wills

Sunlight was filtering in dappled patches through the gently dancing leaves above and highlighting the freckles on Lissa's nose. She had picked a bunch of lavender sprigs and was busy threading them through Kylah's hair as she lay on the soft grass, drowsy in the perfection of the summer afternoon.

Kylah grumbled about the flowers, but secretly she loved them and thought her heart would burst with happiness as Lissa lay beside her and rested her head on her chest. Holding her close, the sun-warmed skin of her lover under her palms, Kylah wished this moment would never end.

But it must. Lissa turned her head to look at her. *There is something you must do. One last task you must complete before you can come with me.*

"I don't want to," Kylah replied, a sensation of unease twisting itself into her gut. "I want to stay here with you."

It is important. Lissa sat up and looked at her. *It is so very important, my love. And you must get up now and do it.*

"No, I'm too tired," mumbled Kylah – a wave of exhaustion drenching her in inertia, pinning her to the grass, unable to move.

"I'm too tired, Lissa – please, just let me sleep."

I know you are tired, my love. Gently, Lissa stroked her face. *And you will sleep soon and be with me forever, but first, there is something you must do. You must do it for me. Please, Kylah, get up.*

"Want to be with you," mumbled Kylah, her eyelids drooping.

Get up, Kylah.

"No, I'm too tired ... must sleep ..."

Kylah! Get up!!

Kylah opened her eyes with a gasp. All around her was the sky and she realised she was lying on her back on the deck of ***The Lissa***. The sounds of battle echoed in her ears and the aroma of lavender was heavy on her senses.

She tried to get up, but the pain knocked her flat again. Crying out, she clutched at her stomach and tasted the sharp iron of blood in her mouth. She was dying. She knew it. Wished with a flare of annoyance that her body would fricking well get on with it. She was tired and she wanted to sleep.

But wasn't there something she was supposed to do first?

Get up, Kylah.

"Lissa?"

Confused, Kylah raised her head and scanned the deck. She was alone. Nylex had gone, and she could only hope he had been successful. That he had managed to destroy the giant cannon and get safely away so he could go home to Fae, who loved him.

Listen to me, Kylah, you must get up. There is one more thing you must do.

Knowing that once Lissa wanted something, there would be no rest for anyone until she had it, Kylah rolled onto her side and managed to heave herself to her knees. The world spun on its axis and she spat blood onto the deck, her hands braced on the smooth planking and her head hanging as she gasped great pants of agony.

Get to the wheel, Kylah. You must get to the wheel.

"Why won't you just let me die in peace," Kylah snapped, but began to crawl, the habit of doing whatever Lissa wanted so engrained she couldn't resist it.

That's my girl, Lissa urged. *You can do it, Kylah. Get to the wheel.*

It took a hundred years, but Kylah finally reached the wheel and used it to heave herself upright, sobbing over the pain that tore at her insides. Gasping, it took a few tries before she could blink the tears from her eyes and open them.

"What the frick!" she gasped. "What the frick is that?!"

It was a monster. The biggest airship she had ever seen. Black and menacing, it bristled with cannons and was squaring up to the Avian fleet – which was in panicked retreat. They wouldn't get far. Casting an eye over the leviathan, Kylah knew this thing had been built for one purpose, and one purpose only – to destroy.

The Dreadnought was the name on its shiny, black hull – and Kylah's heart sank for the Avians because they didn't stand a chance against it.

That is why you must help them.

"Me? What can I do? We have no weapons. There's nothing I can do against any ship, let alone a beast like that."

I am a weapon.

For a moment, the words made no sense. Then the fog lifted in Kylah's brain and it made perfect sense. This was the destination she had always been bound for.

From that afternoon long ago, when her eyes met those of Ronin's annoying baby sister and realised that she was no longer annoying, and certainly no longer a baby. To their decision to build an airship together. To that life-ending instant when she held Eli's body in her arms and watched Lissa's ship go down in a blaze of flames. To Snow coming amongst them and enlisting them in her quest to gain her crown – this was what had awaited her.

And it was all right.

She tried to think. What was the best way to do this? She swung on the wheel and ***The Lissa*** leapt into life beneath her hands.

The safety valve has been disengaged and all the cogs are turned to maximum.

Kylah nodded. Had she done that? Or had the ship done it herself? It didn't matter. It would ensure maximum thrust. It wasn't something she would ever recommend, as the risk of overheating was too great, but now it didn't matter.

"Full speed ahead," she said, and the ship gave a great thrust which almost knocked her off her feet. Clinging to the wheel, she fought down the blackness. Just a little longer. She only had to hold on for a little longer.

At the speed they were going, ***The Dreadnought*** was soon filling the horizon. Dimly she was aware of the Avian ships fleeing from it, parting to move around her, leaving her a clear path to her target.

Aim for the deck. That armoured plating may be too thick to get through, but the deck is wood – wood shatters and burns.

Kylah adjusted their heading. The black ship loomed closer and closer. Kylah's hands begin to slip from the wheel. It was too much. She was too tired. She simply couldn't hang on any longer.

A pair of warm and familiar arms crept about her waist, holding her up and keeping her steady on the wheel. Kylah drew deeply of their strength and focused her eyes forward on their target.

"Darling girl," she murmured. "Is this the end?"

No, my love, it's just the beginning.

And then the world went black and there was no more.

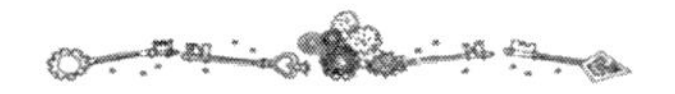

The explosion shook the ground beneath their feet. Ronin and Eli braced themselves against the wall of a nearby building, as all around them, people cried out in terror and pointed skywards.

"W-w-what was that?" Eli cried. "Was it another airship exploding?"

"If it was, it was a big one," Ronin replied.

The soldiers escorting Snow had stopped as well and were looking up at the fireball, concern etched on their faces. But then they turned down a narrow alleyway, dragging Snow with them.

Rushing to the corner, Ronin and Eli were in time to see the last soldier disappear through a stout, non-descript wooden door, which clanged shut behind them. Running to it, Ronin searched for a bolt or a lock or a handle of any kind, but there was nothing.

Growling with disbelief, he ripped his helmet off and ran his hand through his hair in trembling despair. He had assumed the soldiers would be taking Snow back to the palace – a place they could easily gain access to, and in their uniforms move about in unchallenged. Instead, the men had disappeared behind a door that locked from the inside and would be impossible to break down.

"Ronin, w-w-what do we do now?" Eli stuttered.

"I don't know, Eli. We must get in there, but I don't see how. There's no way in."

"I know a way in."

A young man was standing in the entrance to the alleyway, surveying them cautiously through narrowed eyes, plainly poised to bolt at the smallest provocation. Ronin looked at him curiously, then spread his hands wide away from the weapon on his hip.

"Who are you?" he asked.

"It doesn't matter who I am. It only matters that that is the entrance to the Contratulum's stronghold, and even if you could get it open, it wouldn't do you any good."

"Why not?"

"There are ... devices ... implanted in the floor. Should anyone attempt to gain entry who does not have express clearance, they will be triggered. You would both be dead before you even took a step. You wouldn't be much good to her then."

"You know Snow?"

"Maybe," he shrugged. "I know that it sometimes gets cold enough here in Winter to snow."

Ronin stared at him, then something Arden had told him about his first meeting with Barnabus occurred to him.

"And I know that it doesn't only snow in winter," he replied. The young man visibly relaxed and took a small step forward.

"Who are you?" he asked. I saw you following them from the cathedral when they took the queen. Are you Contratulum? Because you don't look – or act – like their normal brain-washed grunts."

"We're not," Ronin told him. "We're with the Avian army, and we're close friends of Princess – I mean, Queen – Snow."

"I met others claiming the same," the young man said. "A blonde woman. Kylah, she said her name was."

"Kylah's alive?"

The young man hesitated at Eli's question.

"She was alive the last time I saw her," he said. "And there was another man – he was on the roof, with the airships. He gave me this." He lifted the edge of his tunic to reveal the knife strapped to his thigh.

"Nylex," Ronin said, and the young man nodded.

"Yes, that was his name. So," he gestured towards the door. "I get you in there, what's the plan?"

"Rescue Snow."

"What about Pontifex Slie? And Mirage – if he's still alive?"

"Kill them."

Without a word, the man turned on his heel and walked away. Stopping at the entrance to the alleyway, he turned to look back at them. "Well, come on then."

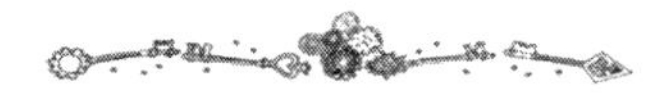

Down that endless corridor with lights flickering on and off above them they dragged her, then out onto a carpeted balcony that ringed an enormous open space. There was an airship at tether here, and Snow's head swam at how great the drop was to the floor below.

Barely giving her a second to catch her breath, the soldiers hustled her along past endless shut doors.

"Please let me go," Snow begged them. "I only want a better life for us all. I promise you won't be punished for working for the Contratulum. I understand you had no choice, but there is a better way. Please, take me back."

"I'm sorry, Your Majesty." The commander of the legion looked at her with something akin to pity. "But you have no idea what you're dealing with. No idea what the Pontifex is capable of."

"I understand he is evil," Snow gasped. "And I know he has dealings with the Power."

"Has dealings with it?" snorted the man. "He *is* the Power, or as like it as it makes no difference."

They reached a door, which opened. They thrust her in and closed the door behind her, and it was dark – so dark – except for a patch of light over the desk at the centre of the room, at which sat the Pontifex, waiting for her, a plate of red apples sitting before him.

"Come in, Your Majesty," he said.

Behind him, his fingers gently resting on the back of his master's chair, stood Mirage. He looked at her and there was something in his eyes she couldn't understand. It was as if he was pleased to see her, but at the same time dismayed that she was there. Then he blinked. Once more the impassive mask she had always known him to wear was in place.

"Come here," Slie ordered.

Snow remained stubbornly rooted where she was – but then he was inside her head. She fought back, raising her barriers as she had done so many times in the past. But he laughed at her and tore them down as though they were made of paper.

"I indulged you in the past," he told her. "When you raised your pathetic shields against me, I allowed them. I was afraid of damaging that brilliant mind of yours, but now I no longer care if I do reduce you to a mindless imbecile. You will obey me."

"N-n-never!" she cried, fighting him with everything she had.

"I said, COME HERE!"

Snow's feet jerked forward. Independent of her mind or her wishes, they lurched her through the darkness into the patch of light where Slie looked at her with those dead eyes that promised her nothing but pain and death.

"Sit down."

She sat and hated herself for it.

"I will never submit to you," she choked out, and he chuckled.

"Oh, my dear girl, you already have."

"You need me to rule the kingdom for you, so you will not harm me," she stated bravely.

"Correction – I needed you, past tense. Now that you have the crown on your head – now that you are the legally anointed monarch – I have no use for you. Although – that is not strictly true. I do have use for one part of you."

"What do you mean?" she gasped.

"Your heart. I need your heart."

"Why?"

"It is the final component needed to complete our clockwork queen. With it, she will be able to attain sentience for a brief while – long enough to pass a law handing complete control of the kingdom over to the Contratulum."

"That creature will never fool anyone."

"Oh, but it will. You see, nobody knows you, my dear. You hid away from anyone who might have been prepared to be your ally. The people will follow you as their rightful queen – but they won't fight for you, because they don't love you."

"Maybe they don't love me yet," Snow retorted. "But they will. I will be a good queen. I want to help my people achieve a better life – one without the foul evil of the Contratulum in it."

"It's too little, too late, my dear. That brief uprising in the cathedral is being handled, and even your grandfather's airships are being dealt with. There is no one coming for you, Snow. No one to help you. It is over. It's merely a question of how painful the end is for you."

He paused and slid the plate of apples towards her.

"Now, my chief technician has told me for optimal results the heart must be beating when it is extracted, which means you must still be alive when we take it from you. But I am not an unreasonable man. I am prepared to spare you such agony." His eyes flicked down to the apples and back.

"Why not have an apple, my dear? Then it will all be over, and you won't feel a thing."

"No," sobbed Snow, as the tendrils of his mind twisted and writhed within her thoughts. "Get out!" she screamed and clasped her hands to her temples. "Get out of my head."

Shouts and yells erupted outside in the corridor, along with the sound of weapons fire and the clash of steel on steel. Distracted, Slie snatched his attention away from her as the door to the chamber flew open and Ronin, Eli, and a young man she had never seen before burst through it with weapons raised.

"Why, do come in," Slie purred. "I have been expecting you."

The door crashed shut behind them, and the men startled and looked about at the darkness.

"Snow!" Ronin saw her and rushed towards her.

"Ronin ... run," she managed to gasp. "It's a trap!"

But it was too late. With a blast of pure Power, Slie smashed the three men to the floor and held them there. Brutally pinned by a force of sheer malevolence, Ronin could only move his eyes and as they briefly met Snow's terrified glance, he saw the resignation there.

She believed they were all dead – that nothing could be done to save them now. Desperately, he tried to smile at her – to reassure her, but all he could move was his eyes.

Fighting with everything he had to raise himself from the floor, Ronin barely managed to twitch a muscle before he was forced to give in and lie panting and exhausted. The thick carpet was warm beneath his cheek, and he could hear the soft moans of the others as they struggled to move.

It had seemed too easy. When he had run into Barnabus and his men in the palace, they had readily agreed to come with them to rescue Snow from the clutches of Slie, and the strange young man had led them down through the servants' quarters and into a quiet passageway. Opening a hidden door, he told them it was Slie's secret entrance into the vast Contratulum base of operations, located under the palace for over a century.

The men on guard had been easily subdued, and the door had been unlocked, but it had only stayed open long enough to admit himself, Eli, and the young man – then it had slammed behind them and they had found themselves totally at Slie's mercy.

"Now then, Your Majesty. Admit it is over. Admit it, and then everything will become so much simpler. Eat the apple, and there will be no more pain, no more fear. Eat the apple."

Behind him, Mirage shifted uneasily, his eyes fixed on Snow. His fingers gripped the chair so tightly his knuckles whitened.

"Eat the apple." Slie pushed the thought into her mind until it was all she wanted. She would eat an apple. They were such beautiful apples. So red and shiny. So delicious looking. Just one bite, she told herself. What harm would one bite do?

She saw her hand reach out and pick up an apple.

"Go on." Slie leaned forward in his chair in anticipation.

She put the apple to her lips, then looked up into Mirage's human eye. A single tear glittered in its black depths. To her fascination, it rolled silently down his cheek. With everything she had, she pulled the apple away from her mouth and dashed it to the ground.

"N-n-no!" she cried, and then Slie was upon her. Barging into her mind with a bullish roar, he invaded all that she was and groped for her. She turned and fled within her mind. He reached out for her, but fear gave her strength. With a pained shriek, she ran.

Retreating before him in her mind, she slammed and locked doors behind her and fled down darkened corridors. But he smashed down the barricades and was hot on her heels until at last, she came to a stout wooden door she had never seen before, and yet she knew it.

There was no lock or key, but as she placed her hand on the wood the door swung open. She entered, and it closed behind her.

Snow looked around. It was her old nursery. The only place she had ever felt completely safe until she had found Ronin's cottage. Wonderingly, she walked over the thickly carpeted floor to the little white bed she had slept in as a child and sat on it.

Snow.

"Mother?" Snow peered into the shadows. "Is that you?"

Her mother smiled, her raven-black hair shimmering in the firelight as she gracefully moved to sit beside Snow. Snow could smell the light fragrance of her skin, and feel the warmth of her breath, as her mother gathered her up in her arms and held her as though she was a little girl.

"Mother, I'm so scared," she whispered. "Slie is out there. He means to kill me and take over the kingdom."

Hush, my darling girl, her mother soothed her and stroked her hair. *You are safe here for a moment.*

"But what can I do? He is so strong – so much stronger than me. I can't fight against him. I can't help the others. I can't even help myself. I'm so weak and useless."

You are not weak, my dearest, and you have never been useless.

"But I have no power against him."

You are Queen Snow of the House White. You are this kingdom's rightfully anointed monarch. You wear the Crown of Purity and you have more power than you can possibly imagine.

"Does being the queen give me power, then?"

Oh, my darling, you have always had the power. You just never knew how to use it.

And then the door burst open, and with a great gasp, Snow opened her eyes and was back in the circle of light facing Slie and Mirage.

"I will never," she said, pulling herself upright in the chair and meeting Slie's gaze with a steely firm one of her own. "Never, submit to you. I am Queen Snow of House White and I order you to stop!"

Reaching deep within herself, Snow found her power – her legacy from her mother, Raven, and her great-grandmother, Starling, and so on back in an unbroken line through all the great and powerful women of her bloodline.

Gathering it up in her hands, she cast Slie from her mind and he cringed back in his chair, his eyes flying wide with shock. Then she was on her feet, and power swirled at her fingertips as she threw back her chair with a flick of her fingers.

She found the thread of Slie's control over the others and snapped it, tossing the tattered remnants back at him with a disdainful smirk. The three men scrambled to their feet and Ronin staggered towards her.

"Snow," he exclaimed.

She turned to face him, and he fell back from the look in her eyes.

"Why is it so dark in here?" she cried. "You scurry about in the shadows like a thief in the night, Slie. Let us see what you are hiding." The Crown of Purity flared in a great, white ball of light that flooded all four corners of the room with brilliant illumination.

"Ye gods," Ronin gasped in horror.

On all four walls of the room were bodies. Desiccated and partially mummified, they hung in cages of iron. Tubing looped from body to body, and a thick, sluggish liquid was creeping from one to other.

"What is this?!" Snow demanded of Slie.

"It's the Council of Elders." It was Mirage who answered. "He must be draining them of their power and using it for himself. The Power demands a great sacrifice of pain and suffering – the greater the sacrifice, the greater the Power you will control."

Mirage looked at Slie in grudging admiration. "No wonder no one has laid eyes on them in years."

Examining the nearest body in horrified fascination, Ronin jumped back when its eyes opened and stared at him.

"They're still alive!" he cried.

"You would do this?" Snow lashed out at Slie in disgust. "All to gain power?"

"To gain such power there is nothing I would not do, no one I would not sacrifice. For such power is intoxicating, and it is strong enough to rival even yours, Your Majesty."

He rose from his chair and suddenly had a hold of her throat with his mind. She couldn't breathe. Desperately, she fought against him, but he was strong, and she panicked.

Her heart pounding wildly, she groped for her magic but couldn't hear it over the rushing of her blood, and her lungs struggling to draw in air.

"Let her go."

Ronin moved towards them, but with a casual flick of his wrist, Slie threw him back against the wall, where he landed amongst the dusty bones and shrivelled flesh of a body. Struggling to stand, he heard a dry whisper from above him.

Kill me.

Looking up, he saw the eyes of the body staring down into his, pleading with an intensity that wrung at his heart. He glanced over at Snow, who was on her knees choking and gasping for air.

Kill me. Stop him.

The words echoed in his mind. Staggering back, his movements slow and clumsy as if he were trying to struggle free of quicksand, Ronin pulled the sword from his belt, and with one swipe removed the poor creature's head clean from its shoulders.

Slie let out a great howl of anger. Falling onto the table, he quickly recovered and tightened his grip on Snow's throat.

"Kill them all!" Ronin ordered.

Eli and the young man staggered to their feet to do his bidding, lopping off head after head whilst Slie roared with rage. With each poor creature put out of its misery, Ronin felt mastery of his body returning and rushed at Slie.

With an evil smirk, Slie held out his hand and squeezed it into a fist. Snow collapsed on the ground – her eyes open and staring at nothing – as Mirage slapped his hand onto the side of Slie's throat, penetrating his jugular with the poison-tipped needle in the middle of his ring.

Chapter Forty

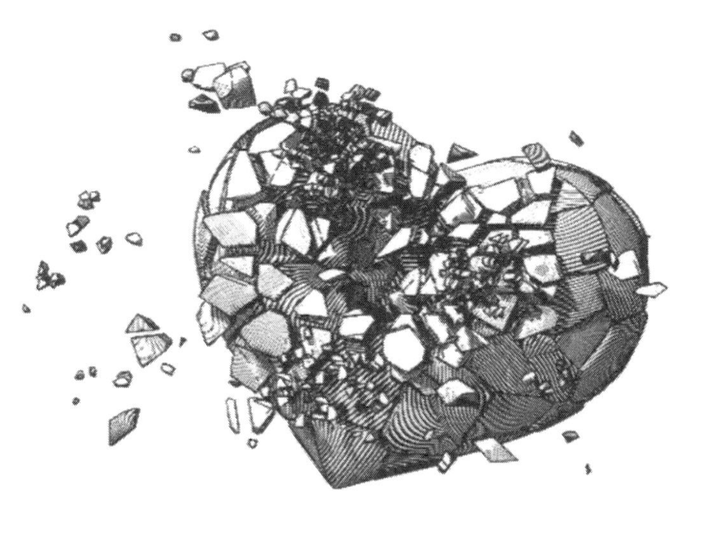

Black Ice

Slie stared in disbelief at his protégé as the poison swiftly spread through his system, and his black and twisted heart ground to a halt. He fell forward, and Mirage gently eased his master down onto the floor. Slie clutched at him.

"I knew I was right ... not to trust you ..." he gasped, then choked as black blood gushed from his mouth, and his eyes emptied of the last spark of life.

"Snow!" Ronin cried, rushing towards her.

"No!" Mirage swept up a hand, and a sheet of black-tipped ice sprang up around him and Snow. "You shall not have her – she is mine."

Ronin stared at the ice in shock. "You are a weather talker," he exclaimed. "Yet I don't feel the taint of the Power within you – so how is this possible?"

"Because I am Dwarvian, and as such my magic is inherent and diverse. All my life I have concealed the full extent of my power from Slie, for fear he would guess my true heritage."

"Let down this barrier, Mirage. If you are truly Dwarvian, then you will not use your magic to do harm – and especially not towards her."

"Don't you understand? All of this is for her. She is mine. She has always been mine, and I shall not allow you to have her."

Fumbling in Slie's robe pocket he drew out a bunch of keys, then crawled to where Snow lay so still and quiet on the floor and gathered her up in his arms.

Standing, he staggered slightly under her weight and adjusted her body, so her head lolled on his shoulder. He ran to the door in the far corner of the room, inserted a key from the bunch and disappeared through it.

"Quickly," Ronin cried. "We have to follow them."

Running to the ice barrier, he pounded futilely on it. But the ice was too thick – no amount of force would shatter it.

"Ronin," the young man put a hand on his shoulder. "The queen is dead. There is no point in pursuing him. It is over."

"Never!" Ronin roared. "He shall not have her. If she *is* dead, which I don't believe, then she shall rest amongst her family and her friends. She shall be with the people who love her," he looked wildly at the other two. "If you won't help me, I shall go alone."

He dashed back to the door they had entered through. This time it opened easily, and he charged out into the corridor to find Barnabus and his men waiting anxiously.

"Ronin," cried Barnabus. "What's happened? Where's the queen?"

"He took her. Mirage took her. We need to get after him and get her back."

"Where did he take her?"

"I don't know. There is a barrier, we cannot get through."

"There!" one of the other soldiers cried. "Look down there."

Far below, Mirage had appeared on the workshop floor. Striding up to the mechanics who were working on the airship, he appeared to be having some sort of altercation with one of them, then simply pushed past the man and strode up the ramp that led to the ship.

Clambering on board, he lay Snow down on the deck then gestured to the terrified mechanics to come on board. When they didn't move quickly enough to suit him, he gestured at one and the man collapsed to his knees, screaming, and clawing at his face until blood splattered the ground. The other mechanics hurried aboard.

"We have to get down there!" Ronin insisted. "We have to get Snow back before he takes off."

"Takes off where?" Barnabus demanded. "We're inside a hill."

There was a grinding and a creaking, and at the far end of the cavern double doors began to open. Ronin turned on Barnabus in despair.

"Is ***The Revenge*** still in dock?"

"If it hasn't been destroyed, then yes."

"I do not understand why you are pursuing them," the young man said, as he and Eli joined them in the corridor. "The queen was beyond question dead. It is over."

"Never!" Ronin grabbed the man by his shirt and shook him. "I refuse to believe that, and even if she were, do you think I would leave her with that creature? What do you think her mother would say if she were here now? Would she not want you to do everything you could to protect her child – or avenge her?"

The man stared at him for a second, then an almost fanatical gleam lit up his eyes. "You are right," he murmured. "I must help you do this, for Queen Raven's sake. It is what she would have wanted. It is the mission she would have given me."

"Then let's go." Ronin demanded and glared at the others. "I am convinced that Snow is still alive, I feel it here." He struck his chest. "So, we go to get her back, and if we find that she is dead, we take revenge on every stinking member of the Contratulum who contributed to her death. Who's with me?"

"We all are," Barnabus assured him.

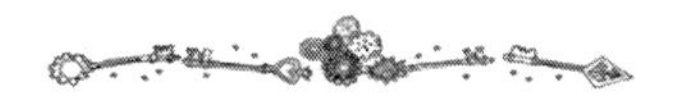

To Ronin's great relief, ***The Revenge*** was still hovering at the end of its docking ropes. As they ran towards it, Nylex's head popped up to survey them over the rail with great relief. They clambered aboard, Nylex raised his brows at Ronin and smiled gently at Eli. To the young lad's surprise, as he clambered over the railing, Nylex clasped him in a warm hug of greeting.

"I'm p-p-pleased to see you too, Nylex." he grinned, then looked around the deserted dock. "Where's ***The Lissa***? Where's Kylah?"

"I'm so sorry, Eli." Nylex awkwardly patted Eli on the back. "The Contratulum launched the biggest and nastiest airship I've ever seen at the Avian fleet. It was monstrous. The Avians wouldn't have stood a chance against it, so Kylah ... well ... she did something incredibly brave. She saved everyone."

"W-w-what did she do?" Eli pulled the oversized helmet from his head and stared at Nylex. "Where is she? Nylex, where's Kylah?"

"She rammed the airship with ***The Lissa.*** She must have opened the engines all the way because she was going at full speed when she hit it, and she blew it to kingdom come."

"B-b-but where is she?" Eli's face twisted as he struggled to process what he was being told.

"***The Lissa*** exploded as well, Eli. There was nothing left of it."

"Kylah's d-d-dead?"

"I'm so sorry, Eli. But her sacrifice saved hundreds of people. The destruction of that airship seemed to knock the fight out of the Contratulum, and the Avian ships have them on the run."

"B-b-but I don't understand. Why would Kylah do that?"

"Because she was one of the bravest people I ever met," Ronin told him, and placed a hand on Eli's shoulder as the boy's face crumpled and he began to sob.

"She was already dying." The young man had been listening with interest and now offered his knowledge like a gift.

"What do you mean?" Ronin looked at him.

"When the bridge fell, she was hurt – badly hurt – inside. I have seen it before, where someone is bleeding into the stomach cavity and nothing short of a miracle can save them. She was dying, and she knew it. This way she ensured her death meant something. She is to be respected, and honoured, for her decision."

"Do you hear that, Eli? Kylah died a hero."

"I don't want a hero," Eli wept. "I want my sister back."

"Come on, Eli," Nylex soothed the lad. "Let's go below deck and see if we can find anything to eat. You know you always feel better when you've eaten something."

"I don't want anything."

"Aren't you hungry?"
"Perhaps ... a little."
"Could you maybe manage a bite?"
"Maybe."
They disappeared down the stairs, and Ronin marvelled at this new and gently sympathetic Nylex who had the capacity to help the grieving boy. Pushing down his sorrow about Kylah, he looked at Barnabus. Whilst they had been talking, he and his men had readied ***The Revenge*** for flight, and the ship was now drifting up and away from the battlements.
"Where to?" Barnabus asked, and Ronin tried to get his bearings.
"East," he answered, and Barnabus nodded, yelling orders to his men who set to turning the ship around onto its new heading. Gently the ship pulled up and away until the whole of the palace and the city was spread out beneath them.
Looking down, Ronin could see how much damage the city had sustained. The two crashed airships had left scars, and debris raining down from the destruction of other ships had damaged buildings and set fires that raged all over.
The city was built on the side of a great hill, and as they floated higher, Ronin spotted another airship far below on a north-easterly heading.
"There," he pointed. "That's them."
The Revenge shifted its course to follow. The Contratulum ship flew in such an erratic manner that it wasn't long before they were gaining on it.
"I would have expected it to be faster," Ronin muttered, and Barnabus handed the wheel over to his second-in-command to stand beside him at the railing.
"I think it's damaged," he said. "That's probably why it wasn't in the battle with the others – it was being repaired."
"Lucky for us then," Ronin replied.
"What are you going to do when we reach them?"
"I'll think of something."
Lower and lower the Contratulum ship flew, and Barnabus shook his head in bewilderment. "What are they playing at?" he muttered. "It's like they want us to catch them."
A small wood was located to the north of the city, and the Contratulum ship was making a beeline for it, flying even lower as it reached the trees. Ronin fretted for the long minutes it took ***The Revenge*** to round the edge of the wood and set off in pursuit of the ship.

A sudden, determined spurt of speed took them by surprise, and Barnabus cursed as the ship sped ahead of them. "Ahead, full speed," he bellowed, and his men rushed to comply, heaving on ropes to trim the fins and adjust the sails.

For long minutes, the other ship pulled away, until a great belch of smoke billowed from the exhaust port and their speed cut by half.

"Steady as she goes!" Barnabus bellowed. "Grappling hooks at the ready."

Soldiers rushed to ready the firing mechanism which would shoot barbed hooks into the side of the other ship and pull it towards them. Slower and slower, the Contratulum ship went until it was barely limping along, and ***The Revenge*** was gaining on it fast.

"Now!" Barnabus yelled and away went the grappling hooks. All but one found their marks. "Stop all engines," he ordered. "Hard to port side."

With a dreadful groaning noise, ***The Revenge*** stopped. The soldiers began to winch in the lines until the other ship was so close, Ronin could see the terrified expressions on the mechanics' faces as they scurried about the deck.

Close enough to jump, Ronin was the first up on the railing and over onto the other ship's deck, followed by Barnabus and some of his men.

"We surrender, we surrender!" Petrified, the mechanics held their hands up in defeat.

"Where are they?" Ronin snarled at their leader. "Where are Mirage and the queen?

"Not here," said the man, then gasped as Ronin grabbed him by the tunic front and lifted him off his feet. "I swear to you, they're not here," he cried. "Mirage put the queen in the cradle and made us lower them down near the wood."

"Search the ship," Barnabus ordered, and his men scattered to obey.

"Which part of the wood?" Ronin demanded, and when the man was slow to answer he shook him again, snarling in his face. "Tell me, or I'll rip your windpipe out. Tell me where he took Snow!"

"Why do you care?" the man gasped. "Wasn't getting rid of her the plan all along?"

"We're not Contratulum, and we do care very much what happens to Snow, so you'd better start talking." Something in Ronin's eyes must have convinced the mechanic, for his face went ashen.

"Soon after we rounded the corner of the wood and were able to lower the cradle without you seeing it, there's a hillock. I saw him carry her body there as we were flying away. That's all I know."

Ronin threw him to the ground in disgust and turned to Barnabus.

"You men," the Commander ordered. "Stay here, guard the prisoners, and fly the ship back to join the Avian fleet. Make sure you signal them well in advance that you are friend, not foe – don't want them to shoot you down, do we?"

"We have to find her," Ronin muttered, and Barnabus clapped him on the shoulder.

"And we will. We have him on the run now and he won't get far on foot carrying ... the queen."

Ronin heard his hesitation and knew what he had been about to say – that Mirage wouldn't get far carrying a body. He glanced at the Commander and realised, by the way he wouldn't look at him, that Barnabus believed Snow was dead as well.

They climbed back on board ***The Revenge***. The grappling hooks were released and wound back in, then Barnabus gave the order to turn the ship around and head back the way they had come. Nylex joined them on deck, followed by a silent Eli. His face was streaked with tears and his cheeks bulged around a ship's biscuit.

"He wanted to be here," Nylex murmured. "He said he wants to help find Snow."

Ronin nodded and gave Eli a gentle smile. The lad blinked furiously and wiped his nose with his sleeve, before cramming more biscuit into his mouth.

Swiftly the ship flew, until the hillock the mechanic had spoken about could be seen rising a few yards from the wood. Barnabus barked orders and ***The Revenge*** slowed to a stop. The cradle was readied, and as soon as it was level with the deck Ronin jumped impatiently inside, followed by Nylex, the young man, Barnabus, and two of his men, and – after a slight hesitation – Eli.

"You don't have to come, Eli," Nylex told him gently.

"Yes, I do," Eli replied with a stubborn shrug. "It's S-s-snow. She'd come for me."

They reached the ground and tumbled from the cradle, weapons at the ready as they rushed towards the hillock. Tussocky grass swished beneath their boots, and high above a skylark warbled its song to the skies. It was a beautiful day, Ronin thought – too beautiful a day for Snow to be dead, so she must still be alive.

As they approached the hillock there was the familiar sound of a skimmer's engine starting up. Frantically they put on speed and raced around the base of the hillock in time to see a small skimmer-like device rise up in the sky through an opening in the hillside.

Desperately, Ronin raised his weapon. The skimmer, with the familiar figure of Mirage sitting in the cockpit, was already out of range – but he fired it anyway, screaming with frustrated rage as the man inside cast him a coolly contemptuous look over his shoulder and then flew away into the wide blue sky.

"Back to the ship," he yelled. "We must get after them."

"Wait," Barnabus put a restraining hand on his shoulder. "That contraption was too small to hold more than one comfortably, and I certainly didn't see the queen squashed in there with him – did you?"

"Maybe he left her in t-t-there?" said Eli. He gestured towards the opening in the hillside as it began to close.

"No, no, no!" Ronin screamed and ran towards it, reaching with his fingertips as the opening slammed shut and the edges melted away into the landscape as if it had never been there at all.

They moved all over the hillside, desperately probing with swords and fingernails, but whatever mechanism existed to open the doorway from the outside, they couldn't find it. Finally, Ronin knelt and placed his hands on the ground, attempting to feel for any flaws or cracks. Further, into the hillside, he probed, until there was a rumble, and a trickle of dirt dislodged itself and bounced down upon them.

"What is he doing?" Barnabus asked.

"Pulling down this side of the hill," Nylex replied.

"He can do that?"

"Oh yes – although I think even if he couldn't, he would still try it to get to her."

The other men moved back, as Ronin forced the earth and rocks apart with his mind. Tearing down the hillside to get to Snow, he clawed and dug with his magic until there was a great rumbling and grinding, and part of the hillside began to collapse.

Nylex leapt forward with Barnabus and dragged Ronin away as boulders and earth slid and tumbled, and a cloud of dirt billowed out, enveloping all, and making them cough furiously. As it began to settle, they saw the entrance. Just big enough for the small skimmer to pass through, it led into a cavern, which narrowed into a tunnel, leading away.

Ronin strode forward into the cavern and looked around. Apart from a narrow bench holding an assortment of tools – presumably for maintaining the skimmer – and several kegs of oil, it was empty. He crossed to the tunnel and peered in.

"Wait until we fetch torches from the ship," Barnabus advised.

"No need," Nylex grinned, snapping his fingers. A light appeared in his palm. "Better let me go first," he told Ronin, who impatiently moved aside to let him take the lead. Nylex took a few paces to where the tunnel took a sharp right-hand turn, the others crowding in behind him.

"It's all right," he called back. "There's a cave here with enough light to see by."

He was right. Beyond the corner, the tunnel widened into a large cave. A small stream wound out from a fissure in the cave wall to empty into a small pool at its heart. Sunlight streamed down through a gap in the cave roof and shimmered on the crystal waters of the pool.

Around the cave were signs of habitation – a comfortable bed, a small table and chair, a shelf full of books, boxes of food, and chests. In the centre of the table sat the Crown of Purity.

"What is this place?" Barnabus wondered out loud.

"It looks like we've found Mirage's bolthole," Nylex replied. "Maybe this was his refuge if things went south with the Contratulum."

"But where's Snow?" Ronin demanded, glancing about the cave in despair. "If she wasn't on the skimmer, and she's not here, where is she?"

"She's here," Eli replied. Standing by the pool he pointed into its crystal waters, and the others crowded over to look.

She lay on the rocky bottom of the pool. Her eyes were closed, and her dark lashes were rimmed with a sparkling layer of ice that stood out in stark relief against the alabaster paleness of her cheeks. Her hands were folded at her waist and her black hair lay in waves over her shoulders. Above her still body, tiny fish darted about in the crystal-clear waters of the pool.

Dropping to his knees beside the pool, Ronin plunged his hands into the sparkling water, then drew back with a sharp cry of pain. He examined his fingertips which were red raw.

"What is it?" cried Nylex, kneeling beside him. "What's wrong?"

"It's ice!" Ronin exclaimed. "She's encased in a block of ice."

And now they could all see it. Around the edges of her body, walls of black ice formed a sarcophagus fit for a queen, with a clear lid of thick ice through which they could see her body perfectly preserved for all eternity.

"We have to get her out!" Ronin cried and again plunged his arms into the water. He groaned in agony as his hands touched the enchanted casket of ice, and Nylex saw streaks of red veins race up Ronin's arms and onto his throat.

"Stop!" he cried and yanked him violently back. "Ronin, stop. It's no good. Mirage has placed a spell on it. You'll never get it out – not without killing yourself."

“I have to get her out.” Gasping with frustrated pain, Ronin held out his hands as the red streaks gradually subsided.

“The queen has a fitting resting place,” the young man stated with a shrug. “All that is left of our mission now is revenge. I say we go after Mirage and kill him.”

“No!” Ronin snapped and leant forward over the pool. For a moment, Nylex thought he intended to plunge his hands once more into the water, and moved to pull him back, but instead, Ronin braced his hands on the slippery rocks at the edge of the pool and closed his eyes.

Long moments passed. The men watched expectantly, knowing by the strain on Ronin’s face and the veins that were popping on his temples that he was doing something – they just weren’t sure what.

Ronin had sent his mind down to the thick black ice that encased Snow’s body, trying to determine the nature of the spell that had made it. Cold. Intense cold. His mind recoiled from its frigid touch. Such ice could not be melted by any fire that man could make.

He sent his mind further and further down into the ground. Stretching the boundaries of his magic, he cried out in exhausted frustration. Then a hand on each shoulder steadied and reassured him, and magic poured into his body in great revitalising waves. He knew it was Nylex and Eli. Uncertain of his intentions, they only knew he needed help, and so they gave it, freely and unrestrainedly.

Deeper and deeper into the ground his mind travelled until he found what he was looking for. A stream of lava so hot it would melt the flesh from a man in seconds was churning and broiling miles below the surface of the cave.

Carefully he teased a thread of it from the stream and drew it up to the surface. Up and up, he brought it, slowly and carefully. Not too much – enough to serve the purpose, but not so much it would rage out of control.

Vaguely he was aware of his heart labouring under the task. He acknowledged that this might kill him, then carried on regardless. Higher and higher he drew the lava until it was mere inches away from the bottom of Snow’s casket of ice.

He fanned the fire until it played over the bottom of the pool in an even stream, unaware that the water in the pool began to bubble and steam as it was heated by the subterranean forces. But Nylex saw it and realised what Ronin was about.

Twisting his head to look at Barnabus, who was staring with fascinated wonder into the pool, he snapped.

“Get ready to pull her out on my command.”

Barnabus nodded and moved closer to the top right-hand corner. The young man and the soldiers positioned themselves at the other corners.

Hotter and hotter the water bubbled, then there was a tremendous crack as the thinner clear ice of the casket lid cracked all the way across, and water gushed in, flooding Snow's body.

"Now!" Nylex shouted, and the men plunged their hands into the hot water of the pool, smashed aside the remaining shards of ice, and grabbed Snow's body.

"Ronin, let go!" Nylex ordered and pulled Ronin away as the men lifted Snow out of the pool and lay her on the ground. Water streamed from her ice-cold body, and her hair lay like fronds of seaweed over her face.

Gasping with exhaustion, Ronin knelt beside her and felt her frozen skin for a pulse, but there was none. Frantically, he searched for a spark of life with his magic, but she was still and empty, and cold – so very cold.

He gathered her to him to warm her. Perhaps it was only because she was cold. She hated being cold. He remembered how she had whimpered in her sleep from the cold, the first night she slept in his cottage. How he had tucked a blanket around her to keep her warm.

"Snow," he cried brokenly, and rocked her body into his, burying his face in her neck and whispering her name over, and over, again "... Snow ... Snow ... Snow ..." as his heart silently shattered into a thousand icy shards.

The other men turned away, not wishing to witness his pain. Sorrow gripped their hearts at the loss of their beautiful young queen. All except Eli. Not understanding the subtlety of the moment, he only knew his friend was sad, so he knelt beside him and placed a hand on his shoulder.

"Ronin. Make Snow better."

"I can't, Eli. She's gone. She's dead."

"I was dead once," Eli told him proudly. "But Grein brought me back."

Slowly, Ronin raised his head and stared at him, memories flooding his mind of that dreadful night five years ago. Of running through the forest with Grein to discover their whole village on fire, too late to save anyone. Of Kylah kneeling on the ground beside Eli's body and screaming at them to help him.

Of Grein feeling for his pulse, then shaking his head. But then Grein had turned Eli onto his back, and then he had ...

With renewed hope, Ronin turned Snow on her side and opened her mouth to empty out the small amount of water from her brief immersion when the casket had cracked. Then he gently lay her on her back, tilted her head and opened her mouth. Kneeling, he placed his lips over hers and blew.

Desperately trying to remember what Grein had done, he blew and blew, then pressed on her chest with his joined hands. *One, two, three, four ...* he counted out loud. How many had Grein done? Was that enough? He didn't know but switched back to her mouth and breathed air into her body.

Her lips were frigid beneath his, and he tried not to think about the last time he had kissed her when they were soft and warm and fitted his perfectly.

On and on he went until Nylex gently touched him on the shoulder.

"Enough, Ronin. Enough. She's gone. Let her go in peace."

Chapter Forty-One

Choices to be Made

There was light beyond her eyelids and warmth. Slowly, Snow opened her eyes and looked up at the bluest of skies that arced gently overhead, with the smallest of fluffy white clouds drifting lazily across it. She was lying on soft grass that was the most intense vivid green she had ever seen. When she turned her head to look at it curiously, it was soft and springy to the touch. Birds were singing, and somewhere a wood pigeon was cooing. She lay for a moment, completely at peace. Was this what being dead was like?

Eventually, she sat up and looked at her surroundings. Rolling parkland lay all around, with a pretty wood behind her, and in the distance, a small stream splashed and burbled in the sunshine. She scrambled to her feet and brushed the grass from her gown.

In the distance, behind a screen of trees, she heard voices and laughter. They sounded familiar, and Snow had the overwhelming urge to see who they belonged to. Lifting her skirts, she wandered barefoot over the grass, stopping every few steps to gaze about her in wonder and draw in a great lungful of the sweet, intoxicating air.

Pushing her way through the trees she came to a clearing with a beautiful cloth-of-gold marquee erected in the centre. Within the marquee was a table laid with delicious food and crystal goblets of ruby red wine. Sitting at the table were a man and a woman.

The man was tall, with dark blond hair and a rugged beard, dressed in royal clothes. He looked up at her approach and gently laid a hand on the woman sitting beside him. She was slender, with raven-black hair which rippled down her spine.

"Mother?" Snow whispered, and Raven turned and held out her arms to her daughter. Rushing forward, Snow threw herself into them with a cry of joy and sobbed on her mother's breast.

"Mother, I was so afraid."

"I know, my darling, but you have been very brave, and now it's all over."

"We are so proud of you, Snow. You have travelled so far and fought so hard. You have proven yourself a true queen of House White." Snow looked at him shyly, but his eyes were kind, and he looked at her with so much love that in an instant she knew him and was no longer afraid.

"Papa?"

"My beloved daughter," said King Elgin, and enfolded the child he had never seen into his arms. Snow snuggled into her father's embrace and lay down all the burdens she had carried for so long. The fear and the worry, and the guilt about her people – she lay them all down and enjoyed the moment of pure love with her parents.

They sat her between them and poured her a glass of the most delicious wine she had ever tasted. They held her hands and chatted with her about her adventures, laughing and crying in turns over all she had endured. Eventually, Snow took a deep breath and looked about her.

"Am I dead?" she asked curiously.

"You are in the place where a choice can still be made," her mother gently told her.

"A choice? What choice?"

"Whether to remain, or go back?"

"Then I choose to stay with you," Snow said, and hugged them both. She took a sip of her wine and a nibble of the most delicious cake that was placed before her.

Sighing happily, she looked around at the gently smiling faces of her parents, at the sky, at the softly whispering trees, at the sumptuous feast laid before them ...

She fidgeted in her seat and placed the cake uneaten back on her plate and pushed it away. Biting her lip, she looked behind her and then stiffened in her chair.

"Did you hear that?"

"Hear what, my darling?"

"I thought I heard someone call my name – only I couldn't have, could I?"

"Love can cross all barriers," her mother told her and smiled lovingly at her husband. "It can break down preconceptions and prejudices, and shine light into even the most determined of hearts."

"Like yours," Elgin said and twinkled at Snow. "Your mother was determined to hate me even before she met me. But from the moment I entered the throne room of House Avis and saw this vision of beauty scowling at me – I knew that she was the only woman on this earth I would ever love."

"And I knew that I would love your father, even if he had not been a king. That no matter how lowly his station, I would still marry him. Because when two hearts are destined to be together, nothing as base as rank and money should keep them apart."

"That's what I told Ronin, but he ..." Snow's voice trailed away, and once again she glanced over her shoulder and frowned. "What do you think I should do?" she begged them.

"Only you can make that decision, my darling," her mother replied.

"But I would say," her father continued, "that there is a man out there who has literally moved a mountain – well, a small hill – to get to you, has dragged up fire from the bowels of the earth to set you free and is even now refusing to give up and let you go."

"Is there? Has he?" Snow looked at them with tears in her eyes. "But if I go back, I'll never see you again."

"Silly girl," her mother said and dropped a kiss on the top of her head. "Did I not tell you that love can cross all barriers? We will always be here." She lightly tapped Snow on the chest. "And we will all be together again one day."

"I have to go." Snow jumped to her feet, looking excitedly at them.

"I know," said her mother and gave her one last hug. "Have a long and happy life, Snow. And never forget that love is always the first and only answer."

"Goodbye, Snow." Her father held her tightly. "I like that young man of yours, and for what it's worth, you have my blessing."

"Thank you, Papa," she whispered into his chest. "That means more than you can ever imagine. Now I just have to persuade Ronin to forget his silly pride."

"Pride is never silly," her father told her, "but it can sometimes be misguided. Now hurry, Snow. The way back won't stay open forever, and the spell that Greta placed into the witch hazel to build a protective barrier around your mind can't last much longer."

"What will happen when the barrier falls?" Snow asked.

"Your mind would be damaged forever," her mother told her, "so run, Snow. Run as fast as you can."

"I love you both. Goodbye," Snow gasped.

She pushed her way through the trees and back out onto the parkland, but the sky was no longer so blue, and a cold wind was blowing through the wood, making the leaves rustle ominously.

She picked up her skirts and began to run, but the wind grew stronger. Tearing at her hair and clothes it beat her back, almost knocking her off her feet as she tried to run.

"Ronin!" she screamed. "Ronin! Help me!"

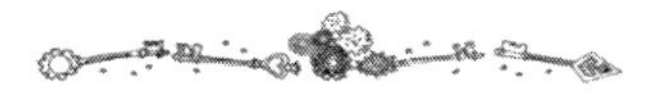

"Enough, Ronin. Enough. She's gone. Let her go in peace." Nylex's words resonated in his brain like ice cracking on a lake. Ronin rocked back on his heels and looked down at Snow's frozen body.

Nylex was right. She was gone. He had been too late, and now he had lost her. Numbly, he allowed Nylex and Barnabus to help him to his feet and lead him gently away.

"You wait outside," Nylex told him. "We will take care of her now. We'll take her back to the city for a funeral befitting a queen."

"No," he ground out. "They don't deserve her. We will take her to House Avis. We'll take her *home.*"

Nylex hesitated, then nodded in agreement, and Ronin turned away in despair because he couldn't bear to see the pity in his eyes. Seeing the Crown of Purity on the table, he picked it up and thought about the girl who had been queen for such a short time.

"It's not fair," he said. "It's not fricking fair."

"Life rarely is," Barnabus told him.

Ronin smiled a twisted grimace of pain and dropped the crown on the table. He turned to leave, then stopped and spun around, a frown of confusion creasing his brow.

"Did you hear that?"

"Hear what?" Nylex asked.

"That voice ... it sounded like ..." Sudden resolve ignited in him and he strode back and dropped beside Snow's body.

"No!" he declared. "I will not accept this. You are not gone. You are a fighter, Snow White. All of your life you have fought to get what you want, so fight now for your life and come back to me."

Raising his fist, he brought it down in a sharp punch over her heart, again and again, then knelt and vigorously blew into her mouth, over, and over, again.

"Fight!" he shouted. "Fight for your life, Snow! Fight!"

He raised his fist, and Nylex grabbed it, yanking him back and away from her.

"Ronin! Stop!" he cried. "She's gone. Accept it."

"Never!" yelled Ronin and lifted his fist again.

Snow gasped. A great gulping for air that shocked all and made them jump back. She gasped again, her chest rising and falling as her heart began to beat, and air rushed into her lungs. Panting, she opened her eyes and stared wildly around at them.

"Snow?" Ronin sobbed and helped her to sit up.

"Ronin? Where am I? What happened?"

"You're safe – that's all you need to know. You're safe."

She nodded and clung to him in confusion, looking around at the assembled men. Her eyes softened when she saw Eli and Nylex and then narrowed in confusion at the sight of Barnabus, the young man, and the other two soldiers.

"Your Majesty," Barnabus said and fell to his knee, his men flanking him as they bowed to their queen.

They went back to the city. At the sight of the battle still being wearily fought, Snow ordered them to fly ***The Revenge*** into the heart of it. She placed the Crown of Purity upon her head, and a blast of pure white light dazzled all who saw it. The Contratulum ships suddenly found that their cannons would no longer work.

Snow spoke to them, and somehow all could hear her words. She told them that Pontifex Slie was dead, Mirage had fled, and that their base of operations had been discovered. That the days of the Contratulum were over, and she offered amnesty and a fresh start to all who would denounce the old ways of darkness, and embrace the new world she planned to create, with light and hope and peace for all.

At the end of her speech, all the Contratulum soldiers and airship crews bent the knee to her as she stood on the bridge of ***The Revenge*** – a slender vision in white, who had vowed to win their hearts. The crews of the Avian ships cheered and offered help to any Contratulum vessel that required it, and the first tentative steps toward peace were taken.

Then Snow went down to the palace. Her palace. Shocked at the damage it and the city had suffered, she vowed to build anew. A better city that would provide home and shelter for her people. Upon learning that a sumptuous feast had been arranged for her coronation, she ordered the soldiers of the Contratulum to carry it out to the people, to distribute it amongst them, and to aid all who required it.

The base of operations surrendered to her forces. The people discovered within were given the same choice as the soldiers – join us or leave House White forever. Most accepted the new regime. Some didn't. These were given clear passage to wherever they wished to go.

Some chose a more permanent exile, and when her soldiers entered the Contratulum workshops, the bodies of the senior technicians were found, still clutching vials of poison.

But all of this took time, and first Snow had to be told of the death of Kylah. Sobbing, she gathered Eli to her and told him he would always have a home with her at the palace, and that his sister and her bravery would never be forgotten.

The Avian fleet docked at the castle battlements and the first to disembark was Robin, followed by her ladies, Franki and Tegan. Vastly relieved to see them unharmed, Snow laughed and sobbed as Robin clutched her up in a fierce hug.

"Told you we'd win your crown for you, Cuz," Robin muttered. Then she stepped back to survey Snow as the new queen hugged

Franki and Tegan warmly. "I must say, it looks good on you," Robin commented, with a wry grin.

Prince Peregrine joined them. Relief that the battle was over warred with sadness in his expression at the steep cost of victory. Taking Snow gently by the hand, he led her back on board his vessel, to where her grandparents were waiting at the other end of a wireless transmission. Seeking the reassurance of hearing her voice, Falcon's own was gruff with emotion as he congratulated her and promised to send House White whatever aid it needed to rebuild its shattered city and heal its broken people.

And of course, Prince Hawk and Princess Jay had to be dealt with. For once united in their hatred of Snow, when their queen strode into the throne room at the head of her army, they were seated on the dais dressed in their finest robes.

Snow stood before them, the stepdaughter and niece they had tried to besmirch and even kill, tall and slender in her white coronation gown, with the Crown of Purity glimmering on her head. They must have known in their hearts that their time was over, yet still Jay tried.

"You are a travesty." Jay snapped. "You are not fit to wear that crown. You will take it off immediately and submit to us as your elders and betters."

"You will not address her Majesty that way," Barnabus barked, and his hand went to his sword. Snow stayed him with a gesture and stepped forward.

"You will leave my kingdom," she said quietly. "This is to be a progressive and equal society, and there is no place within it for the likes of you."

"How dare you speak to us that way ..." Hawk sputtered.

"I dare because I am the queen." Snow retorted. Her eyes flashed black fire at them, and they subsided. "Escort their highnesses to their rooms and ensure they stay there," she instructed Barnabus, and he gave her a bow, his eyes twinkling with approval.

"Yes, Your Majesty," he said.

The problem of what to do with them nagged at Snow until eventually they were offered sanctuary in Larkhaven by King Falcon, on the understanding that they lived quietly and behaved themselves. The offer was made not through any paternal regard on Falcon's part, but more as a way of exiling them far away from harm, and away from Snow.

Then Snow set about rewarding those who had remained true to her through the darkest days. Barnabus she made her Commander-in-Chief, and his men were designated her Royal Personal Guard.

Already, the palace seamstresses were busy making special uniforms of royal purple with a single snowflake sewn onto the breast pocket.

Snow wanted to reward the young man who had played such an integral part in both her rescue, and in the ongoing resistance movement against the Contratulum, set in place by her mother, but he had simply vanished into thin air. A search for him yielded no results and Ronin had the feeling that he would never be found – unless he wanted to be. His mission was complete. Maybe, Ronin thought, he had gone to find what life could be like without a mission and he wished him well in his endeavour.

A day after the battle, ***The Kittiwake*** limped into dock after being patched up enough to fly some very special people to be with Snow. Beaming with happiness, Snow watched Nylex pelt down the dock to snatch up Fae as she clambered off the ship, and hold her so tightly, she squeaked.

"I'm never going to leave you again," Snow heard him murmur to Fae, as she walked past them.

"And I'm never going to let you," Fae told him.

Then Snow was at the ship, laughing as Dog and Cesil were dropped onto the dock. Dog realised there were new people to molest and dashed about investigating the personal spaces of her Royal Guard, much to their embarrassed consternation. Cesil ran about squealing his disapproval of the whole situation.

Arden the cat made much less fuss. Jumping down from the ship, he surveyed Snow with coolly slitted orange eyes, then padded gracefully off to investigate his new domain.

There were Grein and Greta, bringing much needed medical supplies and knowledge to help with all those who had been injured during the battle and to oversee the building of her new hospital. They hugged her, Greta wiping away a tear as she looked about the palace, she never thought to set foot in again.

And then there was Arden. He climbed from the ship and simply held out his arms to her. Letting out a sob, Snow realised how very pleased she was to see him and hurled herself into them.

"Arden. Uncle," she cried, and he stroked her hair.

"Well done," he said. "Well done."

All this, Ronin watched and approved of. But as he saw her step into her role as queen, he saw her retreat further and further away from him, until he barely recognised her as his Snow. With sadness, he accepted that it was fitting, and quietly made his preparations to leave the palace.

He waited a week. Seven days during which he hardly saw her. Then one evening at dusk he slipped from the palace and wandered out into the city. Work had already begun to build it anew, and there was good, paying labour for any who could handle a tool or shoulder a load. Already the people were beginning to talk about a golden age, and every time Snow came down into the city to meet her people and talk to them, which she did frequently, the cheers for her grew ever louder and more genuine.

She would win them over, he realised, and they would love her for it.

"Are you running away then?"

Lost in thought, Ronin hadn't noticed the shadow following him down the street until a voice spoke from behind him. Spinning around, his hand going to his sword, he realised it was the young man standing on a mound of fallen masonry, and relaxed.

"Snow has been looking everywhere for you," he said, mildly. "She wants to reward you for all that you did."

"I do not need a reward." The young man shrugged. "I completed my mission, and that is reward enough. Raven's daughter sits on the throne, and she will be a good queen. I hear the talk in the taverns and the markets – already the people grow to trust and love her. The Contratulum is broken. Soon all their outposts will be defeated and their followers either dead, converted or banished. So, what else is there?"

"Aye," Ronin had to agree. "What else is there?"

"So," the young man jumped down and looked at him curiously. "Which direction are you headed in?"

"West," Ronin replied. "I am going back to the Great Forest and my home."

"I had thought that you and Queen Snow would be together. After all that you went through to save her, I believed that you loved her."

"I do love her." Ronin gave him a sad smile. "But sometimes love is not enough. I can never live in her world, and she can never live in mine, so it is better that I leave."

"Love is always enough," the young man replied. "And there is only one world, which we must all live in as best we can. And as for it being better if you leave – better for whom?"

Ronin did not answer him, merely shifted his pack more comfortably on his shoulder and turned to trudge wearily down the ruined street. He heard the young man fall into step behind him but said nothing. Neither did the young man.

Chapter Forty-Two

The Raven and the Mirror

Dinner that evening had been both merry and bittersweet. Snow was happy to be reunited with most of her friends and to celebrate the wonderful news that Nylex and Fae had blushingly told them. But she could not deny her sadness. Kylah was not there to raise a glass with them, and Ronin was also absent.

All week she had watched him slip further and further away from her until it felt as if they were strangers. Snow tried to manufacture a reason to see him – be with him – but there were always demands on her as queen that nobody else could fulfil.

Occupied from dawn till dusk, Snow would try to catch his eye, to at least share a moment of humour or companionship with him as they used to in the past. But it was like looking through a wall of ice. She could see him, but hammer on the ice as she might, he remained oblivious to her presence.

After dinner, Arden offered to walk her to her chambers, and Eli bounded along behind them. Since Kylah's death, he had remained by Snow's side except when he was with Barnabus and his men. They had adopted him as their lucky mascot and were kind to him in a rough, soldierly manner.

Two of her guards fell into step behind them, and Snow was comforted by their presence. Not that she feared a further attack, but the knowledge that Mirage was still out there gave her pause for thought at times. She had been reassured that he would be found, and that the palace was secure, but still – sometimes she thought of him, and a shudder would run down her spine.

The royal bedchambers that had once belonged to her parents had been opened for the first time in eighteen years, cleaned and refurbished, and were now hers. The guards positioned themselves outside the door as Snow, Arden, and Eli made themselves comfortable around the fire that crackled companionably in the fireplace. Snow poured wine for them and they sat in silence for a while, staring into the flames, each lost within their thoughts.

"Tell us a story, Arden," Eli begged, and Arden's eyes twinkled.

"What story would you have me tell, young Eli?"

"Maybe the one about the b-b-blacksmith and his wife, or the one about the donkey s-s-stuck in the gate?"

"Both excellent tales, and ones that I will tell Snow on another occasion, but now I think I will tell a new tale. You will like this one, Eli, for it's a story about a cake."

"Cake," murmured Eli, and settled down in his chair with a happy sigh, as the flames in the fire shifted higher and swirled into shapes to illustrate the tale Arden told.

Once upon a time, two brothers lived together in a cottage on the edge of the wood. Being amiable and sociable souls, they were much liked within the village, but both brothers had an unfortunate weakness. Both were stubborn to the point of death, and when one had fixed upon something, nothing would change his mind.

Now, one day something happened. Something so small and inconsequential that no normal person would have paid it any mind, yet to the brothers it meant everything. The matter was this. The spade went missing from the shed, and each blamed the other for taking it.

Stubbornly convinced it was the other one's fault, each brother determined not to speak to the other until an apology had been issued, and the tool put back.

On and on this went for days, both brothers refusing to utter so much as a word to one another, and the atmosphere within the cottage became sour and unpleasant. Then one day, upon returning from market, one brother went to the shed to put away the baskets of produce and was astonished to discover the missing spade hanging in its usual place. The other brother, upon going into the cottage, was equally astonished to discover a cake resting in the middle of the kitchen table. A thing of magnificence, the cake was frosted all over with rich buttercream, and it smelt of vanilla and chocolate. All the things one would expect a really, splendid cake to smell of.

Heading out to the shed to find his brother and enquire if the cake was of his doing, he discovered the spade back in pride of place. Meanwhile, the other brother entered the house through the back door and discovered the cake sitting in pride of place on the table.

Instantly, each one decided that the cake was by way of an apology for taking the spade, denying having done so, and then stealthily returning it. And each determined that not one crumb of that cake would pass their lips until the other confessed and made a proper apology.

For days, this situation continued, with both brothers giving the other pointed glares and nods towards the cake. But not one word did they speak, and so each interpreted the other's actions to be an admission of guilt.

Left there, the cake began to go stale, and flies began to inhabit it. Eventually, the kitchen was so infested with their annoying buzzing, that one of the brothers took the cake and threw it on the midden heap – so neither got to eat it.

Later that evening, as each brother was sitting in his own fog of simmering hatred and anger, there came a tap at their door, and it was their widowed neighbour. She had come to apologise for having borrowed their spade without permission, but her old dog had become stuck in a hole under the roots of a tree and had been unable to get herself out.

The old widow had rushed to their cottage to ask for their assistance, but upon finding them both at market she had simply borrowed the spade to dig the dog out herself. Bringing the spade back, along with a magnificent cake she had baked for them by way of expressing her gratitude, she had again found the cottage empty, so had left the cake on the table, intending to return later to thank them in person.

Unfortunately, the next day she had succumbed to a bad cold, so had been abed for a week and was only now well enough to come and explain what had occurred. Thanking them again, she exclaimed that she hoped they had enjoyed the cake and departed, leaving the two brothers staring at one another in mortified realisation and regret for the beautiful cake that, due to their stubbornness and refusal to talk to one another, neither one had even got to taste.

“Well, I think they were b-b-both stupid to have wasted such a wonderful cake.” Eli twisted his face in disgust. “I would have cut the cake and given a piece to my brother and told him I had not taken the spade and that I believed him when he said he hadn’t. Then we would have finished the cake between us and tried to think who else might have borrowed it.”

“You are wiser than either of the brothers, young Eli, and you are quite right. It was indeed a crime to let such a beautiful cake go to waste.”

He winked at Snow, who sat considering his story long after he and Eli had left. Understanding full well the implications, that if she and Ronin did not talk to one another then their ‘cake’ – the love she knew existed between them – would simply go to waste, she determined that first thing in the morning she would find him and talk to him. Even if it meant swallowing her pride, going down on her knees, and humbling herself before him, she would beg him to listen to her, and they would talk.

First thing in the morning.

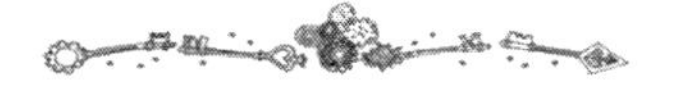

Their way lit by a full moon, Ronin and the young man wandered the streets of the city, always heading west. In no hurry, Ronin found his progress slowing until finally he stopped and turned. Behind and above them was the palace, ablaze with lights, the kindness of the night hiding the damage it had suffered.

"What's the matter?" the young man asked. "Are you thinking of returning?"

"No, it's only ..."

"Only what?"

"A feeling I have. A feeling that all is not well."

There was a flurry of black wings in the moonlight and a large shadow alighted on a nearby garden fence and peered at them with eyes that glittered like fire.

"What is that creature?" the young man gasped, stepping back in superstitious unease.

"It's a raven," Ronin said. "An unusually large one. They do not tend to venture this far into the city, for folks believe them to be unlucky and will drive them away – and I never known one fly at night."

The raven looked at them, seemingly unalarmed at their proximity, and uttered a loud caw, which made them both jump back in shock.

"What is that it is clutching?" the young man whispered, pointing to a shiny object the large bird had clenched in its strong talons.

"Ravens collect shiny objects – like crows and magpies. It must be something it found amongst the debris," Ronin told him.

Curiously, he stepped closer, trying to see what the raven had stolen for itself. It was a mirror – a small, delicate, and intricate thing of beauty.

Plainly the property of a lady, the sort of mirror she would have hanging from her chatelaine maybe, to discreetly check her appearance. Indeed, as he crept closer, he could see a piece of chain dangling from its ornate handle as if intended for such a purpose.

Hopping forwards, the raven dropped the mirror at Ronin's feet. Taken aback, he bent to retrieve it, and the moonlight caught the glass. In the dim light, it cast a distorted reflection of himself. Barely human-shaped, it was but a mirage of a man.

Mirage.

Ronin's head snapped up and he stared up at the palace as the unease he had been feeling swept over him in a tide of warning. Dropping the mirror, he began to run as fast as he could back towards the palace – to Snow.

“Wait!” the young man called, catching him up. “What’s the matter? What is it?”

“Mirage,” Ronin gasped. “I think Snow is in danger.”

Without another word, the young man fell into a swift pace beside him, and their footsteps rang out on the flagstones of the city.

Behind them, the raven took off with a sharp caw and vanished with a flurry of inky black wings into the night.

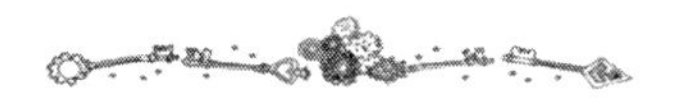

Snow awoke with a start. Unsure what had disturbed her, she sat up in bed and glanced around the large chamber, lit only by the moonlight flooding in through the open window. With hands that shook, she lit the lamp by her bedside and slipped from the bed.

Her long white nightgown whispered about her feet as she padded softly over the thick carpet and went to the window. Stepping through the open door, onto the wide balcony which spanned the entire width of her chambers, she crossed to the balustrade and looked down at the city sleeping below.

Her city.

She would mend its hurts and make it a city to be proud of. Already hundreds had signed up to work on rebuilding, and she had met with the Royal Keepers of the Purse – a meeting in which she had held her ground and forced them to make available the funds she needed.

Snow shivered in her thin gown and turned to go back inside. A large form at the side of the balcony made her pause and take a curious step towards the unusual shape that hunched in the shadows.

Clouds shifted from the face of the moon and light abruptly streamed down, illuminating the balcony, and she saw it for what it was. A skimmer.

Snow gasped with fear. Looking down, she realised that the crystal on her breast had turned black. She ran back into her room, but he was there – as he had always been there, in her mind and her dreams.

He tackled her to the floor, and she landed heavily, knocking all the breath from her lungs. Then he was rolling her over onto her back and the full weight of his body was on hers, crushing her until she could hardly breathe.

One strong hand clamped over her mouth and she felt the rasp of his goatee on her neck.

"Good evening, Your Majesty," he purred in her ear, and Snow struggled in blind panic.

"It's pointless to fight me, Snow," he whispered. "I've come back for you. I thought you were dead, so I encased you in ice so you would stay young and beautiful forever. But then I heard the tales of your miraculous return from the dead."

Snow strained away from the feel of his body pressed against hers, but he was so strong. She struggled madly. Her nightgown rode up and then his knee was between hers, forcing himself closer against her. His breath was hot on her skin as his lips lingered over the pulse that beat like a caged bird in her throat.

Ronin!

She screamed his name in her mind, but he had never felt so far away.

"I never realised you see." Mirage moaned the words into her cheek as his hand roamed over her, feeling her body through the fine silk of her nightgown.

"I never realised what you meant to me until I stood there and watched Slie killing you. As he choked the life from you it all became crystal clear in my mind. We were destined to be together, Snow. You and I. Together we can rule the world and create a dynasty that will live on long after we have gone."

Snow's heart clenched with horror at his words, and she kicked at his shins with her bare feet, but through his thick leather boots they were mere caresses and he chuckled at her attempts to break free.

"That's when I knew Slie had to die, and that I had to be the one to kill him. In a way, by killing him I was fulfilling my destiny. It was always intended that I be the one to kill him. I think he always suspected that, and that is why he never truly trusted me."

Reluctantly, he rolled from her, his hand still firm over her mouth. Yanking her to her feet after him, he gathered her close to his body. His breathing quickened, and to Snow's petrified horror, his glove was replaced with his mouth.

Hard and unyielding, his lips forced themselves onto hers. His hand twisted into her hair, forcing her head back to allow him access to plunder, his arm holding her tightly against his muscular frame.

Gathering her strength, Snow bit down as hard as she could on his lip. His blood was hot in her mouth and he cursed her as she screamed with all her might for her guards waiting outside the door.

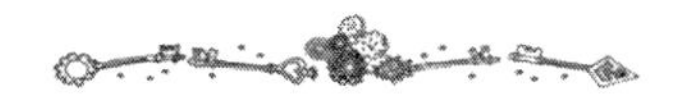

Ronin! He was running up the steps to the royal wing when her cry blasted through his mind in a shout of raw terror and panic. He paused, clutching at his head, then took the steps two at a time, the young man still hot on his heels.

Pelting down the corridor, he saw the two guards outside her chambers look up in alarm, their hands moving to their swords.

"Halt!" one of them cried.

"Ronin? What is it?"

"The queen! I think something is wrong with the queen."

"She has retired to her bed, and none has entered since Arden and Eli left."

"Knock on her door, rouse her!"

"She gave orders she was not to be disturbed."

A scream ripped through the door, and both guards leapt at the handle at the same time.

"Locked!"

"Your Majesty! Open the door! Your Majesty!"

"Break it down!" Ronin ordered.

Obediently the guards kicked at the door, but it was made of reinforced iron, built in the ancient days of warfare and siege, and as such designed to withstand the battering.

Ronin watched impatiently. Quickly realising it would take too long to break through, he turned to the wall next to the door and placed his fist on it.

Vaguely, he was aware of the young man running away down the corridor as he summoned all his powers from within and punched with his fist at the wall.

It shattered, leaving a good-sized hole in the masonry. Again, he drew back his fist and blasted at the wall with his magic. Fuelled by his fear for Snow, he released a wave of angry rage at the wall, and it exploded inwards.

Drawing his sword, Ronin jumped through the hole with the guards at his heels but stopped short at the sight of Snow held fast in the arms of Mirage, with a gun angled at her throat. There was blood on her mouth and her nightgown was torn.

Slowly, Ronin lowered his sword arm, and beside him, the guards did the same.

"Let her go, Mirage."

"I can't. She's mine, so you are going to back away, nice, and slow. All of you."

"You know we can't do that, Mirage. You can't escape, so you might as well let her go and make this easy on yourself."

"He has a skimmer on the balcony," Snow choked. "Ronin ..."

Ronin took a step forward and Mirage pressed the barrel of the gun tighter into Snow's throat.

Ronin spread his hands and stepped back, and the pressure was released enough for Snow to take a deep, gasping breath.

He wondered why she didn't blast Mirage with her powers but then realised that stark terror had rendered her incapable of summoning them. Untrained and unused to her magic, it had failed her in her hour of need.

No – he had failed her, he thought bitterly. He should have begun training her himself, for who else could do it? Instead, he had sulked and pouted because her new duties took her away from him.

"You know I can't let you take her, Mirage. She will never be yours."

"Maybe not," Mirage sneered. "But she will never be yours either."

He yanked Snow towards the window. Her feet dragging reluctantly on the carpet, she was forced to stumble back with him, her eyes pleading with Ronin to do something.

But Ronin knew Mirage was mad enough to kill that which he claimed to desire, and he hesitated, his eyes fixed on the gun.

They were at the window. Mirage paused and smirked at Ronin.

"Don't bother trying to follow us," he said. "My skimmer is much faster than any of your lumbering airships, and I have boltholes hidden all over this kingdom. You could look for a thousand years and never find us."

"Ronin." Snow sobbed, then Mirage was pulling her through the window.

Suddenly, a shadow swung down from above and viciously kicked Mirage back into the room. Caught off-guard by the unexpectedness of the attack, Mirage released Snow, who fell to one side with a cry.

Then Mirage was on the ground, with the young man struggling to hold him down. Ronin and the guards recovered their wits and rushed to aid him, and Snow crawled frantically away from the thrashing, heaving figures.

It all happened so fast.

One second it appeared the young man had the upper hand, but he was no match for Mirage's strength. Mirage flipped the man onto his back and fired his weapon into his stomach at point-blank range.

Kneeling beside the young man's body, Mirage took him by the throat. The man opened his eyes and stared at Mirage with hatred.

Then, in a movement so smooth and swift it was hard to follow, he reached down and snatched the long dagger from Mirage's boot and thrust it upwards into Mirage's heart.

The knife cleaved the human half from the mechanical side, and he twisted the blade and pushed it deeper.

"Told you to leave your weapons at the door, you bastard," he gasped.

Blood gushed from Mirage's mouth as he stared down at the hilt of the dagger protruding from his chest. Arching his back, he plucked it from his body and tossed it away, then fell backwards onto the ground and lay still.

"Check he's dead," Ronin ordered the guards, and they hurried to obey.

Snow scrambled to her knees and crawled to the young man. Cradling his head on her lap, she gently stroked his hair away from his face as eyes of brilliant blue opened and focused on her.

"Raven," he whispered and coughed hoarsely. "I did it. I completed the mission you gave me. Your daughter is crowned queen and is on the throne. Slie and Mirage are both dead. Did I do well, my Queen?"

"You did," Snow sobbed. "You fulfilled your mission magnificently. You have your queen's gratitude and her unending love."

"Love ..." he muttered. "Love is always enough ..." Then his eyes closed, and he lay still.

"No!" Snow howled and held him close, his blood soaking through the fine silk of her nightgown. "I didn't even know his name," she cried in anguish, tears soaking her cheeks. She looked up at Ronin, her face pleading.

"What was his name? Please, what was his name?"

Ronin knelt beside her and placed his arms about her trembling body, looking down regretfully on the face of the young man who had sacrificed so much for the love of his queen.

"None of us knew it," he said. "But he will never be forgotten."

Gently, he drew her to her feet and fetched a blanket from the bed to wrap her in, then swept her up in his arms as she began to shake.

"Dispose of *that*," he told the guards, looking at the body of Mirage with a disdainful curl of his lip. "And treat *him* with the utmost respect," he ordered, inclining his head towards the young man.

"The queen?"

"I will take care of the queen," he told them firmly and carried her from the chamber.

He took her to the room that had been assigned to him. In his absence, a fire had been lit, and he sat on the sofa before it with Snow lying beside him, her head on his lap and the blanket tucked tightly around her.

As she shook with the memory of the encounter, he stroked her hair and soothed her into drowsiness until she lay at peace, gazing into the fire and thinking on all that had happened.

"I need to tell you a story," she eventually murmured.

And she told him the tale of a ragged street urchin who had tried to pick a queen's pocket and ended up being her most faithful supporter.

Loyal even after her death, his whole life had been dedicated to fulfilling the mission his queen had given him – that of seeing her daughter safely onto the throne.

Finally, her voice grew silent, and she slept, knowing she was safe, and that the monsters were all dead. His own eyes growing heavy, Ronin too slipped into slumber, his head resting on the back of the sofa and his arms holding the woman he loved.

When he awoke in the morning, she was gone. Leaving him a note that she had left to dress and to arrange a funeral fit for a nameless hero, she pleaded with him to meet her in the throne room at noon.

Throwing the note onto the fire, Ronin went to bathe and change his clothes, all the while a thought nagging that there was something he had missed.

His mind going back to the previous evening, Ronin pictured Mirage's face – and an older memory surfaced. A recollection of a face from his childhood and a tale he had grown up with.

The certainty growing into a conviction, Ronin went in search of Grein. Discovering him with Greta supervising the construction of the new hospital, he took them both to the room where Mirage lay.

Grein stood beside the body in silence, then drew a deep, shuddering breath and looked away, his eyes suspiciously bright.

"It is your nephew, isn't it," Ronin murmured, and Grein nodded.

"He is the dead spit of my brother. I do not see how he could not be his son." Gently, he touched the mechanical eye.

"I wonder what happened to my brother. How did his son end up with the Contratulum, with a mechanical eye and heart?"

"I might be able to answer that question."

For the first time, Greta spoke and both men looked at her curiously.

"I have been speaking with some of those poor souls who were conscripted to work within the Contratulum against their will. Some of the things they have told me …" She paused and shook her head sadly.

"There is a story some of them tell, of a prisoner many years ago who … exploded – almost killing Mirage and necessitating the replacing of half his heart and his eye."

"Exploded?" Ronin asked in surprise.

"Yes," Greta confirmed. "Exploded. At the time I assumed it to be an exaggeration, but given Grein's talent, I am now wondering …"

"Whether it was my brother …" Grein finished her sentence and rubbed a hand wearily over his chin. "It is possible," he continued. "My brother possessed the same magical talent as I. If I wished, I too could rearrange the cells within my body to create an explosion. Not that I ever would," he hastily added, as the other two stared at him.

"How did he die?" he asked. "Tell me," he added, as Ronin hesitated, unsure whether it was wise to tell Grein the truth.

"He attacked Snow in her chambers," Ronin finally admitted. "He had a skimmer, and he was trying to take her far away. If we hadn't come back when we did. If we hadn't seen that raven …"

"Raven?" Greta's head snapped up in interest. "What raven?"

"In the city. It landed beside us."

"Tell me everything," Greta demanded, so Ronin did. Admitting that he had been leaving was hard, but Grein's eyes were warm with sympathy and Greta nodded her head slowly, her eyes thoughtful.

"This mirror," she started. "Was it about this big?" Her hands sketched the dimensions. "With a gold ornate rim and carving on the handle?"

"Yes, that sounds about right," Ronin agreed, trying to remember what it had looked like.

"I gave a mirror just like that to Raven for her eighteenth nameday." Greta drew a shaky breath.

"What are you saying?" Ronin demanded in surprise.

"I'm saying that the veil between the worlds of the living and the dead is not always as thick as people believe it to be," Greta replied quietly.

"Well, I just hope that wherever my nephew is now, he finds the peace he never found in life," Grein remarked, and Greta's face softened with compassion.

"We will bury him," Greta told Grein and laid a hand on his arm. "We will bury him," she repeated as Ronin stiffened in protest. "Quietly, and privately," she insisted, glaring at Ronin fiercely.

Ronin nodded, then clapped Grein on the shoulder in silent sympathy, and left to keep his appointment with Snow.

For once she was alone, and when he entered the throne room on the stroke of midday, she was awaiting him. Dressed in a simple gown and corset, with her hair unbound, she reminded him of the girl he had rescued in the forest.

It felt that an age had passed since then – that they had experienced so much and travelled so far when only a fortnight had expired.

She smiled at him when he entered and held out her hand. He crossed the room and took it, bending to it with a kiss and a teasing – *Your Highness* – as he had teased her so many times before.

When he straightened, she would not relinquish his hand but pulled him over to the balcony.

"Come with me," she said. "There is something I must show you."

Obediently, he allowed her to lead him, and they leant on the balustrade together, looking out over the city spread far below.

"Tell me what you see?" she demanded, and Ronin looked at the view and considered.

"I see the cathedral, and the rest of the city."

"Yes, but what else do you see?"

"I see that the city has been severely damaged in places."

"It has," Snow nodded. "As has the palace. They are not as they were before."

"You will rebuild them," he reassured her. "Better than before."

"Ronin, you once said to me that you could not live in my world and that I could not live in yours. Well, this is my world now," she swept her hand wide to encompass the whole shattered city below. "And I am asking you to help me rebuild it."

"Snow ..."

"Hush," she said, and gently placed her fingers to his lips. "My parents told me that love is the most important thing there is. That it can cross any divide, and travel any distance, and that when I find love, I should hold onto it with everything I have. So, I am asking you, Ronin, to stay with me as my husband and as my heartmate. Stay with me, and together we will create a new and better world – a world that is *ours*."

Ronin hesitated. Snow released him and turned away, running a trembling hand over her face to compose herself before turning back to look at him earnestly.

"If you can look me in the eye, Ronin, and tell me that you do not love me, then I will let you go without another word. But, if you cannot, then I will fight with everything I have to convince you that our love is worth any price we must pay."

“Snow.” At last, he found his voice. “I think I fell in love with you the first moment I laid eyes on you in that clearing, covered in blood and shaking with fear at what you had done.”

“No, you didn’t,” Snow laughed. “You thought I was a nuisance and you wished rid of me.”

“Maybe,” he conceded, his eyes twinkling. “Maybe it was when you tried to clean a room for the first time and ended up with cobwebs in your hair. I cannot say exactly when it happened, I only know that there is no part of me that is not filled with you. I understand now what Nylex tried to tell me, about how he felt when he believed Fae was dead, and he had thrown away the chance to be with her when he could.”

“You do love me,” Snow stated with confidence.

“Of course, I love you,” he replied, and his voice shook with the sincerity of his words. “But are you sure you want me? I am nothing, Snow. I have nothing. I stand before you with literally only the shirt on my back. You are a queen with the whole world at your feet. You deserve to be showered with gold and jewels. What can I possibly offer you that you do not already possess?”

“Love,” she replied. “Love and trust and loyalty. Things that are precious beyond all the gold and jewels in the world yet cannot be bought. This is what I want from you, Ronin. Indeed, this is what I demand of you. So, I stand before you and ask. Can you give me what I want?”

Ten Years Later

It had been many months since they had managed to slip away to the cottage – the trade negotiations with the mysterious snowy land of House Ursa had taken longer than anticipated – and Snow sighed in exhausted relief when finally, the agreements were signed, and the delegates returned to their ice-bound land in the airship ***Endeavour.***

Now, as she climbed down from the skimmer and took a great lungful of the sweet, pine-scented forest air, she thought how good it was to be back. Arching her back to ease out the kinks a two-hour flight cramped into the back of the skimmer had created, she reached up to take down the squirming body of her eight-year-old son, who was frantically kicking his legs in excited anticipation.

"Mama. Put me down," he begged. Snow gently landed him on the ground and mussed his hair with an energetic kiss.

"Me now. Me now, Mama!" Laughing, Snow reached up for her daughter, swung her from the skimmer and stood her next to her twin brother.

"Can we go and find Uncle Eli, Mama?" they pleaded.

"You certainly can," she told them. "Although he will have heard the skimmer, and he's probably ... ahh, there he is."

A beaming Eli had appeared on the porch of his cottage on the far side of the now greatly extended clearing. Kneeling, he held out both arms, and the twins flew on sturdy legs over the grass to be swept up in his energetic embrace.

"Uncle Eli, Uncle Eli," cried Blanche, her dark hair already coming loose from the ribbons Snow had tied in them that morning. "I have a new puppy, only Papa said I wasn't allowed to bring him in the skimmer."

"And I have a new pony," her twin, Elgin, told him. "And Papa wouldn't let me bring her either."

"What a mean papa you are," Snow teased, holding up her arms to take four-year-old Lissa and set her safely on the ground.

"Well, I didn't see you offering to give up your seat for the pony," Ronin told her, jumping lightly down from the skimmer, and catching her up in an embrace, his eyes twinkling with merriment. "And as for that fricking incontinent puppy – until it learns to control its bladder, I am not getting into any confined spaces with it."

"Language," Snow gently chided him and snuggled into her husband's side as they followed Lissa, who was making a beeline for Uncle Eli, plainly determined to get in on the hug action. Eli straightened as they approached, his delight at seeing them written all over his beaming face.

"Ronin, S-s-snow," he said, and Snow pulled him close in a hug.

Closing her eyes as she leant into the kind of hug only Eli could give, she thought of how much happier he was here than he had ever been back at the palace. Lost and confused after Kylah's death, life at court had been too much for him to handle, and one night he had crept out of the palace and set off alone.

Panicking at finding him gone, Snow sent out search parties, and he had eventually been found going in completely the wrong direction, heading north. He wanted to go home to the forest, he told them. He just wanted to go home.

Finally understanding that keeping him with them was selfish and wrong, and not what was best for Eli, Ronin and Snow came up with a solution that appeared to make everyone happy.

They would take him to Ronin's cottage. He would live there while a new cottage was being built for him, so he could ensure it was built exactly the way he wanted it. Then he would move into his brand-new home and supervise the improvements that were going to be made to Ronin's old cottage, to make it the perfect getaway retreat for Ronin and Snow whenever court duties allowed.

Barnabus had requested that his men have a camp in the forest – a place where they could learn hunting and survival skills, and train recruits. A new clearing was created not far away, and Camp Kylah was established as a training base for all raw recruits – both male and female – who wished to become soldiers in the army of House White. Not that one was needed in these wonderful days of peace, but Snow had been advised by Ronin that it was a good idea to always be prepared.

Eli was in his element – always having a ready supply of new friends to talk to – and knowing that his old friends were liable to drop in at any moment. Although busy with their respective positions as the Minister of State and Minister of Education, Nylex and Fae always made time to visit him – bringing their ever-growing family with them.

Grein and Greta too, whenever their duties at the hospital allowed, would make the short skimmer journey to see Eli. As for Arden – well, Eli never quite knew when there would be a knock at his cabin door, and he would be standing there, with a smile on his face and a new stock of tales to tell.

Snow and Ronin saw Eli eventually lose the confused and haunted look from his eyes and knew that much as they had wanted to keep him with them, it had been the right decision to let him go.

"Right," Ronin clapped his hands. "If we want to get a campfire built, we need to gather firewood – so who's going to help?"

“Me, me!” cried the twins and happily dashed after their father into the forest.

Sitting by the campfire later that night – the children tucked up and fast asleep in bed – Snow sat wrapped in her husband’s arms and sighed with contentment. The fire warmed their fronts as the firelight leapt in their eyes, and Ronin had fetched a blanket from the cottage, which he placed around them to keep their backs warm in the chill of the night air.

Eli had gone to his cottage already, and Snow revelled in being alone with her husband, under the twinkling stars and a crescent moon that looked at them through clouds of dark lace.

“It’s good, isn’t it?” she asked.

He turned to look at her, his eyes warm with love – for her, their family, and the world they had created between them.

“Yes,” he agreed, and his lips brushed gently over hers. “It’s good.”

The End

About the Author

Julia Blake lives in the beautiful historical town of Bury St. Edmunds, deep in the heart of the county of Suffolk in the UK, with her daughter, one crazy cat and a succession of even crazier lodgers.

She has been writing all her life but only recently took herself seriously enough to consider being published.

Her first novel, The Book of Eve, met with worldwide critical acclaim, and since then, Julia has released ten other books which have delighted her growing number of readers with their strong plots and instantly relatable characters. Details of all Julia's novels can be found on the next page.

Julia leads a busy life, juggling working and family commitments with her writing, and has a strong internet presence, loving the close-knit and supportive community of fellow authors she has found on social media and promises there are plenty more books in the pipeline.

Julia says: "I write the kind of books I like to read myself, warm and engaging novels, with strong, three-dimensional characters you can really connect with."

A Note from Julia

If you have enjoyed this book, why not take a few moments to leave a review on Amazon. It needn't be much, just a few lines saying you liked the book and why, yet it can make a world of difference.

Reviews are the reader's way of letting the author know they enjoyed their book, and of letting other readers know the book is an enjoyable read and why. It also informs Amazon that this is a book worth promoting, and the more reviews a book receives, the more Amazon will recommend it to other readers.

I would be very grateful and would like to say thank you for reading my book and if you spare a few minutes of your time to review it, I do see, read, and appreciate every single review left for me.

Best Regards
Julia Blake

Other Books by the Author

The Forest
~ a tale of old magic ~

Myth, folklore, and magic combine in this engrossing tale
of a forgotten village and an ancient curse

Erinsmore

A wonderful tale of an enchanted land of sword and sorcery,
myth and magic, dragons, and prophecy

The Perennials Series

Becoming Lili – the beautiful, coming of age saga
Chaining Daisy – its gripping sequel
Rambling Rose – the triumphant conclusion

The Blackwood Family Saga

Fast-paced and heart-warming, this exciting series tells the story of the Blackwood Family and their search for love and happiness

The Book of Eve

A story of love, betrayal, and bitter secrets that threaten to rip a young woman's life apart

Eclairs for Tea And Other Stories

A wonderful collection of short stories and quirky poems that reflect the author's multi-genre versatility
Includes the award-winning novella – Lifesong

Printed in Great Britain
by Amazon